Curse of the Blood Queen

Also by JM Lee

The Novus Proprius Chronicles

When October Ends
Chasing
Novus Orsa
The Complete Trilogy

The Londinium Saga

Curse of the Blood Queen
Books 2-5 coming soon

Short Stories

Countdown
Featured in "Dark & Stormy: Sixteen Tempest-Tossed Tales"

Rite of Passage
Featured in "Shadows & Mist: Twelve Terrifying Tales"

Mabel
Featured in "Steam & Steel: Thirteen Riveting Tales"

www.jmlee.info

BOOK 1
of The LONDINIUM SAGA

CURSE OF THE BLOOD QUEEN

JM LEE

Paperback & Dust Jacket cover design by GetCovers
Interior art created using Canva Pro
Hardback front cover art by Ayla Ginsberg
Hardback back cover art by Seth Cockerham

Paperback ISBN: 979-8-9917822-0-3
Hardback ISBN: 979-8-9917822-1-0

For more information about JM Lee, visit: www.jmlee.info

Dedication

to those who never got their apology
and chose to forgive anyway

and to the women villainized by history

1

WINIFRED

Though most would find the thought of speaking with spirits eerie, Winifred Fox felt most at home when surrounded by the dead.

"Know that most of them mean you no harm, little one," Death whispered in her mind many years before, when the lingering shadows still made her skin crawl. *"But be careful to trust your instincts. All monsters were human once."*

Now, rays of the late afternoon sun beamed through a set of stained glass windows. Winnie watched a set of men, employed by Madam Stanhope's House of Spiritualists, install their seance table at the center of a quaint family study.

Her beloved's emerald eyes glimmered with concern as they waited. Beatrix, or Bea as she was affectionately known, rubbed Winnie's shoulders in reassurance before she continued to anxiously pace across the room's walnut floors. A throbbing headache only added to the young medium's discomfort, exhausted from a long day's work.

Shadows slowly danced along the walls as the curtains slid shut. The gas lamps were off, only the flickering of candles lighting the space. A heaviness lingered in the air; she could feel it in her bones. The hovering spirit waiting desperately in the void to speak to her family.

As Stanhope's men hung a crimson curtain around the circular mahogany table, the bereaved family entered. A cloud of darkness followed, their grief tangible. Their youngest daughter's cries rang through the house. The mother's soft whimpers echoed in Winnie's ears, the father trying to maintain his composure.

"I appreciate your willingness to help my family, Madam Fox." His words were almost unintelligible, the whites of his eyes red with agony.

"I'd be lying if I said I wasn't a little nervous, Sir. I've never spoken to a soul torn from this earth in such a violent manner," she confessed, taking a seat at the head of the table where a set of ropes waited for her.

"Miss Fox is the best Madam Stanhope has to offer," Bea assured them, stepping toward Winnie to begin a set of extravagant bindings that looked like they could hold an elephant down.

"Why must she be tied up?" the mother questioned, clutching her hand to her chest.

Winnie answered in the way she'd been trained. "The bindings ensure that I cannot…harm you. If I am to become possessed by someone other than your daughter."

The young girl's whimpers turned to a terrified squeal, hiding behind her mother. Much to Winnie's relief, it took only a moment before a nanny entered from the other room, escorting the young girl out.

As Bea pulled the ropes tighter around Winnie's wrists, her amber eyes flashed up to her love who quietly mouthed 'smile.' She couldn't help but scoff in response, knowing such trickery wasn't necessary to commune with a spirit. Winnie had been in contact with the dead since she was a little girl. Surely such thieving schemes weren't worth it. Her dark curls clung to the back of her neck; a mix of summer heat and nerves making her sweat.

The family took seats around the table, the father to the left and Bea to her right. A loving finger stroked her hand, a reminder that Bea was what kept her sane most days. She'd become the moon to Winnie's tide. Whenever the treacherous seas of life threatened to sweep her away, that love brought them back together.

"Please grab my hands," Winnie hummed. "I need to see the photograph of your daughter before we begin."

The father complied as Winnie examined the grainy picture of a fifteen-year-old girl dressed in a modest gown. She memorized the subtle features; the gleaming smile that tried to hide from the photographer and small ringlets that lay on either side of delicate features. The girl was the picture of Victorian middle-class beauty. Something Winnie once was.

"During the ceremony, no one speaks until the medium gives me the signal. We don't wish to call on any nasties, now do we?" Bea's words almost taunted the family. Sharing nervous glances amongst themselves, all three nodded in hesitation.

At last, with the curtain closed around the group and clammy hands grasping Winnie's, they were ready to begin. Settling her mind, she called out to the spirit. Unsure if they'd connect after dying so recently, she waited. Several moments passed when a chill spread through the air, a sure sign a spirit was joining them. Yet, the young girl didn't linger amidst the shadows of the room as though she weren't quite strong enough to manifest.

"I'm having trouble communicating with your daughter. I'm going to meet her in Oblivion," Winnie announced, deepening her voice and drawing out every syllable knowing Madame Stanhope would be proud of the show she was putting on.

Just as every seance before, her soul detached from her body. Floating higher and higher until she was weightless, her consciousness appeared in the world between life and death, the meeting ground for newly departed spirits biding their time.

"There you are," she whispered, seeing the young girl waiting in the void. Nothingness surrounded them, only the glimmer of the girl's own soul lighting her way forward. After squeezing Bea's hand, the family started their questions.

The usuals came first; ones Winnie was all too familiar with. What was it like on the other side? Was she at peace? But given the nature of this girl's death, darker questions quickly overtook the conversation, too desperate for answers to continue asking about the mysteries of the afterlife.

"Did she see the man's face? The one who…" The father's words came to a halt, unable to finish the sentence as the mother sucked in a sharp breath withholding more tears.

Winnie waited for a response, eyes closed and attention in two places at once. "She recalls a derby hat and dark eyes. Believes she will be the first of many," she mumbled, struggling to maintain the connection in Oblivion. Her head once again throbbed thanks to her third seance of the day.

There was a long pause, silence and unease spreading as the family seemed to contemplate what else to ask. This happened often during seances. The deceased's loved ones usually found it difficult to continue communicating when struggling to wade through their grief. In response to the lull, Winnie felt Bea's leg trigger a loud thud beneath the table. The family retreated back with sharp gasps before the surface finally settled again.

Winnie squeezed Bea's hand so tightly she almost hoped it would cause discomfort. She'd expressed her displeasure for such scare tactics, despite knowing that most customers paid more for a good performance. Regardless, it didn't help lessen her guilt. Though she'd been speaking to the dead since she was a child, working for Madam Stanhope was one part born skill and two parts show. A fact she hated.

In Oblivion, the girl's solemn face waited for any more questions.

"Can you tell them something for me?"

"Yes, what is it you wish to say to your family?" she announced, knowing the girl's request was the perfect timing following Bea's trickery.

"Tell them…I didn't feel any pain. That I'm at rest and always watching over them."

Winnie repeated the message back to her clients, whose sobs

only escalated with each word she spoke. "Was it truly painless?" she asked curiously in Oblivion only, careful not to repeat the words aloud for the others to hear.

The girl shook her head grimly. "Eventually, it was. But those first few strikes…the moment the blade hit my stomach. I've never experienced anything like it. But please don't tell them that."

A sharp knocking sounded from outside the door, two of Stanhope's men indicating the family's time was nearly up. Kindly thanking the spirit, Winnie watched as she wandered toward the glowing white light within the void. The familiar smell of Death's lilies overwhelmed her senses, a hello from the entity before departing with the girl's soul.

"She is on her way to the afterlife," Winnie announced, attempting to withdraw her hands, ready to have the ropes removed from her wrists.

"Thank you, Madam Fox. It truly settles my heart to know she's at peace." The mother gently sobbed while Bea unfastened the bindings.

"I'm so glad I could help." Taking a stand and rubbing her aching wrists, Winnie was overwhelmed by the mother's sudden hug. This is why I do what I do, she thought as she gently stroked the woman's back.

"A few extra shillings for you, ladies. We appreciate your services." The father extended his hands toward the two mediums who quietly snatched the coins and pocketed them before Stanhope's men entered the room.

As they turned to leave, Bea's steps came to an abrupt halt.

"Everything alright?" Winnie asked, placing a steadying hand on her partner's back.

Bea didn't respond, only clutched her forehead before her body became hunched and wavering. Winnie pulled Bea's chin up, attempting to assess the young woman, but the eyes that stared back at her were vacant and empty.

"Is it happening again?" she cried, steadying her partner as she nearly fell to the floor. The family and Stanhope's men stared from across the room, glancing at each other as if they were unsure what to do.

"Is she all right?" the mother asked, stepping toward them as she clutched the pearls around her neck. "I can fetch some tea if needed."

"That won't be necessary. But thank you, Ma'am. I suspect it's been too long of a day for us," Winnie reassured.

Bea's eyes slowly regained their mossy hue and locked onto Winnie's. "You!" she cried.

"What's wrong?" Winnie tried reaching for her, though her attempts were met with swats as Bea continued to back away in a frenzy.

"I…I saw! What you…" She eventually stopped thrashing at Winnie and rubbed her head. As clarity settled, she looked back up at her partner with watery eyes. "I'm sorry, Win, I don't know what came over me."

"We need to get you home." As her nerves worked to settle, she reached for Bea hesitantly. *The way she just looked at me… like I was the devil,* she wondered.

Exiting the family's London home, the two ladies' feet met the cobblestone streets to begin their trek back to Whitechapel across the Thames river. The evening breeze flowed past them as Winnie pulled her head of dark curls aside, alleviating the heat from the back of her neck. An eerie silence sat between them before Winnie finally opened her mouth.

"I'd like to leave Whitechapel and live somewhere nice like this one day," she began, waiting to see if Bea would respond. When her partner continued her stoic silence, she proceeded. "I hate hosting seances like that. The seance table feels like a cheap way to frighten people. When I have my own business, I'll just talk to the spirits. I won't use all of the gimmicks and scare tactics to swindle people into paying more money."

At last, she heard a small huff of amusement escape the woman on her arm. Long strands of golden hair blew into her angelic face, which she brushed aside effortlessly. A motion so small and insignificant, but one that made Winnie's heart swoon as she noticed the curvature of her love's lips turned into a small smirk.

"Don't let Stanhope hear you say that. She'll send Oliver after you to teach you another lesson." Her smile fell, a wide-eyed gaze falling back on Winnie.

"I'd like to see him try. I'm not as naive as I once was." With a furrowed brow, Winnie pushed away the surfacing memories.

"We should hand over our tips when we get back. You remember what happened last time." Bea stopped walking, pulling Winnie to the side.

"No one saw us pocket the coin. If we ever hope to rid ourselves of that wretched woman, we have to keep saving." A loving finger brushed the side of Bea's face.

They said nothing as they resumed their walk, only stopping on occasion to point out some of the small shops and oddities they passed on their way back to their temporary home. At last, Winnie could no longer stand the looming question in her mind.

"Are you ever going to tell me what you've been seeing these last few weeks?"

"I'm not sure what to tell you. It's been nothing but strange nightmarish images." That same panic-stricken stare returned, plastered to Winnie's face as if she'd finally seen her own ghosts.

"Perhaps you're like my mother. Her eyes turn milky white when she's having visions," she suggested, thinking back to the many times her mother was overcome with images sent by Fate.

"It's possible," Bea mumbled, almost inaudible had Winnie not been standing so close. "I hope they're mere tricks. The things I've seen you do…"

"Can't you just tell me?" Winnie pestered.

But just as before, Bea merely shook her head and continued on with her secrets.

Upon arrival at the House of Spiritualists, the Madam herself waited for them in the doorway. With a hand as vicious as the snapping jaws of a hound, it waited outstretched. "Make good money, did ya?" As usual, her updo was layered high toward the sky, a hoop skirt almost wider than the doorframe adorning her curvy physique.

"It's with your men. We left a few minutes early due to exhaustion. I keep trying to tell you that three seances in one day is too much for me to handle," Winnie noted, arms crossed over her chest with a sour glare.

"Get used to it, dear. Perhaps try faking it like everyone else. Tomorrow you'll have four clients waitin' for you." Sucking air between her teeth, the Madam examined the two young ladies with her head cocked to the side. "You sure you ain't lyin' to me? I have ways of finding out the truth, you know."

"Why would I lie to you?" Winnie sneered, ready to pass the Madam and head up to their room to retire for the night.

Before they could proceed, Madam Stanhope stopped her once more. "Another letter came in for you today while you were out. I took the liberty of openin' it for you."

"I told you to stop reading my mail!" Winnie protested, rushing toward the letter box sitting near the entryway.

"You should know by now that there's no such thing as privacy at Stanhope's." An almost manic laugh followed the woman's words as Bea's cowering figure rushed upstairs.

"I take it dinner's already put away as well?" Winnie muttered, her eyes glancing over the letter to ensure her mother's pleas didn't include any mention of her family's magic.

"Sounds like you already know the answer to your question, dear," the Madam purred with curled lips.

"Why do you send us on jobs when you know it'll lead to our complete and utter fatigue without bothering to feed us as you promised when we moved in?" Within her balled fists, condensation built as her family's magic stirred. Trickles of water leaked onto the stone flooring, waiting desperately to be made useful.

"Winnie, let's go." Bea's shrill voice called down from the top of the landing, nervous fingers fidgeting with the laces of her corset.

"You're lucky you're one of my most requested girls. Otherwise I'd have thrown you to the wolves already." Madam Stanhope pushed past her toward the house's kitchen with a mocking snicker.

Winnie stomped up the stairs, ensuring her huff of frustration was audible. Slamming the door shut, she walked over to the small floorboard she'd been prying up for weeks to hide her additional earnings. "What the Madam doesn't know won't hurt her," she mumbled, adding the coins to a small leather sack hidden beneath.

"You shouldn't push Stanhope like that. You know what happens when we act out," Bea mumbled, unlacing her corset and removing the bustle beneath her dress which accentuated the ever-so-desired voluptuous figure.

"I don't give a damn what happens to me as long as I get out of this place," Winnie hissed. "Why you accept her poor treatment so easily I'll never understand."

"Not everyone's like you. None of us have rich family back home we can rely on if things turn sour." Sad eyes avoided Winnie, delicate fingers removing jewelry and brushing her hair free of tangles. "The same message as always, I presume?"

Winnie nodded. "My mother is once again begging me to come home. You'd think after a year, she'd accept that I'm true to my word. She knows what she must do to make amends, and yet refuses. So I'll stay put." Her recollection of that night was hazy, the sting of memory-altering magic buried deep in her mind.

"She just loves you, Winnie. Why can't you see that?" Bea mumbled, never turning around to make proper eye contact.

"And you? I worry with all these strange visions you've been having that you've lost your affection for me," Winnie asked, anxiously awaiting an answer.

Bea said nothing, only peered into the mirror playing with something small and metallic in her hands. The moments that passed felt like hours, silence eating away at the connection between them.

"Did you hear me?" Her heart pounded, mind racing as she anticipated Bea's response.

"I wish I could put into words what I've seen and how I feel," she muttered, turning to Winnie at last. Though her words ceased, a small hand reached across the room. Stepping away from her money's hiding spot, Winnie accepted the invitation and embraced her beloved.

"Just tell me what's going on…"

Still, Bea said nothing. The embrace around Winnie became firmer, holding her as tightly as possible as though she'd slip away like sand through an hourglass. When the hold loosened and Bea examined her once more, her lips planted firmly onto Winnie's as a tear rolled down her cheek. She'd expected a quick peck, but instead was met with a surprise intensity. Clutching the sides of Winnie's face, Bea's kiss didn't resemble the usual slow and savored passion. Instead, it felt like a goodbye.

Bea's lips parted Winnie's for a moment, hovering in place. "I'm sorry…I wish I could tell you what I've seen. Wish I could make you understand…"

As if sensing the hesitation, Bea's grasp only tightened. One hand released Winnie's face, the other seizing her by the wrist. Winnie pulled away, amber eyes darting up toward a gleaming metallic shine. Her heart sank when she saw a deadly blade held above her and ready to strike.

2

WINIFRED

"Have you gone mad?" Winnie attempted to pull away, but Bea only gripped her wrist harder.

"I'm sorry! You don't understand! I have to..." Bea's eyes widened, her body shaking with adrenaline as she struggled to maintain her hold.

"After everything we've been through? What could I possibly have done to make you hate me this much?" Tears welled, and her throat bobbed with unspoken curses.

"I don't hate you…you have to believe me! If you only knew!" Bea glanced up at the dagger in disbelief.

"I told you everything! Let you in when I swore I'd never love again. And now you try to stab me in the back? Was this the plan all along?" she hissed, ripping her hand from Bea's.

Bea shook her head as if trying to discredit the accusation. Her face contorted in fear. Wildness lingered among tear soaked cheeks.

Winnie's heart seemed to stop. She glanced at the blade poised to swing toward her. Taking a moment to analyze her escape, her gaze darted between the door and the floorboard where well-earned money lay hidden.

Winnie struggled to find the right words. "And to think I loved you…"

"Please don't look at me like that," Beatrix whimpered, hand trembling as the grip around the dagger loosened.

Winnie shoved her, the blade clattered to the floor. The sound of the Madam's undeniable heavy steps darted up the stairs as Bea fell. With seconds to spare, Winnie lunged for the small sack of money hidden beneath the loose floorboards. When she once again came to a stand and Bea recollected herself, the metallic edge of the blade waited back at her throat.

"What the devil's going on in here?" Madam Stanhope shouted, barreling into the room. Her eyes widened, first on the blade before narrowing in on the sack of coins in Winnie's hand.

"She's been stealing from you for months, Madam! I told her to give you the money! She wouldn't listen to me!" Beatrix's treacherous tongue spewed.

Winnie's pain turned bitter.

"You liar!" she bellowed, snatching the blade from Beatrix's hand and holding it out before her. "I'm leaving."

The Madam squinted scornfully – a brick wall blocking the doorway. "That's my money, you thief!"

Ignoring the woman, Winnie barreled toward her. Madam Stanhope's skirt wrapped beneath her legs as she fell, unable to get up in time to stop the supposed thief. The sounds of Stanhope's voice screeched orders from the landing above as Winnie's anxious feet leaped down the stairs, desperate to escape the house.

"Nasty little pickpocket! Get her boys! Kill her and I'll pay you double for the day!"

The chilling words made Winnie feel more lifeless than the souls she spoke with. Determination took hold, her feet meeting the pavement of London's streets. Heart racing, body sweating, mouth panting. Winnie ran as fast as she could, weaving in and out of the crowds, hearing the sounds of shouting coming from behind her.

A shot fired, the pang reverberating through the streets. Onlookers' cries pierced her eardrums as she ducked behind the masses to avoid being hit. A few more rounds rang out before she heard the muffled sound of orders behind her.

Turning down another street and landing in Bethnal Green, she slowed. Seeming to have lost Stanhope's men for only a moment, Winnie tried to catch her breath. *Bethnal Green is just as bad as Whitechapel,* she thought with a shudder, seeing rows of spirits as they loitered in the shadows.

Not only were the streets filled with the dead, but the living haunted this place too. Brothels, ramshackle homes, medicinal stores, pubs, and makeshift theaters filled with shouting bettors lined every inch as she tried to blend in with the horde. That's when she heard them once more.

Another shot sang, only inches to spare between Winnie and the small bit of metal that rushed past her face. The crowd around her scattered, screams ripping through the street as a nearby innocent met the fatal end of the bullet. Her pace returned to a sprint, desperate for somewhere to hide.

Turning down a nearby alleyway, she took a second to breathe. Her corset dug into her ribs, limiting her ability to fully recover from the chase. Behind her, running steps came to a halt as Madam Stanhope's men approached with the infamous Oliver as their leader.

Slowly, Winnie faced them, fastening the sack of coins into one of her skirt pockets with the dagger still in her hands. "We don't have to do this, gentleman."

"You heard the Madam. Double for your head," Oliver rasped, inching toward her.

"I'll give you all I have. Just let me go!" Her feet continued to carry her back, though she knew she'd eventually run out of space. The men snickered and sneered, a wild pack of hyenas prowling toward her. There was no way of getting out of there alive. Little did they know who they were really dealing with.

"Gali, a little help here?" Winnie prayed in her mind, hoping her deity could hear her.

Feeling the familiar warmth of the goddess's magic coursing through her, she cupped her hands together forming a ball of water.

Shooting it past the men before they realized what was happening, she created a shimmering wall to block their escape.

"I don't want to hurt you," she warned once more.

Another cackle escaped the men's lips as four barrels pointed directly at her, the others ready for hand-to-hand. The gunmen shot a few rounds as panic set in. Drawing on her element once more, she formed a wall of ice between her and the incoming bullets with mere seconds to spare. Deep down, her body ached drawing on that level of power but it was likely the only thing that would allow her to survive.

Using the cover of darkness and their momentary confusion, she snuck around the ice wall. Slipping behind one of the men, she thrust her dagger across the backs of his knees, grabbed a hold of his gun, and pointed it at his head.

"Stop this now! Before you all lose your lives! There's no need for violence," she shouted as the injured man cried out, clutching his legs. Her actions only backfired, the men continuing their ruthless pursuit.

Another round of bullets fired just as Winnie pulled the man in front of her to act as a living shield. Peeking over his bloodied shoulder, reluctant fingers pulled the trigger. By the time she was done, only three were left standing. Tucking her dagger in the side of her boot, she thrust her shield's body toward one of her attackers. Another lunged, swinging a blade wildly at her.

Nicking her forearm, she winced. Smacking either side of his hands, she focused on the weak spots of his limbs, watching the weapon fall to the cobblestone street. Jumping to avoid an attack from the side, she landed a swift punch to the man's face. Retrieving her own weapon once more, Winnie sunk the glistening metal into the man's gut before turning and throwing the crimson weapon at the thug behind her.

I'm sorry, Gali. I wish it hadn't come to this, she called out in her mind, hoping her goddess would understand.

Behind her, only one remained. Oliver. He peered around

the alleyway, seeing the bodies of his fellow attackers littering the ground. "She was right about you." His voice almost didn't carry between them, fear lacing every syllable as trembling knees shook beneath him.

"This is the first time I've seen you scared, Oliver. Didn't think you were capable," Winnie mocked, holding out her hand toward the man.

"Please, we only do what we're told," he cried out as soft waves of water slowly slithered up his torso and neared his face.

"I saw the way you smiled when you 'followed orders.' There was no pity in your eyes," she spat.

Winnie called on Gali one last time, focusing on the writhing water droplets that worked their way up the man's body. Within moments, a ball formed around his face, his hands reaching up while the liquid sloshed around and around.

The seconds that passed felt like a lifetime, Winnie holding fast to her position. A glimmer of guilt sparked, watching the man's terror grow with every second he remained without air. She closed her eyes, holding firm in her stance, remembering the terror she'd endured at the hands of this man. At last, his body fell to the ground with a thud onto the cobblestone streets of Bethnal Green.

A deep breath released, Winnie's gaze jutting around the alleyway as relief spread over her. But that victory was temporary, a soft whimper echoing from behind her. "Show yourself!" she bellowed, turning in a fury.

A mess of ashy blonde hair poked out from behind the corner down the alley, blue eyes gawking at her. A gun sat in this man's hands, though they shook too violently for him to point it at her. It fell to the ground with a clank as his hands raised above him.

Winnie inched toward the stranger, snatching his weapon off the ground and turning it on him. He shivered, examining her with a look she'd never seen before.

"Are you one of hers?" When he didn't answer, she cocked the gun.

"No!" he panicked at last. "I…I was already down here! I'm not one of them! I swear it!" His voice trembled as he tried to straighten himself, peering around at the bodies lying lifeless.

Unsure of his motives, she continued to question him. "Why were you down here, hiding?"

"I…um, it's a long story," he stuttered, his gaze once again fixing on the gun in her hands.

"How do I know I can trust you?" Pushing the barrel into the man's chest, his breath quickened and arms remained above his head in a sign of submission.

Around them, the temperature dropped. The smell of lilies filled her senses, Death slithering toward her. *"You have given me enough work for one evening, Winifred. This man means you no harm. It is not his time."*

Guilt stirred deep within her, lowering the gun away from the man as both seemed to sigh in relief at the same time.

"What's your name?" she asked hesitantly.

"Ezra Watson." A gulp followed his words, lowering his hands slowly.

"Will you tell the police what you saw tonight?" Her words were short, her patience growing thin as the craze from the day began to wear on her.

"N – No. I swear!" His stutters hardly escaped him as he took cautious steps away from her. The same fear she felt was evident in his doe eyes.

"The name's Winifred Fox. Call me Winnie. You live around here? I need to get off the streets." Fastening the dagger inside her boot once more, she examined him.

"No, I, um. I don't live anywhere."

Winnie glanced at his appearance. His hair seemed neatly placed, chin length with soft waves, but otherwise well kept. Typical lower-class attire of simple pants, button down, and waistcoat clothed his body, though they didn't appear to be covered in the usual soot and grime of most street rats.

She turned, ready to leave Ezra behind and find her own way when Death once again whispered to her. *"You will take him with you. You'll need each other in the following years. I have seen what's to come. You'll want an ally like him on your side."*

She released an exasperated sigh, realizing she'd been holding her breath as she listened to Death's words. Turning back toward the stranger before her, she offered him back his gun. "We should stick together. Bethnal Green isn't a safe place."

He peered down at the weapon, eyes still wide when he shook his head in a fury. "I don't want that thing back. You keep it."

With a nod, she fastened it within a hidden pocket of her dress. Snagging his arm, she pulled him toward the wall of water as it crashed down, the sounds of the street beyond joining them once more. "There's an inn just up ahead. I have enough for a few nights. We can figure out a plan tomorrow."

"You wish to take me with you?" he scoffed, pulling his arm away from her grasp. "Just like that? You're not going to kill me?"

"Shall we tell them you're my husband or my brother?" she asked, her mind focused on one thing: survival. Beatrix's face was etched into her mind every moment she closed her eyes, remembering her actions like a nagging bug bite waiting to heal.

A scoff fell from his mouth before he answered "brother," the first sign of his personality shining through.

She chuckled, nodding in agreement. "We'll have to tell them we have different fathers. We don't look much alike," she joked, noting her dark head of curls to his blonde waves.

"Are you a demon?" he blurted, taking another step away from her.

With a chuckle, she shook her head.

"Then what are you?"

"My mother would kill me if she knew I were telling you this, but…" she muttered, almost too quiet for him to hear. "I'm a witch. It seems strange saying that out loud. You're the first human I've told."

"Aren't you worried I'll turn you into the church to be burned? If they still do that…" His words seemed lighthearted, a joking tone hidden beneath.

"Well I am, now," she admitted. "How much did you see?"

"I, um, saw you kill a bunch of people. I've never seen a woman fight like that before." With a shrug of his shoulders, Winnie swore she could see the events unfold within his mind as Ezra stared off into the alley behind them.

"What else did you see?"

"You did something to the last man, but I couldn't tell what. He dropped to his knees as though you'd killed him from several feet away," he finally explained.

"And you won't tell anyone?"

He shook his head. "I have no reason to. I've nothing left. No family to speak of or friends." Ezra's shoulders slumped down, icy eyes peering back toward the spot in the alley he'd been hiding when the mob attacked.

"Then you and I have much in common, I fear." As they inched their way toward the crowded streets, the light of a nearby lamp post illuminated his face and she could more clearly make out his features.

"Don't you work at the bakery?" Her mind raced to the quaint establishment, mornings spent sipping cheap teas and eating small pastries with the woman she thought she loved.

"Not anymore," he mumbled as the two headed off toward an inn for the night.

She paused, unsure what to say.

"Are you going to kill me?"

It took her a moment to realize she'd ignored him the last time he'd asked. She shook her head again, thinking of Death's words. "I think we may be able to help each other. Let's just make it through tonight and we can figure it all out in the morning."

3

WINIFRED

One year later...

Thunder struck up ahead, the promise of a storm looming. Sitting across from the bartender and owner of the pub she frequently visited with Ezra, Winnie couldn't help but giggle as she relayed the widower's messages.

"She says you need to stop flirtin' with the bonny lassies that come in here, Mr. Butch," she teased, mimicking his wife's Scottish accent.

"I knew it was her who knocked that bottle of gin from my hands the other day. Damn banshee cost me a pretty penny."

Butch wiped up some spilled beer farther down the counter before offering Winnie a bowl of the evening's complimentary soup, gray curls falling into his face before brushing them aside. This was their usual arrangement: food in exchange for a conversation with his deceased love. She didn't mind it, especially since his wife was easily one of her favorite spirits to haunt Bethnal Green.

"You should know by now that she doesn't want to see you with anyone else." Spoonfuls of vegetable stew were devoured in seconds, her amber eyes jutting between the ornery spirit and her husband.

"Why can't she just move on already? A man gets lonely, you know."

Winnie grimaced, handing him her empty bowl as he offered her a piece of bread. "You're the one that insists on speaking with her every week," she reminded.

With a heavy sigh and a slight chuckle, he wandered off to care for another set of customers waiting at the bar. Winnie offered the other patrons a greeting nod before focusing her attention back on the bread she tore apart in her hands. For a moment, the world felt like it could collapse on her. Her ears rang and temples spasmed, making her clutch her head with a wince.

"You okay there, Miss Winifred? Seems you and Ezra have been pushing it these last few weeks. Never seen either of you look so ragged." Butch set a small glass of gin before her which she gratefully accepted.

"You're customer number five of the day. I'm beginning to think I'm spending more time with the dead than the living. Never thought I'd be working this hard just to stay afloat," she confessed, guzzling the drink down with a tight frown.

"I noticed he's been working extra shifts at the factory, too. What are the two of you trying to prove?" Carefully, he poured her another glass. When she tried to refuse, he offered her a gentle nod before adding, "It's on me."

"Just trying to get out of this place, already. I've been lucky enough to secure some customers over the Thames, but Madam Stanhope and her lackeys seem to be one step ahead of me at every turn." Taking another shot of gin, the headache slightly eased for a mere second.

"I had some of her boys in here the other day. Easily one of the nastiest crews to ever come through."

She nodded in agreement, recalling the mod that hunted her only a year before.

"Remember that young lad that came looking for you last year?" Her attention perked as he awaited her acknowledgment. "He came in again today. He's been showing up every few weeks lookin' for you. Says there's an issue with your mum and needs you to come home."

Guilty eyes dropped back down to the bread in her hands, knowing the young man he spoke of was her brother, Wesley.

Whether or not her mother still sent letters was unclear, but it seemed her brother was more tenacious than her parents.

"I thought Ezra was your brother?" he questioned, brows scrunched and examining her carefully.

"Different fathers," she lied, overcome by the memories of her family's sudden appearance at the inn she'd shared with Ezra those first few days of friendship. He'd seen her use her powers that night; something her mother would surely never allow.

"Please," she'd begged all those months ago. *"Don't erase his memory. He's become one of my closest friends. My only friend! I can't lose him now."* It seemed Death was right; they needed one another as both battled their own demons.

"Why don't you head home? You look exhausted. I think the sky will open up any minute now," Butch offered gently, pulling her from her memory-filled trance.

With a careful nod, she thanked him for yet another hearty meal. Placing a few stray pennies on the bar, he tried to turn them away. "A tip for the world's best bartender. But only if you listen to your wife and stop flirting with the ladies that frequent your pub!"

A daring smirk fell across her face before she offered the man's wife a quick wink who hovered in the corner of the bar. All Butch did was cackle, tossing a rag at that same corner Winnie eyed.

As she exited the pub, lightning split the sky and a cold wind chilled her to the bone. A few raindrops pelted the top of her dark curls, though thankfully she didn't have far to go. Just across the street, her ramshackle flat waited. Several stories of brick sat on the corner, her home thankfully on the very bottom. Not a single light flickered on the other side of her windows as she approached, fumbling to find her keys.

Entering, she sucked in a deep breath grateful for the level of cleanliness they managed to keep thanks to Gali's magical gifts. Hurrying toward the fireplace, Winnie stocked the smoldering embers to bring the flames back to life. *I'd like to put on a kettle before he gets home,* she thought as she grabbed a teapot from the small kitchen area. Truthfully, the room was just that. A room. No walls for privacy or family studies. Just an open area with two beds, a table, and some cabinetry.

Given that Ezra had originally mistaken her for a demon, she tried to hide her magic from him as best she could. Though he knew very clearly of her natural-born gift to speak with spirits, she didn't dare tell him about the goddess she prayed to or the other elements that could be harnessed.

"Gali? I hope you can still hear me…Can I have some water, please?" Focusing her prayers to the Goddess of Water, she waited. After two years separated from her family's coven, the connection to the deity seemed estranged at best. Attempting to fill the teapot, nothing happened at first. Cupping her hands in front of her, she imagined baby blue light shimmering in her palms as she tugged again and again on her family's magic.

Still, nothing appeared aside from a few droplets. With an agonizing sigh, Winnie tried one last time. Though it felt like running with strained muscles, she managed to call forth a few devastatingly slow inches of water, filling the teapot with enough for both of them to enjoy a small cup of tea before bed.

At once, a furious fist pounded her door. Jumping from her seated position, she rushed toward it wondering if something was terribly wrong. It swung open, a figure startling her as a wild-eyed woman jumped through the threshold. Winnie reached for the pistol at her side, holding the barrel up to a sweaty forehead.

"I mean no harm! Please, I need your help!" The woman's body was frail and timid, shifting nervously from one foot to the other and panting as she peered at the gun.

"What do you want from me?" Winnie questioned, her tone grave. *I know this trick. One minute you'll have me thinking you need help, the next a swarm of thugs will have me beaten and bloodied on the ground,* she recalled.

"You're Miss Fox?" Her thick Irish accent clung to every word as she spoke, arms raised in submission.

Not long after, a man appeared at her side wheezing and breathless. "My God, Mary. You need to start thinkin' clearly!"

Winnie pointed the gun between the two of them, his eyes widening in horror at the realization.

"Please, we're harmless. I just need your help! You're a medium, yes?" Mary rushed, pushing for an answer. She continued to take steps closer as she crossed through the threshold of their home, Winnie attempting worrisome steps away from her.

"Mhm. Mary is it?" Steady hands moved the barrel between the two strangers.

The woman nodded.

"I'm her brother, Liam. I know what this looks like, but we really have no ill will," he panted, an accent just as thick. The family resemblance was uncanny. There was no denying they both had the same mossy eyes and brown hair.

Winnie lowered the gun slightly, still uncertain.

"My daughters…" Mary's voice faltered, wiping tears away.

"I apologize for my sister. She's having a fit right now. Times have been hard," Liam mumbled, placing encouraging hands on Mary's shoulders.

Up ahead, thunder cracked once more. The rain pelted the streets just outside the threshold, the streetlamps casting shadows across the two strangers' faces.

"My daughters were murdered! I need your help. To see them; speak to them. Find out what monster could do…that!" Her words struggled to come out between sobs.

"I can't help you." Winnie's hand lay flat on the door, ready to shut it in their faces. She could hear footsteps approaching from afar as Mary reached for her arm despite the weapon she still carried.

"I've heard of you; how you help people. I already tried Madam Stanhope's and they wouldn't help me. *Please!*" Her sobbing stopped a moment, replaced by insistence.

Just past Mary and Liam, Ezra peered inside. His icy blue eyes searched between his friend and the two visitors.

"Seems strange to point a gun at company, does it not?" With a disturbed laugh, his gaze landed immediately on the pistol in her hands.

"Customers, I presume. No use standing in the rain." Winnie grumbled, ushering the siblings inside.

Ezra watched curiously as the group entered, his gaze darting around the room in a panic. As Winnie led them to the small kitchen table, he rushed around to straighten up a bit.

Around their flat, piles of books and a few stray dishes lay. Their home was overall quite bare, given that most of their money went to rent, food, and savings. Winnie managed to bring some books from her home on spiritualism, one of the few things that decorated the place. She'd traded some seances for warm blankets which would come in handy as the days became cooler, winter slowly creeping up on them.

"I charge a shilling per seance. And I'll need something of theirs. A photo or drawing works fine." She took a seat across from Mary, Liam to her left.

"I haven't any money…but I need your help." Her eyes watered, though her sobs were slowly replaced by frustration.

"I don't work for free," Winnie insisted.

"I can't even pay for food or rent, let alone a seance. I just need to talk to my girls…" Mary pleaded with the medium. When her luck seemed to run out, she turned to Ezra instead.

"You don't have to do this, Mary. You should just try to move on," Liam mumbled, placing an encouraging hand on his sister's back.

"I can't just *move on*. These are my daughters we're talkin' about! I won't rest until I know who did this."

"I saw the stories in the papers. Murders all over London. I can't believe he's been at it for a whole year and hasn't been caught yet. The last two…were they your girls? I've seen them running through the streets with the other kids. I wondered where they were these last few days. I'm so…" Ezra's eyes softened, dropping to the floor to avoid the mother's sadness. The word 'sorry' couldn't seem to choke out.

A crash of thunder sounded, everyone inside jumping in surprise.

"Yes…the most recent murders were. I was workin' at the factory and came home to the police telling me they couldn't do anything."

"They said they would try," her brother mumbled, though he didn't look too sure.

"We're all very aware that the police don't care about the slums of Bethnal Green. Especially not us. They're probably happy to see two less Irish sleepin' on the streets at night." Anger filled her eyes as she spoke.

Liam sighed, digging into his pockets. He pulled out a few pennies and placed them on the table. "That's all I have left."

Winnie reached for them, examining what little he could offer. Just as guilt rumbled inside her, she felt a hand place lightly on her shoulder. Looking up, she saw Ezra's soft eyes, lips in a tight frown, as he shook his head.

Returning the coins back to Liam, he mumbled, "We're not ones to take a man's last coin. You started this business to help people. Please? Do it for me." His scrunched eyebrows and pleading gaze begged her to agree.

Mary's brother nodded graciously, the mother's face brightening with hope.

"When did they die?" Winnie asked, focusing the conversation. She had an early morning, needing to be down at the docks if she wanted to beat her rivals at Madam Stanhope's.

"Last week," Mary whispered. "The police already told me there were too many criminals here to figure out which of 'em did it."

No wonder she's such a mess, Winnie thought. "Calling on

such new spirits can be a bit of a gamble. They may not know how to reach out yet, but we can try," Winnie mumbled with a sigh, her head aching from the previous performances that day. She hoped she could still get through to them despite her exhaustion.

"Please explain to my sister that all of this is a hoax and you can't actually help her," Liam urged, motioning for her ensemble.

She glanced down at the outfit she'd worked hard to procure. Part of her business was looking and acting the part. Though she didn't rely on fanciful crimson curtains and money-hungry gimmicks like Madam Stanhope, she knew she still had to put on somewhat of a show. The crimson robe and cascading, chunky jewelry were all part of it. Her amber eyes glanced around the room anxiously, a strange feeling of dread settling in her gut.

"I assure you, I am not a hoax. We will make contact." A certain stubbornness brewed inside her, ready to prove him wrong.

"Get on with it then," he muttered.

He still doesn't believe me. I'll show him, she thought with conviction.

Mary reached into her pocket, pulling out two stained scarves. "These belonged to them. They wore them when…"

Winnie nodded in understanding. "It'll do just fine." Having their blood was probably more useful than a photo would have been. She could complete the seance without anything tangible, though the items helped her hone in on the correct spirits, rather than be a beacon for every lost soul in London.

"Grab my hands," she said, reaching for Mary and Liam. Holding hands wasn't necessarily a requirement either. Just as the personal items ensured the correct spirits were called, so did the connection to their family.

Ezra took a seat at the edge of his bed across the room, observing. He'd never been one to get involved too much. When available and not working in the factory, his job was to keep an eye out in case things went wrong. In case she needed his attention on her customers while deep in her spiritual trance.

As the mother's clammy hands made contact with Winnie's, a shock radiated through her. *Is that coming from Mary?* she wondered. She'd only ever felt a bolt of energy like that from magical creatures. The storm outside continued to surge, the dim light of the flickering fire making the room feel more menacing. A chill ran down her spine, a sense of dread washing over her once more.

Within an instant, her gut told her to stop.

Winnie closed her eyes, focusing on the girls anyway. Attempting to transport herself into Oblivion, something blocked her. A chill spread through the air, a sure sign she was making contact in the physical realm. There was a tug on the other end, Mary's daughters trying to join them. A faded whisper fell across the room, fire dimming.

"Girls? Your mother's here. Come to us."

The invitation was strong, her heart warming as she felt the girls' approach. They were close, the temperature dropping once more, and then…

Is someone interfering? she wondered.

A crash landed outside, the room filling with momentary light.

"Please, girls! I need to see you!" Mary cried out.

"Only the medium speaks during the ceremony," Ezra said, repeating the warning Winnie always gave. Any sign of distraction and she may end up calling the wrong spirit. He took a stand, inching his way toward the group as if unsure how much to interfere.

Ignoring him, Mary called out, tears streaming down her cheeks. "Please! I need to know who did this to you! I'll do anything!"

The air in the room thickened, weight filling the shadows. Soul-crushing pressure, sitting heavy on Winnie's chest. Mary's daughters dissipated at once, their fear tangible.

Slowly, something shifted.

Stalked.

Closer and closer it prowled, salivating at the mother's torment.

"Someone's here." Winnie's voice faltered.

Shallow breaths turned to clouds as the room froze, a haze glossing over all surfaces.

"Iníonacha? My girls? Please!"

The shadows crept closer around the grieving mother.

"Ezra, stop her," Winnie warned, her tone sharp.

She attempted to pull her arms away to break the connection. It was no use. The mother's grip was like glue. Liam looked around in confusion, Mary's endless tears ceased at last. Books rattled from the shelves and thunder clapped. The hair on Winnie's neck rose as she sensed the darkness spreading in the room.

"I hear something…" Mary whispered.

Winnie turned in confusion, hearing nothing. She tugged at her hands, pulling herself free from the siblings. Trying to stand, shadows grabbed ahold of her wrists and planted them firmly onto the arms of the chair.

"Girls?"

"That's not your daughters!" Winnie warned, continuing to tug harder and harder, the shadows seeming to drain her. She felt lifeless, that *thing* using her energy to manifest.

Soft whispers spread across the room. The smoke encircled Mary, pulling her closer and closer.

"You're drawing it in!" Winnie cried.

Ezra yanked Liam from his chair, pushing him toward the door.

"I need to see them…" Mary said softly. Her vision seemed to glaze over, expressionless and dull. A moment passed before the whispers slowed. Grew deeper in tone.

And at last began to hiss.

"Yes…" she sighed, answering a question no one else could hear.

Air vacated the room, extinguishing the fire on its way out. Every ounce of warmth abandoned Winnie's body as an icy chill spread, the fingers of Death grasping her tightly. Closing her eyes, the medium envisioned her light magic encompassing the entity, suffocating it. Sending it back to wherever it came from. But it was no use. *I've never had to banish a spirit before. I don't even know what I'm doing!*

"We didn't summon you! Whoever you are – leave now!" Winnie exclaimed, scooting her chair back to create distance between her and the entity.

She continued spearing her magic at the creature, though nothing seemed to stick. As if shielded by the mother's pain, it only grew. Drawing on the goddess she'd prayed to since she was a little girl, she called out in her mind.

"Gali, Goddess of Water. I know I haven't kept up with my practice. But…I could really use your help!" Silence sat on the other end of her prayers.

A match flared in Ezra's hands. Illuminating the room just enough, they could see an entity lurking behind Mary. Only her face peered through the wickedness, shadowy fingers grasped tightly around her head. They dug into her skin, eyes closed.

Within an instant, the extinguished fire relit itself. Flickering flames filled the room again, more intense than before. Shadows dance like rioting demons as the sounds of thunder rose.

"Mary!" Liam bellowed, reaching for her.

Ezra intercepted his hand, pulling him toward the door once more. "We need to go!" he ordered, pushing the man further and further, though her brother persisted.

An unearthly moan spread through the room, ensuring Liam's attention stayed on his sister. Winnie shivered, every instinct telling her to *run*. A low grumble fell and the tension in the room tripled. The soft whispers ceased…

Then silence fell.

Winnie let out a small cry, seeing Mary's body begin to levitate. With arms outstretched at her sides, her mouth gaped open. The darkness lifted her by an unseen hand, eyes paling and lifeless.

Ripping the door open and pushing Liam out, Ezra turned back. He gawked at the shadows before looking back at Winnie, precious seconds passing.

"I'll be fine! Just go!"

With a nod, the two men exited before Winnie's attention flickered back toward the possession. Mary's green eyes were blank – as if her life was sucked out. Colors of flames consumed her muted hair, the texture coiling at the invasion. Palpable rage emanated from the floating woman, heating the frozen room. Chills turned to sweat. Whispers intensified. Fierce lines of navy blue painted her skin, the mother's face contorting as a veneer of ancient battle marks embedded into her.

Turning back toward the medium, Mary's head lay cocked sideways as if broken, a fire-filled vacant glare directed at her. The energy pouring from the mother was so dark, Winnie was certain she'd die. She never experienced a spirit as vengeful as this.

"The anger this mother feels…It's intoxicating." She inhaled deeply as she spoke, but it wasn't Mary's voice. Rather than shrill and scared, it was rough and grating – as if she'd spent a millennium shouting.

"Who *are* you?" Winnie stuttered.

A wide-eyed stare followed the entity as she lowered onto the ground.

Ignoring the question, the spirit asked, "What year is it?"

"1871…"

"What of Rome?" The woman's voice seemed to hiss at the mention of it.

The question surprised Winnie. "Rome isn't around anymore… Who are you?"

"You should never question your queen," she spat, voice sure and powerful. Flames blazed in the woman's eyes as she looked to the exit.

"Wait – come back! This isn't Rome!" Winnie cried, tugging at the shadows that still held her. She didn't know what to do, but letting her leave seemed like a grave mistake.

"This will always be Rome..." the queen hissed, stalking toward the door.

Winnie tried one final time to tug at the shadowy bindings and banish the spirit. Anything other than sit and watch the woman leave. But it was no use. Her energy drained as the spirit drew on her power, taking one last piece before finally exiting the flat. Winnie's eyes faltered, dark spots clouding her vision. The last thing she felt was the anger and fury of the queen taking Mary's captive body with her.

<h1 style="text-align:center">4</h1>

WINIFRED

Winnie's mind continued to fade in and out of consciousness. The departure of the queen took the last little bit of energy she had left, leaving her with only her thoughts and regret. Even though the shadows no longer tied her to the chair, she felt she couldn't move. Cemented in place, the ferocity of that entity still consumed her.

Heavy footsteps thudded back into her flat, though she couldn't tell who it was. Between flashes, she could see glimpses of blonde hair and a factory uniform. As soon as she saw his blue eyes, she realized it was Ezra.

"Winnie! What…happened?" Though she could only vaguely make out his words, a mix of colorful language peppered what she could hear.

With nearly every ounce of her magic drained, she knew what she needed to do. Fox Manor was the only place where she'd be able to recuperate and recover from the spiritual attack. Only then could she figure out how to fix her mistake.

"I'll explain later…Where did…she go?" Her words choked from her mouth.

"Mary's gone. Don't know where she went. I saw her speak to someone down the street before disappearing. It was the strangest thing. As if she walked *through* a wall." His gaze searched around the room as if it contained answers.

"Home…" she muttered, trying to hold her head up. "I need

to get home."

"You are home," he tried to say, though a drowsy hand shushed him.

"Fox Manor. I need to get there." Slowly, her vision returned and she could see clearly again. Despite the ringing in her ears and pounding headache, she was steadily becoming more coherent.

"You've never told me where your parents live. Why don't we wait until morning? It'll give you some time to rest. I'll take you then," he suggested, crouched down in front of her.

"No, tonight. I'm drained. I need my family." She leaned forward, almost falling from the chair as she shook her head, trying to clear the fuzziness in her brain.

"I don't understand what you're saying. Drained? I've never seen you like this."

"We don't have to go far…just around the corner," she mumbled, pulling herself to stand as he helped her up.

"They live in Bethnal Green? I thought your family was well-off?" As he supported her weight, he pulled back a little to inspect her carefully.

"Ez, I haven't been…honest with you. Spirits aren't the only things to exist. You know a little bit, but there's so much more." Her words came to a halt, stomach slithering inside nervously.

"I already knew I was living with Merlin. What more could there be?" he joked, a soft chuckle escaping his lips.

"I should've told you the truth sooner. I wanted to keep you away from all of this."

With a scoff, he continued. "You're my best friend, Winnie. Sooner or later, I would've found out the whole truth. Just tell me how I can help."

"We need to get to the alleyway. I'll show you."

Clutching his arm, the two shuffled outside onto the rain-soaked streets. Across the way, a slew of onlookers gawked at the pair as Winnie limped beside him. As they rounded the corner and down an alley, Ezra peered around in confusion.

My mother is going to be furious when she finds out I'm bringing him home, she worried. Her mind thought back to the last time she'd seen her family. To the fight they had over Ezra. Milicent told her to part ways, wipe his memory, ignore him, keep him out of her life. But that wasn't an option for Winnie. No matter what the world threw at them, she knew she'd protect her friend, no matter the cost. But what if this time she couldn't stop them?

"Where the hell are we going?" he muttered, unknowingly standing just before the portal to Fox Manor.

To him, it looked like merely a blocked doorway. With a rusty handle and wooden planks covering the entrance, there was no way to get through. Others in the area certainly tried, thieves and curious children especially. But without the family talisman she wore around her neck at all times, entry was impossible. Magically warded and sealed, Milicent ensured her daughter always had a way home. Even if she only knew the general vicinity of Winnie's location.

"That door doesn't open," he began.

As her hands reached out in front of them, the blockade glowed. The onyx necklace around her neck exuded the same shine, the connection between two worlds joining. She felt a small tug from the other end, closing her eyes as she envisioned the manor.

Though she had little energy left to make the jump, there was just enough. She pulled on her family's connection, her mind screaming at her to stop over-exerting herself. Clutching his shoulder for support, she pulled the two toward the portal.

"Just trust me," she said with a half-hearted smile, weary and tired as she guided him through.

When their feet landed through the threshold and onto the grassy lawn of Fox Manor, Ezra hunched over and clutched his stomach. His groans brought back memories of her first time, remembering the pain and dizziness she'd felt as well. A slew of foul words escaped his lips as he attempted to straighten himself up.

"Where are we?" His voice was strained as he examined the estate.

"This is my home..." she mumbled, seeing the gas lamps on the porch glittering in welcome.

She'd wanted to bring Ezra to the manor for a while now. Wanted him to meet her family the proper way, especially her brother. Fear kept her away, worried her mother would stress the issue once more. Or worse, make her brother use his powers to make her best friend forget her after a year of knowing each other.

Looking around the estate now, memories of her childhood pelted her. Her heart ached, heat building in her throat. She took a deep breath, simpler times piercing her mind. With each inhale, she remembered them – the days before the hustle. The years of ease, of only having to worry about growing up. Nostalgia made her eyes well, realizing just how much she missed this place.

She remembered it all so clearly. Festivals celebrating various holidays. Running through the hallways playing tag with her brother. Meeting her best friends, the Falke brothers, and spending countless hours out on the lake with them. The porch where she'd first discovered she could wield the element of water. Memories of firsts and lasts, love and heartache.

Turning toward Ezra, Winnie couldn't help but notice his blue eyes bewildered, taking in the estate. It was a sight to behold, after all. Massive and gothic, the outer combination of brick and wood stood alongside ornate archways and gabled roofs. The same colonettes that would soon be decorated for Samhain stood tall and grand.

His gaze roamed the flowers blooming despite the days growing shorter and colder. "How the hell did we get here? And... shouldn't those be dead?"

Winnie chuckled, though before she could open her mouth to respond he peppered her with more questions.

"*This* is where you grew up?" His voice was accusatory this time, mouth gaping wide and brows furrowed in confusion.

She nodded reluctantly, still clinging to his arm for stability.

"I knew your family was rich but I didn't know they were *rich*. You mean to tell me you could live *here*, but you choose to live in Bethnal Green?"

"Yes, I wanted…to make it on my own." Her voice stalled a little, shivering from the cold chill.

"I love you, Winnie, but that's the stupidest thing I've ever heard. Look at this place! It's enormous!" A small chuckle escaped him, eyes still roaming the house, a dull ache behind them. "I don't think I've ever seen something this beautiful."

"You're right. And it would've been easier to stay. But I wanted…more." Her head lowered, beginning to walk toward the house.

"I don't know what more you could want. Where is this place?" The two shuffled forward, his arm braced around her for warmth.

"That's an even longer story that we don't have time for tonight."

As they approached the entrance of the house, the heavy walnut door swung open in a fury. "Winnie!" Milicent cried, arms reaching out to her in a panic. "I could feel through the coven's ties that you were drained. What happened?"

Before Winnie could answer, she noted her mother's sudden hesitance. Taking a few steps away from their blonde haired visitor, a cautious hand reached for them regardless.

"I'm fine, Mum." She sighed in relief, accepting a deep long embrace carefully offered, though Milicent's gaze was still fixed on Ezra.

The house's smell hit her immediately as the door stood open. Coffee and vanilla, leather from the couches. Fresh cut flowers. Dirt from copious house plants. It all mingled together and brought back memory after memory, the ache of home knotting in her stomach.

"Mother, you've heard of Mr. Watson," Winnie mumbled, seeing her mother's stunned look.

He nervously reached out, shaking her hand. She took it

carefully, examining him. "I wondered when I'd officially meet you," she said softly, a nervous smile quivering at the corners of her mouth.

"Evening, Ma'am." Ezra shot his friend a strange look, one she couldn't comprehend. With furrowed eyebrows, his head tilted to the side as if waiting for Winnie to explain further.

"Come inside! You two look dreadful!" Milicent shuddered. She led them to the sitting room just off the entrance and urged them to sit.

Winnie examined the rooms, just as she had so many times before. Every plant and ornately framed drawing or photograph on the floral wallpapered walls brought back a sense of comfort she'd forgotten about. Her mother snapped her fingers, a pot of tea appearing on the coffee table in front of them. A startled, wide-eyed gaze fell to Winnie, Ezra in shock of the appearance.

"H – how did she do that?" His voice was soft, merely a whisper.

"Oh my," Milicent exclaimed. "I'm so sorry! I assumed that since she brought you here, she'd told you about…you know." She offered both a cup of tea.

"I knew she could do some things. Making tea appear out of thin air seems…" The words fell flat as he shook his head in disbelief.

"Like I said, I haven't been fully honest with you." Winnie's eyes dropped, a twinge of guilt filling her as she accepted the cup from her mother. The smell of chamomile and honey wafted to her nose. It was the same concoction Milicent always made when Winnie was in distress growing up. Everything seemed so familiar and yet equally so distant.

"In Winnie's defense, we raised both our children to keep quiet about their magic. Though she's the only one of my two that seems to have an affinity for defiance." Milicent offered her daughter a playful smirk above the rim of her teacup as she spoke.

Just like the tea, her mother hadn't changed one bit in two years. Milicent wore the same cotton robe she'd owned for the last decade, her dark hair pinned up out of her face. Her delicate fingers grasped at the same porcelain cups with dainty pink flowers. Those mirrored amber eyes, the ones Winnie had inherited, roamed her daughter settling on the outfit.

"Oh, Winifred." Her sigh felt like a punch in the face. "I know things ended badly the last time I saw you, but I wish you'd come home. Those clothes. They're hardly suitable for a young lady of your standing. And I hate to tell you this, but I've smelled stables that were cleaner than you two."

"I'm here now. For a short time," she said softly, a faint smile over her lips. She shifted on the couch, trying to get comfortable, feeling a little too much and yet not enough.

"Tell me what happened. I could feel you pulling on the family magic to assist you in whatever was going on. If you'd kept up your practice, you might've been successful."

Her face scowled, Winnie feeling like a child during a lecture. As she filled her mother in, Ezra sat quietly sipping his tea glancing back and forth between the mother and daughter.

"She didn't say much. Only that she's a queen and looking for Rome," Winnie explained.

Her friend's gaze rested on the teapot again, Milicent managing to read his mind. Grabbing the handle, she poured him another cup with a welcoming smile. A gracious head bow followed, Ezra scooting back into the couch as if trying to make himself smaller.

"Rome?" Her mother sighed once more, lips twisted in curiosity and brows scrunched.

"I didn't have time to give her a history lesson," Winnie joked.

"I didn't know spirits could overtake someone like that. I mean, I've heard stories at church growing up about demons, but I didn't believe them. Always just assumed they were trying to scare us." Ezra's tone was hushed as his attention drifted.

This must all be so overwhelming for him, Winnie thought with some guilt. She could see the way he anxiously shifted in his seat, straightening his clothing and eyes glancing around the room. He was doing a good job hiding his discomfort from her mother, but she could read him like a book.

"I can't help but wonder if this is tied to the visions I've had," Milicent began, sipping from the last little bit of her tea. "I keep seeing a girl in danger, consumed by flames and chased by hounds. I wonder if your queen is the one after her."

"Do you know where she may be?" Winnie asked, setting her tea cup down and leaning back on the couch as her corset dug into her ribs.

"From the few images I've seen, definitely not London. There wasn't a single cobblestone street in sight. She feels far away, as if perhaps across the seas." Her mother held her hands out, eyes closed, likely trying to sense the girl.

"Is it possible to get there in time? Boats leave every day to get to the other continents but it'll take months," Ezra mentioned, leaning forward in anticipation.

"We don't need boats," Milicent chuckled. "We do need to get there quickly, however. Portaling will be the best option. The full moon just passed, so we're going to need help. Our magic alone won't be enough to open one of such magnitude."

"You know who we can call on," Winnie mumbled, knowing Milicent wouldn't like her answer. Her mind immediately landed on her childhood best friends whom her mother banished two years ago; the catalyst of many events that led Winnie to leave her family home.

"I'm not calling on those boys! I'm still upset with them." She straightened the fabric of her robe and nightgown, avoiding Winnie's gaze.

"It's been two years, Mother! You can't seriously still hold a grudge."

Ezra glanced between the two curiously in a silent plea for more information. Winnie shook her head as if to say, *'I'll tell you later.'*

"Not only are they powerful, you know they'll help us in a

heartbeat. What they did wasn't even that bad! The fact that you banished them to begin with is ludicrous!"

Anger bubbled up in Winnie's stomach. The same conviction she'd felt the night the brothers were banished returned, reminding her why she'd moved out in the first place.

"I'm *not* having that argument with you again, Winifred. There's a lot more to that story than you realize. I will not have those boys here." She shook her head as a severe grimace formed on her face.

"That's why I can't remember that night. Isn't it? You can't trust me with my own memories or tell me what happened!" The events of that evening were muddled in her mind, like wading through quicksand. To this day, no one would confess what happened. And yet still, she knew they'd done something to her memories to keep the truth concealed.

"Who're you talking about?" Ezra asked cautiously, his voice quiet as if to change the subject yet not put himself in Winnie's line of fire.

"The Falke brothers," Milicent said with an exasperated sigh.

"They were once like family to us until my mother overreacted." Winnie's tone was accusatory and harsher than she meant it to be. Even two years ago, she hadn't dared speak up like this.

"We can call on your Aunt Afissa instead. Or even Horace for goodness sake! Anyone but those bloody sirens." She stood, grabbing the teapot to leave.

"I'm calling them. If you don't want them staying here, they can stay at my flat in London," Winnie insisted.

Ezra groaned, likely thinking of two more people in their small, ramshackle home.

"I don't think it's a good idea," her mother grumbled, turning back toward the conversation with a fury. "They will only bring chaos."

"Even Afissa's magic won't be enough to open a portal without the full moon. They're our best chance and you know it. They'd do anything to protect us," Winnie insisted.

"That's partially the problem," Milicent muttered. "Fine. Call on them. But I will keep a close eye on them. I want everyone to stay here at the manor. Every second they're around, I will be watching."

"Scold them all you want when they get here, I don't care. But I felt the anger of that queen. We're going to need allies." Winnie stood up, arms folded across her chest. Though she still felt a little woozy, her stubbornness kept her steady.

"I can't wait to meet these friends of yours," Ezra mumbled sarcastically, eyes flashing to Winnie in concern. They seemed to scream, *'What have you gotten us into?'*

"Winnie, you need to stay here tonight to finish recovering. That entity took a lot from you, I can tell. Even my powers feel impacted. Mr. Watson, you're welcome to stay in one of our guest rooms. But please, bathe first. Get the smell of grime and vermin off of you both before stepping foot into those beds."

Ezra's cheeks flushed in embarrassment. They each nodded, Winnie leading him upstairs as Milicent sauntered toward the kitchen. He followed after her up a set of walnut stairs, a navy oriental runner leading their way.

"This house just keeps getting more and more beautiful," he mumbled.

"Wait till you see the outside tomorrow. It's even better."

Lifting his nose in the air, he sniffed carefully. "Why do I smell," he began, careful to choose his next words. "I smell the bakery."

She remembered the stories he'd told her – the vague reasons he'd ended up kicked out of his home to begin with, which led him to huddle in that alleyway. To this day, he hadn't opened up fully. *I hope one day he'll trust me enough to know the truth,* she confessed internally.

"The house has a tendency to pull out memories. Good ones usually. There must be something about the bakery that stuck with you all this time," she explained.

His eyes darted away from her nervously, shame lingering beneath them. Reaching the top of the stairs, Winnie showed him to the bathroom and then the guest room.

"Your mother doesn't seem to care for me," he admitted, standing just outside the guest room door.

"Give her time. She's like me. Needs to warm up to people, first. I'm just down the hall if you need me." She offered his arm a quick squeeze of reassurance before ushering him through the door.

"This bed is enormous!" she heard from the opposite side of the closed door, followed by a loud gasp.

Chuckling, she wandered toward her childhood bedroom. Entering, she was in awe. Nothing had changed. Her piles of books were still scattered, the same forest green wallpaper covered in drawings and wooden carvings of animals and fae alike. After a much needed bath, she sunk into her bed. The strongest wave of exhaustion she'd ever felt washed over her as the bed pulled her down, tempting her with comfort and relief.

I'm home.

5

EZRA

The crackling of a warm fire woke him first. Sleepy fingers brushed through cotton sheets, spreading from one end to the other with ease. Drowsy eyes fluttered open, mind muddled and filled with confusion. He shot up, forgetting where he'd fallen asleep. His racing heart eased slowly, taking everything in and remembering the night before.

"My god, this place is huge!" he announced to the empty room.

When he entered last night after a long bath, he'd sunk into the mattress without a single thought. Exhaustion overtook him, a tiredness he was all too familiar with.

He took a moment to appreciate the dwelling. All of it. The warm fire, the cozy reading chair next to it. The floral wallpapers and walnut floors. The bed toppled with pillows for style, not just sleeping. In all his life, he'd never had such luxuries. Growing up, he was lucky to have a bed that wasn't shared by several others.

Get up, his mind screamed at him. *You have places to be!* But he took a moment to settle himself, remembering he had a later shift that day. With a final stretch, the same question he'd asked Winnie the night before re-entered his mind: *Why does she live with me in Bethnal Green when she could live here?*

He'd grown up near their current home, just a few blocks away. Memories of running through the mucked up streets, working the paper stands, and trying to bring in every penny possible to survive reminded him that their childhoods were clearly very different.

His stomach rumbled, checking the golden clock sitting on the nightstand with steady hands ticking away as the seconds passed. He panicked, untangling himself from heavy sheets once he realized it was already nine o'clock.

A pair of slippers and cozy robe waited for him, draped over the edge of the reading chair. Neither of which he remembered being there before. An anxious gaze peered around the room, noticing that his work clothes were nowhere to be found. *I hope her mother didn't have them burned,* he thought with a frown, knowing that a factory uniform was one of only two outfits he had the luxury of owning.

Peering into a mirror, Ezra ruffled his hair and straightened his borrowed pajamas. Before he could exit the room, the aroma returned. Those familiar wafts of apples, dough, and bourbon. The smells of the bakery. *I wish the house would stop trying to remind me of that night,* he thought, memories tugging to be set free.

The day he met Winnie surfaced first, a little more palatable than the ones lingering beneath the truth. The fateful night that changed the course of his life. The night he'd lost his somewhat well-paying job and a piece of his heart, only to be kicked out by his mother. He'd blocked much of it from his memory, too weary to linger on the images.

If there was one thing that stuck with him, it was his mother's face. The look of disappointment in them when she found out the truth about him. The disgust that followed had been the source of nightmares for the last year, remembering that look. The words that rang through his mind in an unceasing loop: *"You're no longer my son."*

The thought that he hadn't seen his mother since provided much needed comfort. Now he was free, though waking in a gothic manor, surviving his first possession, and learning about a whole new world he didn't know existed was never something he expected. Strangely, it felt like it was always meant to be this way.

He'd easily accepted the truth about spirits. He had a few

encounters growing up that were unexplainable. Plenty of folks told tales at their pub, trying to earn a few pennies. But it was different than seeing it first hand.

The night he met Winnie, he'd lied to her. About several bits of information. For one, he didn't tell her why he'd been down the alley with a gun in his hand in the first place. Ezra didn't think he'd ever be ready to tell the truth about his intentions.

He recalled his desperate deceptions, unwilling to confess he'd watched her drown a man with no source of water around from fear she'd do the same to him. It wasn't until weeks later that he truly accepted that she had no intentions of hurting him.

Exiting the room and walking through the hallways of Fox Manor, he couldn't help but stop to admire the family photographs. They made him feel…different. Ezra hadn't expected a physical reaction, but seeing their happiness made him crave a childhood he never got to have. Rather than a mother that loved him, he had one that abandoned him, took everything he had. Threw him on the streets to fend for himself.

I'll never forgive her…

Shaking his head, he attempted to throw away the memories as he forced a smile across his face. They'd be the death of him if he let them linger. Walking through an intricately carved hallway, he saw the kitchen just ahead. The sounds of music and laughter met him where he stood, welcoming him.

He stood in awe of the room, large windows standing from the floor to the ceiling just before the cooking area. Gray and white tiles lay beneath his feet, white cabinets and greenery spread throughout the room. The island counter sat with lines of barstools, ready to entertain guests. A small table with three chairs sat by the side of the room, the perfect place to stare out over the scenery.

Through the windows, he saw a line of dense forest humming with life. Birds, deer, insects, butterflies, and all manner of tiny creatures buzzed about just beyond the glass. To the right of the woodline sat a magnificent lake, deep spruce and lush with all types of vegetation. Frogs jumped from lily pads, more insects humming along the waterline. The entire estate seemed to forget that it was currently autumn, winter looming.

Winnie sat at the small table by the window, looking out. Nursing a cup of coffee, she pulled a wool robe around her. Milicent cooked by the gas stove with a young man, the two playfully spooning thin batter onto a warmed pan.

That must be the real brother she mentioned, he thought to himself.

"Look who's finally awake!" Ezra heard a deep voice with a thick American accent coming from behind him.

Winnie's presumed father walked into the room, passing Ezra as he strode to Milicent's side. His friend hadn't mentioned her dad was American, though it made sense. Her accent was never as thick as most in London.

He leaned in and gave Milicent a small peck, ruffling his son's hair and striding back to Ezra. He was the only one in the group who wasn't in pajamas, wearing typical men's fashion: trousers, a white button-down shirt, and a fitted blue waistcoat.

He reached out a welcoming hand, offering a warm smile. "Ernest Fox, it's a pleasure to meet you." He pointed over to Milicent and the boy before adding, "You've met my lovely wife, Millie. That's Wesley beside her. Feel free to call us by our first names. No need for formalities here."

The boy, only a few years younger than Winnie, raised a nervous hand with a shy smile. The father and son duo were spitting images of each other with curly, coffee brown hair and verdant green eyes. As Wesley turned back to his mother cooking breakfast for the group, his smile was infectious. Just as Ernest grinned big and bright, so did his son.

Milicent smeared a bit of batter onto his face, the boy cringing with a belly laugh. Something in Ezra's chest tightened seeing them. *I'll never know what it's like to have a mother worth cooking with*, he thought with a sigh.

"Have a seat. Let me know if you prefer tea," Ernest offered, pointing across from Winnie. He brought over two plates topped with pancakes and jams, hot coffee waiting for Ezra as well.

"You didn't have to go out of your way to feed me. I would've been fine with a piece of bread," he chuckled nervously, waiting for them to start laying out their conditions for kindness.

She offered him a smirk just above the edge of her cup. "I think you'll find that anything you have here will be much more satiating and delicious than anything we have back at home."

Ezra took a careful taste and almost jolted back in his seat. He'd never enjoyed such a deep, rich flavor before. He inched forward in his chair, sitting right at the edge, savoring another cautious sip. A mix of nutty vanilla, the perfect balance of bitter and sweet, danced on his tongue.

"What is this? Why does it taste so good?"

"My parents actually have money for good quality coffees, unlike us," she joked.

"Will you tell your daughter she's being a fool for wanting to stay in Bethnal Green?" Ezra called out, looking to her parents for support.

"We've been trying to tell her that for two years now," Ernest said with a laugh. "She's got her mother's stubbornness. There's no use arguing."

Winnie sneered at her father playfully before Milicent interrupted the thought.

"So Ezra, Winnie mentioned you briefly when you first met, but she hasn't been around much lately. Tell us about yourself."

"What do you want to know?" He didn't particularly care to share too much about his past.

"Do you have family in London?"

Let's see…there's the father who's a drunk. The mother who hates me…

"No…Well, technically but I don't talk to them." He didn't feel right lying.

"Siblings?"

She continued to pepper him with questions as he shifted nervously in his seat. Flashes of images hit him like a ton of bricks. The small button nose, the sounds of soft coos. Teeny tiny fingers wrapped around his pinky when he was only five years old. The doctors visiting when she fell ill. *"We can't do anything…we're sorry for your loss."* The baby with no name, not around long enough to be given one.

"No…no siblings." *Not anymore,* he thought. His answer was simple. Not technically a lie.

Something in Milicent's eyes shifted to sadness as if knowing. "Sorry if I'm intruding. Winnie never brings her friends around."

"Maybe because you nag them with questions," she retorted between bites.

"How did you two meet?" Wesley asked, speaking for the first time since Ezra sat down.

"The same night I cut ties with my mother, I bumped into her on the street. She was dealing with a group of thugs from Madam Stanhope's," Ezra began. *Cutting ties is a bit of an understatement, but they don't need to know the full story.*

Her attention flashed to him in a panic at the mention of the men who attacked her. A quick kick met his shin beneath the table, glaring at him.

"I accidentally saw her use some magic, mistook her for a demon, and then we joined forces," he explained.

"You weren't wrong about the demon part," Wesley blurted, a giggling snort following as his words seemed to tumble aimlessly from his mouth.

Winnie simply glared at her brother. "I think I scared the daylights out of him. But the spirits spoke to me. One in particular. Told me he has a greater purpose here in this life, and that we'd need each other." Her eyes fluttered over the edge of her coffee cup once more, a smile hiding.

Something in Milicent's face seemed to shift, a sort of disdain or disapproval Ezra couldn't quite place.

"We decided to collaborate, focusing on her business. I still work at the factory during the day to bring in extra money. And we've been best of friends ever since," he added, offering her a grateful smile.

Still to this day, there was a part that didn't feel worthy of her kindness. He remembered how cold she could be to some, recognizing the hurt and shielded side of her. It had taken some time to break through her shields, Ezra familiar with the feeling.

Ernest's eyes narrowed on him. "Are you two…?" He hinted at the obvious, Ezra's cheeks flushing.

"No," he choked out.

"Dad!" Winnie's mouth gaped open in mortified disbelief.

"I'm sorry! I had to know. You two do live together, after all." He threw his hands up in a sign of submission, having a seat at the counter to enjoy his coffee.

"We tell people we're siblings, though I don't think the bartender at our usual pub is convinced," he joked.

"Brother is more accurate, for sure. I don't think I'm your type," Winnie mumbled with a soft chuckle.

Ezra shook his head, surprised she'd noticed at all. He'd never told her what his type really was.

"Have you heard back from the Falke brothers?" Milicent asked, placing a few more pancakes on an empty plate.

Ezra peered across the room, mouth salivating thinking of having more. *I couldn't possibly impose,* he thought. As if reading his mind, she offered him a warm smile and placed another on his plate.

"Haven't heard back yet, but knowing them they'll just show up." A nervous huff of something resembling a laugh escaped Winnie as she took another pancake as well.

"I need to know more about these two," Ezra teased, digging into the second helping of breakfast.

"They're old friends of ours," her brother began, joining Winnie and Ezra.

Milicent's eyes seemed to roll at the mention of their names.

"Mum doesn't particularly like them all that much."

"Now, now – it's not that I don't like them. Don't make me out to be some awful person," she said, her words flustered. "I simply don't like the trouble they always cause. Especially with *that one*," she finished, pointing to Winnie.

Her face blushed as she attempted to retreat within herself.

"I'm sure they'll be here in time for the portal. Good thing too, because Afissa is dealing with selkies, and Horace is dealing with the aftermath of the full moon. You know how hard it is for them." Milicent's face scowled at the thought.

"Why is that?" Ezra questioned, searching for anyone to answer.

"Horace and his people are Lycan," Wesley added, pouring himself a cup of coffee.

"Like the legends?"

"Yes, like the legends. I'll fill you in later," Winnie mumbled, getting up from her seat. Her cheeks were still flushed as she placed her dishes in the sink.

"Where're you going?"

"I'll be in the sunroom reading. Come find me when you're ready." She offered Ezra a smiling nod meant to reassure before exiting.

Ezra glanced between her family members – strangers and yet so friendly it was alarming to him. As the morning went on, he found they had a knack for drawing out his outgoing side. They continued to ask questions about his past, though less serious ones.

Small inquiries about hobbies and interests, where he'd gone to school. What his knowledge of magic was. He felt almost embarrassed to admit he had none. All he knew was what the church had taught him as a boy growing up and the occasional tall tale from travelers in the pubs.

It wasn't until they left the kitchen that he realized he enjoyed talking to them. Strangely, he welcomed the barrage of questions. They felt like the kind of people he could rely on. The kind that wouldn't turn their backs on him when he needed them most.

6

WINIFRED

Warm autumn sun hit the backs of the mother-daughter team, a cool breeze dancing through the air. Milicent and Winnie sat atop their family's stone slab altar used for rituals, perfectly centered between the house, woods, and lake.

Not a soul knew where the altar came from, with edges worn from hundreds of years of wear and tear. Ancient runes and symbols were carved around the edge of the stone, acknowledging all manner of ancient Gods and Goddesses. In the center sat an ornate compass, each cardinal direction accompanied by its correlating element.

With eyes closed, Winnie tried to picture the mystery queen. While her mother searched for the young woman, she called on Death for help locating the lost entity. Though her powers were still recuperating from the previous night, she could feel her family's connection coursing through her veins, strengthening her search. Still, she felt blocked. Like something was keeping her from sending her search out far enough.

"Concentrate," Milicent scolded, squeezing Winnie's hands tightly. "Your energy is scattered. This much time away has made you lose some of your potency."

An hour had passed with absolutely no information gathered on either search.

"I'm sorry, Mum. I've been so focused on work lately," Winnie muttered.

"It's more than that. I can sense the strained relationship with your goddess. Your born skill lives strong within you, but your elemental magic has taken a toll. You need to mend your relationship with Gali, and soon. Our lives may depend on it," she scolded gently. Only her mother knew the perfect balance between disappointment and loving care.

Winnie nodded silently, her eyes dropping heavy with guilt.

"What's got you so scattered?" Milicent released her hands for a moment, searching for new answers unrelated to their goal.

"You're sure he's the one?" she asked solemnly. Winnie's gaze darted toward Ezra, seated alongside the large windows of the sunroom.

"From my visions? I'm almost certain." Her mother's pensive stare looked out over the lake, almost like she couldn't bring herself to look back at her own daughter.

Winnie's mind raced back to the year before – to the conversation she'd had with her mother. To the fight that made her not want to return home until her ruinous seance.

"What did you see that makes you so sure he's the one?"

Milicent let out a small sigh. "I remember blonde hair, but no face. A sense of deep love and compassion. And pain…I can't be sure, but something *will* happen to him. And others if we're not careful. He's in danger."

"I can protect him," Winnie insisted, lips tight in a frown. "I won't let anything happen to him."

"Fate has a way of making sure they get their way," she reminded. "Though, if you stood any fighting chance, the estate would be the safest place for him. I can't promise you'll save him, but I understand why you feel the need to try."

"I don't know why you feel your visions are a sign to give up. They should be treated as a warning. To stop the events from happening." Nerves swirled around in Winnie's chest as she spoke.

Milicent sighed, a calmer response than Winnie had anticipated. "I've learned over the years that my visions almost always come to pass. Fight as hard as you want, but at the end of the day you have to accept the truth. There have been very few times where I was successful in stopping them. ”

“But you have been successful at least once before. That’s the only hope I need. Why else would Fate send you visions? Otherwise there’d be no reason to receive them at all.”

Her mother shrugged. “Perhaps you’re right. Or perhaps I am, and he’ll get hurt either way.”

“I don’t care what you think. Visions are a warning. He’s like family to me and I’ll do anything to protect him.”

“Careful what you say, Winifred. Fate also has ears and they’re always listening.”

Milicent’s eyes landed back on Winnie, her mother’s face softer than expected. She was anticipating anger or frustration, but instead was met with understanding. Perhaps a year away helped both of them.

“Can he stay?” she asked after a moment of contemplative silence.

“Yes, but I’d keep him away from the Falke brothers. Those two are reckless enough as it is. No need to get your friend involved.” Her head shook with a disapproving frown, messing with the cuticles of her nails.

“Why won’t any of you tell me what happened two years ago? Surely a reckless prank wasn’t enough to get them banished? They were once like sons to you. How could you just cast them out? Especially after they lost both parents,” Winnie challenged, tears welling as the memories tried to tug at her mind.

“Some things are best left unsaid, my dear. Perhaps your gentle mind wouldn’t like the answer to that question.” Her scowl continued, avoiding Winnie’s gaze.

“Gentle mind? I don’t think you know me as well as you think you do,” she scoffed.

“There are things that you’re just too young to understand.”

“Too young? I’m nineteen, about to be twenty! I’m an adult!

Thoren and Kane are both around my age and they know what happened. Hell, even Wesley knows and he's the baby of the family! That's the worst excuse you've ever given me."

Silence fell between them before Milicent reached for her daughter once more. With a huff, Winnie set aside her questions knowing she'd never break through that thick skull of her mother's. *If I were her sweet, darling boy, she'd tell me right away,* she thought with a grumble.

"We have more pressing matters to worry about. Let's try again."

"Let me try drawing on your powers. Maybe I can bring the queen's spirit forward and talk some sense into her. Get her to move on before she gets the girl," Winnie suggested.

"I don't see why not. I'm not getting anywhere with my visions." A huff of frustration escaped her lips as she relaxed, allowing Winnie to tap into her energy.

She closed her eyes, concentrating and visualizing the queen. Calling out to her nameless foe, Winnie pictured the woman in front of them. Drawing on every ounce she could, she tried and tried to no avail. The queen seemed either unwilling or unable to be called forth with her spiritual powers. Just as she was about to give up, the air around them stirred.

Autumn leaves rattled in the trees. She felt her mother squeeze her hands in encouragement as the air chilled. An icy wind picked up and the temperature dropped, the warmth of the sun no longer heating their bodies.

Nearby, a pile of decaying leaves swirled into a human-sized tornado at the center of their stone slab altar. The two women scooted back, making room for the sudden presence. Milicent searched the area, though only Winnie's paling face could see the entity before them.

"Who is it?" Milicent asked frantically.

"Mary?" she gasped, rising to her knees before the woman peering down at her. "Why are you here?"

Her mother remained quiet, a curious gaze still seeking out an entity she'd never recognize.

"With the Queen using my body…I've been cast out." Her voice was a mere whisper, fading as she spoke. "I don't have much time. She notices when I disappear."

"Where is she?"

Mary's image flickered in place, the connection with Winnie weakening with every passing second. "Chicago…with descendants. They've been conspiring for much longer than you realize. They've done terrible things, even in the short time I've observed. It's not just them. They have masses of creatures on their side. You have to stop her…"

Shivers rattled Winnie's spine, thinking of the carnage that vengeful spirit could cause. "What do you mean by descendants?"

"Some distant cousins of ours. She needs blood. I don't know what she plans, but she needs lots of it. As many ties as she can find."

"We think she may be going after a young woman. Have you seen her target anyone?" Winnie pleaded with the spirit, sensing that her departure was nearing.

Mary nodded silently, eyes soft and sorrowful. "That's what brought her to Chicago in the first place."

The silence between them was deafening. The woman's spirit slowly faded before Milicent called out to the nothingness before them. "What's her name? The Queen's?"

But within moments, she was gone. The leaves settled around the two, the air returning to the previous temperature. The familiar warmth of the sun returned, shining through the trees.

"She's in Chicago. How the hell did she get all the way to America so quickly?" Winnie muttered, throwing her hands around her in frustration.

"I heard you mention descendants. They must be quite powerful. Or part of a coven. Or both. I wish I knew what they were planning. I don't think you comprehend the position you've put us in." Milicent stood, shaking debris from her dress.

"I know, I don't need a lecture. I remember you telling me that one day a seance would go wrong," she admitted begrudgingly as she, too, took a stand. "Without the full moon, will our collective powers be enough tomorrow?"

Winnie's bare feet stood at the center of the altar as she contemplated their next move. They'd created portals to closer locations, using anything from tree stumps to mirrors. She'd never created one to the other side of the world before.

"I hate to admit it, but with the help of the Falke brothers, we should be able to pull it off." Milicent's face continued to scowl, eyes searching the estate.

"They should get here any minute. I sent word last night," Winnie added as her mother headed for the manor.

Milicent mumbled something unintelligible before entering the sunroom. Ezra poked his head out, awaiting her signal before coming outside. She'd told him to wait, worried he'd disturb their concentration.

As he approached, he chuckled and pointed at her bare feet. "Can't do that in London."

She laughed softly, mind in the clouds, as they walked toward a small table sitting at the edge of the lake. Before sitting down, he squeezed her shoulders in reassurance. A soft, half-hearted smile fluttered his way before she tapped on the empty pitcher sitting on the table.

At first, nothing happened. Ezra's eyes looked her over in concern, likely wondering what she was doing. Winnie shifted in her seat, squinting and trying to focus. Another tap and a few drops slowly appeared. She huffed an exasperated sigh, trying once more. This time, half the pitcher filled with cool liquid.

"That's incredible," he said softly. He looked around as if expecting the water to have come from somewhere else.

She'd been careful not to use such magic in front of him before from fear of freaking him out. It seemed that worry disappeared after last night.

"I used to be better at using my element. Unfortunately, I've let it go to waste." Heavy guilt caused her gaze to shift away from her friend.

"Stop beating yourself up and just focus on getting better," he urged with a playful nudge. She offered him a sideways smile before he continued. "Does your entire family have these powers?"

"I'm the only one who wields water. We're fortunate that each of us works with a different elemental deity. Otherwise we'd need to bring in other witches for big rituals like the portal." Her eyes continued to wander as she explained.

"Deities?"

She nodded. "I work with Gali, Goddess of Water. My mother with Ina, Goddess of Earth. Wesley wields fire, thanks to Aelius. And my father uses air, working with Caelus. They're the original four. The ones who created…everything."

Ezra's eyes widened in realization. "So everything I learned growing up is…wrong?"

"Not necessarily. There's truth in all religions. All deities exist in one form or another. If you read any religious text, you'll find commonalities in them all. Not many know of our true creators. It boils down to nature and the elements."

She offered him a warm smile as his mind seemed to race.

"Can anyone learn?" This time, his voice sounded eager.

"I'm not sure, actually. Certain gifts you must be born with. Like my ability to see spirits or my mother's visions. But I never considered if a human could wield the elements. I suppose you could always try to earn one of the Gods' favors." She glanced at him curiously, realizing that he seemed to be taking it all better than she'd expected.

"Any luck finding new information?"

"Chicago. That's where the girl and the queen are." She couldn't help but stare out over the water, lost in thought.

"This…portal. It'll get you there in time? To save her?" he

asked, pouring two cups of water between them.

"I hope so..."

The two sat silently sipping for a moment before he interrupted her thoughts.

"So..." he began, drawing out the vowel sound, a sly smile forming on his lips. "Tell me about these two brothers. Wesley mentioned some history between you and one of them. I need details."

He poked at her shoulder impishly as her cheeks flushed a little from embarrassment. Winnie rolled her eyes, trying to hide a sheepish smile. "There's really nothing to tell. I was in love with one of them...like a fool."

"Love is never foolish," he rushed to say, glancing out at the mesmerizing lake. "He never returned your feelings?"

"There was a time when I thought we would be together. But then I ruined it and chose someone else." She fiddled with the rim of the glass in her hands as she spoke.

"Samuel?"

She forgot she'd told him about the young man before Beatrix who'd ripped her heart out and eaten it like some foul beast. Winnie nodded solemnly. "I chose Samuel over him and it was the biggest mistake I ever made. Our friendship suffered, and he's barely spoken to me since."

"Are you still in love with him? After all this time? Even after Beatrix?" He examined her curiously, crossing his arms over his chest.

"I do love him, yes, but not the way I used to. I sometimes wonder if I ever truly loved him in that way. The Falke brothers were my best friends growing up. I've missed them terribly. I feel awful about the way things ended with Thoren. And then with everything that happened with my mother..."

Winnie shivered, setting the cup down and pulling her knees up to her chest. Ezra took his jacket off and draped it around her. Though she refused at first, he insisted anyway.

"It sounds like you need to apologize. The guilt will eat away at you if you let it. I know all too well how that feels." He took a seat once more, crossing one leg over the other and slouching back comfortably in the chair.

"You're probably right," she mumbled.

"You need to send me back to London. I worry if I show up late, they'll replace me at the factory." He took a stand, beginning to walk toward the front of the house.

No, he can't go back! It's not safe!

"Why don't you just stay here?" she suggested, legs rushing to get to his side.

"I'll gladly come back at the end of the day once my work is done. Will you come get me?"

I could tell him about my mum's vision, but it may only scare him off, she worried. "Or you could stay here. I'm sure my dad can find some work for you to do and he'll pay you just the same." Her tone was desperate and yet he didn't seem to pick up on it.

"I'll be fine out there. I happen to like staying busy," he said with a chuckle. "You'll come get me then?"

Winnie let out a small sigh as they neared the portal back home. "I'd rather you stay here. It's safer."

"I'll be fine. I've made it this far. One more day in the 'slums' won't hurt me." His dimpled-smile beamed across his face, examining her curiously at her sudden nervousness. "Besides, someone's got to scare the mice away or we'll need to start demanding rent from them."

Winnie let out a stressed giggle. "Alright, if you insist. I'll send Wes to come get you when the time is right."

He stood atop the portal, ready to rejoin the Londoners. "I know you'll find her, Winnie. Don't be too hard on yourself."

Nodding in thanks, she rubbed her onyx pendant, picturing their ramshackle flat and sent him back. She chuckled softly as she heard a quiet gasp, Ezra teleporting to their flat just as the sound of footsteps appeared behind her.

7

WINIFRED

Behind Winnie, a deep voice called out. "And who might that have been? The man whose jacket you're wearing?"

It didn't take long for her to recognize who it was. She turned, seeing the two Falke brothers standing at the entrance of the manor. Thoren, the boy she'd once loved, standing silently at the door. Kane, his older brother, walked toward her with arms outstretched.

She ran to greet him, a small squeal escaping her lips as he lifted her in a tight hug and twirled her around. Though they hadn't seen each other in two years, it seemed so natural to fall right back where they'd left off.

"I can't believe how long it's been since we've seen you!" Kane's deep hazels examined her, resting on Ezra's jacket.

"I can't either!" she began, smile wide and beaming. "That was a friend of mine – Ezra. I imagine you'll meet him soon."

"You look incredible! The last two years have been kind to you," Kane added before she looked past him and toward his brother.

"And you? No hug for me?"

Thoren glanced between her and the door, hands tucked away in his pockets before deciding to finally saunter toward her. As they stood before one another and she reached up for a quick hug, their heads collided with a small thud before deciding perhaps a hug wasn't necessary.

"It's good to see you, Winnie," he mumbled before returning to his post on the porch.

"You two have changed quite a bit as well!" she added, examining them both.

The last time she'd seen them, they were more like scraggly teens. Now they stood tall and proud, living up to their species' reputation. Afterall, sirens were known for their beauty.

Outside of the obvious changes – thicker facial hair and more tattoos covering their olive-toned skin than her mother would approve of – they were still the same Falke brothers she'd grown up with. Thoren still had his dark combover, facial hair neatly trimmed short. Kane's on the other hand was more wild and loose, though he'd cut it shoulder length since last she saw him.

Looking at the oldest brother, so many fond memories came to mind. Whether she recalled the hours of goofing off, swimming on the lake, or training, she thought back fondly. Kane's same hazel eyes examined her now as though she were a rare diamond. She'd forgotten how his gaze translated to adoration, lips curled into an almost delicate smile revealing that familiar playfulness she'd missed in the years apart.

"Why don't we get you two inside? Wes and Mum spent all morning preparing," she suggested, motioning for the door.

The three of them stepped into the house, wandering silently to the kitchen. At the entrance, Milicent stood with a frown on her face and arms folded across her chest.

"Thoren, lovely to see you. *Kane,*" she began, pointing to the sunroom.

He lowered his head, walking to the room to have a private conversation. Winnie and Thoren were left in the kitchen, exchanging some sort of silent conversation as neither spoke a word.

"What do you think they're talking about?" she asked, trying to ease the tension a little.

"Probably my brother's stupidity the last time we were here." He shifted from one leg to the other, arms fiddling at his sides as though he didn't know what to do with them.

Coming from the sunroom, she could hear her mother's stern tone and yet couldn't make out any words. Kane didn't seem to say much, merely let her vent. Then at last, his voice came through loud and clear.

"I'll be on my best behavior."

"Both of you better be!" She scolded, pointing toward the table where a plate of pancakes waited for them.

"In my defense, I didn't do anything," Thoren interjected, the first smile of the visit cracking across his face. A glimmer of who she'd once known…

"I hardly call setting the manor on fire 'nothing.'" Winnie's mother scoffed as she watched the two of them.

Kane's eyes rested on the plate toppled with one of his favorites. "Momma Millie! You remembered!"

"I have half a mind to tell you not to call me that," she scolded. At last, her face eased. "But, a promise is a promise. Before you pulled your little stunt, I did say I'd always have pancakes waiting for you two. And though it pains me to say this, I do appreciate both of you for helping us right this matter."

Her scowl seemed to soften, seeing the two young men grab plates and jars of jams. They took a seat, scarfing down the breakfast. Winnie could see the motherly affection rekindling in Milicent's gaze, likely remembering all those years of the wild Falke brothers causing trouble on their lands, stealing the hearts of the Fox family.

"Do you not have food at home?" She put a basket of fruits on the table, then grabbed a pot of coffee and served them just as she always did when they were children.

"We're fed, but nothing beats the breakfast at Fox Manor," Kane mumbled between bites.

"Thank Wesley. He's the one who did the majority of the cooking this morning." She walked past Winnie, giving her a look that indicated she should perhaps leave them to eat.

"You two settle in. Come find me when you're ready to catch up," Winnie said, turning toward the hallway.

"Won't you come sit with us?" Kane asked with a small pout. "It's been a while since we've seen you. Last I heard, you began as an apprentice in London. Come," he insisted, pulling the chair out for her.

"Who told you that?" she asked, taking a hesitant seat between them.

Thoren's gaze shot to his brother with reddish cheeks as if they were having their own internal conversation. "Must've read it in one of Wesley's letters," the youngest brother finally added.

Slowly, she filled them in on the last two years as they ate. Winnie took care to skip over some of the nastier parts of living in Bethnal Green, specifically the lower-class housing and the mucked up streets that had a habit of clinging to her boots and the rim of her dresses.

"So what of this 'Beatrix' you worked with?" Kane followed up.

"She…betrayed me," Winnie paused, unsure how much she was willing to let herself relive. "We spent a great deal of time together working for Madam Stanhope. Their version of seances was nothing like the real thing. But it was something I could do for myself."

Memories of learning the craft together, no matter the money swindling, reminded her of the fun she'd had with Bea. Images of cozying up in front of a Yule fire, kissing under a cotton candy summer sky. Then, that fateful night. Deep in an embrace, only to see the sharp end of a blade ready to dig into her back.

Kane nodded, head cocked to the side to examine her as Thoren's eyes remained glued to the food on his plate.

"We were in love, you know. At least I thought so," Winnie confessed.

A quick cough escaped Kane's lips, a strange look on his face. "I didn't realize…"

"I told you there were more people like me," Thoren interjected, offering Winnie a kind smile before returning his focus to the coffee in hand.

"I'll never understand what changed to make her suddenly hate me so much," she confessed.

"From all you've told me, I'm surprised this 'Bea' still lives to tell the tale." Kane's humor turned dark, eyes narrowing in on her as if sensing how much it hurt to think about those days. "So you've been working on your own since then?"

"Mostly. I met Ezra that same night. After he mistook me for a demon, we decided to rent a small flat together. He helps me here and there where he can, mostly bringing in money from the factories in London." She placed her empty cup on the table as the two brothers finished their plates.

"Perhaps your friend knows something about you that we don't," Thoren teased, at last opening up. "I look forward to meeting him."

"I'm really glad you two are here. You didn't have to come after..." She almost couldn't finish the words dancing on her tongue.

"It's been a few dark years spent away from you, if I'm honest. Our time back home in Greece was...eventful." Kane pushed his fork around on his plate, messing with the last crumbs remaining.

"I don't think we should get into that," Thoren warned with a tight frown.

"Dark years? Even darker than the invasion?" Winnie tried to recall the vague stories she'd been told. Tales of war and sorrow, of the Falke brother's and the destruction of their family and home.

"In some ways, yes. I spent the last two years truly lost. I'm almost thankful we didn't know each other during that time," he admitted.

Thoren's foot kicked his brother below the table, silencing Kane at last.

"Perhaps when you're ready, you'll tell me all about it." Carefully, she placed a delicate hand atop his own in an attempt to comfort him. An action she never would've thought twice about before this moment.

"For now, let's focus on getting your queen," Thoren scolded, though she couldn't tell who his reprimand was targeting.

"You'll have to excuse me. I need to prepare for the portal."

As Winnie exited the kitchen, the sounds of soft mumbles caught her attention. She paused outside the kitchen door, a nosey ear listening in.

"Why are you such an ass? We can tell her the truth!" Kane's voice was an accusing whisper.

"I'm not being an ass! She doesn't need to know what you did! Wesley said," Thoren countered, though his words were cut short.

"Wes doesn't always know what's best. She deserves to know what happened that night."

"And what happens when she never forgives you for what you did?"

A long pause filled the air between the brothers, Winnie holding her breath trying to remain unnoticed.

"I think she'll understand. Samuel…" Kane's words were interrupted this time.

"Lower your voice! Samuel is none of your concern. Or anyone's for that matter. Leave. It. Be."

The sound of a chair backing away from the kitchen table with clattering dishes in hand sent her into a frenzy, rushing to exit the house before they could catch her eavesdropping. As she collected her offering for Gali, her mind spun wondering what secrets may lie between the Falke brothers that neither wished to share.

8

WINIFRED

"We will be quick – we'll go in, get the girl, and come right back. We don't know if we'll run into this queen, but need to be prepared for anything," Ernest said, briefing the family the following evening.

"I want to come with you," Wesley insisted. "I've gone on missions before. Why can't I come this time?"

"You know what your job is, Wes. You have to go get Ezra after we leave," Winnie added, placing a sympathetic hand on his shoulder.

He shrugged it off with a grunt. "He's not needed here and you know it. Getting him is pointless. You're just trying to get rid of me."

"He's in danger out there in London. By bringing him here, you're helping me protect him," she retorted, eyes pleading with him. She hadn't stopped worrying about her friend since she sent him back the day before.

"Do as your sister asks, Wesley," Milicent chimed in, standing behind her daughter in defense.

"Did you just disagree with your favorite child to take my side?" Winnie sneered.

"Fine," he grumbled, taking his spot at the stone altar.

The remaining family took their spots around the slab, each stationed with their correlating element. On the outside of the circle, Thoren and Kane waited as well. It was now dusk, the sun setting and streaking the sky with wonderful reds, oranges, and pinks of autumn.

Winnie checked the altar one last time to ensure everything was set. A few inches of icy water created a mirror effect, looking up to the heavens. Lines of salt for protection decorated the altar, outlining the runes. An array of crystals sat on the outside of the circle, drawing power from the earth as well.

At last, it was time to begin. As with all previous rituals, Wesley was the first to go. Facing East, he placed a lit candle gently on his point. He was careful not to disrupt the water too much, leaving his offering of fire. The symbol on the altar glowed, accepting his contribution.

In the palms of his hand, he attempted to summon the element, a small flicker of flames glimmering. It was the most he'd ever been able to conjure – the element never fully accepting him for anything other than the family's rituals.

As the East claimed its offering, Winnie proceeded next facing the West. She offered a chalice of water from their lake, the symbol on the ground lighting with acceptance. She reached deep within herself, summoning the water deity to guide her as she attempted to create a ball of water in the palm of her hand. She felt resistance at first, Gali not responding.

"I'm sorry. I know I haven't been doing my daily devotions or offerings. I wasn't trying to disrespect you. Please help me! I need to fix this," she thought in her mind, sending her thoughts toward the goddess she'd worked with since she was only ten years old.

At last, her fingers tingled and a bead of liquid formed, turning to a swirling hurricane in the palm of her hands.

As if sensing her depleted energy, the Falke brothers began their siren song. Their voices emanated soft vibrations, the Fox family pulling on the intoxicating power.

The symbols of the East and West glimmered, the portal eagerly waiting to open. Ernest proceeded next, facing North. In his hands, he held an offering for his element: air. Kane had given him one of his feathers years ago to use for such special occasions. The symbol glowed, waiting for the final piece as a small tornado of air funneled in the palm of his hands.

Milicent stood last, facing South. She held a bundle of flowers in her arms, picked from her garden just that morning. She placed them down on her spot on the altar, a ball of running vines forming between the palms of her hands. The final element glowed, Earth receiving her offering.

Each member of the family said a silent prayer in their head as the Falke brothers stood along the outside, humming soft purs. Their voices caused the water inside the altar to reverberate. The energy surrounding their prayers was enough to make the air feel electrifying as they took a step inside.

Their feet slowly soaked by the water as the Fox family quietly concentrated. Walking from each direction toward the center, they sent their elements forward into the middle where they would meet. If their intentions were pure, they would soon open the portal.

As the elements met in the middle, each collided with the other, consuming each other and morphing into a ball of glowing verdant energy. At the center, the family held hands forming a connection. Their thoughts raced toward Chicago, envisioning the place they'd spent the afternoon familiarizing themselves with through pictures and books. As their minds became one and elements merged, the glowing ball of energy slowly lowered toward the ground.

The stone slab slowly heated, a soft rumble coming from beneath their feet. *This is going to work,* Winnie thought hopefully, before sending one last burst of power between the four of them as the portal opened.

Sitting at the bar of their usual pub, Ezra chugged down a pint of frothy beer. A live musician sat inside, playing wild tunes that he knew Winnie would have enjoyed if she were here. He thought of the last day and a half as he ordered a second. Staring down at the bottom of the empty jug, he regretted missing work the previous morning. Arriving at the factory late, he'd been informed they'd already replaced him.

I should've known all good things come to an end...

As Butch topped him off, those familiar brown eyes glanced over him. "What's got you so quiet?" he asked Ezra, setting down the jug of beer with a concerned look. A strand of gray curls fell in the man's face, pushing them away quickly before wiping up a small spill with a rag.

"Just a lot on my mind, Butch." A weary glance met the older gentleman.

"Where's Miss Winifred tonight? I'm due for my usual date with my wife," he followed up, offering a gentle nudge to Ezra's shoulder.

"Off saving the world probably," he said glumly. *Of course I'm not needed for that.*

He'd expected Winnie to get him yesterday, but alas she didn't. He couldn't help but wonder why even bother to come back and get him at all. She had more important things to worry about compared to her *human* friend.

The walnut doors to the bar swung open wildly, Ezra peering over his shoulder in alert. At first, he thought perhaps an already drunken hoard of Englishmen were entering, ready to cause trouble. It happened often and he was known for keeping the peace. If words didn't work, he knew exactly how to end the squamishes by any means necessary. Any regulars of the pub knew not to trifle with him.

As Ezra turned, he realized that it was not a mass of drunks, but instead a wild-eyed man, clothes bloodied. Everyone inside stood to their feet, rushing to the door and windows to peer outside.

"There's," the man began, a terrified stutter interrupting his speech. "There's been another murder," he finally managed to wheeze, pointing outside.

The entire pub emptied into the streets. A unison of gasps omitted from all men and women who'd just been inside enjoying their evenings. Three men were in the middle of trying to remove a teenage girl from a nearby lamppost. She looked to be about fourteen years old, dressed in a nightgown as if ready to go to sleep. She was hung limply from the top, her stomach gaping open and head bobbing as the men continued removing her.

I know her, Ezra realized. *She was one of the factory girls.*

As they lowered her down, the contents of her innards spilled from the incision across her stomach. Onlookers gagged, the smell of death heavy in the air. Some retched the contents of their evening orders on the side of the streets, a dull murmur spreading amongst the spectators. In an attempt to pay the girl respect, one of the men laid his coat across her body.

Ezra couldn't help but stare. He'd witnessed death before, but never so bloody. With the coat draped over her, she almost looked like she was merely sleeping. His heart ached, a pit churning in his stomach as he thought of the girl's family – if she had any. One of the familiar young boys that roamed the streets ran up beside him.

"No, Jack! Don't look!" Ezra ordered, turning the boy away.

He looked down, realizing the child's eyes were glued on the girl regardless. Before he could say anything else, the boy ran for it, off down the street and back toward the brothel where his mother worked.

How many more children will need to die in order for this killer to serve some justice? The thoughts raced through his mind, conviction settling in his stomach as the image of the girl singed into his mind.

Ezra examined those that stood gawking at the sight of the dead girl. It wasn't until his eyes locked with a man across the street that a chill ran over him. The stranger's face was still, as if unbothered by the sight of death.

He wore a derby hat pulled low to cover most of his face, though as he wiped his cheek, a smear of blood was left behind. Ezra couldn't help but notice him slipped something in his pocket, the reflection of metal gleaming in the light of the lampposts. In only moments, the stranger sauntered off down the alleyway.

"Stop that man!" Ezra's mind screamed at him to do something, knowing deep down who he'd just witnessed.

He attempted to push through the crowd, too many Londoners standing around.

"Get out of my way!" he bellowed. "I see the killer! Let me through!"

Down the street, police hats rushed down toward them. Everyone around simply stared, afraid to move from the safety of their numbers.

The killer became a phantom in the alley, walking away with such ease that it was obvious he felt no man or woman could touch him. Ezra continued to struggle, trying to push his way through the crowd when he felt a hand grasp his shoulder tightly. He turned, seeing Wesley standing behind him, doe eyed and nervous.

"I came to fetch you…like Winnie asked." His eyes rested on the girl.

Ezra turned back once more, but the killer was nowhere to be seen. "I need to go after him!" he shouted, still pushing against the line of onlookers.

"No, we need to get back. Winnie and the others will return soon," Wesley insisted, pulling on Ezra's sleeve toward the alleyway where the portal to Fox Manor stood.

He grumbled, feeling defeated. Another day, roaming the streets. Another day with more opportunities to kill again. *I'll stop him…if it's the last thing I do.*

9

WINIFRED

Rushing wind whipped past Winnie's ears, muffling her parents' voices. The heat of Chicago compared to London was unbearable. Peppery and dry, it seemed unusual for October. Back home, the days were crisp and serene, the calm before the harsh cold of winter.

"I'll never get used to portals…" Ernest grumbled, hunched over and gagging. For as long as Winnie could remember, he'd never been one to prefer this method of travel.

"The weather is…dreadful," Winnie commented, pulling off the scarf around her neck. They'd dressed for fall, now peeling away layers to keep from sweating to death.

Walking through the streets of Chicago, wooden planks squealed beneath their feet. The city was made of brick and stone, but mostly wood. Buildings, shanties, houses, and businesses lined the area. To the side, the Fox family could hear the Chicago River rushing past as they examined their surroundings. The hustle and bustle of the city seemed similar to London, both with robust nightlife.

"How on earth are we going to find this girl? There's too many people!" Winnie questioned, taking in the overwhelming amount of inhabitants.

"Quiet now; I need to concentrate. The energy is much less scattered here. I can feel her nearby." Milicent's arms were outstretched in front of her, mentally searching.

The locals of Chicago meandered carefree, casting odd stairs at the woman wandering around with her eyes half shut and arms in front of her. *Maybe I can ask Death to help me find the queen,* Winnie pondered. Her gaze roamed the streets, seeing the spirits of both settlers and indigenous people wandering around alongside the living.

"What does she look like again?"

Milicent's eyes shot open, glaring at her daughter. She huffed before saying, "I can't see much of her. Dark hair and a dagger at her side. That's all I've been given." She brought a demanding pointer finger to her lips, shushing them once more.

"Are we sure she's in the city?" This time her father dared to interrupt Milicent's concentration.

"I don't think so. I can feel that she's a bit further out. I'm sensing animals surrounding her."

With a nod, Ernest and Winnie followed after Milicent. Their pace quickened, reaching a less populated area farther away from their portal. In the distance, Winnie could make out an outline of a barn, the sounds of mooing cows not far away. Her skin prickled, sensing the danger looming in the air. This dreadfully hot evening, she couldn't help but feel Death's presence as though they conspired with Fate, both intent on disaster today.

—•(((●●●)))•—

THE MYSTERY GIRL

The wooden slats of the barn groaned as movement inside shifted. The shadow of a young woman peeked through a small opening, eager to see. She knew right away this barn belonged to Mrs. O'Leary.

Though she didn't know the family well, she knew *of* them. Rumors were spreading, drawing her out this night – searching. Tales of enormous hounds and other nightmares haunted Chicago and Melinda was determined to find out more.

She attempted small, quiet steps as she peered inside. She'd witnessed a strange, animalistic figure darting through the streets and followed it here. Her family warned her not to go out…to stay put. But she had a gut feeling she needed to do something, anything, to protect her city. It didn't sit right with her to wait around and do nothing while the people of Chicago were in danger. She'd spent her life preparing for a fight. Now was her chance to prove herself.

The barn's wood smelled musty, years of damp conditions eating away at it. The heat this October night was suffocating, her dark brown skin glistening with sweat. Though she wore loose trousers and a button-down, she still felt overdressed for such weather. She'd thankfully pulled her thick, coiled hair out of her face, alleviating some of the heat from the back of her neck.

More movement inside caught her attention swiftly. Quietly it prowled, the farm animals peacefully unaware. The figure heaved, standing on back legs, looking eerily human. As the beast stood, the figure of a man took its place. From darkness he appeared, shedding his wolf's skin. As he turned, the animals inside shrieked realizing they were trapped with a monster.

"Have you found her yet?"

In the corner of the barn, Melinda could hear the sound of a woman's voice. Her chestnut eyes darted, searching for the source. Something about the lilt of it sent shivers down her spine, despite the heat surrounding her.

"It wasn't hard. She came looking for me," the man grunted, turning to face Melinda with a wicked grin.

His features were harsh yet handsome, as if the beast's appearance had melded together with his. A barbarous scar ran down the side of his face, cutting straight through his electric blue eyes.

She let out a small gasp, thinking she'd been quiet and unnoticed. Turning, she was ready to dart. Before her feet could leave the ground, an unseen hand grasped her waist tightly. Its grip was molten, even hotter than the heat of Chicago.

"Let me go!" Kicking and thrashing, Melinda was dragged into the barn by this hidden force. She tugged and pulled, trying to free herself. The invisible clutch was too great. The animals inside continued to cry as if they could sense the evil within.

"I've been looking for you," the woman sang, pulling Melinda closer to meet her gaze.

Her coiled red hair seemed to float around her as if she were a goddess. Melinda had never seen something so fierce. Power and anger emanated from the woman in waves, heating the room. The young woman panted, breathless from the crushing weight of the grasp around her waist.

"Who are you?" Her voice wavered as fear took over. She was mere inches from the red-haired woman, close enough to feel violent breath on her skin.

"I am your executioner." Something behind the strange woman's eyes blazed in fury, her pupils shrinking and flames encompassing them.

"You got the girl. End this already so we can move on," the man said, his voice low and husky. He looked around anxiously as if expecting company.

"You were a hard one to find. You don't look like him, though." She examined the girl, searching for similarities.

"Like who?" Melinda choked out. She glanced around the barn, looking for anything or anyone to help her. Her dagger was fastened at her waist, though the grip that held her made it impossible to get to.

"Your ancestor, General Paulinus. I expected you to look more like him." Her gaze dropped, a twinge of guilt or some form of human emotion lurking within them. "You're the only one I could find. It seems that his bloodline has seen tragedy even without my interference."

The hand that held Melinda in place tightened, her vision blurring. She could feel the blood pumping through her veins stalling, the grip too tight. The air in the room continued to rise in temperature, suffocating her. The animals squealed in their confinement, bucking and pushing against the walls to try and escape. Embers fell around the woman holding her.

The beast noticed and with panicked eyes, tried to subdue the smoking hay that lay strewn across the floor.

"What're you doing? Chicago hasn't had rain in months. You'll burn the whole damn city down!" His words were quick and pleading as he stomped on more falling sparks.

"Let it burn. Let it *all* burn," she hissed.

"That's not part of the plan," he bellowed, eyes wide as the embers turned to flames.

The woman moved her hand, pulling Melinda over the simmering sparks. Thrashing and resisting, the girl was pulled over the inferno regardless. As the flames continued to build, the soles of her shoes melted and fabric singed.

Melinda cried out in pain, the beast turning for the exit. Noticing what looked like escape, the woman snagged him.

"Where do you think you're going?" Her words slithered from her mouth, rage tangible.

"This will only draw attention to us! You can't just burn an entire city down…" he choked out. He grasped for his neck as though an invisible force also held him tight.

"Let them find us. If you're not willing to die for my cause, you're not worthy to begin with," she seemed to scold.

As the two assailants spoke, the flames continued to lap at Melinda's feet, now bare and sizzling.

"Please, I didn't – do – anything!" Her feet kicked and eyes pleaded, but it seemed to fall on deaf ears.

The beast ran from the barn, escaping the demonic flames just in time before becoming consumed himself. Off in the distance, Melinda heard howls as the animals inside shrieked. Just beyond her redheaded attacker, she could make-out shadows. Movement seemed to sneak behind the lashing flames, inching closer and closer.

A soft creek sounded behind her before a small herd of cattle charged from their stalls. One of the cows ran wildly, thrashing its head as it attempted to avoid the flames. Barreling into the woman, Melinda fell to the ground as the hold around her momentarily faltered. With only seconds to spare, she leaped from the burning embers and snatched the dagger from her side, ready for a fight.

Before she knew it, the clasp resumed but she was prepared this time. As the woman pulled her closer, she slashed, making contact immediately. Her attacker's blood spilled as she withdrew the blade, the hold around her finally dropping.

She hit the ground with a *thud*, skin immediately sizzling. Melinda cried out, adrenaline urging her to keep moving. Her bare feet hissed as she ran for the exit, wondering where the red-headed woman had gone. She searched on her way out, only to come to a halt as the woman appeared between her and escape.

"You're not going anywhere," she boomed.

Melinda examined her in horror. The blood from her wounds was now smeared on her face – battle markings adorning her visage. She looked even more sinister with lines of crimson decorating her devilish face.

I'm going to die, she thought as she took a step back. The flames lapped at her like a thirsty dog. The fabric of her shirt and pants slowly singed. She knew she needed to move now or risk being engulfed entirely. Darting eyes landed on a set of shadows behind the queen – a hopeful sight.

Her red-haired attacker stood unsuspecting, the silhouettes growing closer. Melinda wanted to cry out, unsure of their intentions. The figures cleared, revealing three individuals: a man and two women. They flanked him on either side, hands resting on his shoulders. A commanding reach stretched toward her attacker.

The woman's arms ripped to her sides within an instant, letting out a fiery shriek as the flames danced behind Melinda. She was frozen in place, unable to move as the group continued to approach.

"Go!" the man yelled, studying the flames.

She didn't need to think twice before her feet dashed. As she ran, the fire attempted one last time to nip at her heels. She ran as fast as she could, the adrenaline the only thing keeping her going as the skin on the soles of her feet screamed in pain.

WINIFRED

"Go!" Ernest yelled to the girl – the one they'd been searching for.

Winnie could feel as he drew on their strength to amplify his powers. He was holding off the flames as best he could with a forcefield of air, yet tendrils of power leaked through his shield. Behind his wall, the fire only seemed to blaze brighter as they fed on the oxygen.

I should be the one creating force fields, not my dad. My element would do better against fire, Winnie panicked.

She watched as the girl limped past them and toward the inner city. They knew the Queen was here in Chicago, but hadn't expected this. She scanned the rising flames, imagining all the worst possible outcomes.

"Go after her," Ernest yelled to Milicent. "We'll keep her at bay for as long as we can," he finished, pushing an invisible force back toward the deranged spirit.

Milicent withdrew from her husband and daughter, taking off after the girl. Winnie and Ernest held tight, summoning everything in them to keep the queen at bay.

With splayed arms, she slowly turned. Flames blazed, air suffocating. Heat nipped at the family, doing everything in their power to keep her contained. Neither of them knew how she was moving. The bindings should have kept her steady. Yet still she turned – her face revealing a wicked glare.

"Helping the girl only puts you and your family in danger," she warned.

"You can't have her!" Winnie shouted, her voice strained as her father continued to pull on her strength. She could feel their powers dwindling with every breath.

Ernest flashed his daughter a knowing glance, his eyes darting after Milicent. Winnie knew what that meant: it was time to run. Time to push one last time and hope the magic held their attacker off long enough to get a head start.

Winnie took a deep breath, preparing herself for the amount of energy needed. Ernest drew on every last bit of power he could muster, throwing it toward the Queen. A wall of wind stood between their escape, holding her tight for precious moments.

"You can't run from me. I will find you! I always keep my promises," the queen bellowed, waiting to be set free.

Feet pounded on the hard ground, Winnie running as fast as she could. She was breathless, the power stripped from her. Creating the portal and then that…

"Just keep running," Ernest yelled.

The wall that held the queen captive at last faltered. She stepped out from it, a wave of darkness surrounding her. The flames continued to surge, moving forward like warhorses. Howls of beasts sounded from the rows of buildings behind her. She ran after the group, quickly joined by a small pack of beasts just behind her.

Winnie's eyes flashed back once more, seeing the flames beginning to spread. Like a wave of fury, they consumed the surrounding buildings. Growing and growing, devouring everything in their path.

"Millie! Get her! We need to get to the portal!" Ernest roared, throwing his hand out in an attempt to slow her enough for his wife to catch up.

Around them, businesses, houses, establishments – it all engulfed in crimson flame. Chicago screamed, its citizens crying out in panicked pain.

"We can keep you safe! But you have to come with us now," Milicent shouted over the cries of the city.

Shrieks ripped at Winnie's ears, innocents trapped in buildings unable to get out. Families pounded on windows, desperate and trapped. Flames circled buildings, ensuring no one escaped. She looked around, horrified. Too many to save, not enough time. Seconds felt like hours, decisions weighing heavy on her. *If only I had control of my damn element!*

"We can't stop," Ernest yelled, as if sensing his daughter's hesitation.

Winnie slowed, coming to a complete halt. Her eyes roamed the terror, unable to move.

"I know you want to help, but we have to go. There's nothing we can do." Her father's face was desperate, pleading for her to continue toward the portal home.

"Break the windows," she ordered, picking up her pace once more.

Ernest nodded, sending one last burst of telekinetic power through the area. Windows shattered, families beginning to escape. He guided the shards away from the innocents and toward the beasts that funneled into the streets of Chicago.

The queen turned the corner, searching for the girl. The glass slowed the hounds but didn't seem to touch her at all. She ignited more and more of the surrounding buildings as she spotted Winnie and her family. They were near the portal home, unsure if the flames would break the connection back to Fox Manor.

How many will die tonight? Winnie wondered, the shrieks of the innocent echoing through her mind. *How many will lose their lives because we didn't help them?*

The vengeful queen ran after them, getting nearer. Winnie swooped to pick up a shard of glass, hurdling it toward her. It sunk deep into the woman's chest, eyes flaring with rage. Ripping it from her body, she held it up to her face.

The moments that passed felt like a lifetime.

Winnie watched as the woman mumbled something, the gleam in her eyes wicked as the blood oozing from the weapon darkened. Whispering her final curses, she hurled it back like a javelin.

Flames rained down from the heavens as the shard neared. Though she attempted to dodge the glass, it was no use. Winnie's arm burned as the Queen's blood made contact with hers. Gaze flashing down, she ripped it from her impaled forearm.

Blood swelled and she could hear the Queen's voice sounding through her mind.

"You're mine now."

Her whole body shuddered, feeling the entity's essence slithering its way through her. Searching, as though it were ready to attach itself. Her feet pounded once more, nearing the portal. She glanced back one last time, eyes connecting with the Queen's. They were the last thing she saw of Chicago before leaping through the portal and toward safety.

The transition home was not as smooth as it was on the way there. Rather than stepping through, it felt like they were shoved.

"Close it!" Milicent cried out as their feet hit the ground of Fox Manor.

The Falke brothers sat lazily around the ground, scrambling to their feet when the Fox family came through. Wesley and Ezra ran up along the side of the house, likely arriving back from London.

Everyone worked together to remove the offerings, disturb the water, and ruin the salt designs that had taken all afternoon to create. Each member of the Fox family stood at their cardinal directions, arms outstretched and ready to take back the sliver of powers they'd sent out to create the portal previously. As the passageway closed, the family's attention ripped toward the sound of a scream.

10

WINIFRED

Winnie frantically searched for the source of the scream. The young woman they'd rescued attempted to get to her feet, crying out in pain. She looked around in terror, eyes resting on Wesley. Something in her gaze shifted as she examined him, backing away more and more as the group grew closer.

Milicent approached cautiously, trying to calm the girl. Before anyone could say anything, she whipped the dagger from her side and started slashing. She scooted on her bottom, the burns on her feet too great to stand.

"Stay back!" She held the blade out in front of her, hands shaking as the adrenaline slowly wore off and pain set in. Her eyes fluttered open and closed, fading in and out of consciousness.

"We don't want to hurt you," Wesley said softly, hands out in front and voice gentle.

Winnie shot him a warning glance to which he nodded in understanding. He continued to inch forward as the girl slashed at him once more.

"I don't know what you are! I don't know how I got here! Stay back!"

Her brother's piercing green stare examined the girl curiously. Winnie couldn't help but watch as the gears in his brain seemed to turn, looking like the spitting image of their father. His dusty brown hair lay in a permanent state of dishevelment, his goofy smile absent as he got closer.

She knew it wouldn't take much for him to calm her. Over the years, they'd realized his powers were different from the others. He couldn't see spirits or manifest objects. Nor was he telekinetic like their dad. His powers were more of an emotional matter – quite literally.

From an early age, her brother could alter the emotions of others. One simple touch and they felt however he pleased. As he got older, his powers grew until eventually, he could even alter memories. A fact that she learned the hard way.

"Can I look at your wounds?" His voice was calm and gentle as he inched toward her carefully.

She jerked back, slashing at his hands. Behind them, Thoren let out a small sigh of frustration. Parting his lips, he sang his siren song, taking control of the situation. The girl's expression glazed over as the dagger dropped from her hands.

Reaching out, Wesley placed a calming hand on her forehead, guiding her back as she passed out. At once, she was in a deep slumber free of fear and pain.

Her thick, jet black coils lay across her face, covering her. Wesley moved a lock aside, revealing the features beneath. She had a strong jaw and tight lip as she lay unconscious. Thick lashes lay over closed eyes, indicating they had some time before she would wake.

"I had it handled. You didn't need to do that," Wesley grumbled, shooting Thoren a vexed glare.

Approaching, the siren bent down and offered to pick up the girl. Winnie's brother helped her into his arms, walking alongside as the rest of the group followed.

"We need to dress those wounds," Milicent stated, examining the girl's feet and legs that dangled.

"Does she have family?" Thoren asked, peering over his shoulder at the rest of the Fox family.

"We didn't get a chance to ask. I imagine she does, unless the fire took them out or the queen got to them first," Ernest answered after a slight pause.

Milicent ran ahead to open the sunroom doors, a flick of her dainty fingers causing the entire house to light in welcome. Winnie followed behind with Kane at her side, her hand clutching her forearm. He motioned down at her arm in concern. He never needed to open his mouth for her to understand what he was trying to ask.

"It's just a small cut. It can wait," she lied with a half-hearted smile, covering it with a tight grip.

As they entered the sunroom, a cot waited ready for the injured girl. Thoren set her down gently, turning to see Milicent running back into the room with her healing ointments in hand.

"Don't you want us to try healing her first?" he asked, calling his brother over.

Milicent's scattered mind seemed to keep her from forming words, her hands motioning down at the girl in hurry before both brothers joined on either side. Her mother crouched down next to the girl, watching and waiting for the sirens to begin their healing songs.

As their lips parted, soft euphoric melodies escaped them. Ezra glanced toward Winnie in awe before examining the brothers again more carefully.

"I probably should've told you about their abilities," she admitted, taking a seat at last. The muscles in her legs eased, thankful for a small bit of rest.

The group watched as nothing happened. Thoren and Kane tried again and again, though their magic didn't seem to make a difference. Winnie knew it could be done; she'd seen them heal before.

"Plan B," Milicent rushed, beginning to remove scraps of fabric to examine the wounds.

She glanced at her husband, Ernest offering clean water and rags. The brothers took a seat with Winnie in the corner of the room, a set of gothic loveseats and chairs awaiting company. She stared out the window in shock, seeing the faces of those she couldn't save every time her eyes closed.

"So many people died tonight. And we didn't save them." Her voice was merely a mumble, her words only audible to Wesley who sat directly beside her.

"You didn't have a choice…you were outnumbered," he added before scooting back on the couch and making himself comfortable.

"It's a wonder she made it through the portal at all," Ernest mumbled as they examined the girl. Her feet were heavily burned, the backs of her arms, legs, and torso severely blistered as well.

Thoren and Kane took a seat across from the Fox siblings, Ezra still standing to the side. He looked unsure what to do or where to stand. As he shifted nervously from one foot to the other, he straightened his clothes and brushed his hair out of his face. Seeing his discomfort, Winnie attempted to call him over though he seemed too mortified by the girl's wounds to hear her.

"You look hurt," Kane mumbled, examining Winnie once more as her parents focused on the girl.

"The queen got me. I'll get some ointment in a few minutes." She maintained pressure on her arm, trying to hide the severity.

With his usual stubbornness, Kane removed her hand from the spot where the glass met her arm. She couldn't bring herself to look down at it, only noting his widening eyes and look of horror as he turned her arm around and around to assess the damage.

"It's just a scratch," she tried to joke, though the memory of the queen's voice slithering inside her mind made it difficult.

"You need to have your mother take a look at that," he ordered, his tone urgent for reasons she didn't quite understand. Shooting up from his seat, he pulled at her hand toward her parents.

Pulling her arm from his grasp, she clutched her head as waves of lightheadedness washed over her. A part of her didn't want to look at it, the burning she felt making her stomach churn.

"Don't ignore me, Winnie. This needs attention," he seemed to plead as she ripped her arm from his grasp.

"I'm sure I'm fine," she insisted, though she got up and approached her parents only to satisfy his demands.

As she walked toward them, she glanced down at last. The shard of glass hadn't done too much damage, but the sight of the wound almost sent Winnie to the restroom to hurl. The gash was beginning to darken, thick navy blue veins sprawled from the area as if spreading through her body. Something dark seemed to be coursing through her veins like a parasite. A small, nagging fire sat at the pit of her stomach. A mere fraction of the rage that belonged to the red headed warrior queen.

Milicent straightened her back, eyes closed as if concentrating. "Something's wrong… I can't quite place my finger on it."

"Millie," Ernest began, noticing Winnie's wound. "Millicent, look!" he urged, tearing her mother's attention away from the girl.

In a panic, she got up from her crouched position. Shaking fingers reached for Winnie's arm as she asked, "When did this happen?"

"Right as we were leaving Chicago…"

Milicent shook her head in alarm. "What did she use? Was there blood on the weapon? Did you see her do anything specific before attacking you?"

Overwhelmed, Winnie replayed the images in her mind before finally answering each of her mother's inquiries. At last she added, "I saw her whisper something to the shard before…"

"This has to be a blood curse. I've never seen one in person before, but I've heard of them. They're almost impossible to reverse." Her voice was merely a whisper as alarm overtook her.

"Don't give up so quickly," Ernest muttered to his wife, taking Winnie's arm to examine. "We can try a few things. Perhaps start with some herbs and the sirens, then move on to more unconventional methods. Salt baths, tonics, talismans even. We have options. We just have to find what works. Nothing is invincible and everything has a weakness."

Though his eyes looked panicked, his face offered her a warm smile of reassurance. *My dad – always the rational one,* she thought.

"Millie," he began, pulling the base of her chin up to meet his gaze. "You continue working to heal this girl. I'll go patch up Winnie."

"Did you see how many beasts she had?" Her voice was stifled, eyes watering.

Ernest nodded. "We'll get help from the others, don't worry. But for now, I need you to focus. Precious time is passing and this girl needs your help."

Winnie's mother nodded, getting back to work. Ernest grabbed Winnie by the arm, guiding her to have a seat. Cleaning her wound, he continued to examine it.

"You really think it's a blood curse?" She couldn't bring herself to look at the others; too embarrassed to admit she'd allowed this to happen.

"It certainly looks like it. This queen sure is powerful. I hope you understand what you've gotten us into."

Her father didn't scold her often, but his words seemed to hit her like a ton of bricks. He finished cleaning her wound, applying some of Milicent's healing ointment.

"Stay here. I'm going to get something that should stop the spread for now."

Ernest took off upstairs, headed for the family's study. Within a few moments, he returned with a bundle of dried purple flowers in hand.

"What's that?"

"Vervain – purifies and protects against evil. I figure it's our best bet right now," he explained, placing some of the dried flowers over the ointment.

Wrapping gauze around her arm, Winnie flinched as pain speared through her whole body. The feeling of the flowers against her skin burned, as if the curse was rejecting their magical properties.

"It's going to hurt like hell, but it should keep the curse from spreading for now," he replied with a small nervous chuckle. He sniffled, Winnie realizing his eyes watered and sadness sat behind them.

A tear rolled down her cheek as she leaned forward and grabbed her father. Sinking deep into his embrace, her emotions flowed freely. The faces of Chicago haunted her vision, the sounds of the attack and the fire playing through her mind like a relentless, broken music box. He merely held her tight, squeezing her in reassurance.

"Will it kill me?" Her words were soft and solemn, quiet so no one else could hear.

"No, Winnie Bear. I won't let it."

11

EZRA

The next morning, Ezra stood in the sunroom watching from a distance as the Falke brothers kneeled on either side of Winnie. They'd ceased their haunting siren songs for a moment, her back arched and tear stained face crying out.

"Again!" Milicent shouted.

"Stop!" Winnie pleaded, her eyes flashing to each brother.

"We can't stop! Again," her mother urged, stomping her foot with impatience at the brothers' hesitation.

Kane offered Winnie's arm a gentle stroke of reassurance before both sirens expanded their mouths, low baritone notes escaping their vibrating throats. Deep, gentle hums encompassed her, causing her to seeth in her place.

She gripped at her arm, fiery pain coursing through her veins once more. From where Ezra stood, he couldn't help but notice the lines beneath her skin glowing like embers every time the healing songs began.

"We can't keep doing this," Kane insisted, wiping away a running tear from Winnie's cheek.

"We have to do *something*. We can't just let the infection spread." She pointed back down to Winnie as if ordering them to begin again.

"Every time we start, the infection spreads a little more. I think we're doing more harm than good! I won't keep hurting her!" Kane helped Winnie to a seated position, arms braced around her for support.

His glare was fierce, staring her mother down. Ezra examined the group, seeing the anguish in Milicent's eyes as she stared at her daughter. It was clear that it ate away at her not knowing how to help.

For a moment, he stopped to imagine how it all worked. Watching the brothers sing was mesmerizing. He couldn't imagine how it could possibly hurt her if they were meant to heal. A year ago, he'd probably assumed they were angels given their divine appearance and the way they carried themselves.

Thoren in particular caught his attention – the way his hazel eyes seemed to examine everything so carefully. He hadn't officially met the Falke brothers the night before. The group came barreling back through the portal just as he and Wesley returned from London. With the fear surrounding their new guest, he hadn't had time to exchange pleasantries.

Winnie's brother entered from the kitchen, perched alongside Ezra in the doorframe. He bit at his nails, leg shaking with nerves, tugging at the cravat around his neck.

"Are they truly trying to heal her?"

"They're trying to…by using magic to purify her blood," Wesley explained. With every leg bob and mutilated cuticle, it looked like he wasn't comfortable in his own skin.

"Your mother mentioned they're…" Ezra began, trying to recall the conversation from the first night.

"Sirens," he hurried, tapping an anxious finger against his cheek.

"Like the mermaids?" Curious eyes roamed both brothers, looking for any sign of scales.

"No," Wesley chuckled, the question easing his tension for a moment. "Think older than that. There are mermaids and other sea-dwelling creatures, of course, but the brothers are a more archaic species. Have you not done your history lessons or read of Odysseus?"

Ezra glanced away from the young man without saying a word on the subject, knowing an education was a luxury he hadn't been afforded.

"They're the originals – from Greece. Instead of being half fish like the merfolk, they're half bird…technically."

"Half *bird?* I don't see any feathers," he whispered, hoping not to offend the two brothers should they hear their conversation.

Thoren's eyes shot up at the comment, a slight chuckle escaping him. He wandered over, Kane and Milicent tending to Winnie.

"Expecting a beak and plumage, were you?" Thoren asked, his chin held high with a cocky grin. Ezra couldn't help but notice a slight accent to his voice, though his English was overall quite stellar.

"Shit, you weren't supposed to hear that! I didn't mean any offense! I'm so sorry," Ezra stammered.

Milicent and Kane exchanged a few words before he left the mother-daughter duo alone to speak for a few moments. Deep belly laughs escaped him as he overheard Ezra's panic.

"No offense at all," he assured, stepping next to his younger brother.

Ezra couldn't help but notice how massive they were. He'd always been tall, but they towered even over him. He felt strange and utterly helpless. So human compared to everyone else here.

Kane held out a hand, introducing himself officially. Ezra reached out to Thoren next, who's arrogant smirk remained but didn't return the favor.

When he pulled his hand back in defeat, Ezra finally asked, "How does the humming…work?"

"We picture what we want in our minds, set our intentions, and begin to sing. Any form of music works. Humming, singing…" Kane rambled.

Thoren cut him off. "Why don't I just show you?"

Ezra peered over to Wesley as if asking for guidance. The young man shook his head, the words *'I wouldn't if I were you'* plastered on his face.

Despite the look of warning and an eye roll from Kane, he nodded. Ezra waited a moment, but at first nothing happened. The siren took a deep breath before emanating soft, tenor melodies.

Bliss spread across Ezra's mind, calming him and making him drowsy. His senses drifted away, his body weightless, his nose surrounded by those same smells and memories from that night. A warm fire. Apple cider. Bourbon. The images tied to those smells tugged at his mind, begging to be set free. Those deliciously sensual reminders of who he truly was which Ezra worked so hard to repress.

Surrounded by bliss and pleasant smells, he was suddenly snapped back to reality. He shook his head, realizing what happened.

"What…" he began, rubbing his temples.

"That's how it works. Imagine what other lovely memories I could pull out of you if we had the time." Thoren's gaze was wicked, cheeks flushed, as he crossed his arms across his chest.

Ezra didn't have time to process what happened before the siren returned to Winnie's side.

"Just ignore him. He's just puffing those feathers you were hoping for," Kane said with a nudge to Ezra's side before returning to Winnie.

He shook his head, still dizzy and in shock. The realization of what happened hit him like a ton of bricks. Then, one of Wesley's earlier comments pulled his attention back to their previous conversation.

Distracted from his thoughts, he asked, "Wait…did you say mermaids are real too?"

Wesley chuckled and nodded, before adding, "If you've read about it in a book, it has existed at some point in time. Whether they still exist is usually in question. It seems the Gods have a way of smiting those who disrupt the balance between our worlds." He wandered back over to his sister, checking in with Milicent to offer help.

Ezra maintained his distance, unsure where to go. What to do. He didn't feel like he belonged. He hoped he'd find his purpose eventually, but for now he felt useless. He glanced up, making eye contact with Thoren. Ezra had a hard time reading his body language, something playful lurking behind the siren's eyes. Needing some air, he wandered through the side of the sunroom toward the lake.

Outside, it was still early morning. Birds chirped and bugs hummed throughout as a low fog hugged the dewy grass. Not too far from the house was the edge of the woods. There was a peaceful presence with him outside as if this was Utopia. He still didn't understand the mechanics of the estate. Winnie had only told him it was shielded, a safe space for beings of all kinds in a world that generally didn't accept magic.

Ezra took a seat at the small table near the water. He glanced out over the lake, enjoying a few seconds of peace. For once in his life, he didn't have anywhere to be. No job to rush off to, no one needing him in that moment. *I'll have to begin looking for work when all of this is over,* he thought.

In his mind, he couldn't help but think about the coffee he'd enjoyed the other morning. His mouth watered at the thought before a canister appeared in front of him in an instant. The surprise of the delivery caught him off guard, causing him to almost fall back out of his chair.

"Are you trying to scare me?" His words echoed to no one in particular, speaking to the house as it played its devious little tricks. Reaching out to the pot hesitantly, he worried it would move on its own.

"Coffee doesn't usually bite."

Ezra looked around in confusion, trying to locate the sound of an unfamiliar female voice.

"Down here!"

He searched once more, noticing a hand sticking from the water. A woman floated at the edge of the lake near a few rocks, one arm perched with her head braced gracefully on her hand.

"Who are you? Where did you come from?" Ezra asked, getting up out of his chair. "It's way too cold for a swim this time of year! You'll freeze to death!"

She peered toward him, milky white hair slicked back and soaking wet. A pair of wide-set eyes examined him curiously, a green-blue as deep and soulful as the lake she sat in. Within seconds, Ezra noticed something. Shimmering scales lined her pearl white skin, glistening by the light of the sun.

"You're new here," she said as she hoisted herself into a seated position, a delicate smile seated beneath her button nose. She looked to be about Milicent's age, perhaps a few years older judging by her smile lines. As she took a seat atop the rocks, he noticed something more alarming than her scales. A tale flopped out of the water, sky blue and glittering like pearls.

"M–Mermaid?" *I know what Wesley said, but…it's real. She's real. Hearing it and seeing it are very different things!* His mind raced in a panic.

"Milicent didn't tell you I was coming, did she?" Her eyes were soft and reassuring, as if she were used to this kind of a reaction.

Behind him, Ezra could hear a set of shuffled feet approaching. He turned, noticing Winnie limping her way outside.

"Afissa!" She helped the woman out of the water, her tail turning to a set of scaled legs. The mermaid shook herself off, wringing her hair to expel any excess moisture. Afissa's torso was covered in a corset made of shiny material, similar in color to an abalone shell. Gold trim lined the sides in decorative swirls, small pearls sewn into the edges.

"This one hasn't seen a mermaid before, has he?" Her voice was more playful this time.

"I – I'm Ezra," he stuttered, stretching out a hesitant hand.

"I don't bite either," the mermaid said with a smile, offering him a whole-hearted shake.

He half expected her skin to be slimy, but it felt like a normal, damp hand.

"Wait till he meets Horace," she joked with a playful growl.

"I'm sorry for gawking…you're just so," he began, though he didn't know what to say to finish his sentence. *Beautiful? Strange? I'm not sure what's appropriate to say.*

"Of all the creatures you'll meet, us merfolk are certainly one of the more…unusual looking," she nodded in agreement, pointing to the scales adorning her skin.

He sighed quickly, feeling a little relieved.

A soft *whoosh* came from the other side of the house, Winnie alerting at once. Her posture straightened, brows furrowed in concentration before a smile finally broke.

"Right on time. That must be Tara!"

She walked toward the front of the house, still slightly limping from the agonizing siren songs she'd endured only moments before. As they rounded the corner, Ezra's eyes landed on a woman about their age with a massive dog at her side.

"You're here!" Winnie squealed, hurrying with arms outstretched.

A long-legged, strawberry-blonde stood in front of Winnie, offering a tight hug. Long braids hung down the back of her sturdy figure. *She looks like she could hold her own in a fight,* Ezra thought. Her pale oval face was peppered with freckles, olive green eyes gleaming with a wide smile. The dog next to her walked up beside Winnie with a playful nudge, though its appearance oddly sent chills down his spine.

"My sweet boy!" Winnie wrapped her arms around the massive, gray-black beast that Ezra imagined to be more wolf than dog. Its imposing height was outdone by sweet, tawny-yellow eyes. As she scratched, clumps of fur rained down onto the grass.

"So I'm guessing you're Tara?" Ezra mused, holding out a hand. "And this must be…Horace?" He got down to the dog's level, rolling laughter coming from the three women.

"This is Cricket, not Horace. Don't ever let him find out you mistook him for a beast," Afissa explained as she finished her giggles.

Tara stood, stroking the dog's head roughly as she examined Winnie's friend.

"This may be insensitive to ask, but…are you magical too?" As he questioned, his gaze landed on Cricket who seemed to carefully inspect every inch of movement.

"Nope. Plain ol' human," she said, taking a small theatrical bow. He noted her Irish accent immediately.

Ezra sighed quietly in relief. At least there was one less magical creature to keep track of.

"You probably shouldn't ask people that, though. One day, you'll ask the wrong creature," Tara added.

"Forgive me, I'm still trying to figure all of this out," he mumbled, straightening his waistcoat. He turned, heading back toward the house. *I think I need a break from meeting new people.*

——◦(((●●●)))◦——
WINIFRED

As Ezra disappeared, Afissa turned to Winnie. "Is that the infamous friend?"

Winnie shook her head. "He's inside."

She felt a little guilty, suddenly. Though she realized she could've told Ezra the entire truth about her and her world sooner, she hadn't warned him about all of the visitors and their capabilities. Hadn't warned him about the siren brothers and the tricks they could play, or the house that liked to fulfill wishes by surprise. Hadn't warned him about the scaly friend of her mother's come to help. She kicked a rock at her feet with a sigh of frustration.

It landed just past a flower, its head drooping. She squinted to focus on it before she plucked it from the ground. Upon examination, she realized that it was dying. One of her mother's ever-blooming flowers…withering away.

Her eyes flashed around, looking for more. She didn't see any, the others still untouched by whatever magic was causing the terrible sign of trouble.

"What is it?" Tara asked, watching her friend dig through beds of flowers. Beside her, Cricket dug as well though he seemed to be doing it for fun rather than attempting to be helpful.

"The flowers shouldn't be dying," the mermaid explained, kneeling next to Winnie.

She shot to her feet, racing to find her mother. Tara, Afissa, and Cricket ran after her, each passing Ezra as they rounded the corner of the house. Without hesitation, he took off after them to see what the commotion was about.

Winnie burst through the sunroom doors, catching her family and the Falke brothers by surprise. She walked straight to her mother, shoving the flower into her face. Winnie stood, one hand on her hip and breathless, everyone in the room looking at her in concern. Kane's gaze flashed to Tara, turning away with a blushing frown.

"Why are you showing me a dead flower when we clearly have new guests to welcome?" Milicent asked her daughter, plucking the delicate dying thing from her hands. She examined it, as if trying to sense anything wrong. "Is this from our estate?"

Winnie nodded with haste, wiping a bead of sweat from her brow.

"Where was this?"

"The front door. Only one. Aren't they spelled to be eternally blooming?" Winnie panted, pacing the floor in front of her mother.

Milicent nodded, dropping the flower to her side.

"I can only imagine this has something to do with your blood curse." She motioned for Winnie's gauze-wrapped arm.

"Blood curse? How the hell did that happen?" Tara exclaimed, grabbing her friend's attention.

Winnie simply ignored her. "What would this have to do with my arm?"

"The estate is tied to our family. If any one of us is injured or harmed, the land will reflect it. I can only imagine this will be the first of many things to die." Milicent's words stumbled from her lips, eyes weary.

"We can keep trying to cleanse her blood," Kane said sorrowfully, turning back to the group.

Winnie noticed as his gaze continued to avoid Tara, her friend trying to get him to pay attention. *It's like she likes watching him squirm,* Winnie thought.

"As you so plainly stated earlier, that didn't work. We'll need to do some research and figure out where to go from here. This is truly a terrible sign…We need to find out as much as we can about this Queen as well. Winifred, fill in our guests on the situation. Wesley, help them find rooms to stay in. I imagine we have many long days and nights ahead of us," Milicent rambled, headed off to the family library.

12

WINIFRED

A little after midday, the group sat around in the family's library reading text after text on ancient queens, curses, blood ties, or anything else that seemed relevant. Anything to figure out how to solve the problems at hand. *This is all my fault. I never should've done that seance in the first place,* Winnie thought as she flipped through page after page.

Their family library was massive with towering vaulted ceilings and walnut wood. Exposed beams up top were the perfect place to hang plants. Winnie's eyes shot toward her reading hammock in the corner, remembering the days of simplicity. Back when her only worries were regarding the words on a page.

Winnie took a break from her research for a moment before examining Ezra. His face stared in fascination at Afissa, her shimmering scaled face glittering just in front of the fireplace. She didn't seem to notice his insistent fixation, a book on curses in her hands.

"You stare at her any longer and you may turn to stone," Thoren mumbled in Ezra's ear.

He jumped back in surprise, though Winnie wasn't sure if it was because of the comment or the proximity of her other friend. She watched curiously as Thoren chuckled lightly, Kane shaking his head in disapproval. Winnie opened her mouth to explain before Ezra seemed to figure it out for himself that the siren was joking.

"You're cruel," he grumbled.

"Remind me one more time," Tara began, the entire group releasing a sigh of frustration.

"We've been over this several times already!" Thoren's scowl rested on the redhead in disdain.

Beside her, Cricket lay curled at her feet. His ear perked, as if waiting to see if she'd want him to take care of the siren. He was trained for such tasks, afterall. Tara unapologetically shrugged, turning to Winnie awaiting answers.

"She was here for Rome. Mary mentioned she was also looking for the descendant of the general who defeated her. Thankfully we found her just in time."

"You've heard her explain this a million times. Stop asking her to repeat the damn story," Thoren moaned.

Still, Tara seemed to ignore his frustration. The gears turned in her head as she thought of new questions. "Given the time period, your queen was likely a druid. You say she commanded fire in Chicago?"

Winnie nodded silently.

"I feel like I know exactly who you're speaking of… I just wish I could remember her name." Tara rubbed her temples feverishly.

"Here's one possibility: Queen Boudicca?" Milicent mumbled, flipping through the pages of a book.

Something in Winnie's gut stirred hearing that name. The air around her seemed to thicken as her heart raced in anticipation. Soft whispers of the dead slithered toward the group, though no one else could hear them.

"Warrior queen…60 AD. Led a massive attack on Rome," Ernest confirmed, reading over Milicent's shoulder.

"I know of her, but it can't be! She's a legendary hero. Not some murderous psychopath," Tara exclaimed. Her gaze landed on each person in the room, as though she hoped someone would agree with her.

"According to this, she killed thousands. Men, women.

Children even," Ernest retorted.

Milicent's eyes continued to race over the pages.

"Doesn't sound like much of a hero to me," Kane mumbled.

"No, you don't understand. She's a symbol. An icon! Against oppression. Feminism! You have the wrong lass." Tara's arms folded across her chest in disagreement as she stumbled over her words.

Cricket, seeing his owner becoming upset, took a stand from his lazy position before her. Nudging her lovingly, Tara let out a soft sigh as she scratched the dog's head.

"I don't know, Tara. I'm connecting a lot of dots here," Ernest said softly, pointing toward the page. "She burned three cities to the ground. The last one was Londinium, what we call London today."

Milicent turned the page feverishly, her eyes landing on something. They widened a moment, catching Winnie's attention.

"What are you looking at?" she questioned, leaning forward in curiosity.

"Her final speech." Milicent released a long sigh as Ernest lay a hand around her shoulders for support. Her mother quietly read aloud. "We, the people of the Iceni, are used to women as commanders in war."

As her mother spoke, something deep within Winnie seemed to awaken. The veins beneath her gauze wrapped arm burned hotter than the embers of the flames across from her, the bandages falling away to ash. Her head shot back, eyes lifeless and void as the air around them hummed. It grew louder and louder as it mimicked the sounds of the group's anxious heartbeats.

Midnight blue veins slithered from the wound, decorating her arms and face. A bandana of war paint slithered across the bridge of her nose, eyes still vacant. The sounds of thumping hearts ceased and turned to drum beats. The lights dimmed, fire lowering to a simmer.

Losing control of her body, Winnie suddenly chanted the remainder of the speech from Boudicca's final battle. However, her voice was not her own. Deep and hoarse, it was the voice of the Warrior Queen. Her body floated, overtaken by the soul that bombarded her. Flooded with rage and vengeance, Winnie saw it all.

THE QUEEN

Looking out, Boudicca was in awe of her army. Hundreds of thousands marched with her, their goal unified: revenge on Rome. Revenge for the oppression her tribes and others had faced. Retaliation for her daughters. Retribution for anyone without a voice.

Rage simmered in the pit of her stomach. Her back still welted, daughters still recovering. General Paulinus thought they could get away with it. Little did he know the power of a mother's rage.

"We, the people of the Iceni, are used to women as commanders in war," Queen Boudicca began, banging a spear across her shield.

Her troops stood in awe of her untamed presence, her fiery red locks blowing in the wind. Anger and grief fueled her blazing vengeance.

"But I am not just fighting for my tribe, or a long line of noble ancestry. I am fighting as a mother. A woman. A leader. For my lost freedom, my bruised body, and my outraged daughters," she bellowed.

The energy spread throughout the Iceni's warriors as she continued.

"Nothing is sacred from the Romans due to their pride and arrogance! All are subject to their greed and violation. They will scourge these lands, burn our homes. Take our families! But by the hand of the vindictive gods, we are what haunts them now! We will win this battle or perish. That is what I, a woman, will do!"

She thrust her spear toward the sky as her people howled and cheered, their conviction palpable. The vitality of the army was intoxicating, the masses of soldiers ready to fight.

The field butted up to a dense woodline where Romans stood, trapped. Nowhere to go but forward. They stood in triangular formations, a line of shields ready to block any incoming attacks. Lines of war machines stood behind them, readied to fire.

On the Iceni side, carts sat filled with women and children along the outskirts. The groups were ready to watch their people's victory. Boudicca's army stood fierce, a gargantuan force of fur, chainmail, spears, and swords. Blue lines adorned their bodies and faces, ready to drive forward at their queen's command.

"Savages!" General Paulinus shouted, only adding to the Iceni people's rage. "More women than warriors!" he shouted again, riling up the soldiers close enough to hear him.

A wave of passion continued to spread like wildfires through both sides. The more he shouted, the more Boudicca wanted to fight.

"They do not stand a chance against us…" she mumbled to herself.

Her daughters standing next to her looked at their mother in wonderment.

"You will defeat them," one daughter said furrowing her brows with a devilish smirk. "That's what we warriors do, is it not?" she asked, grabbing her younger sister protectively.

Pride glimmered in the mother's eyes. No girl should have to endure what they did, and yet here they stood.

Prasutagus, my love, you would have been proud, she thought, wondering if her recently departed husband could hear her.

Both girls wanted to fight and she understood the need within them. It was the same rage that burned inside her. But she wasn't willing to risk it. Wasn't willing to accept their fate, should they fail and Rome won this battle. Didn't want to accept they may endure worse than they already had. She was optimistic, but she wasn't foolish.

"The time has come," she said, looking down at both girls. She grabbed them by the sides of their faces, bringing them in forehead to forehead.

"What will happen to you if…" her eldest began.

"If I do not find you after the battle, you must *run*. Do not tell anyone your names or where you came from. Protect each other. Ensure no one can hurt you ever again."

The warrior queen's face softened, looking down at her girls. The youngest's eyes welled, looking around, too afraid to show weakness in front of an army.

"I don't want to leave you, Mommy," she cried, leaping into the queen's arms.

"You have to, my darling. I have to do what is right for my people. Just as I must fight, you must run." Her eyes shot across the field, seeing movement behind the Roman lines. "We do not have much time. You have to go."

Both girls embraced their mother, unsure if this would be the last time they'd see her. They whispered soft 'I love you's' before heading for the outskirts of the field. In Boudicca's mind, she called out to anyone that could hear her. Any gods or entities that may take pity on her daughters.

"Protect them. Protect my girls and I will be forever in your debt," she thought, sending her prayers into the high heavens.

Once they were safely past the carts and on their way, Boudicca turned to her general. Nodding, she gave the command.

Her army formed their lines, ready to charge as soon as they were told. She looked back at her girls one last time before clearing her throat, taking a deep breath, and focusing her full attention on the general as she climbed onto her horse's back.

She raised her hand, dropping it with force – the signal.

"Charge!" she bellowed, waving her arms in a forward motion.

Those around her howled as they plowed ahead, signaling to all others that the time to attack had finally come.

Holding spears high toward the sky, others banged their swords across their shields as if mimicking the anxious heartbeats of the Roman soldiers they neared several yards away. For every two Romans, four or five bloodthirsty Celts were ready for them.

Boudicca's army neared the Roman lines, their anger and frustration tangible. The Romans stood in their formations, holding fast to their training. Boudicca heard the shrill squeal of a whistle, though she didn't know what the sounds meant. She didn't particularly care either.

They stood in lines, hiding behind their shields like cowards. Boudicca wondered why their oppressors were not moving, but she commanded her army to continue on. As they moved toward the Roman lines, a wave of spears and arrows showered her army. Many blocked the first attack while others fell to the ground, trampled by angry warriors.

A frustrated huff escaped her lips as she slowed her horse. She watched as her army continued to charge forward, disregarding the waves of arrows and spears hurdling their way.

Another shower of death rained down, landing behind her army's lines. A mass of unsuspecting warriors fell, those around them pressing on with only one thing on their mind: survival. It wasn't long before another wave of arrows launched, this time covered in flaming cloth. Their armies hadn't met face-to-face yet and somehow they'd already managed to take out large herds of soldiers.

The Romans may have fancy war machines, but they can't match our passion, she thought as she whipped the reins of her horse and urged it forward.

The queen felt her heart ready to beat out of her chest. With every hoof beat, her blood pumped harder. Her face felt hot, flushed. Anger boiled inside her. She was ready to finish what she started. They'd already succeeded in Camulodunum and Verulamium. Now, Londinium would burn as well, one way or another.

Within moments, the two armies finally collided. Every ounce of fear she may have felt was turned to rage and solidified with every swing of Roman weapons. All she had to do was remember what they'd done to her daughters, to her. It was enough to fuel her crusade.

A Roman soldier neared as she struck him through the neck with her spear. Blood spurted from the wound, the man clutching the protruding weapon with wide doe eyes. She tugged, though the spear was stuck. Letting go, she withdrew her sword from her side.

She looked out, hearing the screams of her people. Cries of anger. Of pain. Watching as her army fought, she realized her warriors were funneling. The Romans didn't attack, merely held their lines.

Another wave of fiery arrows rained down, Boudicca blocking one with her shield. Her people continued to press on, trying to break the ranks of the Romans. Occasionally, the shrill sound of a whistle caused movement amongst their oppressors. And then, back to their formation they stood.

Behind the triangular Roman lines, a mass of horsemen surprised the Iceni and their allies. Attacking her from the right, Boudicca fell from her horse and onto the wet, muddy battleground. The horsemen swung their long swords and spears down at her, Boudicca narrowly avoiding fatality. Getting past their armor was difficult but not impossible. She aimed for ankles, knees, necks. Anything exposed that could be struck.

She soon realized she needed space and time to examine the battleground. To understand what was happening. She sprinted to the back lines, horsemen following her. The Iceni around her barely noticed as she passed, everyone fighting for their lives.

The carts filled with women and children were terrified statues. The battle crept toward them, dangerously close. Swiftly, she pulled herself up onto a wheel of a nearby cart to look out over the fields. Their numbers were dwindling, waves of flaming arrows sinking into the chests of her warriors. The horsemen continued their ruthless pursuit, the Iceni turning wildly unsure where or who to fight first.

"No!" she grumbled aloud. *We were supposed to win! Their*

cities were left defenseless and now here they stand – ready to defeat us? Anger burned in her chest, a festering feeling inside her broiling. Just as the Roman cities had burned for days, so did her rage.

A group of Romans neared the onlookers, slaughtering the women and children who didn't have time to run. Masses came to their defense, though the carnage was too great. As her army gradually faltered, some turned to flee. She watched as they tried to escape, trapped by the very carts they'd placed to watch the spectacle. Romans stabbed her warriors in the back before their feet ever lifted off the ground to climb.

A pit formed in Boudicca's stomach as she engaged with nearby soldiers on foot. As she skillfully ducked one strike, another came hurtling down. Blocking it with her shield, the force of his attack caused her to slip into the bloodied mud. Falling to her knees, she held the shield trembling overhead as blow after blow rained down. Her muscles screamed, holding fast. One wrong move and it was over for her.

The soldier jabbed at her stomach, Boudicca narrowly avoiding the lethal strike. Falling to the ground, she rolled back into a fighting stance. Lunging at the man in front of her, the blade slipped into the skin of his neck like butter. Crumbling to his knees, she only had moments before the next continued his attack. A group of nearby Iceni warriors came to her defense, joining her in the fight against the hoard.

Slowly, the Iceni realized there was no escape. Death waited with a cruel grasp on every fallen man, woman, child, and animal as the Romans continued their brutal attacks. The sounds of squelching bodies and manic cries for help deafened Boudicca's ears.

From her side, Boudicca could hear a man's voice call.

"Your time is running out, Savage Queen."

General Paulinus sat atop his horse, never having stepped foot on the battleground.

Coward, she thought. He didn't bother to engage when they'd attacked her tribe. Why lift a finger now?

"Come join me on the battlefield. Show your warriors if you're worthy. If I, *a woman,* can fight, so can you," she mocked.

As she spoke, the last of her warriors fell at her feet, slain with ruthless savagery. Her eyes glanced around the field, seeing the last of her people picked off. Romans plunged their blades and spears into the bodies of her people, leaving no survivors. Showing no mercy.

"You are not worth my effort." He spat at her in disgust, his saliva landing at her feet.

Soldiers surrounded her, no one around to aid her in this last fight.

Capture isn't an option, she thought.

Nervous eyes looked between the soldiers before her.

"You know what you have to do," a slithering voice whispered in her mind.

Paulinus examined her carefully, as if trying to anticipate what she'd do next.

"I need to know that my girls will be safe," she called out internally, wondering if the strange voice could hear her.

"You may win the battle today, but eventually Rome will fall." Boudicca gritted her teeth, pointing her sword directly at the general.

"Do it," the voice coaxed in her mind.

"My daughters?" she called out desperately to the thing crawling through every inch of her body.

"For a price…" it purred.

"Your oppression will cease – and when your army fails, know that I will be waiting for you in hell."

Grabbing the hilt of her sword, she drove it into her stomach and twisted. Ripping through her intestines, she fell to the ground. Kneeling, staring up at him. Watching as he laughed at her. Rage only exploded within.

"Whatever the price may be, I'll pay it," she agreed at last, hoping that strange entity was still around.

"No matter how many lifetimes it may take me, I will ruin you. You and your entire lineage," she cursed, the world around her fading.

The last thing she heard as the pain ceased and the euphoria of Death's grasp spread was…

"The Savage Queen is dead!"

WINIFRED

Winnie's body shot forward, saliva and vomit spewing from her foaming mouth. She flailed around aimlessly, unsure where she was.

"Who am I?" she cried out, grabbing hold of her body and feeling for any sense of normalcy.

Winnie couldn't be sure she was herself again as her vision slowly focused. All she could see were specks of darkness, the light from the library's smoldering fire slowly leaching its way into her eyesight.

A hand stroked the back of her head, cradling her with fierce protection. The smell of her mother's floral perfume enveloped her, bringing her back to reality. As her eyes fluttered open, she realized Ernest and Wesley sat on either side nervously. She'd never experienced such an intense vision before. One where she was ripped *into* the memory. Not guided or shown, but snatched. The wound on her arm continued its luminescent shine, the soft voices surrounding her still haunting.

"It's alright," Milicent purred, continuing the calming strokes.

With an endlessly racing heart, Winnie's vision at last fully recovered. Her friends' faces stared back at her, some pacing, some frozen in shock.

Ezra paced in the corner of the room, wide-eyed and terrified.

"What the hell just happened? That was worse than what happened to Mary…"

"I saw," Winnie began, though the words choked her.

Cricket came to her side, nudging her softly as she hugged the mutt's neck for comfort.

With the taste of vomit still fresh in her mouth, her eyes darted to the teapot sitting on the table. Kane, noticing her gaze, grabbed her a cup. She offered him a gracious half-smile as she took a few quick sips and continued.

"I saw her final battle," she managed to say, gazing down at her arm.

The veins coming from the gash were more pronounced now. As if the vision had intensified their connection. She swooshed the liquid around in her mouth, trying to drown the bitter lingering taste.

Winnie recited what she saw, recounting every scream and sound she heard as she described the battle. She'd never been in a battle herself, only small scrimmages.

"I never want to see or hear that again. I could even smell it. The stench of Death…" she muttered, rubbing her throbbing head.

Pacing, Tara mumbled, "I guess I was wrong. Sounds like we have the right lass after all."

"I'll continue doing more research," Wesley offered softly. His eyebrows scrunched upward in worry as he squeezed her shoulder.

"Let's get you cleaned up." Tara sighed, helping Winnie to her feet.

Ernest took a stand and motioned for Winnie's arm. "I'll get more Vervain."

"I think we all need a little break," Milicent sighed at last, watching as pockets of people exited the library. "We can reconvene in a few hours in the bar for dinner after we've all had a moment to rest."

Before leaving the room, Winnie turned curiously to notice Thoren and Ezra sharing words. Tara pulled at her arms, coaxing her down the hall before she could stop and listen in on their conversation.

13

WESLEY

Page after page and still Wesley couldn't find any information on how to stop a blood curse. Only vague notions of spells uttered or carved into candles, but nothing about two souls connecting. With a deep sigh, he tossed the book aside. No one seemed to have the answers to their questions. No one seemed to know how to help his sister. Sitting in an armchair by the window of a guest room, the girl they'd saved lay sleeping quietly before him.

This room was rather bare with deep silky blue walls that reminded him of the night sky. Soft silver curtains hung over a massive window, letting in light and casting rays of afternoon sunshine onto her sleeping face.

On the desk in the corner, a wad of thick paper and pencils had appeared. *I wonder if she likes to draw. Or write perhaps,* he wondered, trying to predict her story before she woke.

Wesley was eager for her to finally come out of the magical slumber. The last year since his sister refused to come home, their mother held a tighter grip on him. Didn't allow him to leave the estate as often to see his friends from school. She'd never been one to shelter him, but he couldn't help but feel a little suffocated as Milicent grew more and more worrisome.

Grabbing a newspaper from the nightstand summoned from Chicago, he reviewed the article on the front page. Tales of the ravenous flames outlined by survivors of what they now called the 'Great Chicago Fire' worried him. It seemed they didn't stop, spreading more and more by the hour.

Pulled from his contemplations, the young woman stirred in her bed. Her arms stretched out around her, rubbing sleepy eyes. As if she didn't remember her injuries from the attack of the queen, she woke peacefully. Chestnut eyes fluttered open, landing on Wesley who sat staring at her by accident.

She's going to think I'm a creep, he worried, jumping from the chair with a wild look on his face as she inhaled sharply to scream. He stretched his hands out as if to fend off the incoming shriek.

"Don't scream! You're okay!"

She paused for a moment, releasing the panic deep down in an exasperated sigh. Her eyebrows furrowed as she looked at him.

"Are you watching me *sleep?*" Her face pinched in disgust, voice shrill.

"No! Well, I guess it looks that way doesn't it?" Wesley rubbed the back of his head, unsure what to say. "I thought you'd be waking up soon, so I wanted to wait for you. Didn't want you waking up alone in a place you were unfamiliar with. I swear I didn't sit there the entire time!"

His voice was defensive, an awkward smile across his lips as he contemplated any possible way to make the situation less strange.

She glanced down at her lower half, covered by blankets. As she pulled them off, she gasped at the sight of gauze-covered legs.

"Why can't I feel anything below my waist?" she cried, her hands shaking and eyes pleading with Wesley for answers.

"I," he began, unsure he should tell her the whole truth. "I blocked your pain. And made you sleep. I didn't want you to wake up uncomfortable," he explained, pulling the chair up to the side of the bed to have a seat next to her. "I'm Wesley by the way."

Softly, she extended her hand as though uncertain of his kindness. "Melinda. Where exactly am I?"

"Fox Manor. Somewhere safe."

"No, where *am I?* Some woman told me that we'd be going through a portal."

He was taken aback by her sudden calm demeanor. The casual

mention of portals was just as surprising as the way she now acted.

"Just outside London." A nervous gulp accompanied his words.

"London? As in *England?*" she clarified, sitting up straighter in bed. Her thick American accent accentuated each word.

Wesley merely nodded.

"My family must think I'm dead. How many people died in that fire?" She covered her face with her hands, rocking in place.

"We aren't sure yet. Word has it that the fire may still be burning, destroying half of the city."

"*Still* burning? How long have I been asleep?"

He stuttered, the tone of her voice almost resentful. "Only a day. But, I just made you sleep so you wouldn't feel the pain," he offered, hoping she'd understand.

"Regardless of your intention, you still made me do something I didn't want to do. Maybe I wanted to be awake to meet the people that would be dressing my wounds," she scolded.

"I'm sorry," was all he could muster up. "And I'm sorry about your family. I hope they're alright."

"God, I hope so too," she muttered, looking at the bedside table. Within an instant, a glass of water appeared. "Portals? Randomly appearing water glasses? What else are you going to throw at me?" she mumbled, reaching for it cautiously.

Wesley chuckled. "We can send word to Chicago if you'd like. Try to reach out to them?"

Nodding, she took a quick sip. "Yes, as soon as possible. I need to know they're okay. Can't we bring them here? Since you say this is a safe place?"

"We had to close the portal so the Queen couldn't come after us. Unfortunately, we have to wait to open it back up," he tried to explain.

Something in her eyes stirred – an anger he wasn't expecting.

"You steal me from my home. Rip me from my family during a crisis. And now you tell me I can't get back to them?"

"We're just trying to help…" he mumbled. He slouched with

his hands covering his head.

"She tried to warn me," she began.

There was a long pause, Wesley merely waiting for her to process her thoughts.

"She begged me not to go out. And I did it anyway. I followed that beast right into a trap." As she spoke, her fingers messed with the cuticles around her nails, eyes cautiously examining the room. "Did a lot of people get hurt?" Her gaze flashed to him, the sun illuminating the specks of green and brown in her dark eyes.

He paused for a moment, unsure what to say. At last, he just handed her the newspaper he'd been reading. As her gaze raked over the words, she stared back at him in shock.

"All these people…because of me?"

"You can't blame yourself," he tried to say, unsure if there was anything to truly take away the guilt she felt. "If it helps, they're blaming it all on a cow."

Melinda scoffed. "Mrs. O'Leary's cow did this? Not a chance. If anything, that animal saved my life. Ran straight into that woman and gave me a few seconds to spare."

There was another long pause.

"Remove whatever it is that you did to me. I don't care if I feel the pain. I don't want to be under anyone's influence. And I want to see your real face like I did the other night," she insisted, stretching her hand out to his.

Wesley hesitated.

"Are you…" he began, abruptly interrupted.

"Do it!"

He sighed, obliging her wishes. He grabbed her hand, surprised to feel them calloused. *I wonder what kind of training she's been doing all these years to have such rough hands,* he thought.

Taking a deep breath, he removed the shields. The pain returned as she gripped his hands with a vengeance. Something in her face changed as she looked at him. Fear, he quickly realized.

"Put it back!" she cried, hands patting at her wounds as if it would help dull the ache.

Without thought, he agreed. She sat quietly for a moment, staring off over the room.

When her gaze landed back on him, she asked, "What *are* you?"

"Excuse me?"

"Your face is…different." Her tone was cautious, examining him curiously.

"What do you mean?" he asked, walking to the mirror to examine himself. He pushed the skin of his face around, nervousness brewing in his stomach.

"You didn't look…human." Melinda's breath turned shallow and fast, eyeing him cautiously.

"Everything looks in order to me." He turned back to her as her brows softened and she seemed to relax. Regardless, she still squinted in the slightest suspicion.

"Your face was…featureless. Like you had no identity at all." Her voice was softer this time, leaning forward in curiosity rather than concern.

"Perhaps the pain messed with your vision," he offered, walking back to her side of the bed. "The others are eager to meet you if you're feeling up for it."

"I don't know if I can walk on these feet," she admitted.

Wesley knew she wouldn't feel an ounce of pain, but imagined it was still a bad idea to put pressure on the healing burns. Then, an idea popped into his head. He ran to the door, pausing a moment as if thinking of something. When he opened it, a wheelchair sat on the other side. Carrying her out of bed and placing her into the chair, Wesley and Melinda headed for the family bar to meet with the others.

Winnie lay in bed, somewhere between consciousness and sleep. Her eyes drooped heavily, exhausted from the vision she'd received. But for the first time in her life, they didn't feel like visions from Death. She felt like she was actually there. Like she was the spirit that haunted Boudicca, viewing the queen's life through her own eyes.

Tara moved about the room, unpacking her things and making herself comfortable. A snug, single bed stood across from hers by the fireplace, provided by the house.

Not only did they want to catch up since they last saw one another, Milicent agreed it was a good idea to have someone keep an eye on Winnie. Just in case things got…worse.

Cricket lay lazily in front of the fireplace in her room, stretched out embracing the warmth. Small snores escaped his lips as he snoozed, paws twitching as if dreaming of running after squirrels.

Winnie's room was slightly more chaotic than many of the others of Fox Manor. Her mother put such an effort into keeping the house organized and tidy, and yet Winnie liked it a little more cozy. Her mother didn't agree one bit – she called it messy and wild.

The two always argued about the disorganized book piles, plants, and cluttered decor. Deep spruce walls surrounded large windows peered out over the lake. It was the perfect place to sit and read or watch the animals outside. Or even just exist without feeling like she had to be somewhere doing something.

She's decorated the frame around the window herself. Carvings of mushrooms, fairies, and other woodland creatures lined the wood. Every square inch reminded her of the forest just outside.

Winnie was desperate for a nap, hoping it would fight off the gnawing headache. However, sleep didn't seem to come to her. The scenes and sounds of the battlefield haunted her, Boudicca's final words burning a hole into her mind. She couldn't help but wonder who it was that spoke those tempting words moments before the queen's death.

Slowly, her eyes became heavy and mind drowsy. As she slipped into unconsciousness, she heard soft murmurs all around her.

"My queen…" A voice whispered, far off and almost unintelligible.

Winnie sat up, aware she was not alone. And no longer in her room, either. Surrounded by darkness, she couldn't see anything. Only the soft whispers could be heard through the void.

She quickly realized where she was – Oblivion. A place she often intentionally visited for clients. Rarely did she visit in her dreams uninvited.

"My queen, my love," he hissed again.

"Who's there?" she called out into the abyss.

"My love, come," he whispered again. His voice was closer this time; less of a hiss and more of a beckoning breath.

Winnie opened her mouth again, though nothing came out. She felt like she was floating, weightless and observing.

"Prasutagus…" she heard as Boudicca's voice seemed to come from her body, two spirits simultaneously inhabiting it.

Winnie's emotions blended into Boudicca's as though they were one person. So many layers she hadn't expected.

Grief – the loss of her husband. Her tribe. Her life. Her daughters' innocence.

Anger – the need for revenge singeing her soul.

Longing – to be at peace. To let go of the rage that nagged at her.

Entrapment – knowing she'd made a deal that she now needed to complete.

"My Queen, come to me. Rest," he hummed softly, ever so calm.

She stopped for a moment. She couldn't see him, but she could feel his presence near hers.

"Rest?" Boudicca said aloud, unsure if she was talking to him or herself. "I cannot rest until Paulinus is dead."

Winnie tried to call out to the two entities before her, though neither seemed to realize she was there. As if trapped in yet another memory, she could only watch the two discuss.

"My love, my queen. Please. Rest," he begged once more.

Winnie could sense him getting closer, but the notion of rest infuriated Boudicca. The queen's spirit moved restlessly inside the more he implored her.

"I can't do that…"

Winnie felt as Prasutagus's soul pulled away from them.

"I will be with you one day. But not until I have finished what I started. I always keep my promises." A wave of rage emitted from the queen's spirit, Prasutagus expelled from the area.

Scenes formed in front of them. Boudicca's soul watched as hundreds of years passed. Time didn't seem to work the same here. The years passing were mere seconds before her. General Paulinus's lineage forming and falling with every generation. Tragedy followed them, the queen's curse a living force working against the unsuspecting family.

It wasn't until Winnie heard a soft cry for help that she was pulled from the general's descendents. "Please, I have to see my girls!"

I recognize that voice, she thought.

Mary's grief was intoxicating to the queen – Winnie could feel it. The pull toward her was strong. And something about her oddly familiar, Boudicca recognizing a tortured soul.

Coming from the other side, more beckoning calls sounded. "Our ancestor – Queen Boudicca! Come to us!"

In the distance, two figures called out from the void. Behind them, flames rained down and beasts prowled. But Boudicca was drawn to Mary regardless. Winnie felt both sides tugging at the spirit, trying to bring her forth. But nothing could break her concentration on the mother. Another woman having felt similar pain.

She felt Boudicca's spirit plow through the veil, toward the mother's cries.

At once, she could see it.

The seance.

The night everything changed.

Hovering above the kitchen table, her full attention on Mary and the kindred revenge she craved.

Boudicca reached for the mother and then…

Winnie jolted up in bed, panting. She peered down at the slithering navy snakes that jutted from her healed wound. Only a scar remained, the lingering traces of the queen's blood curse moving over her skin like a living entity.

Tara lay in bed, peacefully sleeping with Cricket curled up on the floor in front of her. A soft whisper sounded through the room as she got up.

"Help her rest…" the voice called. Prasutagus, whispering through the veil.

She couldn't see him anywhere, only sensed him nearby.

"I'll do my best…" she mumbled. She wasn't sure it was possible, having tasted a sliver of the queen's rage. Nonetheless, she knew it was the only option.

14

EZRA

Turning to the side, Ezra checked the clock sitting on his bedside table. Eight o'clock. They were supposed to meet in the family's bar for dinner an hour ago! After the debacle in the library, he couldn't help but fall into a deep, nightmarish sleep.

He remembered many things from the dreams that haunted him: the dead girl, guts spilling onto the streets of London, the blank expression on her face. The sounds. The squelching of blood and organs. The cries of onlookers. And at last…the eyes of the man who'd committed the crime. He couldn't get any of it out of his head. Even awake, he could see it all again just by closing his eyes. He'd witnessed death before but never like that.

Winnie's appearance in his dream stuck with him as well. The murderer's face had shifted and slithered, becoming hers. Some unknown thing using her for its own wicked games, making a mockery of his fear. He vaguely remembered speaking to the creature.

"What are you?" he'd asked.

"I am Death." When he didn't respond, only looked at the creature with Winnie's face in horror, it continued. *"You are marked, Ezra Watson. She will not be able to save you."*

It was with that final sentence that he was jolted from the dream, violently as if he'd been thrust out of it by an unseen hand. Though the memories of those words faded, an uneasy feeling sat in the pit of his stomach.

He didn't know what any of it meant, but one thing was for sure: the children of London needed help. The idea of a killer running around gnawed at his mind, unable to think of anything else.

Shuffling out of bed, he slipped his boots back on and rushed toward the mirror. His hair was disheveled, the ashy strands flying in all directions except the way they were meant to lay. He ruffled them a bit, realizing that only a bath could fix this mop.

Adjusting his clothes, another thought popped into his mind: *What am I even doing here?* It was becoming increasingly obvious with every passing second that he didn't belong with the rest of them. Why Winnie was keeping him around, he didn't know.

And yet still, there he was. Trying to fit in. Anxious about the way his hair looked. Wondering if his clothes were nice enough to take a seat in a bar that would likely be more furnished than every home he'd ever had combined. Unsure if he was worthy enough. Feeling inadequate compared to the magic beings that surrounded him. His racing mind continued as he exited the room.

The sky was already dark outside, shadows cast along the corridor. The dim gas lamps were on, but it still felt eerie as he shut the door behind him. Once again the memories of that girl pelted him, his stomach queasy as he heard something creeping behind him.

The hair on his neck stood, hearing the groaning of the floorboards. His shoulders tensed, afraid to turn. It wasn't until he heard someone clear their throat that he nearly jumped out of his skin.

"Jesus…" Ezra said through clenched teeth. His fist lay at his side in a tight knot as if ready to pummel any entity that would dare mess with him.

"Did I startle you?" Thoren's tone was filled with sarcasm as he approached, leaning against the wall casually on the opposite side. His dark hair looked messier than before, hazel eyes glancing around the hallway. They seemed darker now in the dim light of the hallway; more specks of earthy brown encompassing his irises than Ezra previously noticed.

He thought back to the library. The words that Thoren spoke. *"You're doing a good job trying to hide how panicked you are."* He couldn't help but feel like the siren's words were a punch in the gut then, though they seemed more gentle now looking back.

With shaky knees, the siren had tried distracting him as they walked to their respective rooms. Told him tales of Winnie as a teenager meant to amuse, but Ezra's mind was still fixed on those vacant eyes of hers.

"It's just you…" Ezra let out a sigh of relief, his fist easing again as he wiggled his fingers.

"I'm sorry if I've been a bit cruel to you so far. I realized when I saw you in the library that this must all be terribly difficult to accept. And yet, I've been a total ass. I'm told that's my specialty." Thoren stretched out a welcoming hand, finally ready for a formal shake.

Ezra let out a slight chuckle, shaking the siren's hand carefully. The siren's grip seemed to linger a moment, mouth opening and closing a few times before finally releasing the hand he held.

"I haven't introduced myself properly. I hope you'll forgive me."

Thoren motioned down the hall as the two walked toward the bar. Though they were still upstairs, the sound of music flowed toward them, a beacon to follow.

"I can be a bit protective of Winnie. My brother especially. We've been friends for quite a few years now and…"

Ezra cut him off. "I understand, you don't have to explain. I've only known her a year and I still think I'd do anything for her."

Both chuckled, continuing their walk slowly as they spoke. Thoren was slightly behind him, the hallways too narrow to accommodate both side by side.

"Winnie speaks very highly of you," he added as they reached the stairs.

Ezra paused, unsure what to say. As they made it to the bottom, Thoren continued.

"Given that my brother and I are so protective, I have to ask…"

"My God, can a man and woman not be friends without romantic feelings?" His words were quick with a huffed sigh of frustration.

"Hit a nerve, I see…"

"No, I'm sorry. It's just, we've been asked this almost constantly since becoming friends and moving in together. We tell others we're siblings. That's not…I'm not…"

Ezra ceased his rants of frustration as Thoren held his hand up.

"Take a breath. I saw that memory of yours. I know exactly what you mean," he added with a devilish smirk, leaning in as if to spill his secrets.

Ezra's stomach sank, a rock in his abdomen that likely wouldn't move. "You…saw them? I didn't think you'd be able to actually see my memories when I agreed to have you invade my mind."

Thoren nodded, the feline grin on his face widening. "You and I may be more similar than you realize."

His pace quickened as they snaked through the hallways, leading to a doorway off the entrance. The sounds of laughter and music filled his ears, the smell of ale and stew wafting through the air.

Thoren leaned in, ready to open the door. He turned, seeing Ezra's hesitation.

"Come, now. There's nothing to worry about. Unless Winnie gets too drunk and starts *trying* to sing opera. That's when you know the night is over. She's a perfectly fine singer but she's aggressively alto. When she tries to hit those soprano notes, it'll make your blood run cold."

The siren snagged Ezra's hand, dragging him into the bar. As his feet stepped through the threshold, he was met with a mass of cheers from those inside. His heart fluttered as grateful eyes passed over everyone.

WINIFRED

Inside the family bar, Winnie sat with Tara and Melinda across from the fire. Cricket lay sprawled in front, enjoying warmth and relaxation. In the other corner, Milicent and Afissa sipped wine while catching up on each other's lives since they'd last seen one another. Her father and Wesley sat with Kane, discussing the brothers and their time in Greece since the two-year ban.

A pot of vegetable stew bubbled over the fire, the smells of hearty deliciousness wafting through the air. She'd finished her dinner a while ago but found herself craving more of her mother's cooking as she enjoyed a drink or two. Though, the rumbling in her stomach certainly dimmed her appetite a bit.

After some research, Wesley gave her a tonic of sorts filled with herbs and roots that had no business being mixed together. Bitter wormwood, grassy nettle, fiery bloodroot. Plus a few others he didn't bother to mention. Put together, the taste was disgusting.

"Wesley says you plan to send a letter home?" Winnie's attention turned back to Melinda, serving her another helping of stew as well.

The young woman, about the same age as her brother, seemed to be healing well. Though she didn't dare walk on her burned legs, she managed to join them for dinner.

"Yes, I hope they're alright. I don't know what I'll do if they're not." Gloomy eyes examined the stew, a spoon pushing the contents around while deep in thought.

"Tell us about your family," Tara prodded.

"They're not technically my family. In all honesty, I have none. But the people I live with took me in at a very young age. Taught me everything I know." She shrugged, as though the thought alone didn't bother her in the slightest.

"I'm sorry to hear that," Winnie mumbled.

"I've never known any different. Miss Leona and the other children back home have become my family. I had an uncle, but he passed a few years ago. He always said that our family was cursed. Maybe he was right." Melinda took the last few bites of her stew before straightening herself, adjusting the corset cinching her waist.

"Do you know anything about Queen Boudicca?" Winnie asked, racking her brain to connect dots that didn't quite form.

Melinda shook her head. "I wish I could help, but I really am clueless."

"We'll figure it out," Tara reassured, seeing her friend's concern.

Just outside the bar, two figures formed behind the frosted glass doors. The handle jiggled before Thoren stumbled in with a deep laugh, dragging Ezra behind him. Everyone around cheered, welcoming the two into the family's bar. It made her heart happy to see everyone so welcoming. His face lit up, the energy of the group lifting him.

"You made it! I was beginning to worry about you!" She ran up to him, pulling him to the table to sit with the ladies. "Ez, meet Melinda!"

He nodded at her, a soft smile gracing the young woman's lips. She seemed stoic and shy, like she either didn't get out to gatherings often or found safety in keeping parts of herself hidden.

"How are you feeling?" Taking a seat across from the girl, Ezra reached for an empty glass.

"Fine – beaten and healing, but fine. I should be back on my feet soon," she replied, shifting in her seat uncomfortably.

"Do you know anything about this queen?" he asked, pouring himself a glass of frothy beer as Winnie handed him a bowl of soup.

"Already asked her, Ez. Just enjoy the night," Winnie joked, handing him her cup to receive a top off.

"Winnie's been telling me all sorts of things about you," Tara said to him with a sly grin.

"Hopefully not too much…"

"Only bad things, don't worry." Winnie offered him a quick wink before sitting back down across from him.

"You really haven't spoken to your mam since she kicked you out?" Tara's words slurred a little as she spoke, several glasses of gin and beer mixing to create an overly outgoing version of her.

The whole room seemed to still, turning toward the group in front of the fire.

"That's a conversation for a more sober time." He seemed to shrug the comment off, thankfully, eyes fixed on his glass.

Winnie jabbed Tara in the ribs with a tight frown.

"So, Melinda," he began, seeming eager to take the attention off himself.

The room returned to its usual conversations as each pocket continued talking amongst themselves. Melinda's gaze fluttered toward him above a cup of steaming chamomile tea.

"Did I already miss your story?"

"Kind of." She huffed a quick, nervous laugh. "There's not much to tell. You already know I'm from Chicago. I was out hunting beasts the night they found me. Until that horrible woman got a hold of me." Her eyes darted down as if she, too, was haunted by the image of her.

"Huntin' hellhounds," Tara scoffed. "What a brave lass you are!"

"What are they?" he asked between bites.

"Horrid beasts. They can shift from man to wolf at will. Their disease spreads like wildfire; a single bite and you'll find yourself howling at the moon," Thoren called across the room, taking a quick shot of gin.

"I've heard tales of them, but I thought they were bound to the moon cycle." Melinda's brows furrowed in confusion.

"You're thinkin' of Lycans – two different beasts," Tara clarified, pouring another glass.

"There's some debate about that," Winnie added. "We aren't sure how the hellhounds came to be, but some speculate they originated from Lycan. It's caused a bit of a rift in the magical community."

"Who taught you to hunt?" Ezra asked in curiosity.

Melinda's pause was concerning. Her mind seemed to search for answers. With every second that passed, Winnie's curiosity peaked.

"My uncle. The one I lost a few years ago. Taught me everything I know before he passed."

Winnie's eyes dropped, a twinge of sadness following. She had half a mind to offer a seance, but thought perhaps those were out of the picture until she could fix her last screw up.

Kane took a stand, walking to their table and topping off his drink. Placing a hand on Winnie's shoulder, he said, "We'll have to put you to the test once you're healed. The Fox siblings and I have been sparring for years. It'll be fun to work with someone else for a change."

Winnie sneered, thinking back to years of training with him. Originally, she'd worked with Thoren. It wasn't until she ruined things that she and Kane grew closer.

"I love a challenge," Melinda affirmed, her voice sure and confident. It seemed with each passing moment, she warmed a little more to their outgoing group. "How do all of you know each other?"

"Well," Tara said with a giggle. "They've all known each other since childhood. Except for that one." A sloppy finger pointed at Ezra. "I've been a part of this chaos for three years now."

Kane's face turned red with embarrassment. He rushed back to his seat, grabbing his beer and beginning to guzzle it down. Winnie's eyes met his, and though she felt some pity at first, it quickly faded as she recalled the memories of the day she met Tara.

"I was passing through London, sittin' at a pub and talkin' to a cute little blonde lass. When suddenly my dress was soaked. Some befuddled idiot spilled his drink on me." She shot Kane a devilish smirk.

"Yes, let's relive this night once more for the few people who haven't heard the story…" Kane mumbled into the bottom of his drink.

"He *insisted* on buying me a new one. This, of course, cost me my date. A few hours pass and he claims he wants to take me home. He pulls me to a random alleyway where I'm sure he'll kill me if he weren't falling over himself, drunk. And that's when I have to drag his giant ass through a portal, winding up here at Fox Manor."

Ezra's eyebrows shot up in surprise, looking around as though he were trying to gauge other's responses. Melinda's cheeks flushed, letting out a nervous chuckle between sips of soothing tea.

"And that is why we no longer go out when the Falke brothers visit," Milicent snapped, tuning into the conversation. "Can you imagine? Trying to bring a stranger into our home for a one-night fling?"

Her question was directed at Afissa, though the whole room seemed to laugh. Everyone except the siren in question, of course.

"I'm sure we can cause just as much trouble by staying here," Thoren announced, leaning back lazily in his chair.

Winnie couldn't help but notice his eyes rested on Ezra, sensing tension between the two. Her friend's gaze darted away, almost choking on his drink as he set it down.

"You should be thanking me!" Kane ignored his brother, taking a stand to defend himself. No one in the room seemed to know where he was going with his statement. "Because of me, Winnie met one of her closest friends!"

"He has a point…" she muttered.

"Just so I understand; Kane has a tryst with a stranger and you become her best friend?" A playful grin sat on Melinda's face.

"Yup," Winnie said with confidence. "I woke up the next morning, came downstairs, and there she was. Sipping coffee in our sunroom."

"What a shock it was when that pot appeared out of nowhere! I'd heard tales of magic from the Quinn women in my family, but never seen it with my own two eyes." She rubbed the necklace around her neck, glancing down at it as if lost in memory for a moment. "Although, I wouldn't necessarily call it a tryst. One would need to actually stay in the room for it to be considered that."

"But I thought you two…" Winnie started to say, though Kane shook his head.

"Long story…" he grumbled.

"What happened after?" Melinda asked eagerly.

"Nothing." the siren's face was glaring down to the bottom of his cup, the beer finished and empty again. He looked like he could drown himself in that glass if he wanted.

"I wasn't ready for anythin' serious," she added, bracing her head on perched elbows.

"So after that day, you two just became friends?" Ezra questioned, pointing between Winnie and Tara.

Both giggled with quick nods.

"Tara stayed for a while after, given that she's a bit of a wanderer. She spent some time exploring the woods and trying to learn about the fae and other creatures out there," Winnie continued.

"That's where I found Cricket! I tried to make friends with the crows, too, but they wouldn't have me." Tara motioned for her sleeping mutt as Milicent rolled her eyes in the corner of the room.

"We've tried to explain to her that what she found is not a dog, but she doesn't want to listen to any of us," Milicent added, swirling her wine.

Ezra's eyes flashed nervously back to the heaping pile of fur and fluff. "What…is he?"

"He's an angel, that's what he is! I found him as a little runt, and he's never done anything to hurt me or those I care for. Now, the same can't be said for anyone that attempts to harm me, that's for sure."

"Mother's face was priceless when Cricket came home. She insisted the creature be put back into the woods, but Tara had already named him and made him a collar," Winnie chuckled, Tara's face blushing.

"But you still haven't answered me. What is he?" Ezra's tone was more rushed, anxiously watching Cricket laying in front of the fire. As though the dog knew, he glanced back over his shoulder, staring at her nervous friend.

"He's a black shuck. *Not* a dog!" Milicent insisted, though Tara rolled her eyes.

"Like the legends? The beasts that roam England and are a symbol of death?" Ezra gulped, backing away from the dog who's tawny yellow eyes examined him carefully.

"He's my pet!" A determined fist slammed on the table a moment, firm in her opinion.

"He hated Kane and Thoren in the beginning," Winnie added.

The youngest Falke brother scoffed from across the room. "He still doesn't care much for me to this day."

"That's because you're insufferable," Kane mumbled, eyes still fixed to his glass.

"Just because you hoped to bring home a girl and she left with an actual beast doesn't mean you have to take it out on me," his brother joked, slapping him on the back.

"I love that this is the topic we've chosen for tonight's conversation," Kane mumbled.

Wesley next to him giggled, a hiccup following. He hadn't said much of anything, only taken in one too many drinks.

"Thanks to everything that happened with Tara, no one will let him live it down. He's been a little sour ever since," the siren's little brother explained.

"Since we seem to be making people uncomfortable, I have to ask: why were you two banned?" Ezra's eyes flashed to the two sirens to gauge their responses.

"That's a long story but..." Thoren began, though he was

quickly interrupted.

"Momma Millie. Shouldn't you be the one to tell that story? Since you know it so well?" Kane's gaze darted toward her mother, a certain edge to his voice no one had expected. A history there that no one knew.

She cleared her throat, a look for surprise plastered across her face like she didn't quite know how to respond.

"Why don't I?" Ernest added, sitting forward in his seat. He took one last swig of gin before beginning. "These two have always been trouble makers, let's be honest."

The room erupted into laughter. Even Ezra and Melinda joined in with the rest.

"Since they were boys, they've always gotten into everything. One night we went to the pub and both brothers stayed behind. Millie wouldn't let either come because she didn't want them causing trouble. So, naturally, Thoren snuck into my office and stole an expensive bottle of whiskey. He flew onto the roof, drank half of it, and in a fit of stupidity, set the damn house on fire."

"I wanted to see if I could use some of the elemental magic I was trying to learn. Turns out I don't use air like most sirens. I connected with fire. It's no wonder it took me so long to gain my element. I was seeking out the wrong deity for years." Thoren's brows raised, hands hiding a small smirk as if remembering that night.

"So Thoren's setting the house on fire. What was Kane doing?" Ezra asked.

"I'd be curious to know as well," Winnie muttered, recalling her hazy memories.

"Some things are better left unsaid," Milicent cut in.

"There's more to the story and you know it," Kane accused with a scowl fixed on Milicent once more.

Before her mother could respond, Ernest leaned in and mumbled something to the siren. Slowly, his temper seemed to fizzle out. Winnie could hardly make out what was being said, but one word seemed to stick out to her.

"Protecting? Who were you protecting?" She raised her voice above the conversation at Kane's table, everyone seeming to look at each other in confusion.

"It doesn't matter…" Kane mumbled, pouring himself another glass. He avoided her eye contact as he took a swig.

Ernest patted him on the back before checking on Wesley. By now, he'd laid his head on the table, passed out. The lull continued, eventually everyone returning back to their quiet conversations.

"At some point, I do need to have a more serious conversation with you," Ezra said at last, breaking the silence of his table.

"What is it?"

"The night you went to Chicago…there was another murder. Right outside our pub."

The room quieted once more, listening to him speak.

"That's terrible…" she whispered.

"I saw him, Winnie. I saw the killer. I couldn't get through the crowd in time to catch him. You should've seen what he did. He gutted her like a damn fish right outside our flat." He took a deep, long sip as if trying to drown the memories.

"I'm so sorry you had to see that…"

"It was one of the girls from work. She was *fourteen*. I'm going after him. I won't let another innocent die." He placed his cup down, a stern look on his face as if he wouldn't allow anyone to change his mind.

"Ez, no. You can't go out there looking for some murderer. That's how you get yourself killed!" Winnie looked around the room for backup from anyone who'd take her side.

Her eyes rested a moment on her mother's, pleading for help. Milicent looked away, avoiding the talk all together. *What if this is how it all happens?* Her anxious thoughts swirled around in her mind, a never-ending storm.

"We can't sit here and do nothing. I won't hide like some coward."

"If you go out there, you could get yourself killed. I refuse to let that happen!"

Before the two could continue their conversation, Thoren interrupted. Getting up from his seat, he stopped just behind Ezra with a supportive hand on his shoulder.

"Why don't I join you? I'll help where I can and ensure you have backup if needed."

"He's not some helpless baby," Tara added, looking at Winnie in disbelief.

"I didn't say…" she began, though she was cut off.

"He won't get himself killed if I'm there. I have a feeling we'll make a great team," Thoren said, peering down at her friend.

Why is everyone against me right now? If only they knew…

"We don't have time…the queen…" she tried to say.

"You need time to research her and figure out what to do. The children of London don't have that luxury," Ezra interrupted.

She felt like she could scream – tired of not finishing a sentence.

"I just don't want to see you hurt…either of you."

"We'll be fine," Ezra reassured, grabbing her hand and offering it a quick squeeze. "I want to go tomorrow and start looking," he added, glancing back at Thoren.

He nodded in agreement, returning back to his table with Ernest, his brother, and a snoring Wesley.

"This one's had too much," Ernest barked through laughter, patting his son on the back.

"I think I'm ready to head to bed as well," Melinda said softly, glancing toward the door.

Milicent and Afissa stood, the mermaid grabbing hold of the wheelchair's handles as Winnie's mother opened the door to the bar. Both helped her to her room, retiring shortly after. On the other side, Ernest nudged his son, coaxing him to stand. He pulled Wesley's arm across his back, the boy walking limply as they headed off as well.

"I think I'll retire, too," Ezra mentioned, taking one last sip.

"I'll help you find your room." Thoren got to his feet, waiting for him at the door.

"I can find my room myself. I'm not *that* inebriated." And yet, the siren didn't seem to listen. Only beckoned him out through the door.

At last, only Tara, Kane, and Cricket sat in the room with Winnie. The ladies wandered upstairs, leaving Kane alone. His eyes were still fixed on that glass in his hands, mind seeming to race ever since the conversation about the house ban.

"Goodnight," Winnie called as they left, though he didn't respond. A twinge of sadness flickered in her chest at the complete disregard.

Once in her room, she prepared herself for bed. Tara immediately removed her corset and laid down, Cricket sighing as he curled in front of the fire once more.

Winnie reached down, scratching beneath the animal's chin. "With the amount of sass from you, little Cricket, one would think you live a much harder life." The mutt's face turned to what looked like a canine smile, enjoying a few scratches before she continued to ready herself for bed.

She'd only let her hair down and removed her jewelry when she heard clumsy footsteps down the hall. With Tara snoring in bed, she poked her head into the corridor. Kane stayed only one room down, stumbling as he seemed to turn in circles.

"What are you doing, you drunk?" She giggled, closing the door softly behind her.

He continued to turn in circles, ignoring her question at first.

"Are you having trouble finding your room?"

"Do you hear it?" His voice was merely a whisper, hand on his chest and eyes closed.

She glanced around, the silence of the house eerie. Before she could even open her mouth to speak, he reached for her. Carefully, she grabbed his hand. He spun her around, a soft squeal of joy escaping her lips as he grasped her waist and hand, beginning to sway.

"Close your eyes. You'll hear it."

As she did, she felt a wave of emotions wash over her. Memories flooded her mind, the time spent with Kane a welcomed reminder that she'd missed him terribly the last two years. She focused, trying to hear it. And then…there it was. Soft keys played throughout her mind, a familiar tune she once knew.

"Is that what I think it is?" She giggled, opening her eyes to meet his gaze.

"A song without words," he nodded. "The same song we used to obsessively listen to when we were younger. I never tire of this melody."

His face rested carefully on the side of her head, eyes still closed as they swayed. She pulled back a little to examine him.

"You've changed so much since I last saw you." Standing this close, she noted the lines in his face that had formed in the two years apart. The way his skin feathered near his eyes as he smiled down at her. The familiar smell of his soap, light and sweet like springtime air. One of few things that hadn't changed since they'd been apart.

"You as well," he chuckled. "You've always been beautiful but you're different now. More…radiant. There's a glow about you that you didn't have before. Your energy is magnetic," he added, twirling her around once more.

I'm not used to this version of Kane, she thought as her cheeks flushed a little. He'd never complimented her so forwardly before. Perhaps it was the alcohol or the years away, but she welcomed this new side of him.

"We should probably go to bed," she said softly.

"Won't you dance with me a moment longer?" His face seemed to plead with her.

She almost pulled away but something told her to stay. Instead, she laid her head on him as they continued their quiet dance, listening to the slow steady rhythm of his heart beneath his chest.

"I missed you," she said softly, attempting to pull him in closer as they continued their sway. Seeing him here again made her realize that a piece of her had been missing these last two years. And perhaps it was simpler than she thought to fill the void.

There was a long pause before he finally answered, "As did I."

He twirled her once more, a hint of sadness in his eyes as he bowed, offering her a quick kiss on the top of her hand.

"Milady," he joked in an attempt to hide that sorrow, his lips pursed to imitate a posh London gentleman.

"You're ridiculous." A beaming smile graced her face as she watched him stumble to his room.

"Goodnight, *Winifred.*"

"You know I hate it when you call me that!" Her words were met with deep belly laughs as he wandered into his room, shutting the door with Winnie still in the hallway. She waited a moment, unsure how to feel. Their friendship didn't quite feel the same as it once did, though at the same time she wondered if nothing had changed at all. He was here now, and that was all that mattered.

15

WINIFRED

Lying in bed, Winnie tossed and turned. Relentlessly, memories of her past kept her up well into the morning, remembering it all. The night of the banning reminded her of the heartache she'd felt. She kept wondering how painful it had been for the brothers. Wondered what the true magnitude of the betrayal was for them.

Kane had played it off, haughty and upset when Milicent informed them the next morning. Thoren's face told a different story. He'd been silent, refusing to say a word with his eyes fixed on the ground in a sort of shame Winnie hadn't expected.

As those images resurfaced in her mind, others came forward as well. Reminding her of the pain she'd caused him a year before the banning. The night she'd chosen a boy named Samuel over him. Before she'd made that fateful decision, there was a part of her that knew for certain they had feelings for each other. But Fate had other plans.

Two years before the banning, the Falke brothers spent time away, dealing with their own battles at home. Between the invasion of their island and a sickness that fell upon their mother, neither had time to write to her as they usually did. As the memories tugged at the tear ducts in her eyes, she reminded herself: *I didn't know what they were going through…*

The year apart with no word from either left Winnie heartbroken. So when a boy at school expressed his wish to court her, she happily agreed. In her mind, Thoren had lost interest. It couldn't hurt to seek comfort in someone who actually wanted to be with her.

The night they came back to the manor, injured and orphaned, was the same night she came home from her date. She turned over in bed, pulling her pillow up over her ears as if it could block out the cries she'd heard. She tried to remove the memory of Thoren running away from her, anguished and defeated. The look of worry on Kane's face. Unsure if he should go after his brother. Back to a broken land where they'd witnessed so much of Death's work.

She continued her courtship with the boy from school for another year. During that time, Thoren stopped speaking to her almost entirely. Both brothers still visited, but only Kane spent time with her. He was the only friend she had left, aside from Tara, until her mother banished them. *It's a wonder they want to help us at all after all that's happened,* she thought.

When her eyes slowly shut, a set of new images appeared. The night she'd ended her relationship with Samuel. The boy who broke her heart, destroyed her trust. The one unworthy of her love. Who spent so much of his time trying to convince her she was the problem. The same night the brothers were banned. But these seemed different than the ones she remembered. There was a layer of fog over the evening, her mind muddled as she tried to remember.

Tugging, she realized. Bits and pieces. Kane was there – that she was sure of. Running into Wesley as she stepped inside the house she was also sure of. With her tear-stained face and freshly bruised cheek, she suddenly knew with absolute clarity that she saw both of them that night.

And yet she couldn't remember what happened after. Wading through those memories felt like walking through hardening cement. Like someone didn't want her to recall the truth. The harder she tried, the deeper into her sleep she fell.

The next morning, she rolled over – groggy eyes searching for her usual waiting pot of coffee by her bedside. For the first time in well, ever, it wasn't there. She sat up, noticing Tara and Cricket no longer in the room. The canister sat by her friend's bed, a cup sitting next to it with a bit of pink lip stain around the rim.

She swung her legs over the side, regretting the quick motions. With a throbbing head, she rubbed at her temples feverishly. Her stomach twisted, the tonics sloshing around inside her and gnawing at the infected blood coursing through her veins. Pushing the feeling down, she fixed her hair in a messy braid and pulled on a robe before following the smell of bacon down to the kitchen.

As Winnie entered, she saw her mother making the usual recovery breakfast – bacon, eggs, and freshly baked bread. Her mouth salivated as the smells wafted her way, though she reached for the pot of coffee first. She couldn't help noticing Ezra immediately, stirring the eggs around in the pan as Milincet coached him. A wide, beaming smile sat across his dimpled face, one she hadn't seen in quite some time.

Kane sat alone at the small table by the window, munching on bread with a squeamish face. His eyes were fixed outside, looking out over the lake.

"Good morning, my dear," Ernest said as he prepared a plate for his daughter.

She offered her father a gracious smile before taking a seat next to Melinda. Her wheelchair was out of sight, the young woman sitting freely along the counter enjoying her food.

"I assume you're all healed?"

Melinda nodded happily. "I've seen better days, for sure, but your mother's ointments work wonders!"

Winnie pecked at her food, stomach still queasy. As she took a sip from her coffee, Ernest brought over another vile of foul tonic. Begrudgingly, she took it and chugged the contents, ready to hurl from the taste.

"You look like you've had better days as well," the girl joked, pointing to the bags under Winnie's eyes. "My uncle back home says you should drink raw eggs when you're sick from booze."

"Honestly, I wish it was the alcohol. This blood curse is taking a greater toll on me than I expected."

"They wouldn't call it a curse if it was a pleasant thing," Melinda joked.

She seems to be warming up to us, Winnie thought with a chuckle.

"You aren't going to say good morning to me?" Kane called from his side of the kitchen.

Winnie waved lazily, her head still throbbing. "How are you feeling today, you drunken fool?"

"Better than your brother!"

Ernest cackled before adding, "He's been heaving his guts out all morning, the poor kid."

Melinda leaned in closely, lowering her voice so no one else could hear. "Why do Kane and Thoren have…wings? Are they angels?"

Winnie's eyes darted to the siren curiously, trying to understand the question.

As if reading her mind, Melinda continued. "I can…see things others can't. But I've never seen creatures like them before."

"Not angels; sirens. Unless angels are known for causing trouble," she chuckled. "What else can you see?"

Melinda huffed, glancing around the room. "I see the spirits that surround your family; your ancestors guiding you. Tara's too. I can see the scaly one's tail. Your blonde friend is a little more clouded. I gather his fate isn't yet determined."

Winnie's eyes narrowed in curiosity, trying to decipher it all.

"No wonder you were so scared when you first got here. That's a lot of information to take in all at once. What did you see when you saw the queen?"

"Nothing. Only darkness." She shuddered, likely reliving those moments in her mind.

"We're going to protect you," Winnie said, placing an encouraging hand over the young woman's.

"I know." Melinda offered a warm smile, sure of the family's promise.

Ezra turned, placing another strip of bacon on Winnie's plate. "And how are you feeling?" she asked him.

"You know me – always have to be sharp." His cheeks perked, turning back to the stove.

It's nice seeing him…content, she thought. "Where's your brother?" she called to Kane whose mouth gulped down another cup of coffee.

"Out by the lake," he said between bites.

Winnie pushed her food away, stomach still too queasy to consume anymore. She exited the kitchen and shuffled out of the sunroom. The cool October breeze hit her immediately, yellow and orange leaves falling to the ground as she pulled her robe around tightly.

She approached Thoren with caution, his back to her as he stared out over the water. He turned, eyes dropping as if expecting someone else.

"Good morning," he mumbled, snatching a rock from the ground to toss into the lake.

She greeted him before saying, "I don't feel right about you two going off to chase a murderer."

"Why are you so worried? We can handle ourselves." He cocked his head to the side to examine her carefully.

"It's a long story…just please. Be careful."

"I won't let anything happen to him. Any friend of Winifred Fox is a friend of mine." He offered her a soft smile, the first she'd gotten in a long time.

Silence stalled their conversation, a lull brewing tension before she finally spoke once more. "I really missed you…" She reached for his hand, though he backed up before they made contact.

"I missed you too," he mumbled, though he seemed to refuse

to look at her.

"I," she began, unsure where to even begin.

I'm sorry I wasn't patient enough? I'm sorry I chose someone else? I'm sorry I ripped your heart out when you needed me most?

He put his hand up to stop her as if anticipating this conversation. "You don't have to say anything, Winnie. It's fine."

"No, it's not Thoren. I hurt you. I've felt guilty about it since that day you came back. Just…let me apologize. Please."

"You're right. I needed you and you weren't there for me. So what? That was three years ago. Move on."

Behind them, she heard the sunroom door swing open. Before Thoren could wander off to whoever exited, she stood between them.

"Move on? Like you moved on? Should I just start being an asshole to you too, then?" Anger bit at her tongue, words coming from her mouth she wasn't expecting.

"Seriously?" He scoffed. "You're going to call *me* the asshole when *you're* the one who chose someone else?" A muscle in his jaw flared as he gritted his teeth.

"I didn't hear from you for a whole year! I thought you moved on. I sent letters that you never responded to!"

"I was in the middle of war!" His words echoed through her. "Besides, I never got any letters. Kane got his, *of course.* But I got nothing. Either way, if you really cared for me the way you thought you did, you'd never have entertained someone else in the first place."

"I was *sixteen.* All I needed was reassurance! You have no idea how much the guilt has eaten away at me since that day. You have to realize that I never wanted to hurt you."

"And yet you did it regardless. You ripped my heart out, all for some slag who only courted you for a year."

"Accepting his courtship was the biggest mistake of my life," she cried. "He *destroyed* me. Treated me in ways I didn't know were possible for someone who supposedly loved me."

"Don't change the subject and try to make me feel bad for you. I can accept that you chose someone else, but I will not pity you."

There was another pause as Winnie looked past him, noticing Ezra's gaze on them. He waited outside the sunroom as her eyes welled, tears slowly falling down her face.

"Do you still love me?" Thoren asked at last. His mouth was clenched tight, fists balled at his side.

"W–What?"

"Do you…still *love* me?" The words seemed to pain him, trying desperately not to be uttered.

"I – " She attempted to explain. Tried to say something. Anything. But nothing would come out. The word 'no' danced on her tongue, but she didn't know if she was brave enough to admit it.

"That's what I thought." He trudged away, shaking his fists at his side, and rolling his neck a few times. At last, he stood in front of her friend, back turned to her and unwilling to acknowledge her tears.

Winnie glanced between the two and the front of the house, choosing to run. Away…far away. *Anywhere but here,* she thought as she ran. She reached her portal back to her flat, jumping through and landing back in the alleyway of Bethnal Green. The familiar smell of smog and mud hit her nostrils as she hastily walked toward the front of the building. She heard footsteps, following her as she approached the door.

Turning, she was surprised to see…

"Kane?"

"I saw you running away crying. I came to make sure you were alright," he said, placing a hand on her shoulder.

She glanced between him and the door, wiping away tears as onlookers passed by and gawked. A young lady in her nightgown? Speaking to a fine young man, unchaperoned? If there was one thing she'd learned about Bethnal Green it was that the people loved a juicy scandal.

"Let's go back to the manor," she rushed. She pushed him toward the portal, though he stood his ground.

"No, let's go inside and talk." He offered her a gentle smile, reaching for the handle and taking a step into her flat. Winnie stood in the doorway awkwardly before finally shutting the door.

"I know, it's not much…it's harder than I thought to make it in London." She took a defeated seat on the edge of her bed, glancing around at what little they owned.

"It's not much, but it's yours." His face turned, softening as he noticed how upset she was.

As his eyes met hers, she couldn't hold it back any longer. Her sobbing intensified, Thoren's words ringing through her mind.

"Did you two finally have the talk?" He took a careful seat next to her, placing an arm around Winnie which she sank into. Moments passed before he pulled her in tighter.

"Your brother's an ass," she choked out.

"Yeah, that's why we love him," he joked. The word 'love' only made her cry harder. "I wish you two would've talked a long time ago. I know you both have been holding that in for a while."

She sat in silence, unsure what to say.

"He still cares about you. Not in the same way, but you'll always be family to him. His pride is too wounded to admit it."

She huffed, wiping away a few tears as she sniffled.

"Once you both cool off, I'm sure you can work things out. Be friends again."

She nodded carefully, getting up to pace the room. "We should go back to the manor."

"Why the rush?"

She pointed around, thinking: *Shouldn't it be obvious?*

"You need to give yourself more credit, Winnie. It's hard making it out in the real world. This might not look like much to you, but it's more than most have."

Winnie's eyes dropped, thinking of poor Mary and her daughters. To the others who wandered the streets at all hours of the night, desperately searching for shelter to stave off the cold, grime, and hunger.

"You should be proud of yourself." He placed his hands on either shoulder, leaning down to meet her line of sight.

"Nothing has gone the way I planned it," she grumbled.

"Nothing ever does," he laughed. "You should still acknowledge how far you've come."

"You've always been so kind to me," she mumbled, their eyes locking once more.

"That's because you mean the world to me." Only a moment passed before he pulled her in for a gentle hug.

She placed her cheek on his chest, a flutter of happiness moving about inside. "I'm glad you're here. You didn't have to come help us after the way my mother treated you."

"If the Fox family needs me, I'll be damned not to assist. Same goes for my brother." He hummed softly, placing his chin on the top of her head.

"Why won't any of you tell me what actually happened that night?" Lifting her head, she met his gaze directly. She didn't need to explain which evening she was referring to for him to understand.

"Your mother's right. Some things you don't need to know," he mumbled, avoiding eye contact and letting go of her to step away.

"Drunk Kane didn't think so."

"Well, Drunk Kane is a whole different person." His cheeks flushed as he spoke.

"Do you remember making me dance with you?" A few giggles escaped from her as she wiped away another runaway tear.

"I did *what?*"

"Mhmm, twirled me around like a ballerina."

"That's embarrassing…" His words were soft, slightly more than a mumble. "Why don't we go back and get some rest? I know those tonics have your stomach upset. You look like you didn't sleep at all last night."

"I'm done resting. Can we train like we used to?"

He chuckled. "For you – anything. Just know I won't go easy on you like I used to."

She scoffed. "When did you ever go easy on me?"

The two continued their back-and-forth banter as they exited her flat. Just down the alleyway, Thoren and Ezra walked through the portal. Winnie rushed past them both, back to the manor before either could say a word.

16

EZRA

Stepping through the portal, Ezra bent over and heaved once more. "I'm never going to get used to these damned portals," he groaned as Thoren offered him a quick pat on the back.

Looking up, he witnessed Winnie's tear-stained face as she rushed past them. He'd watched something go down between her and Thoren but hadn't dared to ask about it yet. Kane waved awkwardly, stepping through the portal just behind her.

Ezra glanced over to the onyx pendant around Thoren's neck, almost identical to Winnie's. "Does everyone have one of those?"

"Anyone that goes to Fox Manor often." His tone was short, eyes resting on the portal as if wondering if he should go back.

"When will I get one?" his voice was soft, almost embarrassed to ask.

"When you're considered family, I'd imagine."

Though his tone was void of any emotion, Ezra couldn't help but feel like the siren's words were a punch in the gut. The two made eye contact before Thoren's face softened, the scowl dropping at last.

"I'm sorry, that was cruel. It was meant to be a joke, but I think I may be all out of those. I'm sure they'll fashion you one on the next full moon."

"Did I manage to make you feel a human emotion? That may be a first," Ezra said with a half-hearted chuckle. There was a slight pause before he finally asked, "Why does everything have to depend on the bloody moon?"

"That's when they're the most powerful and the moon's energy can be drawn upon. My brother and I find ourselves more powerful during that time as well."

Turning the corner of the building, Ezra entered the flat first. He paced around the room as Thoren took a seat at the kitchen table. There was a lull, his mind racing as he thought back to the night of the murder.

"Where do we even begin?" he finally asked, throwing his hands to his side. "Maybe this was a bad idea. I only saw his face. How the hell are we going to find him in all of London?"

"Let's just think. We should probably start with the police; find out what they already know."

"Why would they give us that information?" Frustration brewed inside, thinking only of the possible victims of the madman running around these streets.

"I can be very persuasive," Thoren answered with a smirk, pointing to his throat.

"Ah, yes. How could I forget that pesky power of yours?" Ezra couldn't help but roll his eyes, thinking back to the morning he'd witnessed them first hand.

"How many people were at the pub the night you saw him?"

"Quite a few. Mostly regulars." Ezra took a seat across from Thoren, elbows braced on the table.

"We should try and find them. Question them too. If they're regulars, I'm sure they'll be back." Thoren slouched back in the chair comfortably, eyes roaming the room, then Ezra at last. His gaze was piercing, those warm hazels examining even the smallest of details with an unexpected intensity.

"We can try but I doubt any of them saw the man. They were too afraid the night it happened. I pointed him out, but no one would look or let me through to chase after him."

"Once again, I can pull out any necessary information. Even if it's hidden deep in the subconscious."

"Sounds like you're stellar at invading people's privacy." Ezra's words came out with a surprise bitter bite.

Thoren held his hands up in the air in a sign of submission. "I offered to show you my powers, and you said yes."

"I didn't think you'd be able to *see* one of my more intimate moments," he retorted. "Winnie doesn't even know about that night."

"It can be our little secret." A mischievous smirk sat on his face, eyes darkening with wicked amusement.

With a racing mind, Ezra finally asked, "Why are you helping me?"

"You're a friend of Winnie's. Therefore you're a friend of mine." His answer was simple and direct, but then... "Plus I can't let you get yourself killed. Winnie wouldn't be able to live with herself if that happened."

A pang of sadness hit Ezra, greater than he expected. "Why do you do that? Feel the need to compensate with such cruelty when you clearly have the ability to be kind?"

Thoren was taken aback. For once, he seemed to sit speechless, unsure how to answer. "Kane and I… We had a difficult upbringing. I know it's no excuse, but I sometimes find it helps."

With a nod, Ezra replied, "My childhood was a nightmare too, but you don't see me being an ass."

Thoren chuckled, deep and low. "I do wish to be your friend. Even if I am as intolerable as my brother says."

"That may be a bit harsh. Somewhat of a jerk, sure. But not intolerable." Ezra studied the siren carefully, trying to read him. "What happened? Back at the house? I saw you two talking."

"We've both needed to be honest with each other for some time now. I think we're finally moving past everything that happened years ago. I just hope our friendship can still be salvaged," Thoren explained, leaning forward once more.

The two men sat in silence for a few moments. Ezra took deep breaths, realizing being home brought back feelings of restlessness.

He still hadn't told Winnie he'd lost his job. *Soon,* he reminded himself, *when the time is right.*

"Ready to go?" Thoren's words pulled him from a flustered trance.

As they walked the streets of London, the usual grime clung to their boots. A cool autumn breeze flowed through the streets, a few of the nicer shops decorated for fall. Ezra couldn't help but notice women gawking and giggled to one another as Thoren passed.

They gawked at Thoren, whose well-tailored clothing hugged his muscular body. His fitted dress shirt was tucked neatly into his trousers, a pair of suspenders holding a pistol at his side. He looked wealthy compared to most gentlemen walking the streets, attracting attention from just about anyone who passed. Pangs of jealousy surprised Ezra, realizing he hated seeing the way Thoren's flirtatious smile welcomed the attention he received.

Around the corner, they approached the Bethnal Green Police Station. It opened earlier that year, already seeing a fair share of crime and murders as the men watched over the lower-class. The large brick building sat on the end of the road, the streets outside busy with life.

"When we go in, you do the talking. I'll do what I do best." Thoren pointed to his throat once more.

"What do I even say?" Ezra asked, panicking as they neared the door.

An officer stood outside, looking at them suspiciously. Thoren offered a quick smile before turning to Ezra with a glare. No sound escaped his lips as he mouthed, *'Calm down!'*

Ezra shook his hands at his sides as they entered, sauntering up to the receptionist behind the welcoming desk. She looked to be in her late 40s, staring at them over thick-rimmed glasses, her hair in a neat bun. Her dark navy gown rustled as she stood, waiting for either to speak.

"We'd like to meet with the inspector," Ezra began.

Thoren glared at him once more, the receptionist looking at them in confusion with her head cocked to the side.

"Whoever's investigating the murders of the young girls," he clarified.

Before the woman could open her mouth in response, Thoren hummed low and soft. Her eyes glossed over, face dulling to the point of no expression. Though Ezra looked at the siren in panic, he merely motioned with his chin to follow her as she walked toward the back of the station.

She led them to an office as the siren continued his quiet songs. They walked, not a soul turning to look at them as Thoren's voice cast a protective bubble around them away from prying eyes. It was as if they were invisible to the rest of the police station.

The woman opened a door, motioning for them to enter. "Thank you, darling," Thoren purred, offering her a charming smile.

When he stopped humming, her face cleared and she realized where she was. "These two, um, men are here to see you," she mumbled, still dazed from the siren's trance.

"And who the hell are you two?" The inspector's voice barked at them, angrily rising from his chair. He was short and looked like he frequented the pub often. Wearing a classic suit, his greasy combover matched a thick mustache that wiggled as he spoke angrily.

"We're…" Ezra began, eyes flashing to Thoren.

"Reporters! We're here for information on the murdered girls."

"How many times do I have to tell you damned people that there will be no questions answered!" As he shouted, he picked up a cigar and lit the end of it.

"Please?" Thoren asked, a sly grin spreading across his face as he began to hum once more.

Ezra felt the room vibrating as the musical notes grew louder and louder. The inspector's body shook as if fighting the control, his lit cigar falling onto the desk. Thoren seemed to push a little harder, the man's face dropping as if he finally gave up.

"What do you want to know?" He was suddenly compliant, tone monotone and eyes glossy.

"What do you know so far of the murderer?" Ezra rushed.

"Not much. For the last year, he's been seen all over London wearing a dark derby hat. He has scruffy facial hair and wears a long overcoat even on the hottest of evenings," the inspector mumbled.

"Where was he last seen?"

Thoren motioned to hurry. *Is the inspector fighting the siren song? I didn't think that was possible,* Ezra wondered.

"Whitechapel. By the open markets, mostly. Though he's been seen everywhere by now. Just the other day, right here in Bethnal Green."

"Is there a connection between the girls?" Ezra's last question came out of his mouth, sour and bitter.

"No…some poor, some rich. Only thing in common is their age. And all females."

Thoren let up on his song, the inspector blinking wildly. "That'll be all, Inspector. Thank you for your information,"

He hurried Ezra out of the door before the man could regain his witts.

"Ida!" The sound echoed down the hall from behind them as they rushed for the exit. The receptionist rushed past the two men, glaring at them. "How many times have I told you not to let reporters back here?"

Ezra could still hear her being berated as they exited the station. "Sorry Ida," he mumbled to himself, the two turning the corner.

"Whitechapel," Thoren mumbled. "Let's see what some of your pub friends have to say and maybe we can stop by there before heading back to the manor."

The day continued as Thoren and Ezra headed back toward

the pub. They sat inside for a while looking for regulars but didn't come across any. The siren bought both a slice of bread and some soup, to which Ezra felt rather embarrassed.

"I can buy my own lunch," he'd said begrudgingly as Thoren topped off a glass of beer. The siren only seemed to smirk, enjoying the meal anyway.

"We should probably wait until the evening and come back. None of them are going to be out drinking this time of day. Everyone's too busy working," Ezra added, spooning the last of his soup into his mouth.

"If you wanted to spend more time with me, all you had to do was say so." The words tumbled from Thoren's mouth as if he hadn't thought them through. Blushing a little, he took a sip of his beer before straightening himself back out.

With flushed cheeks that hid a small smile, Ezra took a second to think before changing the subject. "You say your family is from Greece?"

Thoren merely nodded silently, eyes locked on Ezra over the rim of his beer glass.

"How is your English so good?"

With a thoughtful smile, the siren explained. "Our dad was a Brit. Met our mother on his travels and fell in love."

"And he chose to stay in her home to raise you two?"

Thoren paused for a long moment, the gears of his brain turning before finally nodding again. "Perhaps if we'd come back to England, they might still be alive today. And Kane and I wouldn't have grown up too quickly."

Ezra was unsure what to say next. More human emotion than he'd ever witnessed from Thoren lay behind his russet eyes, set ablaze by the memories of anger and sadness. Finally, he broke the stillness.

"I do appreciate you coming with me on this fool's errand. You didn't have to help me."

"Helping you is my greatest pleasure." A soft smile graced his dangerously beautiful siren lips. "See? I can be kind afterall. Now, let's go to Whitechapel. Ask around if anyone's seen him. Maybe we'll get lucky, find the bastard, and end him quickly."

"End him? Shouldn't we turn him over to the police?" Wide eyed and astonished, Ezra merely stared at him.

"And give him the opportunity to escape? Not a chance. We do it right, for the sake of London's girls," he said matter-of-factly, pointer finger tapping the table.

"I want justice as much as anyone, but I never planned on killing to do it. You're different than I thought you'd be," Ezra mumbled.

"Different how?" Thoren braced his head on a perched elbow, examining him carefully.

He said nothing.

"You may not like it, but I do what needs to be done. For the greater good."

Ezra continued his stoic silence as he brought their bowls and cups over to Butch for cleanup.

Exiting the pub, the two wandered down the streets toward Whitechapel. The walk was quite significant, but the afternoon breeze was pleasant and the smells of the slums not too pungent. He cringed, however, realizing where they'd have to pass in order to get there.

"That's the place, isn't it?" Thoren asked, his chin jutting toward the small bakery sitting at the corner of two streets.

"I wasn't planning on ever walking down this way again. Hurry up," he rushed, his pace quickening to get past.

Thoren met his stride, slowing only when he did.

"It's not something to be ashamed of, you know?" His words came out soft and gentle, a kind hand reaching for Ezra's arm.

"Not according to my mother. Or society. I was literally raised in shame. I really don't want to talk about what happened," he finally snapped, rushing to continue their trek toward the markets.

"Ezra, stop a second." Thoren reached for his shoulder, pulling him to the side out of the way of pedestrians.

"I don't want to discuss this with you. Or anyone for that matter!"

"You have to at some point. You can't let it eat away at you. There's nothing wrong with you. So your mother doesn't approve? Fuck her! You don't need people like that in your life!"

"Why do you even care?" Ezra shouted, his voice reverberating through the alleyway behind them. He was taken aback when he noticed the hurt look on Thoren's face.

"I, too, lived in fear for a time. I know how debilitating it can be to hide. You must learn to surround yourself with people who accept you, and let go of the ones who don't approve. They're not your family if they can't love you for who you truly are." Thoren placed an encouraging hand on Ezra's shoulder.

For a mere second, he released a sigh that felt like years of pent up anger flowing free to the breeze, carried away to be forgotten.

"I suppose it is nice to have at least one person who knows the truth. Even if you did acquire the knowledge through nefarious means."

Thoren shook his head with a chuckle before saying, "When you're ready, know that I'm here to listen. The open markets. Up ahead."

The two reached Whitechapel, examining the pedestrians and vendors scattered about. Countless men were dressed as the inspector described. Derby hats of different sizes and colors sat atop dozens.

"No wonder the police haven't found him yet," Thoren speculated, pointing around at the crowd.

"I should recognize him if I see him." Ezra's words were merely a mumble as his eyes searched.

Walking through the street, they passed vendor after vendor. If it wasn't live animals being sold, it was textiles, food, spices, cosmetics, cheap coffee, or the occasional fish sandwiches. A mix of smells and sounds filled Ezra's ears, the energy of the crowd overwhelming as everyone hustled. They continued their trudge forward, Thoren's attention snapping to a child behind him.

"I wouldn't do that if I were you," he grumbled, letting go of the child's hand.

"Bloody pickpockets," Ezra mumbled. He was quite familiar with the little thieves that roamed these streets. There was a time long ago when he'd almost become one himself.

Thoren straightened back up, eyes darting around. "Do you feel that?"

"Feel what?"

"Someone is watching us," he whispered, though the sounds of the market almost drowned him out.

The siren peered around the market, looking for anyone with ill intentions.

"There," he finally said, motioning his chin toward a vendor down the road. It was torn and tattered, its colors dingier than the rest.

Before Ezra could ask for clarification, Thoren was already storming into the tent with a fury he hadn't expected.

"Who are you?"

Inside sat a group of men and women, leisurely relaxing and enjoying carefree conversation. Their belongings looked rather rugged, the men with unkempt hair and the woman dressed scantily clad. Their eyes raked over their new visitors, judgment and mocking laughter following.

"Who's asking?"

One of the men stood, his appearance quite memorable. Electric blue eyes pierced Ezra, a rugged scar lining the side of his face. Raven-haired locks hung loosely around his square jaw. *I can't tell if he's alluring or terrifying,* Ezra thought to himself.

"You first." Thoren's tone grew impatient.

The man's icy eyes shimmered seeing the tension in the siren's body, jaw clenching as he gritted his teeth.

"The name's Alaric," he sighed, stepping in closer to make eye-to-eye contact with Thoren.

It was like watching two alphas face off. The hair on Ezra's arms stood, unsure why Alaric gave him such creeps.

"Thoren. What is your alliance?" he spat. The only thing separating them from attacking each other was a slender table with small nick-nacks for sale in front of them.

Alaric scoffed. "To myself and my people."

"*Who* do you work for?" Thoren enunciated his words, patience running thin.

"The Queen. You know her?" Alaric's words were playful this time, a cocky smile across his face. "You sirens think you can come in and run the place. My Queen will have your head for your petulant attitude toward me," he said, stepping back to examine them both.

"You work for Queen Boudicca?" Ezra clarified with a gulp.

Alaric merely nodded his head. The group under the tent cackled, muttering and whispering cruel words about 'the human' amongst them.

"You think we're scary?" Alaric asked Ezra directly. "Wait till you see the Queen with all of us at her side," he sang, arms outstretched.

"Keep him out of this. I'm the one talking to you," Thoren insisted, grabbing a hold of the man's shirt and pulling him in closer.

Alaric's demeanor changed as the siren's grip on his shirt relentlessly held on. Ezra shuddered as a low growl escaped him and his glare seemed to darken.

"Where is she?" Thoren followed up, his daggered eyes piercing the man.

"The hell do I know? She goes where she wants. We just wait for orders," Alaric said lazily, tugging his shirt from Thoren's grasp.

"So you're just her little bitch then?" Thoren mused, cocking his face to the side with a grin.

"Watch your mouth, siren, or you'll lose that pretty throat of yours. Can't do much singing without vocal chords," Alaric threatened, his hands gripping the table in front.

"Let's go," Ezra hurried, tugging at Thoren's arm.

"This isn't over," the siren warned, stepping out of the tent.

He never turned his back on them. Alaric simply shooed them away as if he couldn't be bothered with them any longer.

"What the hell was that?" Ezra asked, their pace quick, almost sprinting from the market.

"Hellhounds," Thoren answered. "She was working with them in Chicago, too. Now she has some in London. Their bite is one of the most infectious diseases I've ever seen. She could build an army overnight if she wanted to."

Ezra's mind raced. "Some days, I truly wish I could go back to blissful ignorance."

"We need to go back to the manor and warn the others."

Ezra nodded, the two jogging through the streets. Thoren turned and looked on occasion, searching for any hounds that may follow.

Approaching the portal, Ezra mumbled, "I wish we would've gotten more information today."

"We found more than you realize. We know where the murderer is and we know who the queen is working with. I wouldn't be surprised if they were there looking for the murderer, too. Boudicca is connected to Mary, after all."

"I hope I never run into them again."

Thoren placed a sympathetic hand on his shoulder. "I know you've seen a lot in the last few days. Probably more than you ever thought imaginable. When it all becomes too much, just remember you're on the right side. You're one of the good guys now. We need you in this fight."

For a mere moment, the siren pulled him into a tight embrace. Ezra's hand hovered over his waist, unsure what to do at first. At last, he returned the hug, a sigh of relief escaping him as Thoren merely held him. When they finally pulled away, he couldn't help but notice the way the siren's hazel eyes examined him carefully, tracking every motion he made. A wave of comfort washed over him as Thoren continued to hold onto his hand, pulling him toward the portal.

Ezra tilted his head side to side, contemplating. "Is it too late to back out now?"

Thoren chuckled. "I'd say so. When we get back, we should really work on training you. Get you caught up to the rest of us. Just in case."

He rubbed the onyx necklace around his neck with closed eyes. As the portal glowed, he held his other hand out for Ezra to grab. Nervous fingers grasped the siren's, pulled in tight with their bodies flushed against one another before they stepped through the portal and back toward the safety of Fox Manor.

17

WINIFRED

Sunshine beamed down on Winnie's back. Though a cool autumn wind should've chilled her, she'd been sparing with Kane all afternoon. Beads of sweat dripped down the side of her flushed face, breathless and exhausted.

She remembered all of her training from their time together before the dreadful banishing. However, fighting with her element had taken a serious toll. Trying to pull on those powers felt like running with torn leg muscles. Every ounce took a tremendous amount of energy from her, the curse of the queen coursing through her veins.

"Winnie!"

"If you yell at me one more time, I might just lose it! What do you want now?" she groaned, the veins beneath her cursed skin glimmering like lava.

Her usual light-hearted friend was nowhere to be found. Instead, he was focused and harsh. Clearly growing tired of her faltering powers. "Stop looking down at your feet and just move! You're thinking too much!"

They'd spent the last thirty minutes working on combinations: punch, punch, block. Kick, punch, shield. Only her shields didn't seem to be coming up.

"Everything feels off! I can't help it! This damn curse!" She held her arm up to remind him what she was going through.

"You've spent more than a decade using your element and

somehow you manage to lose it all in two years!"

Kane's arms whipped around him, a concentrated scowl on his face as he held up a shield of wind. He worked with the typical element most sirens possessed: air.

"You can create shields all you want. Seeing you successful only reminds me that I can't get Gali to acknowledge me!"

She'd been trying for the last few days and barely heard back from the Goddess of Water. Meditation, daily devotions, offerings to the altar she'd once used regularly. And still nothing since the portal. Praying to the void was beginning to grow tiresome.

Kane lunged forward, ready to strike. Without thinking, Winnie held up her hands in a defensive position. A glimmer of magic sparked in the palms of her hands. Though she didn't create a shield, a wave of gushing water sprayed out over Kane. Within moments he was soaked, the outlines of his decorated skin peering through the wet fabric.

"I take it back. I think I can hear her laughing right now," she teased.

"Yes, because being wet will stop your queen from killing us all. She'll be so uncomfortable she'll just give up," he grumbled. "Let's just work on weapons."

As Kane reached for a towel on the ground to dry his dripping face, the door to the sunroom opened. Wesley stepped out first, Melinda on his arm as she carefully walked on tender, healing feet.

"Hey, you two. Mind if we watch? Melinda's been telling me about her training growing up. She promises to kick my ass once she's completely healed," he said with a shy smile, helping her into a chair.

Kane shrugged, wringing the bottom of his shirt of excess water.

"That's fine. Have you written to your family yet?" Winnie picked up a spear lying on the ground, turning it around herself playfully.

"Just did this morning. I hope to hear back from them soon!"

Melinda pulled her knees up to her chest, bracing herself from the cold.

Silently, she mouthed to her brother, 'Jacket! Give her yours!' He glanced around in confusion, shoulders shrugging and hands out in front of him. Winnie merely rolled her eyes in response.

Kane turned, seeing the spear she held. With a chuckle, he added, "You never change, do you?" Grabbing a sword from the ground, he had one hand free to wield his elemental shield.

"A sword against a spear? Isn't that cheating?"

"You're the one that picked it. There may come a time when you have nothing and your opponent has everything. You've got to be ready to fight like hell." He positioned himself into a readied stance.

Winnie prepared her spear in front of her. Though Kane had brute strength which helped him in hand-to-hand combat, she was smaller. Faster. She moved with feline swiftness, evading strikes up ahead. She swung around the back, ready to strike with the edge of her spear at his knees.

A wall of air blocked her path, Kane swinging his sword above her. If he hadn't stopped, her head would've tumbled to the floor.

"You're still hesitating. Stop thinking and just fight."

She nodded, readying herself once more.

Lunging forward, she speared at his ribs. He leaped back, avoiding the edge of the blade. Swinging his arms up high, he moved to strike down on her once more. Dodging, she dropped to her knees and rolled behind him. Before he could think to shield, she batted at the backs of his knees once more. Stumbling forward, he fell to the ground with a deep laugh.

"That's the Winnie I know." He rolled onto his back, peering at her sideways.

Seeing him smile like this…it reminds me of when we were younger, she thought.

"You two look exhausted," Wesley called out, drawing her attention over to them.

Sitting on her knees still, Winnie felt a small gust of wind push her over. She fell onto her back, staring up at the sky.

"I'd recognize that magic anywhere," she giggled, glancing to her side.

"Take a small break. You've worked hard today." He nudged her slightly, offering her an encouraging smile that threatened to melt her.

"I may be out of practice, but I can handle myself just fine," she mumbled, counting the clouds trying to hide her blushing face.

"I never once doubted you. But you have to get your element back up and running. I know we all keep saying it, but it's your most powerful asset." He rolled onto his stomach, hazel eyes watching her carefully.

Memories rushed through her. Years of growing up, training, bonding. Having the time of their lives.

Just behind them, Tara opened the door and shouted, "Lunch is ready!" Cricket exited the house, running wild laps around the yard in excitement.

Winnie rolled over and took a stand. Kane peered up at her playfully, something mischievous in his eyes she hadn't seen in a long time. Before she could even think twice, she called forth the elements inside her. For once, it didn't take long before a ball of water came hurtling down on him. Though he'd barely dried off the first time, he now sat soaked once more.

"Winifred…" he said through gritted teeth.

At first, she worried she'd upset him. Goofed off too much or pushed things too far. It wasn't until she realized he was trying desperately to hold back laughter that she squealed and ran. Rushing to his feet, he chased after her. Only moments passed before sopping wet arms wrapped around Winnie. A shrill cry escaped her lips, her body shivering from the cold as he lifted her into the air.

"You wanted me to work on my element," she giggled, mustering up as much innocence as possible.

"Don't use me as a target!" His words could hardly escape him as laughter cut through each word.

He put her down at last when Wesley let out an exasperated sigh. "Are you two done?"

Winnie turned, face flushed and still giggling. Parts of her were soaked, the cold settling in around her.

"You better not track mud into the manor or Mum's going to be furious," he mumbled.

Winnie rolled her eyes as she followed the others inside, stomach growling and ready for food.

It was past supper time, Thoren and Ezra still in London. Winnie paced the entrance room, worried sick something happened. *Did the murderer get them? Or worse – the queen?* She could only imagine what horrible things that entity would do to them if she got the chance.

Just outside, she heard the familiar portal sound opening – a welcomed rush of air so distinct she knew it had to be them. She sighed in relief, running out to greet them. Ezra reached out to her, accepting her embrace with a heavy exhale.

Her eyes met with Thoren's, though she ignored him completely. Instead, she grabbed her friend by the arm and led him inside to have a seat in the kitchen.

"Thank goodness you made it back in one piece!"

"I promised you that I'd keep him safe," Thoren reminded her softly.

"Did you find him?"

Both shook their heads, Ezra's gaze dropping in sadness and disappointment.

"We found some of Boudicca's lackeys though," Thoren added, taking a seat next to Ezra at the kitchen counters.

The two men recounted their day as the other members of Fox Manor slowly trickled in, getting bits and pieces. At last, they landed on the most important detail: hellhounds.

"She has hounds in Chicago and London. That can't be good," Milicent mumbled, standing across from the two young men and offering them food.

They each graciously accepted, eating as they continued to answer a barrage of questions.

"The leader – Alaric – did he have intense eyes? As in, *really* intense blue?" Melinda asked curiously.

Thoren nodded between bites.

"If he had a scar, it's the same one I saw in Chicago." Her gaze shifted away from the group. Winnie could only imagine what she must be going through; the images that likely replayed over and over in the girl's mind.

"They have portals open. It's the only way. She has to be working with a coven," Winnie added.

Milicent nodded, a scowl across her face.

"And it's just…*us?* Against this queen and her army of monsters?" Ezra's voice cracked, motioning at each person with his spoon.

Silence stilled the kitchen, the tension tangible in the air. Winnie could feel her heart beating right out of her chest, realizing he was right.

"Maybe not…" Milicent said at last. "I'm working with Afissa to try and get her army to help us. They're busy dealing with their own battles, but they may be able to help. Horace will be here with his Lycan as soon as he can."

"How are Lycan different? Aren't we just adding more beasts to our problem?" Ezra's tone seemed bleaker than Winnie expected.

"Hellhounds are vicious, contagious, foul creatures. They aren't bound by the moon cycle like the Lycan who only change three days out of the month. They're unruly at that time, but not as aggressive. Through the generations, they seem to have calmed down a little," Thoren explained.

"Are they contagious too?"

"No. The only way you get more Lycan is by having babies." A smirk formed on the siren's face.

Pockets of conversation rattled through the kitchen as Winnie stood in silence. Her eyes glanced at each person, thankful they were there. Terrified thinking she would be the reason they might get hurt or be in danger.

Her thoughts raced through her mind until finally she asked herself: *What if this is the last time we can all just sit and eat together? What if this is…it?*

18

EZRA

Knowing the queen was building an army, everyone worked to sharpen their fighting abilities over the coming days. Though most had their own elements to wield, magic wasn't foolproof. There was always a chance it could falter or be tampered with. Having additional means for protection was vital. At least that's what Ezra was told.

He joined them daily, trying to catch up with a group that trained their entire lives for events like these. Unease sat within him, nervous tapping fingers and fidgety feet trying to listen to the directions of those training him.

Kane and Thoren took turns working with Ezra, though truthfully he found the older brother to be the better teacher. Thoren was more of a distraction, always commenting and making jokes. The one good thing he taught Ezra was how to use literally anything as a weapon.

"If you're down on the ground, use everything around you to gain the upper hand. A fistfull of dirt in the eyes or even a throat punch could give you precious seconds to regain yourself. Don't be afraid to go for the groin, either," he'd coached with a wink.

Though Ezra was sloppy, having only been in a few bar fights or street brawls, he at least knew some moves. He knew how to punch, something Thoren found out quickly.

"Hit me!" the siren coaxed, trying to gauge where they needed to start.

"I don't want to hurt you!" Ezra huffed, knowing he had a mean right hook.

"Come on! Show me what you got! Punch me! Pretend I'm the prick at the bakery!" Thoren's words continued to taunt, the mention of that dreaded place setting Ezra ablaze.

At last, he snapped. Landing his fist right in the siren's face, Thoren stumbled back in surprise rubbing his bruising jaw.

"I – I'm so sorry!" Ezra stepped forward, his hand grabbing the side of Thoren's face to examine the forming welt.

"Don't tell me you're beginning to care for me," he teased, guiding the hand away. He held it a moment before finally releasing it. "Sirens heal quickly. I'll be fine in an hour. But I'm glad to see you can at least punch well. Let's talk weapons."

"I've never really used them before. Never needed to. I always carry a knife on me in Bethnal Green, but usually waving it about and acting like a madman is enough to scare someone away," he confessed.

"Have you ever used a pistol?"

Ezra's gaze dropped away from Thoren's quickly, afraid to answer that question.

"I had one. Never used it thankfully. Didn't like the way it made me feel to own it," he mumbled, searching through the weapons rack at the side of the house.

"When we're done here, you'll practice. They're quite handy when you're in a tight situation. I can show you how to disarm a gunman, too. Let's try swords and shields first, shall we?" He picked up a long sword, handing it to Ezra.

The weight of the metallic blade surprised him, grasping it firmly with both hands.

"I'm meant to hold this *and* a shield?" Ezra scoffed, passing the blade back and forth.

With a deep laugh, Thoren nodded. "If you were more skilled, I'd say we could skip the shield but I think it's best you practice with it. You never know when you'll need to fend off an attack."

"Isn't this all a bit ridiculous?" he asked, tossing the sword to the ground.

Thoren examined him carefully, brows scrunched.

"You're all incredibly magical beings. The beasts we're meant to fight are as well. There's no way a human like me is going to survive this kind of fight!" Rubbing the back of his head, nerves bubbled inside his stomach.

"Tara's human. She kicks ass. So can you," he tried to say.

Ezra cut him off. "She's been training her whole life. I don't want to be compared to her."

"Not true. She only started three years ago when Kane drunkenly brought her back here," he explained, bringing new information to light.

"But I thought…"

"She's an excellent fighter, yes. She's put in a lot of time and effort to be trained. She began with us before we were banished. Then continued her studies elsewhere. She's an excellent fighter, and you will be as well. But moping around isn't going to get you trained."

"I don't have three years to catch up to her," he muttered.

"So you'd rather sit here and complain, rather than get started and have even the slightest chance of surviving this?" Thoren grumbled, clearly growing upset with Ezra's hesitance.

"I just…I don't want to die. Not like this." At last, the words slipped from his mouth.

Something in Thoren shifted, taking those words to heart. Setting his sword down, he stepped forward. A hesitant hand reached for Ezra's arm, giving him a light squeeze of reassurance. He avoided the siren's gaze for a moment, but Thoren made it impossible. Commanding attention, those hazel eyes pierced Ezra's as his words sunk in, an angelic voice wrapping itself around his mind.

"Listen. There isn't a single person on this estate that's going to let that happen. Stick with me, and I promise I'll protect you. You have my word. I won't let anything happen to you."

For a moment, he felt like he could lean in and hug the siren. Repeat the same feeling he'd had in front of the portal. Place his arms around Thoren and pull him in close. Instead, he merely stood in silence.

"Now pick up that damn sword, and let's get started." Thoren landed a playful, lighthearted slap on his face, not intended to harm but rather insight a bit of rebellion in him.

He spent a great deal of time showing Ezra the ropes of the sword. Teaching him the basics before they ever started swinging. Bracing himself in front of Thoren, Ezra held the weapon in various positions as the siren showed him different ways to swing.

Deep down, despite the excellent guidance he received, he found it hard to concentrate. The feeling of Thoren's body pressed up against his sent nervous flutters through his body, making him clumsy and jittery. The feel of the siren's breath on his neck sent nerve wracking shivers down his spine, threatening to overtake him entirely. It took everything in him not to stumble on his words, hiding a blushing face as they continued their training.

"You're a good teacher when you're not being a smartass," Ezra teased after they'd finished practicing a set of combinations that involved more footwork than he'd been prepared for.

"You're a good student when you're not being a whining baby." A taunting feline smile fell across Thoren's face.

At last, it was time to actually fight. Ezra swung his sword up above, ready to strike. Thoren blocked it with the edge of his blade, kicking at his midsection. He fell to the ground, stunned.

"That wasn't what you taught me!" Ezra jumped back up to his feet, readying himself once more.

The siren chuckled, eyes wicked. "Your cheeks are flushing. I rather like seeing you flustered."

Before Ezra could even blink, Thoren removed his shirt. Wiping a bead of sweat from his brows, he tossed the shirt to the side. Layers of intricately tattooed art swirled over his chest and arms, catching Ezra's eye. He wondered what it would be like to examine them closer, wishing to know the stories behind every delicate line and detail.

"See something you like?" he teased, smacking Ezra with the flat side of his blade. "Concentrate."

Ezra continued his attempted strikes, trying desperately to follow the combinations he'd been taught. Thoren swatted away the attacks effortlessly, stepping to the side as Ezra charged toward him.

"You're getting ahead of yourself." Moving back and forth between both feet, the siren stood ready to keep the fight going. The cocky smile across his face only riled up Ezra more, wanting to get at least one good swing at him.

"I can tell there's more in there. Release it! Let it all go," Thoren taunted. Ezra jabbed at his stomach as he jumped back with only a few moments to spare.

"There you go! Now you're getting it! You have to get angry! Use that to drive your strength!"

"I don't want to actually hurt you!" Ezra snapped, avoiding an almost deadly blow from the siren.

"I wouldn't let that happen. Trust me," he mocked with a wink. "Get angry. Come on! Think of all the people who made you feel ashamed! Pretend you're fighting them, not me!"

Ezra swung again. "Stop trying to mess with my head!"

Thoren barreled into him again, knocking him to the ground. He hovered above Ezra, an arm stretched out to help him up.

"You are such an asshole!" he yelled, swatting at the outstretched arm. Behind them, the sound of the sunroom door opened slowly.

"Everything…alright out here?"

Ezra turned to see Winnie standing at the doorway, examining them both curiously. Her attention snapped to Thoren, a frown on her face seeing her friend on the ground. Despite not wanting help, the siren helped him up at last. But not before grabbing his arm and pulling him in tightly to say one final thing.

"Your anger can be your greatest weakness or your strongest weapon. You decide if it consumes you." When he released Ezra's hand, he offered a cocky nod. "Good job today. Practice shooting. I'll see you in a little while to continue."

Ezra sighed, thrusting his sword into the dirt.

"Are you okay? Did he hurt you?" Winnie asked, checking him over.

"Just my pride. I'm alright," he admitted.

"I was watching you two from inside. There seemed to be a lot of…talking. For a training session at least. Is there something going on?"

"Everything's fine," Ezra snapped.

"Are you sure? Things seemed rather…explosive." Her brows furrowed, tilting her head to the side to understand.

"He just likes to get in my head, that's all," he finally added before picking up a pistol and practicing his shots. Bullet after bullet missed the target, another grumble of frustration leaving Ezra's lips.

Across the field, his gaze locked with Thoren's who sat by a nearby tree sipping water and watching carefully. When he noticed Ezra looking, that same arrogant smile waited, jutting his chin toward the targets as if to tell him to 'focus.'

"If something's going on, you'd tell me right?" she asked at last, picking up a pistol as well, and aiming for the targets across the field alongside him.

"What could possibly be going on?" His question was innocent, though he knew it was somewhat of a lie. Deep down, he wondered how much she knew. What she could sense between them.

"No matter what, you can tell me. I won't be upset as long as you're honest with me," she reassured, placing the pistol down to turn toward him.

With a nervous chuckle, Ezra finally mumbled, "There's nothing, Win. He's just being Thoren."

Her eyes squinted at him, still unsure. At last, she dropped the issue and continued practicing her shots alongside him, offering the occasional advice to aid in Ezra's accuracy.

19

WINIFRED

Days passed as Winnie continued her work. Praying to Gali, hearing back on occasion and her element growing slowly back to what it once was. Days of training, researching, foul tonics, painful siren-song induced healing sessions. No matter what they tried, nothing seemed to fix the curse coursing through her veins.

The queen's spirit latched onto her thoughts, sending signals of panic and dismay on occasion. She could feel the queen doing everything in her power to connect. To communicate. Winnie fought every night, but the pull to learn about her, understand her, made her curious.

Winnie lay in bed, eyes fixed on the ceiling of her bedroom. The voice of Prasutagus, Boudicca's love, kept her up yet again.

"I've been trying to tell you she won't move on and yet you still won't leave me alone!" she called out to an empty room.

After a few days of his relentless outreach, his voice seemed to grow weaker. Instead, Boudicca's voice rang through her. The warrior queen whispered.

All. Night. Long.

Winnie couldn't sleep, the threats and pleas from the spirit restless and relentless. As Winnie's mind drifted off, Boudicca's voice remained.

A void of nothingness surrounded Winnie as she sat up in

bed. *I'm in Oblivion again,* she thought, searching the void for the queen. She seemed to end up there a lot, Boudicca's spirit pulling her in on a regular basis. She knew what this meant. The spirit wanted to entice her with the offer of another memory.

Off in the distance, she could see a small glimmer of light. Exiting her bed, she moved toward it. But then she remembered, her feet weren't needed here. Floating along the darkness, her spirit detached momentarily.

Either my powers are expanding, or the curse is killing me, she thought.

Boudicca stood in front of the opening, sorrowful eyes peering through. "I'm not here to fight. Or threaten." Her monotone voice seemed lifeless, a deep regret lingering in her tone.

"Then why are you here?"

"I want to show you my pain. I want you to truly understand." This was one of the first times Winnie had seen where the queen wasn't shouting. Anger didn't fuel her words, but instead the deepest remorse.

I should run… get out of here while I still can, she thought. And yet, she found herself reaching for the queen's hand.

Examining Boudicca, Winnie could see her for more than just a warrior queen. Wife. Mother. Compassionate leader. The legend Tara spoke so highly of. All clouded by rage and vengeance. But not here. Not now. This time, she was merely a woman in pain. Reaching out from the other side for someone to understand her.

"It'll be easier to stop you if I don't know your story," she whispered aloud, realizing she'd meant to think those words rather than speak them.

"But doesn't it kill you to know?"

Despite her body's signals to run, she grasped the woman's hand tightly, allowing the connection to form. Her body became Boudicca's in an instant. Seated above her, she could see everything as if she'd taken the queen's form. Their minds and bodies crushed together, Winnie's forearm screaming as the curse's connection only strengthened. Every ounce of emotion the queen felt, she did too. And then, Boudicca shared her pain.

THE QUEEN

Boudicca sat in her lodging, staring at a simmering fire. The warmth brushed her skin but she couldn't feel it. The only thing she felt was grief. An empty void where her heart once laid.

The love of her life was dead.

Prasutagus.

The thought of hearing his voice threatened to drown her in sorrow.

"Mother, I think they're here." A voice so soft and innocent poked its head through, Boudicca's eldest daughter warning her.

She knew this day would come. The pact was officially over. The Iceni were no longer protected from Roman acquisition. The minute her husband died and left the tribe to their daughters, she knew they would come for them.

I don't think he thought of the position this would put our girls in, she thought, knowing that two young girls would never rule while Rome was in power.

Boudicca nodded her head, exiting the tent. "Get your sister and hide. I don't want them to see you."

She prepared for this. Her body was dressed in fighting leathers and chainmail, her face painted in bright blue war paint. Her generals waited outside, prepared to stand at her side. Lines of soldiers adorning red uniforms and glimmering helmets marched, the sheer number of them overwhelming as the queen took it all in.

"They sent this many just for a simple seizure of assets?" Her general whispered to her, standing at her side.

"Let me speak to them first," Boudicca ordered, her fighters nodding.

Leading the Romans rode a smug man with a serpentine smile across his face. He didn't bother dismounting his horse, greedy eyes peering down at her in distaste. That same rapacity peered around the tribe, devouring every ounce they had to offer.

"General Paulinus, I take it?" she called. He offered her a slight nod before she continued. "If you respected me at all, you would dismount your horse and introduce yourself properly."

Ignoring her, he stated their business. "We are here to take what was promised to us long ago," he spat, staring down his nose at her in disgust.

"My husband left these lands to us; me and my girls, and…"

"I do not give a damn what his wishes were! He does not have a male heir, therefore you have no right to rule this tribe."

Her people's silence shocked the queen as alarmed faces peered at her.

They're watching me. Looking to see what I'll do…

"I can rule as well as any man," she said, spitting up at him. "I will not give up my tribe just because you feel you have the right to rule all of Britannia!"

"That's where you're wrong, Savage Queen. Rome is far superior and will rule *everything*." His lips curled once more into a devilish smile.

Boudicca opened her mouth to respond. Before a word could be uttered, he continued.

"Take her. Show her what we do to rebels."

Iceni generals surrounded her in an instant, ready to protect their queen. The sheer number of soldiers made them all but useless. A few swings and they were left beheaded or on their knees, forced to watch as Romans moved in on their queen.

She fought hard and yet it wasn't enough. She aimed for knees, heels, throats. Any exposed tissue. She managed to get a few good swings in before her sword flew from her hand, disarmed and forced to surrender. But they didn't stop there.

Soldiers tore at her body, ripping her clothes and armor off.

Exposed and bare, she stood in front of her tribe, mortified. Her heart sat in her throat, ready to wail or heave; she wasn't sure. Her mind screamed to beg for mercy, and yet she knew that wasn't an option.

Shackling her wrists, lines of soldiers held her chained to the ground. Cries of pain echoed through the tribe – the Romans taking turns whipping her. Her back swelled, red-hot fire spreading across her skin. Eyes pleaded to the sky – to anything in power listening to her cries. Anyone to help end her defenseless misery.

As adrenaline kicked in, the pain of others echoed through her mind. She could barely see above the lines of soldiers surrounding her though she could feel it. The heat of the flames consuming her home. The cries of men, women, and children as soldiers ransacked the village.

"Do what you want with me! Leave my people alone!" Her voice shook, anger urging her to stand. As trembling feet lifted her body, another crack of the whip brought her back to her knees.

"What do we have here?" The sound of a soldier's voice sounded from behind Boudicca.

She froze, unsure if they'd found her girls. Too afraid to look, to make a sound, she waited. Her heart sank to her stomach, adrenaline pumping as seconds felt like a lifetime.

Behind her, Boudicca could hear her daughters crying out as soldiers dragged them from their hiding place.

"No! Leave my daughters alone!" Her voice bellowed, echoing over the sounds of her tribes' screams of terror. "Do whatever you want to me! Kill me! Take my tribe! Don't hurt my girls!"

"Oh, I see we found something to finally make the Savage Queen falter?" Paulinus's eyebrows raised with a cocky grin, wickedness in his eyes.

Her whole world shattered. The air around her too thick to breathe. Her limbs numb and eyes burning. *Not my girls! Is anyone out there listening? Please!* Her prayers rang through her mind, wishing to every god or goddess she could think of to help.

"These two *savages* are meant to rule?" Paulinus scoffed, looking at the two up and down.

Standing between Roman soldiers, the youngest shivered in fear, her bladder relieving itself as her eyes streamed.

"There's only one thing a woman is good for," Paulinus mocked, glaring at Boudicca.

She could see the thoughts racing through his mind. He'd beat them, that she knew. But…he wouldn't stoop so low, would he?

"No!" Boudicca cried. "Take me!"

Thrashing at the chains binding her to the ground, her wrists bloodied and bruised. Soldiers held her steady, cracking the whip at every sign of rebellion.

Paulinus turned to the soldiers holding the girls. She saw his hesitation, eyes flashing to their mother. Any sign of humanity left as he offered them a slow nod. The soldiers hauled off the girls. All Boudicca could hear was their screams.

Her heart sank.

Rose again.

Sat in her throat.

Fire in her lungs as she screamed out for them.

Rage burned behind her eyes, throat hoarse as she called on everything inside her to rip at the chains relentlessly with no end in sight to the helpless cries of her daughters.

At last, their voices went still. Boudicca's own cries ceased, looking for any sign of them. Through the crowd, they were nowhere to be seen. For a moment, she wondered if they were dead. She almost hoped they were. To survive such an attack as a woman was a fate worse than death.

"What have you done?" Her voice rang through her tribe, searching for answers.

Ignoring her question, Paulinus dismounted from his horse. "*This* is all women are good for."

He crouched down in front of her, grabbing the sides of her face with force as their eyes met.

"Your daughters are not leaders. *You* are not a leader. Without your husband, you are no better than a worthless mare. Remember this day. Remember the sting of your back and the utter despair on your daughter's faces. Remember all of this if the notion of rebellion crosses your mind. For I promise you, the next time it will be far worse than this."

Paulinus turned to the few remaining tribesmen and women. Their faces paled at the sight of their queen, a heaping mess on the ground dressed in blood and bruises.

"Take a look at your *queens*. Realize your alliance should be with one place only: Rome. Remember this day as the one we tamed you savage beasts. Brought you into the light and led you to salvation!"

Lines of soldiers cheered as they moved out. Minutes passed, though it felt like lifetimes. Boudicca sat slouched, unable to move. Unable to speak. Not a soul dared budge until every last soldier was out of sight. Though the tribe still burned, the silence amongst them was deafening.

Boudicca's general ran to her side, unchaining her and offering her a blanket to cover herself. Unsteady legs lifted the queen, braced by the general beside her. Weak eyes washed over the tribe, landing on her girls. Huddled together, Iceni women and healers surrounded them in a protective bubble. Their vacant faces stood stoic, unable to move. Eyes staring into the void, voices speechless and mute.

"My Queen – we must tend to your wounds," one of the healers called, approaching her carefully.

"No..." Her voice was merely a mumble at first. She shouted again. Rage fueled her, adrenaline shielding her from pain and starting a fire in her unwavering soul. "No!"

Those around her glanced between one another, scared and unsure.

"Today, we were weak. Today, we allowed them to come and plunder us. This will not be our story! Let this day be a lesson to you all. The next time you see Roman soldiers, you attack so viciously their bodies match the red of their uniforms. This fight is not over. They cannot have what rightfully belongs to my daughters! We will take the fight to their cities and burn their towns to the ground! We will let the sounds of their cries echo through the streets as we kill every. Last. One of them!"

Those around her watched in awe and terror as she spoke.

"Let's take the fight to them! Who's with me?"

A muffled shout of agreeance sounded through the crowd.

"I said – who's with me?" Her voice bellowed through the crowd, the tribe's energy set ablaze by fiery vengeance.

WINIFRED

Expelled from Boudicca's mind within an instant, Winnie returned to the deep dark Oblivion. She wanted to cry and scream, though nothing seemed to come out. Her mind still reeling from what she'd seen. What she'd felt. What they'd gone through. Though she returned to her own body, her back still tingled with pain as though the beating had been her own.

A tear streamed down her cheek, opening her mouth and closing it again. "Why would they... how could they?" Words at last escaped her lips but nothing seemed to make sense.

Across from her, Boudicca stood solemn and silent. *Strong... too strong,* Winnie thought. Unable to allow the full effect of those feelings penetrate her.

"They are monsters. It is in their nature."

She placed a hand on Winnie's shoulder for comfort.

"Why did you show me that? I didn't want to see that!" Sinking into herself, Winnie cried. Emotions flooded her as pangs of images and feelings inundated her senses.

"I needed you to understand. Realize why I'm here. You saw my final vow the day of the battle. I made a deal. And I cannot rest until I've finished what I started. You understand my pain now. And you will give me the girl."

Boudicca's face shifted. No more sorrow, only anger. That same fire filled her eyes once more, brows furrowing in determination.

"Who did you make a deal with?" Winnie took a step back, hoping to create distance between her and the queen.

Boudicca shook her head. "I cannot say."

For a moment, only silence sat between them.

"Give me the girl."

"I can't do that," Winnie whispered. "I can't let you kill her. She didn't do anything to your family or your people."

"She is his descendant. Just as betrayal and brutality is in his nature, so it will be in hers. The same ruinous blood that ran through his veins runs through hers. No matter what karmic lessons her lineage has learned, she must pay for what he did."

Boudicca stood close enough to Winnie that she could feel the ghostly breath on her skin. The fire in the queen's soul heated her, the energy palpable just as it had been the first night they met.

"I want to help you move on…but I can't give Melinda over. I'm sorry…"

"Then you and your family will experience the same level of pain as mine. And when the loss becomes too great to bear, you'll hand her over like a pig ready for slaughter," Boudicca hissed, pushing Winnie back and through the void.

Thrashing, screaming, crying – Winnie's vision was dark, still trying to recuperate from the emptiness she felt being there. Oblivion was no place for the living. If it weren't for her intimate relationship with Death, she'd have withered away long ago. A strong set of arms grasped her tightly. All at once, Winnie realized she was trapped.

Rearing her head forward, she threw it back with as much force as she could muster. With her vision still slowly returning, she bucked harder to get the hands around her to cease. She shuffled off to the corner of the room, knees pulled up to her chest and eyes still blurry.

"Ow…" The distant sound of a man's groans came through at once.

Winnie squinted before whispering, "Kane?" Finally, she blinked a few more times and her vision fully returned.

He sat on the ground, cupping his bloodied nose. "Yup," he muttered, standing to grab a handkerchief. "That's one hell of a headbutt you have there."

Winnie thought to stand, to check on him. To apologize. But she couldn't bring herself to do anything other than remain hiding and huddled. The images the queen showed her played over and over again in her head. She glanced at her arm, the navy veins turned to swirls wrapping themselves around her wrist. They seemed to slither like snakes, shifting with her movements.

"Are you alright?" Kane took a seat next to her, nursing his nose as she sat speechless. "I heard screaming from next door and came running."

Her mind continued to race, unsure how to answer.

"Winnie?"

"Boudicca…She came to me. I saw…" Her words struggled to come out. A tear rolled down her face as she worked through the information. Sitting quietly, Kane merely examined her curiously.

"What did you see?"

"The Romans. The attack. What they did to her and her daughters." She opened her mouth to explain further, but he merely held his hand up.

"You don't have to go into detail. I can guess what you saw. I've read the history books."

"You don't understand, Kane. I was Boudicca. I saw everything she saw. I felt everything she felt. It was like I was her for those memories," she said with a shudder.

"It's okay, you're safe. You're at home and you're *not* Boudicca. There's nothing to be afraid of here," he said, reaching over and pulling her in tightly.

"I understand her…why she did it. Should someone dare destroy my family like that, I think I'd want to do the same." Her brows scrunched together, eyes avoiding Kane's gaze.

"That's what makes evil like her so dangerous. She's only human. Given the right circumstances, anyone can become a monster," Kane whispered, pulling her face toward him with a gentle hand.

"She's going to kill us if we don't give her Melinda," Winnie whispered softly, afraid someone might hear her.

"By now, you know me, Winnie. I won't let anything happen to you or your family. No one hurts the people I love." A moment of pause sat between them. "I will protect you, I promise," he said at last, cradling her tear stained face in his hands.

Winnie tried to remain strong, but it wasn't long before she crumbled. The world around her turned to tunnel vision, the anger and grief of the queen breaking down her carefully curated walls as she merely sobbed. When it finally ceased, she glanced down at her cursed arm, slithering blue lines dancing on her skin.

"Maybe we should just…give her over," she whispered once more, the navy lines flaring luminescent orange in anticipation.

"That's not an option, love. We're meant to protect her. We can't hand her over to be killed," he replied, his voice firm.

"I know you're right. I don't know why I even said that… I'm just so scared to lose you. All of you."

Kane got to his feet, helping Winnie up. He led her over to her bed, motioning for her to get in. "Why don't you lay back down. I doubt your sleep was restful."

Softly, he tucked her in. Her eyes flashed around the room, realizing they were alone.

"Where's Tara?"

"I saw her and Ezra headed toward the portal earlier." He took a seat at the edge of the bed, examining her carefully. Picking up her arm, he inspected the lines as they moved away from his touch.

"I don't think I can sleep. I really don't want to be alone." She peered up at him, pleading and hoping she didn't have to actually ask what she wanted to.

A small smirk fell to his lips. "I can stay with you until you fall asleep if you'd like."

Walking around to the other side, he scooted in beside her. She turned, watching him carefully, trying to drown out the deafening cries of the Iceni people.

"I'm sorry I woke you..."

"Stop apologizing," he chuckled. "I'm sorry if I scared you by grabbing you like that. You were flailing all around; I was worried you'd hurt yourself."

"Stop apologizing," she echoed, a small smile cracked on her face. She wiped away tears, sniffling softly. All she could see when she closed her eyes were the flames of the tribe and the beastly smile of General Paulinus, Melinda's ancestor.

"The more I'm back at Fox Manor, the more I realize just how much I missed spending time with you. More than I thought possible..."

As he spoke, a wave of calm spread over her body. The horrors she'd witnessed eased in her mind, temporarily forgotten. All she could feel was that moment – huddled under the blankets with Kane at her side. A sense of comfort and familiarity she hadn't realized she'd been missing the last two years. It wasn't long before the light of the room faded and she once again fell into a deep slumber.

20

EZRA

Heavy footsteps thumped along the ground as Ezra chased after Tara, her stride long and almost sprinting toward the portal. Cricket pranced beside her, as relaxed as she was. Coming to the front of the house, he couldn't help but notice the flowers withering away. A dark omen, he'd been told, telling of treacherous days to come.

Less than an hour ago, she'd suggested they go back out to the pub to question the regulars regarding the murders. Though Ezra didn't think it wise, he obliged. Feeling a little stir crazy, he'd run to Winnie's room to see if she wanted to join them. Knocking on her door gently, he'd opened it to find her sleeping soundly in bed. He imagined that the day's training had taken a toll on her physically and mentally.

"Are you sure it's safe to go back without the others? Let's at least bring Thoren or Kane. Just in case…"

"You have to loosen up, Ez. We'll go to the bar, talk to some folks, have a few drinks, and come right back. We don't need the sirens to question a few blokes. What's the worst that could happen?" Her tone was carefree, mimicking the calming breeze that flowed through the evening sky.

"What's the worst that could happen? Did you really just say that? Are you trying to jinx us?" He glanced around the estate one last time, a feeling deep in his gut screaming to stay back.

"Give it up, friend. You're coming whether you like it or not," she said with a devilish smile.

Reaching for him, he reluctantly grabbed her hand as they stepped through the portal together. Arriving in the alley behind their flat, the thick London smog once again grasped around his throat. Being on the Fox family's estate made him realize more and more the effects of pollution. Even Cricket's nose inspected in the air, sniffing in horror at the smells that radiated throughout the street.

Bethnal Green is awfully quiet tonight, Ezra thought as they trudged down the side of the building. He pointed out their flat as they entered the pub. The inside felt moodier than usual, the lights low and fewer patrons this evening.

"Now this is the kind of place I could get in trouble at," she mumbled to Ezra, offering him a sly smile.

"Something's off," he whispered, more to himself than anything.

A few of the regulars looked up, seeing Ezra and offering welcoming nods. One or two held up their glasses in greeting as they passed to the back of the bar.

"Winnie wasn't kidding when she said you spend a lot of time here, was she?" She took a seat at the counter, Cricket facing the doorway. As he protected his owner, the sweet smile of his faded into a predator's scowl. No one dared mess with her with that beast sitting in wait.

Ignoring her comments, Ezra took a seat. "Butch, what's going on? Where is everyone?"

"You haven't heard?" the bartender asked, raising an eyebrow.

"Of?" Ezra shook his head in response, a glass of frothy beer waiting for him.

"Rumors. Strange creatures roaming the streets of London. Half man, half beast." The old man's face dropped in sorrow, looking out at his few customers.

"Have there been more murders?" Ezra was too stunned to even entertain the idea of taking a sip.

Butch nodded. "Doubled since last I saw you. Never thought

I'd see the 'slums' shut down, but everyone's in hiding. Except for the few brave blokes you see here tonight. Seems they're waiting for a fight." His words seemed to choke out the word 'slums,' sorrow and sarcasm mixing for a strange sense of dread.

"Still young girls?"

"No, not anymore. They don't seem connected at all. They're thinking it's a group now, gutting people all over London."

Alaric, Ezra thought to himself, shuddering at the thought of the pack of hellhounds he'd met.

"I'm surprised you didn't ask when you were here with that tall fellow. How've you not heard of this? And where the devil is Miss Winifred? I haven't been able to talk to my wife in quite some time." The bartender's eyes narrowed in on him, then flashed to Tara.

"I've been…" he paused. *What's a believable answer? I can't say I've been on a magical estate.* "Working. Out of town."

He could feel Tara's stare digging into him as he stumbled over his words.

"Do they know where these beasts are? Where they may be hiding?" Tara asked, snatching Ezra's untouched beer for herself.

"Who's this? And why's she got a mutt in my pub?" Butch grumbled, motioning for the redhead.

"Friend of Winnie's," Ezra mumbled, accepting a new glass from the bartender.

Butch huffed a small sigh of frustration before finally answering her question. "There's rumors, but no one's sure. About an old abandoned factory just outside of Bethnal Green. People been sayin' there's all manner of screaming coming from inside the ol' place. No one dares go in." Sad eyes dropped to the surface of the bar, wiping away nothingness as if to stay busy.

"I think I know the place you're talking about. We should let Winnie know." Ezra's attention turned back to Tara, motioning for the door.

She shushed him, her face deep in her drink. "We can have

some fun before we run back to Mummy. Live a little!" She seemed to dare him with her words.

Ezra rolled his eyes, turning around in his seat to face the entrance. *If times are as dangerous as Butch says, better have an eye on every soul in here. Can't trust anyone right now,* he thought.

As he turned, his gaze landed on a somewhat familiar face. Deep brown hair, mossy green eyes. Though dark circles clung beneath them now, as if the man hadn't slept in the weeks since they'd first met each other. Given that they hadn't spent much time together, it took Ezra a moment to realize who it was.

"Hey!"

Waving at Tara, Ezra motioned for her to stay put. Mary's brother's eyes widened, realizing he was approaching fast before darting through the door.

"Hey! Wait!"

Chasing after Liam, they went down street after street. When they were no longer anywhere near his flat, Ezra realized he'd never been down this area before. In fact, he'd avoided these parts, knowing they were worse off than Bethnal Green.

The hair on his arms stood, the chill in the air moving like a forcefield. Something wasn't adding up. *Why would Liam run away from me?*

"Stop! I need to talk to you!" Ezra yelled, chasing Liam down yet another alleyway.

The man stopped, only because his escape was blocked by an iron gate. He turned to look at Ezra, a bewildered sense of fear in his eyes.

"You should've stayed back at the bar." His words seemed to shudder, low and threatening.

Every ounce of Ezra's being tingled, sensing the danger lurking behind him. He turned, seeing a pack of men and women. At the front of the group stood Alaric, the leader amongst beasts.

"The man's right," the blue-eyed, dark haired man hissed, looking Ezra up and down. "Not so tough without your bird to protect you." He laughed, the group behind him cackling like hyenas.

"I don't want any trouble," Ezra began, putting his hands up in submission.

"Shame, because we do! Can we kill him now?" a woman crooned, stepping up to Alaric's side. Her tone was almost sweet and childlike. The glimmer of unusual violet eyes glittered like fireflies in the moonlight. She shared similar features to Alaric's, the same raven hair straight down her back.

"Our queen wants him alive," he reminded.

There was a pause. Ezra tried to read his face, figure out what the beast was thinking. The moments that passed felt like a lifetime, waiting to discover his fate.

"Alive, not unharmed."

The pack of hellhounds circled Ezra, some human while others changed into their beast forms. Swinging wildly, there were too many to know who to hit first. He grasped for his side, realizing he didn't bring a single weapon with him.

He tried taking deep breaths – tried recalling the training with Thoren. Adrenaline pumped through his veins, the hounds circling him like prey. The sky seemed to fall down on him, mind heavy with panic.

Two grabbed at his arms, holding him tightly as the others took turns swinging at him. Aiming for face, ribs, stomach, groin; they hit any place that would cause great harm. Though only a few moments passed, it felt like an eternity. The hits too quick to even suck in a sharp breath. Alaric held up a growling hand, and at once the beatings stopped.

"I said alive, dumbasses," was his only response, indicating with his hand to have the group bring Ezra with them.

They dragged him toward the open street, spasming muscles clenched as he held in his cries. Adrenaline coursed through him, fiery pain unbearable. He'd survived plenty of beatings in his lifetime – growing up lower-class wasn't easy. But nothing was comparable to the sheer force they held within their beastly fists.

Ezra could hardly see through the blood that streamed down his face. He attempted to look back at Liam who avoided him in shame. His entire face swelled, lips bloody and eyes blackened within moments. *Surly I have broken ribs,* he thought as they moved him, his midsection screaming out for relief.

Rounding the corner, he saw her. Boudicca stood in the center of the street, floating in the air like a deranged angel. Another hoard of hellhounds stood behind her. The surrounding orange-hued glow made her look like an ember in a fireplace. The queen's stoic face landed on Ezra as the hounds dropped him in front of her.

"I told you not to roughen him up too badly," she said, though she didn't seem sincere.

"As requested. We know he's in contact with Paulinus's descendant," Alaric said with a grumble.

Boudicca nodded as the group of hellhounds backed up away from Ezra. He could feel heat emanating from her as though she were a living flame.

"Stand."

He attempted to muster up the strength, though his entire body screamed. So much that he could not manage a single ounce of movement. Boudicca grew impatient, flicking her wrists. An invisible force grabbed Ezra by the neck, hurdling him to his feet. The grip around his throat burned; he could smell charred flesh as the grasp tightened. Scratching at his neck, he attempted to release himself to no avail.

"When I say stand, you *stand.*"

Her voice sent shivers down his spine despite the blazing hand that still held him tightly.

Ezra attempted to open his mouth and speak, though it was no use.

"Where is your friend?"

When she realized he could not speak with her fiery hand

around his neck, she viciously slammed him into the ground. Ezra could have sworn he heard a loud crack, the sound of one of his legs shattering.

"You're no use to me if you do not answer my questions," she roared.

He grabbed at his leg, in such pain he couldn't even muster a scream.

"The girl! Where is she?" Her voice boomed through the streets of London, windows and buildings shuddering at the force of her anger.

"Safe from you," Ezra spat. *If I'm going to die anyways, I won't tell her a thing. I won't let them get killed because of me.*

"Feeling rebellious are we?" she mumbled, a small chuckle in her voice. "Let me show you what happens to those that disobey me."

She turned, the group of hellhounds behind her parting ways. Ezra glanced past them, seeing a dark figure floating in the air, writhing and attempting to set himself free.

"Do you recognize this man?"

The figure floated into the light of a nearby gas lamp, illuminating his face. Ezra squinted through the pain. The minute he saw that face, the mustache, the disheveled hair, he knew. The killer's fear was palpable in the air, pleading eyes resting on Ezra as if he'd be the one to save such a monster.

"You found him…" Coughs of agony escaped his lips as he attempted to get on his knees.

"I did. This man has spent the last few days with me. We've been having all sorts of fun, haven't we?" she said, running a finger down his cheek.

As she did, the mere touch of her skin against his set the killer's face aflame, burning him viciously. He let out a muffled scream, the rope around his mouth stifling the cry.

"Why would I care what you do to a murderer?" Ezra spat, finding the strength within to sit up all the way.

"It's not what I'm going to do to him that matters. It's what's going to happen to you if you do not bring me that damn girl." Her voice was calm and even. As though nothing could bother her.

"There's no chance in hell we're giving her over." Anger bubbled in the pit of his stomach, a fierce protective energy replacing the pain surging through his body.

With an emotionless shrug, Boudicca flicked her wrist. The murderer's body lifted into the sky, still wiggling to free himself.

"One," Boudicca began, snapping her fingers.

Within an instant, the man's clothes were torn from his body, leaving him entirely exposed. It was then that Ezra could truly see the damage they'd done, wondering how he could possibly still be alive.

"Two," she continued, her voice calm.

A piercing cry shattered the streets, the man's gut ripped open and spilling onto the cobblestone before Ezra.

"Three," she sang. Her final snap finished the man off, the entirety of his skin ripped apart from his body leaving only muscle and tissue exposed. The man's screams turned to gurgling cries, though he still twitched for several moments after.

"That's for you, Mary," Boudicca mumbled.

Her magic tossed the murderer's body aside, the hellhounds lunging. Ezra could hear the lapping of blood and the ripping of tissue as they indulged their animalistic instincts.

Dry heaving, the smell of death clung to the air as he attempted to avert his eyes. Blood and tissue covered the ground, bleeding their way closer and closer to Ezra.

"Oh come now, don't be dramatic. The things he did to those girls – he deserved worse than that," she said, her voice blunt and cold. "That, my dear boy, is what I'm going to do to you if you don't help me get your friend here."

Ezra shuddered, knowing she was true to her word.

"I'll never give up my friends," he insisted, attempting to scoot back away from the approaching queen.

"What do you not understand?" Her burning talons reached toward him to raise him off the ground once more.

Some of the hellhounds turned, watching to see if their next meal would soon arrive.

"You don't have an option. You either bring me the girl or you die."

She lifted him once more, feet dangling like the murderer's had been just moments before.

"Then I guess I'll die," he said softly, saying a silent prayer in his head. *I'll protect them. All of them. With my last dying breath…*

Boudicca chuckled, though it was not one out of amusement. No, it was out of frustration. He wasn't sure if she would actually kill him now. She needed him to get to Melinda.

"You're a stubborn lad, you know that?" she mumbled.

The hellhounds that had turned their attention to Ezra resumed feeding, bored and tired of waiting.

"You won't kill me," Ezra began, choking on his words. "You need me."

Boudicca shook her head. "I don't need anyone," she confessed, raising her hand as if to snap.

This is it.

He knew the second she released her fingers, his life would be over.

Memories flashed in his mind – the sister he'd barely known. The family who abandoned him. The bakery. Meeting Winnie. The night of the seance. The days spent at Fox Manor since then. Thoren.

My life was never one to brag about. Is this really how it's going to end?

TARA

Sitting at the pub counter, Tara finished the last of her beer. Ezra left a while ago. *Should I be worried about him?* As the thoughts entered her mind, the pendant around her neck glowed. The Quinn family necklace, passed down through generations. A warning from her ancestors that she needed to be vigilant.

At her feet, Cricket whined. Nervous paws tiptoed on the wooden floors, yellow eyes burning red-hot, nudging her anxiously and looking toward the door.

"What is it, bud?" Her eyes flashed up. *Between the necklace and Cricket...*

Leaping from the barstool, the two headed for the alleyway. Stepping into the chill, she turned around wildly.

She glanced down at Cricket before commanding, "Find him!"

As though the mutt could understand her, his sniffing nose darted around the streets. Taking off, Tara followed. Her senses sharpened, a dagger drawn from her side and ready for anything.

After some time running, a glowing aura appeared around the corner. The young woman and her dog came to a screeching halt, hiding to assess the situation. A metallic stench wafted toward them, and she knew they didn't have much time. Cricket nudged her, his sweet eyes replaced by shimmering rubies, teeth bared, hackles raised, and ready to attack.

Carefully she peered around the corner, seeing a pack of hounds huddled over a heaping pile of something she didn't want to see. *Is that...* Before she could finish her thought, she watched as Ezra lifted into the air by the queen's magic. *He's alive. Thank the Gods.*

With a racing mind, she schemed. She didn't have long. Only moments sat between Ezra's death and her actions. She watched as the Queen's hand raised, forming into a snap. His eyes closed, seeming to accept his fate.

A sharp whistle escaped her lips, Cricket lunging toward Bouddica. As the dog leapt, so did Tara. Working together, Cricket knocked into the queen and tore at her magically controlling arm. The redhead peered back at the hellhounds, realizing she had mere seconds before they would notice their queen was in danger.

Tara plunged the dagger into the woman's chest, running for Ezra. *I can protect him from her magic if we're together,* she thought. Cricket ceased his relentless, shredding grip as Boudicca ripped the dagger from her chest and swung it at him to evade another razor sharp bite before casting it aside.

Another whistle sounded, the dog grabbing the dagger. Dropping it off in front of his owner, he ran down the street back toward the portal.

Boudicca examined the wound to her chest. "It'll take more than that to kill me, girl."

Tara pulled Ezra up to stand, the man limping and almost falling back down. One of his legs bent the wrong direction, his body crumbling beneath her.

She shuddered before snatching her weapon. "I thought you were a hero…"

The queen cackled. "I am, darling. Just not yours." She lifted her bloodied hand, strips of flesh dangling as she snapped her fingers once more.

The pendant around Tara's neck glittered. She could feel the pull of the queen's magic trying to end them, but her ancestor's protection was too strong to be outdone. An astounded scoff followed as Boudicca tried again and again.

"I need you to be strong just a little while longer," Tara hurried, pulling Ezra to stand once more.

"I'm tired…" he mumbled, eyes blanking. He seemed to fade in and out of consciousness, barely able to comprehend what was going on around them.

Down the street, paws came running once more. Cricket leapt

through the air one final time, catching Boudicca off guard just long enough for Tara to pull Ezra toward the portal home. He mumbled unintelligible words, but limped along regardless.

Cricket was supposed to go to the portal and stay there! Damn dog, where is he now?

The sound of Boudicca's commanding voice boomed, shouting threats toward her hellhounds. Howls pierced her ears as they continued to shuffle down the street, each step closer and closer to the portal. Thundering waves of hounds followed behind them, ready to devour their flesh.

21

•((●●))•

THOREN

Sitting inside the sunroom, Thoren and Wesley played yet another round of chess. He'd wanted to go to bed a while ago, but the young man kept begging him to play 'just one more game.' *This reminds me of first meeting him as a little kid, running around driving all of us older kids crazy,* he thought.

A moment passed when they heard the sound of the portal opening in front of the house. A scream followed, sharp and ringing through the house like an alarm. Darting for the door, the two sprinted around the side of the house. Tara held a blade up high, ready to crack into the skull of a hellhound.

"How did that thing get in here without a family pendant?" Thoren shouted.

A shrill yelp escaped its muzzle, falling lifeless to the ground and shifting back into its human form. Tara lunged toward the ground, someone lying equally as lifeless. Thoren's eyes flashed down seeing a head of blond hair, bloodied and still.

"Ezra?" Thoren dropped to his knees beside the man. He felt his whole body go numb, any warmth drained and replaced by an icy rage. "What the hell happened?"

Tara's sobs echoed through him. The lids to Ezra's puffy eyes were sealed shut by trauma. His clothes torn and bloodied, parts of him bruised and bent the wrong way. Bones broken, skin scorched. His neck burned to a deadly crisp, his breathing barely audible.

"Wesley! Get your mother! And Kane! We need healing!"

Thoren's words were sharp as he cradled Ezra in his arms.

Parting his lips softly, he started his siren song. The same soft lullabies he'd heard as a child growing up encompassed the man, trying to heal him. "It's not working! I need my brother!" he shouted.

Thoren turned his attention to Tara, waiting for her to get up and look for Kane. She did nothing, only seemed to stare at Ezra as despair drained from her eyes.

"This was Boudicca, wasn't it?"

"Yes. And hellhounds…" she muttered, looking back at the portal. "London's crawling with 'em."

With a grumble, Thoren accepted that his siren song likely wouldn't work. Carefully, he picked Ezra up and ran toward the sunroom. Tara darted ahead of him to open the doors, eyes wild and checking behind them for more hounds that may have broken through the wards.

"Cricket's back there! He didn't come through the portal."

"I'll get him. Right after I kill every last one of those damned things. Make sure Milicent starts healing him!"

Gently, he placed Ezra on a cot which appeared at the center of the room, just as it had the night they brought Melinda to the house. Checking the man over one last time, he leaned down.

"I promised I'd protect you…" The words came through as a mere whisper, his head rested on Ezra's chest, wishing desperately for an answer.

With a loud huff, he stormed out of the sunroom and toward the portal. Snagging a sword on his way out, he prepared for a fight. As with every brawl, he released his wings. Scars lined his walnut-brown feathers, having seen many battles in his short lifetime already. As the anger in him blazed, his hazel eyes turned to luminescent amber, the fire in his soul ready for anything. His voice now amplified by the release of his true form.

Before stepping through the portal, Thoren paused a moment. Taking deep breaths, he readied himself, not knowing what was waiting for him on the other side. At last, he stepped through.

When his feet landed on the streets of Bethnal Green, his entrance was so quiet and subtle that the swarming hounds didn't notice him. They ran around the sides of the building, likely looking for passage to the manor.

Baritone notes escaped his lips, jaw wide as the deadly sound waves reached the beasts' ears. Wildly turning in circles, the hounds clutched their heads and cowered on the ground. It wasn't long before they began to shake violently as pain coursed through their bodies. Screams pierced the night, blood vessels in their minds bursting as the melody became too much. A heaping mass of enemies fell to the ground in an instant, taken out by the siren's song.

Thoren felt the draw on his energy, wondering if he should've saved it for later. He looked out at the chaos of bodies, a few still moving. Driving the edge of his sword through their skulls, he picked off the few remaining. Stalking toward the end of the street, he could hear more down the road.

Rounding the corner, he saw her. The woman responsible for Ezra's condition. Boudicca turned toward him, a daring smile across her face. Alaric stood at her side, nervous eyes flashing toward his queen at the sight of the siren. Thoren's lips parted once more, ready to end or incapacitate them. Anything to keep them from hurting anyone again.

Before a single note left his lips, Boudicca and her minion disappeared. Walking through the brick wall of one of the buildings, the two were gone in an instant. Thoren darted into the sky, wings flapping furiously and landing him before the portal in moments. He placed his hand where they'd escaped, realizing only the hard brick now stood where they'd just exited.

A swarm of hellhounds surrounded him at once. Their eyes landed first on the closed portal in front of him, eager to escape. Two brave souls lunged first. As they jumped, he reached under the belly of one and slammed it into the other. With a swing of his sword, both beasts suffered fatal wounds to the stomach. Their innards spilled onto the streets of London while the others readied themselves.

Another set lunged at him, ready to attack his sides. As Thoren dodged one, the other barreled into him. His wings flared, lifting their bodies into the sky to give the siren time to collect himself.

Grabbing the beast by the skull, he dove down with such force, the ground shook as the wolf's skull cracked under the pressure. A ball of fire formed in his hand, catching the second attacking hound mid strike. Within moments, it ran away yelping and crying as endless flames lapped at its dark fur.

A ring of fire barreled toward the remaining few from Thoren's outstretched hand, fur and skin set ablaze as he swung his sword toward them. Ripping into their guts with the edge of his weapon, he finished them off before the flames could.

Another small pack appeared down the street. Seeing their fellow hellhounds as living torches and bleeding on the ground, they turned to retreat. Thoren parted his lips again, making his enemies stop in their tracks as though they were frozen in place.

He stalked over toward them, his blade dripping as it sliced through the limbs and necks of the hounds staring motionlessly into the void. With his attention fixed on the hounds mesmerized in front, he didn't have time to react when another came from behind and latched onto his shoulder.

A yowl of pain rang through the street, Thoren's attacker ripping at his flesh. Leaping into the sky, his wings flapped as he catapulted them up. Spinning around and around, the hound lost its bearing before plummeting to the ground. Thoren watched from the sky as the beast crashed into the cobblestone below, blood pouring down his arm from his bitten shoulder.

His eyes raked over Bethnal Green, the streets once again vacant other than the bodies he left convulsing or deceased. Lowering to the ground, he called out.

"Boudicca? Alaric? Show yourselves, you cowards!" Silence

returned his taunts as he let out an exasperated sigh. Whistling, he called out once more. "Cricket?"

Down one of the alleyways, a small yelp sounded. Thoren ran, seeing the shuck huddled beneath some rubble from one of the businesses.

"Come on, beast. Let's get you home to Tara."

He coaxed the mutt out gently, sensing the hesitation. As Cricket crawled out from under the debris, Thoren noticed the creature's bloodied limp immediately. Grabbing Cricket by his collar, Thoren hummed softly. He thrashed suddenly, taken aback by the siren's magic.

Slowly, the wounds on the mutt's leg healed. Cricket whimpered, licking at his back leg realizing it was no longer injured. Leaning down, Thoren was met with a swift lick to the face of thanks.

"Maybe now that I've saved you, you can stop growling at me all the time," he chuckled, leading Cricket back to the manor.

The travel through the portal felt like hours instead of seconds, each moment passing bringing up every worst possible outcome. Seeing Ezra's mangled body shattered him more than Thoren expected. The promise he'd made just the other day rang through his mind, reminding him that he'd failed.

The manor appeared before him once more, Cricket running off ahead to reunite with Tara. Thoren could hear Ezra's screams from outside before dashing toward the house. Entering the sunroom, the man lay thrashing and writhing in pain.

Tara's eyes landed on Thoren's bloodied clothes, then his wounded shoulder. "What happened? Are you okay?" She raced toward him, attempting to examine the injury.

"Get away from me." His voice was a low growl, eyes still fiery as she backed away. "You're the reason he's injured. How could you be so stupid to go out without help or proper weapons? This is your fault."

Tara trembled, stepping away from the siren. Cricket stood

between them, growling at Thoren in warning. It wasn't until Ezra released another blood curdling cry that Thoren finally simmered down and took a seat beside him.

"I need you to hold still," Milicent begged, attempting to apply ointment on his neck.

"Take it easy, she'll make it better," Thoren whispered, clutching his hand.

"Let me," Wesley interjected, placing a nervous hand on Ezra's chest. He closed his eyes, attempting to use his empathic magic to ease the pain. Regardless, the man still clung to his neck and his cries didn't lessen.

"Shouldn't that put him to sleep?" Thoren whimpered, holding onto Ezra's hand tighter as if his own life depended on it.

"Her magic is foul. Corrupting. Those burns are…different. We need to pull out all our cards. Wes, go grab my bag from the attic," Milicent ordered.

He nodded, running toward the stairs.

"Will he make it?" Thoren's voice was soft, trembling in fear.

"I think so. Wesley is getting some of my strongest medicines. I save them for the rarest forms of magical healing necessary. At some point, we need to take a look at your shoulder, too." Her eyes flashed between Ezra's wounds and Thoren's.

"I can wait," he insisted. As the siren's words escaped his lips, Ezra's body stilled. "Ez?" His voice echoed through the room, pulling the man's hand up to his face. Tears streamed from his eyes, pleading to Aelius to save him. The God of Fire didn't respond to his prayers.

"Wesley – hurry!" Milicent's words met the boy on the stairs as he leapt from them and slid to their sides.

"What's happening?" Thoren cried as Ezra's body began to convulse.

"No, no, no! Stay with us!" Milicent dug through her bag with shaking hands.

Blue eyes flashed open for merely a moment, fluttering around the room in confusion. A mere second of consciousness helped him connect with Thoren's gaze.

"I don't…want to die anymore," he choked, voice cracking.

"Stay with me, Ez! Stay with me!" Thoren clutched onto Ezra's hand like his own life depended on it, mind muddled and shattering with every breath that slowed.

Milicent pulled a necklace from the bag, stuffed with leafy greens and flower petals. She pulled the pendant around Ezra's neck, placing her hand on his chest and reciting soft unintelligible prayers.

"That should keep him steady until the ointments have time to start healing," she explained, eyes opening and sniffling.

"That's all you have?" Thoren's look of astonishment seemed to upset her. "You're one of the most powerful witches I know and all you can muster up is a few plants and some gaudy trinket?"

"Don't underestimate the power of herbology. They may be the very thing that saves his life," she scolded.

He could tell by her tight lips she was unappreciative of his statement.

Ezra's breathing went from rapid uneven movements to slow, steady huffs.

"He's going to need lots of rest, but I think he'll make it," she reassured. "Let's take him up to his room to recuperate."

Thoren nodded before picking him up, Milicent leading the way upstairs toward Ezra's room. Carefully, they changed him into clean clothes, applying ointments onto any remaining wounds they found. As they cleaned one of his legs, Thoren noted how horribly disfigured it was as it curved to the side.

"Will he walk on that again?" Thoren asked, applying the last of the balms.

"If we leave it as is, no. We should hold a healing circle. It'll require everyone's energy to cure this magnitude of injuries, but it's the only way he stands a chance of returning to his old life."

Milicent approached Thoren from behind, placing an

encouraging hand on his shoulder. She led him to the chair in front of the fireplace where he reluctantly took a seat. Tucking his wings in at last, he turned to see her removing strips of fabric from his shoulder.

"Something got you pretty good," she noted, dabbing at the wound.

Thoren flinched before adding, "Thank the Gods sirens are immune to hellhound bites."

"I've never seen you like this… storming off to fight. You're acting like your brother. What's going on?"

"Ezra's a good man. I could've protected him if I'd been there tonight."

Milicent nodded reluctantly. "Are you sure there isn't more?"

Thoren's gaze dropped away from her, as if trying to hide the truth.

Moments of silence passed between them as she continued working on his wound. When he didn't answer, she added at last, "He'll be okay. I'll ensure we do everything we can to heal him. He weaseled his way into the heart of this family. No one dies on my watch."

Offering her a soft smile, Thoren looked back at Ezra. His breathing was raspy, chest moving up and down steadily.

"Get some sleep. He'll still be here in the morning," Milicent said before heading off for the evening.

22

WINIFRED

Waking the next morning, Winnie's groggy eyes landed on the back next to her in bed. Her gaze transferred around the room, expecting Cricket's panting face directly in front of her. Instead, Tara's bed still sat unbothered, no sign of the fluffy mutt or his owner. She sat up, surprised to see Kane still with her. Huddled under a small blanket, he shivered.

The violence of Boudicca's memories still haunted her. All night, she saw the queen's daughters. Their expressionless faces as they stood in shock after the attack. Her heart raced whenever she closed her eyes, remembering how it felt when every lash of the whip slashed across her back.

A small smile and sleepy eyes peered up at her as Kane turned over. Hurriedly, she ran her fingers through her hair in an attempt to make herself look less like a baby raccoon, wondering if she had terribly baggy welts under her eyes from crying most of the night.

"Morning, love. Sorry I stayed. Tara never came back. You said you didn't want to be alone, so…" His voice trailed off as he sat up, pulling the blanket around his shoulders.

"Thank you for staying." Her gaze dropped, guilt settling in her stomach.

Lazy arms stretched above as he let out a grumbling yawn.

"I'm sorry I hurt you as well. And that you slept the whole night cold. You could've come under the covers with me."

"I'm pretty tough. Experienced worse things in my life." He

offered another soft smile before it dropped carefully. Leaning in, he grabbed her arm.

"It looks worse, doesn't it?" She almost didn't want to know.

He moved her arm around in the sunlight, carefully examining. "It's settled in. Only one final piece and the link will be permanent. We need to keep you away from the queen. And you can't keep communicating with her, either. It'll only strengthen the connection you share."

"What's the final piece?"

"Blood," he began, carefully stroking the scar from the initial wound. "Yours. If she gets it, you're done. You'll never be able to escape her."

A shudder wracked through her body, withdrawing carefully. She examined the navy lines encompassing her forearm that moved like a living being.

A polite knock tapped on the door. Kane's eyes flashed to Winnie in a panic, likely realizing what a young man in her room all night would look like to others. Swiftly, he jumped from the bed and opened the door. Wesley stood on the other side, dark bags under his eyes like he hadn't slept all night.

"Everything okay?"

"I need to talk to Winnie…" Her brother's words were hardly audible. Sorrow sat behind them, avoiding her as she rushed toward him.

"What happened?"

"Tara and Ezra went out last night…" His words trailed off, mouth opening and closing though not a sound escaped him.

Winnie urged him to speak faster, flustered and worried.

"Wes! What happened?"

Her brother's gaze dropped to the ground, followed by a small sniffle. He maintained his silence, only looking away as if he couldn't form a single thought.

Storming off, Winnie darted downstairs. Pacing around the house, she looked for her friend. "Ezra?" Her frantic calls echoed through the house but she didn't hear his usual cheerful voice in response.

Entering the sunroom, she saw Tara curled on a loveseat, Cricket pacing in front of the door to go outside. "Tara?" she said softly, opening the door to let the shuck into the fields beyond their house.

She whispered her friend's name once more as drowsy eyes opened cautiously. Tara blinked a few times, a look of alarm spreading across her face as she saw Winnie.

Before she said a word, she burst into tears. Falling into Winnie's arms, she sobbed. "It's all my fault!"

"What happened? Is Ez okay?" Winnie's heart raced, thinking of every possible outcome.

"He's hurt. Really badly. All because of me! I shouldn't have dragged him out last night!" Tears continued to stream down her face, reaching for her friend.

"He's upstairs?"

Tara nodded, chaotic huffs and sharp inhales following.

Ignoring her friend, she hurried upstairs. The memories of her mother's vision swirled in her mind, alongside guilt.

Reaching Ezra's room, she saw Kane waiting outside in hesitation.

"Go!" She urged him forward, unsure why he was stalling.

"Maybe you should," he began, though she swiftly cut him off.

Pushing past him, she barreled into the room. Wildly, she scanned the room and took everything in. The smell of ointment and gauze. The metallic musk of blood. Her eyes settled on Thoren, asleep in a chair in front of the fire. As Kane woke his brother slowly, Winnie hesitantly walked toward her friend.

At first, she couldn't bring herself to look. Kept her gaze fixed on the headboard, the ceiling, the bedding around him. Anything besides the man she cared for crippled in bed. When her eyes finally landed on him, a sharp cry escaped her lips.

Both eyes blackened. Bruised. His lips split and oozing. Throat wrapped in gauze, hiding a disastrous wound she didn't want to acknowledge. Ezra's breath was barely audible, raspy and knocking at Death's door.

She placed a hand on him, wondering if she could sense him. Sense his spirit.

"Please still be in there somehow," she whispered. If he soul detached, there was no saving him.

Closing her eyes, she focused on him. Called out his name into the void. Used her sensitivity to call forth his spirit. When nothing answered, she sighed in relief. For now, a small sliver of hope ached in her chest.

She fell to her knees at the edge of the bed, unable to speak. Tears streamed down her face, blame and guilt weighing heavy on her.

On the other side of the room, a groggy Thoren woke at last. His own shoulder was wrapped in gauze, Winnie wondering what the hell happened.

He walked to her side, grabbing her hand and pulling her to stand.

"I'm so sorry I couldn't protect him." His voice faltered, tears welling, as he pulled her in for an embrace.

"Why him?" was all she could mumble to no one in particular, wondering if Death could hear her cries.

KANE

Headed downstairs, Kane left Winnie and Thoren to talk. If he told them what he knew, they'd likely never forgive him. He entered the sunroom, seeing Tara slumped on the couch. She held her forehead to Cricket's, consoling herself.

"Please don't start, too." She sighed breathlessly with bloodshot eyes. "I've had every member of this house express their anger and disappointment with me. Especially Milicent. I don't think I can take one more person hating me right now. I know I messed up."

Kane took a seat next to her. "Trust me, I know that feeling all too well. Please tell me you got *something*. Anything to make this all at least a little bit worth it."

She nodded carefully. "They're hiding in an abandoned factory in London. Got some portals strewn about too, it seemed."

"That's something, at least. I wish I could say we all make mistakes, but I'm sure you're aware this is more than a mere error in judgment. Next time, think it through first. You're not here on vacation. From here on out, you're always in danger."

"I don't know how they'll ever forgive me," she sighed, wiping her nose with a sniffle.

Kane paused for a moment, unsure what to say. At last, he leaned his back against the couch.

"Can I confess something?"

Tara's gaze darted toward him in concern.

"I heard the screams last night. And I did nothing. I chose to stay with Winnie, even when it likely wasn't the right decision to make." He fiddled with his hands, glancing around the room to ensure no one else in the house could hear.

"I doubt you could've done much. Thoren's voice didn't work at all. The queen's magic was too strong." Placing a sympathetic hand on Kane's, Tara offered a half-hearted smile.

"I think a part of me will always choose her over everyone else. And maybe that's part of my problem."

Taking a stand before she could respond, Kane exited the sunroom. He didn't wear a jacket, the chilled wind rushing past him as if to greet his exit. Taking a deep breath, he worked through the guilt that nagged him.

"Caelus, please! Is there anything I can do to help Ezra?" He prayed to the God of Wind in his mind, though silence sat on the other end. Only regret seemed to stare back at him.

23

MILICENT

Days passed and Ezra showed no signs of improvement. They were running out of time. The wounds still bled, the bones still cracked. The burns on his neck endlessly cried out for healing that Milicent's ointments or the sirens' songs couldn't provide.

Seeing him in bed, anger stirred inside her. She wanted to yell at her daughter. Say 'I told you so' and remind her of the visions she'd had when the two first met. But at the end of the day, she knew it wouldn't help. Instead, she sat at his side day and night, praying to the Gods, Death, and Fate…begging for him to be spared.

With his hand in hers, Milicent decided: tonight was the night. The moon was finally full, their family the most powerful it would be all month. Without hesitation, the entire group agreed. No matter the cost, no matter how much it would drain them, everyone was in agreement that Death could not have his soul.

Winnie and Wesley worked with her guidance to create the circle on the family's stone slab altar. In their entire lives, they'd never encountered injuries requiring one of these rituals. Milicent instructed them, explaining it the way their grandmother taught her when she was young.

"As you place the crystals down, you must envision the healing energy entering the circle. Only positive thoughts of relief can come from you as you're working. Not a single bit of negativity or it won't work."

Her two children nodded, following their mother's instructions. With each crystal placed around the edge, she too envisioned glowing verdant green energy while she prayed to Ina, the Goddess of Earth.

Once intricate layers of salted swirls adorned the stone and crystals lay around the outside in a circle, Milicent resorted to begging. Reaching out to their ancestors, the Gods, anyone listening, she pleaded.

"He's a good man. He has a greater purpose! This can't be the end of his story! Please, help me. I beg of you. To anyone listening. Don't let him die."

That night, the full moon glowed in a cloudless sky, twinkling stars glittering over the lake just beyond. Winter was fast approaching and the family could feel it in their bones as the wind nipped at them. Bundled in layers, everyone aside from Afissa stood around the circle.

The mermaid returned home, attempting to talk her husband into helping the Fox family by providing an army. Milicent knew how precarious their relationship was. Despite the fact that Afissa was his queen, she could almost feel it in her gut that the man would say no.

Stepping out of the sunroom, Thoren gingerly carried Ezra in his arms. His solemn face hadn't seen a smile in days, worried sick over Winnie's friend. Milicent could sense the connection between them, wondering what her daughter would do when she found out. He laid the broken man in the center of the circle atop a bed of blankets, the raspy breath ringing through Milicent's ears.

"Before we begin – some guidance. Think *only* of healing Ezra. The power of the circle has the ability to show you other truths, but your focus must be on him. Any sign of wavering concentration and it may not work." Milicent nodded to each member, even the participating humans, reaching out toward her husband and son at her sides.

Winnie, Thoren, Kane, Melinda, and Tara joined, a sharp sting each time their hands connected to each other. The sirens began a low, healing hum. Sound reverberated throughout the group, the connection intoxicatingly strong with everyone together on a full moon. Each participant closed their eyes, mumbling soft prayers to any deity they chose. Even the humans amongst the group contributed their energy in place of actual magic.

"Please, Ina. Help him!" She hoped her goddess was listening tonight. *"I've been a faithful servant. Done everything you've asked. Devoted my life to you. Help me. Help him!"*

Milicent could feel the pull of energy from her core deep down, tapping into the well of magic their family's coven shared. With the vicious damage of the queen, it would take nothing short of a miracle to pull this off.

—•((●●●))•—

EZRA

Surrounded by nothingness, Ezra continued to float. There were no smells here. No sounds or other beings with him. The loneliness he felt was one he was all too familiar with. The same feeling as waking up in a dream, time frozen and everything cold.

He'd been here for what felt like days with no escape in sight. His thoughts raced, soul spinning in circles of boredom. He couldn't remember much. He tried desperately to recall, not knowing how much time had truly passed. Occasionally, he'd receive a few glimpses of what happened – how he ended up here.

A glass of frothy beer. The snapping jaws of a beast. The glowing flames behind Boudicca's eyes. And then Thoren's words. *"Stay with me."* A pleading beg that tore at his heartstrings.

When the dullness of this place wore him down, he yelled into the void, "Is this all there is? I've always done my best to be a good man! To help people! This better not be the afterlife!" His voice echoed through the space, no answer in return.

Though he lacked any sort of physical form, he could feel his heart beating anxiously in his chest. It felt far away, a truly curious feeling. Behind him, he felt a pull. Glowing ivory light drew him in, the most luminous energy he'd ever seen. The first signs of anything living since he'd arrived.

The glowing light slowly dimmed, a being appearing before him. He couldn't see much at first, but he sensed the strange creature immediately. "Come, Ezra Watson. It's time." The voice was a soft slither toward him, beckoning him to rest.

He glided toward the light, though quickly stopped.

"Wait, I'm not ready." He tried to back away, the space between him and the light growing shorter. Thoren's words once again rang through his mind, one of very few remaining tethers to earth calling him back.

"There's no use fighting. You've been brave, but it's time. Just like you've wanted for so long. Don't think we haven't heard your pleas." Their voice floated toward him, wrapping around him like a soft embrace as the smells of lilies wafted through his nose.

"Who are you?" He almost didn't dare ask, afraid he already knew the answer.

Deep down, Ezra felt his heart settle. The anxious beating eased as the being gripped harder. A wave of euphoria washed over him, mind settling.

"Was it always meant to happen this way?" he asked softly, his voice a mere whisper.

The creature merely shushed Ezra softly, wrapping him in white light and drawing him closer. Just as his soul readied itself for the journey ahead, something snapped him out of his strange blissful trance.

"Stop!" A booming call pierced the darkness, the light retreating with a hiss.

Ezra's essence turned, seeing a figure waiting. In all his life, he'd never seen anyone so beautiful. With skin and hair made of moss, she moved as a living breathing embodiment of vines and flowers. Thick hair laid down the front of her body, covering her as small insects scuttled around. Dragonflies fluttered near her, snakes and other creatures slithering around her body. Piercing blue eyes examined him carefully, a motherly affection pulling him closer to her.

"Who…" Ezra was speechless, drawn to her energy.

"Ezra, darling. I've come to fetch you. It's not time to rest just yet."

Her words echoed through his being, his chest growing tight as warmth spread through him like his blood once again pumped furiously in his veins. He turned back toward the light before moving away from the lily scented creature.

"You're here to bring me back then?"

She nodded, holding out a mossy hand. Her icy blue eyes pleaded with him to return, drawing his spirit toward her.

"I don't want to die anymore." The words came back to him at once. Not merely a statement, but a promise.

Accepting her hand, he felt a sharp pull. Back down. Further and further, the void lessened and suddenly he was washed with… *pain.* Like he'd never felt before. His eyes flashed open, peering up at the night sky. A soft glow loomed around him, though he was unable to move. Carefully, he hovered above the ground.

Ezra tried to turn his head, though he was only met with more anguish. Flashes of the attack came back to him. Snippets of images that he'd forgotten in the void. The hurt, the terror. The thought that he was going to die and more ready for it than he cared to admit. Until he saw…

As his body straightened, his eyes landed on Thoren. Glowing light filled the siren's body, though no one seemed to notice. Behind him, behind all of them, stood a line of souls. At first glance, Ezra's heart raced, terrified of the dark figures hovering behind the group. When his mind settled, their faces slowly regained features, generations of amber eyes glowing back at him.

The Earthly woman roamed along the treeline, watching carefully. In his mind, he heard her words: *"You must choose, Ezra Watson. Choose life. And never accept Death's call again."*

Carefully, painfully, Ezra attempted to answer her. When not a single noise escaped him, he merely nodded.

"I want to live," he cried out in his mind, hoping she could hear him.

Within moments, just beyond the Earthly creature, small flecks of light glittered along the woodline. A whole new world opened up to him and he could see it all.

His swollen eyes slowly eased, the bruises lessening. The pain all over of sore and torn muscles softened until only warmth encompassed him. His leg gently snapped back, though he felt no pain.

Any lesions left behind by the hellhounds healed, softness taking their place. He felt weightless, held by the coven's magic. The last to heal were the burns on his neck. The sharp stinging eased, leaving behind a small trace of the devilish magic that held him days before.

Slowly, his body lowered to the ground. Atop what felt like new legs, he shook himself out. *It feels good to be in my body again,* he thought. Down, hanging around his neck, a small onyx pendant of his own now lay.

His eyes peered up once more, the glow around Thoren still there but easing. The spirits around the circle faded slowly, the Earthly woman morphing into the surrounding woods, gone in an instant. The family's soft prayers continued before Winnie met his gaze.

Connecting with her immediately, a beaming smile broke across her face. He offered her a soft, dimpled grin, thankful for his second chance.

"You did all this for me?"

The prayers ceased as the remaining members ceased their

trance-like focus. Winnie looked to her mother who nodded, granting permission to break the circle. Happy tears streamed down her face, running toward him. She wrapped herself around him tightly, unwilling to let go. A soft cry escaped his lips as he too cried tears of delight.

"Of course we did! Did you really think you were allowed to leave us like that?" Winnie's words were interrupted with happy sobs, burying herself in his chest.

Before he knew it, the rest of the family was right there. They reached around each other, holding on tight. His heart thumped joyously in his chest, overwhelmed by sheer adoration.

The group parted, Winnie running to her mother in thanks. As they split, only Thoren was left standing before him. At first, he said nothing. Only looked Ezra over carefully.

"You're okay." His words were barely audible above a sigh of relief.

Careful, shaking hands reached toward Ezra before examining his scarred throat. A trace of Boudicca's devilish handprint still lingered, the mark of her dark magic a reminder of what he'd been through. Thoren's hand moved from his throat to the side of his face, cupping it softly. The lingering touch sent warm rays of sunshine through Ezra's body, chasing away Death's chill and welcoming him back to the living.

"Seeing you that way… It made me want to die. Or tear this world apart to bring you back," the siren admitted softly.

"Knowing you were here waiting for me made me want to live. You were one of only a few tethers that I was able to follow back." Relief spread over Ezra, realizing there was so much more he wanted to say. All in good time, he promised himself.

Placing his forehead to Ezra's, Thoren released another sigh of relief as a small smile graced his lips. A single tear streamed down the siren's cheek before strong arms reached around and held him in a tight embrace. Just when Ezra thought he'd let go, Thoren maintained the steady hold as if he never wanted to let go ever again.

When he opened his eyes again, he realized Winnie stood staring at them curiously. She approached from the side, placing a hand on Thoren's back. Suspicion laced her words as she asked, "Everything alright?"

"Thank you," was all Thoren could say, reaching down and offering her a quick embrace as well.

Only moments later, Ezra found himself in yet another pile up, enveloped in more love than he'd ever experienced in his life.

24

THOREN

Spending the last few days by Ezra's side was torture. Worried sick, Thoren wondered if he'd ever talk to the man again. Ever see those dimples light up with a cheeky smile. Ever notice the way his icy eyes flashed between Thoren's lips and soft gaze nervously with flushed cheeks.

As the rest of the family retired for the evening to recuperate, the two sat along the woodline. Thoren had no intention of spending even a moment away from Ezra, grateful for the Gods and the Fox family's magic that those treacherous wounds managed to heal. It seemed strange that the human could see the fae now but he thought nothing of it, too distracted by thankfulness to give a damn.

"So they're… fairies?" Ezra glanced back at Thoren, laying on his belly inching closer and closer.

Thoren nodded. "One of many types."

He laid lazily next to Ezra as memories of running through these woods with his brother and the Fox siblings popped into his mind.

"You don't want to touch them," he warned, seeing Ezra reaching for one.

"Will it kill them? Or me?" Nervous hands retreated in an instant.

"No," the siren chuckled. "But they do bite. Stings like hell, too. They're quite feisty when provoked."

"You sound as though you speak from experience."

That smile, those dimples. If I could capture this moment and keep it forever, he thought as nerves fluttered in his chest.

"Growing up here, Kane and I would dare each other to mess with them. Don't know how many welts Milicent had to treat from fae bites." A deep belly laugh escaped him, thinking of the trouble they'd gotten themselves into as young teenagers.

Ezra merely laughed as well, head tilting as he continued examining the fluttering fae.

"I can't begin to tell you how relieved I am to speak to you again. Seeing you like that almost killed me," Thoren admitted, scooting closer to Ezra's side. Once again, he reached toward the scars that lined the man's throat, wondering if there was a way to ensure those went away for good.

Ezra pulled the siren's hand away from his neck. "You have to stop looking at this bloody scar. You'll make me self-conscious," he joked, though it seemed half-hearted. Looking down, he examined Thoren's hand curiously as if seeing the world with new eyes.

"Nothing could ruin you," Thoren mumbled, pulling Ezra's gaze up toward him.

As their eyes linked, Ezra's cheeks once again flushed.

"What is it?" the siren asked with a chuckle, brushing a finger along the rosy sides of the man's face.

"Nothing, you just…you keep surprising me. Every time I think I have you figured out, you change. Open up a little more. Become someone I could…" Ezra's words slipped from his mouth, interrupted by the sounds of footsteps approaching from behind.

"Hey you two!" Kane called, stopping at the edge of the woods. "I wouldn't mess with the fairies if I were you."

"I already warned him, brother," Thoren grumbled, glancing over his shoulder.

"Thank the Gods you're feeling better! We were all worried about you," Kane said through panting huffs.

"You say it as though the man had a simple cold." Thoren's

words came out with a bite, wishing his brother hadn't interrupted their talk.

Ignoring his comment, Kane asked, "Did either of you see anything strange during the circle?"

Ezra glanced at him sideways, curiosity peaking. "I saw a lot of strange things. Spirits, glowing lights. Some woman made of bugs. If I didn't know any better, I'd think I'd just come off of the massive trip," he said, a bewildered expression plastered on his face as if reliving the moment.

"Glowing lights? Hm, okay. I wonder…"

"Kane. What do you want? We were in the middle of a conversation," Thoren urged, now refusing to look back at his brother.

"Sorry, I'll leave you be. I'll catch up with you in the morning." With a hurried pace, he took off once more.

A lull in the conversation set in before Thoren suggested they head inside to the bar. The late October wind picked up around them, chilling each to the bone. When they entered, the siren snapped his fingers and a raging fire took hold in the room's fireplace.

He couldn't help but notice the way Ezra jumped back in surprise before wonder passed through him. As they settled down in front of it on the rug, he offered Thoren a glass of gin before pouring one for himself.

"Will you tell me more about the bakery?" the siren asked at last when the tips of his fingers and toes no longer ached from the cold.

Ezra paused, contemplation running through his mind.

"You don't have to, I was just curious," he hurried to say, almost wishing he hadn't opened his mouth in the first place.

"Of all the people, I want you to know," Ezra admitted at last, though he still stalled. "As you know, I was working there. With the baker's son."

"If you don't want to tell me," Thoren began again, reaching for his hand and pulling him in closer.

"No, it's okay. I want to tell you. I've just never given myself the chance to think about it before. But…I want to get it off my chest." A few more moments passed before he continued telling his story. "We got along great. After a few months working together, he surprised me. With that kiss. The one you saw. Unfortunately, it was the same time his father popped in for a surprise visit. He rarely came to the bakery at night, but of course he did that day."

Thoren recalled the smells of the memory. The bourbon apples cooking over the gas stove, ready to fill pastries. The scent of scones and other treats lining trays to cool, ready to be sold the next morning.

"His son pushed me away. Said I came on to him. The baker dragged me down to my mother's house and told her their version of the story. Everything went downhill from there. She never even let me explain." Solemn eyes dropped to the ground as Thoren felt him pull away slightly.

"That's when your mother kicked you out? And Winnie found you?" He stroked the back of Ezra's hand gingerly, a soft reminder he wasn't alone.

Nodding, he continued. "My mother kept everything I had. Didn't leave me a penny to my name besides the few I had in my pocket from work. I lost it all. Including my will…" His words stopped abruptly.

Thoren inhaled sharply, knowing he didn't need to finish his sentence to realize what words would come next. "You're here now," he added, wiping away a quiet tear rolling down Ezra's cheek.

"Winnie and I found each other when we were both at our lowest. The very place she fought Beatrix's mob was the same alleyway I intended to…end things. For a moment, I thought she'd do it for me given how terrified she was after they tried to kill her. But instead, we became friends. And as odd as it was to simply fall into companionship with her, it strangely felt like it was always meant to be that way." Memories replayed behind Ezra's eyes as he stared into the fire, thoughts threatening to overtake him.

"The Fates must've known you two would need each other," Thoren added, trying to draw the man's attention away from his endless staring.

"I knew that night I couldn't hide who I was any longer. I'd always known, but never knew anyone like me. When I was young, I pretended. Told myself I was some sort of abomination for wanting what I did. When you're raised poor, you go to school at the Church. And they make it very clear how they feel about people like me. So I hid. But I don't want to do that anymore."

Thoren's heart broke seeing him so desolate. "Like I said before: there's nothing to be ashamed of. I think sometimes I take for granted how accepting my family was. I'm sorry you had to go through that alone."

"So, the history between you and Winnie?" Ezra asked, though there didn't seem to be an end to the question.

"You don't always have to pick a side. You can enjoy both, you know," Thoren joked, seeing the confusion on the man's face.

Ezra sat silently for another moment before adding, "It feels good to tell someone."

"Thank you for trusting me." Placing an encouraging hand on Ezra's, Thoren offered him a warm smile.

"I've been so worried everyone would hate me when they found out who I really was," he admitted.

"No one here would do that. Trust me. Of all the people in the world you could tell, there isn't a single person here who would do such a thing." Offering Ezra's hand a tight squeeze, Thoren leaned down toward him.

"Fear can blind you…" he mumbled, eyes fixed on the fire in front of them.

Grabbing the base of Ezra's chin, Thoren brought his gaze up. When he was sure Ezra truly saw him, he leaned in a little further.

"I lied to you, you know." A coy half grin fell across his face as

Ezra scooted back to examine him with concern. "I said I wanted to be your friend…"

Ezra's mouth opened one or twice, unsure what to say. Without a word, he shuffled up to his knees, moving in closer to Thoren. His breaths quickened, cheeks flushing, seeming to understand.

A curious hand reached for Ezra, running slow fingers through his ashy hair. The man's eyes flashed nervously to the door, perhaps worried they'd be interrupted again. It wasn't until those icy diamonds landed back on Thoren's face with a calmness the siren had never seen before that he knew.

"And what is it that you want?" Ezra whispered.

Thoren thought his heart could beat right out of the chest, weeks of nerves bubbling to the surface. As delicate fingers traced the lines on Ezra's face, down to the dimples on his cheeks, he felt he could explode watching as the man leaned into his touch.

Silence stilled between them, Thoren too stunned to say anything. Ezra reopened his eyes, his gaze flickering down to the siren's lips and back up again. As the quiet built between them, Thoren swore he could hear their hearts beating in tandem. The word *you* sat on his tongue, though couldn't muster the courage to be set free. All the cocky arrogance left him, only this moment remaining.

One of Ezra's hands reached for the fingers laying delicately in his hair as the other cradled Thoren's face. Inching forward, he finally planted a soft kiss with trembling lips on the siren's. It was careful at first, as if still afraid. But within mere seconds, the fear melted and desire took hold.

Thoren reached around him, pulling Ezra in closer. Though not an inch sat between them, he felt they weren't close enough. Pounding hearts synchronized and what felt like a millennia of heat came crashing through them. The siren continued to run his hands through those silken blonde strands, knowing how desperately he'd craved this feeling since the moment he'd seen Ezra, his jacket draped around Winnie and standing on the portal ready to return to London.

At last, their kisses slowed and Ezra leaned back to examine the siren's face. A small smile graced his lips, slowly spreading until his entire body seemed to glow in excitement.

"I've been wanting to do that for a long time," he whispered, placing another delicate kiss on Thoren's lips.

He chuckled, grabbing ahold of Ezra's face and bringing him in closer once again. As the evening went on, he found himself counting every tiny detail on Ezra's face, kissing those darling dimples every chance he could get.

25

WINIFRED

Laying in bed, Winnie contemplated lazily whether she should finally get up. It wasn't unusual to be drained after a ritual, but she'd never felt this drained. She could tell during the healing circle just how much of the family's magic was accessed by the way her head now throbbed and her limbs seemed to lay lifelessly at her sides. Even the mere thought of tumbling from bed was exhausting.

Nonetheless, she got up. It was mid-morning, the chirping of birds waiting for her outside. With any luck, perhaps she could sneak in some devotions to Gali today after leaving an offering down by the lake. As she contemplated what she would bestow the goddess this beautifully cheery morning, she fastened her corset strings tight, laced her ankle booties beneath a modest skirt, adjusted her long-sleeve shirt to cover the protruding veins of her blood-cursed arm, and tucked away her wild curls into a neat bun.

Wandering the halls, the quietness of the house was a welcomed sound. With so many visitors, it seemed rare to have such little noise. She knew her parents would still be in bed until noon. Given that her mother was the leader of the family's coven, she'd be the most tapped for energy today. Any sort of magical exertion called for her father's own tradition: breakfast in bed, carefully prepared with love and a handful of hand-picked wildflowers on the side.

Approaching the kitchen, the serenity was brutally disrupted with the sounds of Cricket's endless barking coming from the sunroom. The noise echoed through the house, followed shortly after by Tara's booming voice.

"Quit hypin' up my dog, Kane! Everyone's still tryin' to sleep!"

Winnie chuckled. If anyone was to rile up a beast, it was him. Her feet stepped down into the kitchen, eyes landing directly on Thoren and Ezra seated by the windows. In their own little world, they almost didn't notice her as she entered.

She listened for a moment.

"Can you go caroling?"

"You mean: Can I sing without killing anyone?"

Ezra's question was met with deep belly laughs before Thoren finally noticed her entrance. Under the table, their feet rubbed together and eyes roamed each other. Such adoration she'd never seen from Thoren. As Ezra turned, the happiness in his face dropped instantaneously. Then it clicked…

"But you said…" she began, unsure where her sentence was going. Thinking back to the several times she'd asked, a simmering rage slowly burned deep down.

"Winnie, wait!"

Ignoring her best friend's call, she darted for the door. Standing in the front lawn of Fox Manor, her eyes jumped from the portal to the house wildly. The flat wasn't safe anymore, that much was sure. But maybe she'd risk it to get away.

With her attention glued on the portal, the sound of the front door swinging open caused her to jump. Her face heated, heart pounding in her chest, blood boiling. A rage she'd never felt before, deep down attached to the very essence of her soul.

Footsteps approached quickly, then slowed as though caution took over. Ezra's voice sounded muffled through her ringing ears, her blood running too hot to comprehend much. She felt his hand reach for her, though quickly recoil as if the slightest touch of her skin against his was molten.

When she turned, she noticed Ezra standing behind her, hand shaking as if to cool a burning ache. With a glance down at her dress, the fabric surrounding her arm singed, revealing embers beneath her skin.

"Winnie! Talk to me!"

She waited for a moment, none of his words making it past her ears and into her brain to be comprehended. Then at last, she managed to speak. "You. Lied." The words came out of her mouth sour, a furious temper only growing.

"No, I…Can I just…" His words struggled to come out, choppy and unsure where to begin.

"I asked you. Several times! If something was going on. You said no!"

Ezra stopped trying to speak for a moment, rubbing his forehead as if trying to choose his words carefully.

"What's going on between you two? Tell me the truth or I swear to the Gods I'll…"

Before she could finish her sentence, he cut her off. "You'll what? Feed me to the hounds? Happened once already!"

Taking a step back, she asked again, "What's going on between you two?"

"I don't know exactly. We haven't quite…figured that out yet. It isn't as simple as asking to court someone for us."

Stillness settled into the conversation, both refusing to look at each other. At last, he finally turned back toward her and confessed.

"We kissed last night."

Tears stung the backs of her eyelids, threatening to unleash a rage so potent she tried to keep it held within.

"How…could you do this to me, Ez? You lied to me!" When she finally glanced back at him, the familiar burn of tears met her gaze.

"I don't know what to say, Winnie. Other than that I'm sorry. I'm so *incredibly* sorry," he stuttered, taking steps toward her once more.

"After everything I've done for you? For us? You go off and kiss someone that I cared about? You knew what he meant to me!"

He continued reaching for her, as if trying to draw her in for a hug, but every time their skin touched, he retreated with a hiss as the lava running through her veins only intensified.

"What about what I've done for you? For both of us? I've worked just as hard as you, Winnie! We've both busted our asses to make things work in Bethnal Green. Don't pretend to be the savior here!"

Winnie scoffed, unsure what to say.

"Have you ever stopped to consider why my mother kicked me out? Did you even think about me in all of this? You've never had to keep such a secret to yourself. One that burdened your soul, making you want to die rather than just tell the truth."

Ezra's eyes watered, tears forming behind his lids. Winnie remained silent, knowing if she opened her mouth she'd say something she'd regret.

"I wanted to tell you *so badly,* and when the words wouldn't form I wanted to *die.*" His voice cracked, raw emotion spilling out.

Something in her chest broke, the tears set free to stream freely down her face. Covering them and turning away, she didn't want him to see her cry.

"Do you want me to ignore him? Never see him again? Disregard the feelings we have for each other?" His questions were rapid fire. When she didn't respond, he continued. "Your friendship means the world to me, and if you were to tell me you would never speak to me again if I didn't end things with him, there is a part of me that would consider it for you. But I have *finally* found someone who understands me. Someone who sees me for who I truly am!"

"I see you," she tried to say, her voice softly quivering as she turned back toward him. This time, she was the one to reach out for him.

"No you don't, Winnie. You think you do, but you don't. You couldn't see the real me, crying out for help and wishing someone would just *realize* who I was. I've longed for a love like this. You have no idea what I've been going through this past year! All I've ever wanted is to be accepted."

"I've always accepted you, Ez! You think I couldn't tell you weren't interested in women? We've been best friends for a year. We've spent every waking second together! Did you seriously think I wouldn't notice?" Pacing in small circles in front of him, her mind whirled anxiously.

He stood silently in front of her, eyes roaming around the property as if avoiding her gaze.

"I figured you'd just tell me when you were ready! I didn't think you'd steal my childhood crush! You could've told me there was something there between you two. But you didn't say anything. When I asked if there was something going on, you lied to my face and stole the man I loved."

"That's just it, isn't it? *Loved,*" he retorted, enunciating the final word. "Maybe you had feelings for him at some point, but you can't tell me your puppy love has lasted this long. Especially after you chose someone else."

Winnie took another hesitant step back. "I don't even recognize you right now, Ez. You *lied* to me. You know what I went through with Beatrix and Samuel, and you still chose to keep this secret from me. I knew everyone else would hurt me eventually, but a part of me assumed you were the exception."

With a huff of frustration, he countered. "I never wanted to hurt you! Can't you see that? This isn't about you! I tried to hide for so long, and it felt so good to open up to someone. I spent what felt like days trapped in complete darkness. When I woke up in that circle, I saw him. He was literally glowing like an angel and something just clicked. I knew I couldn't hide anymore."

Winnie closed her eyes, her heart softening a moment.

"Okay," she said quietly, stepping toward Ezra. "I don't want you to end things."

A sigh of relief escaped from him.

"That was cruel of you to assume. All I've ever wanted was for you to be happy. For you to feel comfortable enough to finally let me in and tell me the truth. I'm sorry if I ever made you feel like I wouldn't accept you. Because trust me, Ez, I accept you. I love you! You're my best friend!"

Finally standing before him, she was able to place her hands on his arms folded across his chest. They dropped to his side, furrowed brows softening as he took in her words, though nothing came from him.

"If he is your happiness, then I want nothing more than for you two to be together. But please know that your lies cut me deeply. It will take some time for me to forgive you."

Ezra nodded. "I'm sorry, Winnie. You have to believe me when I say, we didn't want to hurt you. We just want to be together."

"I know," she whispered, heading back inside the house solemnly.

Before closing the door to the front of the house, she watched as he continued to stare down at the onyx pendant in solemn contemplation. To her left, she realized Thoren and Milicent stood at the windows. Her gaze met the siren's, though he avoided her completely before she trudged her way upstairs and back toward her room. To hide, to cry – she wasn't sure.

Her mother's soft whispers floated up the stairs, and Winnie couldn't help but overhear. "To be honest, I've always loved you two together."

It took a moment to realize what her mother was saying, the sting of betrayal only deepening with understanding. Only a few seconds passed before Milicent's footsteps followed up the stairs and back toward her room.

Entering the bedroom, Tara now lay across her blankets reading a book with Cricket curled up in front of the fireplace as usual. Winnie joined them only for Cricket to approach her and place his forehead on her leg in comfort.

"What's wrong, lass?" Tara asked, jumping off the bed and over to her friend's side.

"Thoren…and…Ezra," Winnie mumbled between sobs.

Tara continued to stroke her back softly, shushing her with a motherly calmness. "I had a feeling there was something there between them. They'd been so chummy before the attack. And the way Thoren reacted when he saw Ezra hurt… This is a good thing, though. Why are you crying?"

Winnie's words struggled to come out, her sobbing interfering with her ability to form a single thought.

"I thought you were over Thoren. What's the big deal?" Tara ceased her gentle strokes, straightening to examine Winnie with a sternness she hadn't expected.

"I…don't know. I assumed…" The words refused to come out, choppy and soaked with her tears.

"Assumed what? That he'd never find someone else? I expected more from you. Honestly, Winnie. I don't want to be harsh here, but there's no reason to be crying!"

With a few sniffles, Winnie wiped her nose and face. "I didn't think it would hurt this much. To see him happy with someone else. Especially one of my best friends."

"When Ezra told you… what did you say?" Hesitantly, she reached for Winnie's shoulder, pulling her attention back over to her. "I got the sense that he wasn't 'out' yet. Please tell me you reacted better than this."

"It was terrible, Tara. I was horrible! That was the worst fight we've ever gotten into!"

"You have to fix this! We did not just host a mind-melting healing circle for him just for you to ruin your friendship the very next day!" With a tight frown, she crossed her arms over her chest.

"I don't know how! We were both so cruel to each other."

"You can always fix things, Win. It's never too late. Let your anger settle, and be very careful how you approach those two the next time you speak. I know how scary it is to tell the people you love who you truly are. I guarantee that confession was more terrifying than the attack was." Tara's eyes softened, placing a sympathetic hand on Winnie's shoulder.

"What if he hates me? Never wants to speak to me again?" she whispered, too afraid of the answers.

"That's his choice. He's allowed to feel that way. But something tells me that given some space, you two can mend things. Ezra's a kind soul. I think you both just need to calm down."

Winnie nodded, laying back down in bed. Her mind wandered, replaying the fight in her head over and over again before sleep finally fell upon her.

26

MELINDA

Melinda sat in front of her armoire, fixing her hair in tight braids for the day. She looked in the mirror, having a hard time recognizing herself. She was not one to back down from a fight, and hiding in Fox Manor felt a lot like giving up.

Days passed and there was still no word from her family. Thinking back to Wesley's instructions, she worried she hadn't sent the magical letter correctly. There were only two possible reasons she hadn't heard back: she completed it wrong or they were dead. *Or option three, my very religious family refuses to participate in such practices,* she tried to remind herself.

As she finished fastening the ends of her hair, she couldn't help but recall the young man's kindness. Unlike the others at Fox Manor who were boisterous and full of drama, Wesley was gentle. A little shy. Someone she could see herself spending time with when all of this was over.

She was also beginning to realize that her gift was both a blessing and a curse. Melinda constantly felt the dreaded presence of the Queen around her, thanks to Winnie's deadly connection. That same looming darkness followed Melinda everywhere she went in the house, as if eyes were always plastered on her movements. It seemed there would be no rest in a place like this.

Looking in the mirror, she thought of Wesley's curious face. She'd seen glimpses of a strange figure beneath his skin, though he remained well hidden from her. Never in her life had she met someone who could escape her gift of true sight, though somehow he managed. Through the corners of her eyes or small reflections in the mirror, he revealed an unseen face. One not like the rest.

Though the notion originally terrified her, she'd been overcome by a strange sense of understanding. Maybe she didn't need to know what his true face looked like. She enjoyed the veneer he did share, that same goofy smile always waiting for her whenever she entered a room. No one in the house was 100% human, so why expect it from him?

Fastening the last of her corset laces and pulling a warm coat over her dress, Melinda exited her room. Passing Ezra and Thoren in the parlor off of the entrance, she could tell something happened. With a careful nod, she greeted them.

"Did I miss something?" she asked hesitantly, seeing the way Thoren comforted Ezra.

"Nothing, just some truths finally coming out," the siren retorted before refocusing on the blonde.

Watching them interact, a small glimmer appeared. The same one she'd noticed the days leading up to the healing ceremony. She examined them curiously, noticing the way twinkles of light seemed to surround them whenever they were near each other. It was something she'd only seen on rare occasions, a connection shared by very few.

"I'll leave you to it," she mumbled. As she exited through the front door, Wesley waited for her on the porch. "Where are you hauling me off to today?"

Turning, he straightened himself and tugged nervously at his jacket to free it of wrinkles. Mid-morning sun rays illuminated his face, those green eyes gleaming as he smiled wide at her. "A quick visit to a blacksmith in town and then some sightseeing. We have to be sneaky though. And quick. Do you have a weapon on you?" He glanced nervously behind her as if worried someone would realize they were about to leave.

Melinda nodded, patting the pistol at her side hidden beneath layers of fabric. "Should we be going back to London with hellhounds crawling everywhere?"

"It's quite a big city. We should be fine as long as we're both vigilant. Plus we're using a different portal. It'll take us to the opposite side of the Thames. My mother thinks she closed it long ago. I haven't had the heart to tell her I've been sneaking out for months." He picked up a wooden crate, motioning for her to follow him to the side of the house and into the woodline.

"Does anyone know we're leaving? The last thing I need is for your family to kick me out while Boudicca is hunting me!"

"Perhaps." A devilish smile crossed his face, the first signs of rebellion she'd seen. "My mother just went back upstairs to rest. She'll be in her room for a few more hours. Gives us time to get out of the house for a while."

Carefully, she followed after him. Glancing back at the house a few times, Melinda wondered if all of this was even a good idea. Leading her to the edge of the woods, she watched as Wesley approached two arching branches. Rubbing his onyx necklace, the space between glowed shimmering blue as swirls of light welcoming her through.

When he reached for her, she wondered if she'd catch a glimpse of his face again. But instead, their hands interlaced and he pulled her through the portal, only the glowing lights surrounded her.

When they stepped through the other side, Melinda marveled at the sights before her. London reminded her a bit of home, though the cobblestone streets and large brick buildings stood out the most. Chicago was made mostly of wood, something the papers attributed to Boudicca's destructive fires. Pedestrians walked alongside streets as crowded as any city, carriages circulating through. On the other side of them, the Thames river rushed past. This was merely another detail that reminded her of home, missing her family dearly the more she admired.

Linking arms with Wesley, the two strolled down the street until they eventually came across a blacksmith. He'd nodded to the storekeeper when delivering the package, as if they'd known each other a lifetime, before rejoining her outside.

"What was in the box?" she asked curiously.

"A dagger. Kane brought it for Winnie. Her birthday is coming up," he muttered. Though his words seemed like they should've been laced with happiness, his eyes told a different story.

"He brought her a gift? That's so sweet. Why take it to a blacksmith?"

"He's done some work for us in the past. Has a knack for adding enhancements to weapons for us magical folk," Wesley explained quietly, eyes darting to each passing person.

"I wonder how it is that I've gone my whole life without realizing all of this is real," she admitted as the two walked to a small bench on the side of the street.

"I find that surprising as well, especially with your gift." He tilted his head to the side, examining her carefully.

"The woman who predominantly raised me – Miss Leona – she always said my gift was from God. She claimed the holy spirit was the one guiding me to see the true faces of others. I don't want to tell her she's wrong," Melinda mumbled, fiddling with her fingers nervously.

"Then don't. If there's one thing I've learned about all of the deities that exist, it's that they don't care which name you pray to. Just as long as you're a good person." He offered another of many smiles, warm and calming as he nudged her playfully.

"I'm sorry, but I have to ask… Your face. Why is it different?" A small huff of relief escaped her, finally releasing that nagging question.

He paused for a moment, staring off down the street as if unsure what to say. "I don't know, honestly. I haven't a clue why I'm different from my family, I just know that I am. I'm sorry I don't have a better answer for you."

"When did you find out?"

"When I was about six I started noticing I was different. My face would on occasion change when my emotions got the better of me. I learned to control it, eventually," he finally admitted, the aura around him clouded in shame like irksome gnats on a hot summer's day.

"That's strange," Melinda mumbled. "Why did you lie the first time I asked you?"

"Anyone who's ever seen my true face, I've made to forget. Another of my pesky powers. I've always been afraid someone would discover the truth and I'd lose them all."

She sat with the news for a moment, unsure how to respond. Torn between shock and pity, she wasn't sure how to feel.

"So none of them know?"

"As far as I can tell – no. My mother's caught on a few times but I've always taken the memories away."

Another pause followed, the two sitting in silence.

"Please don't make me forget," she said at last.

Wesley's face shot towards her in shock, as though the mere notion was one he'd never considered.

"I won't tell anyone, I promise. But please don't ever mess with my mind the way you did when I first got here." Placing a delicate hand on his forearm, her eyes pleaded with him.

Glancing down at her touch, a half-hearted smile graced his lips. "I promise."

"When this is all over, I'd like to show you around Chicago. Get to know you a little better. I haven't had many friends growing up," she confessed, hoping she wasn't being too forward.

Inching away from her slightly, Wesley's demeanor changed. "We just need to focus on getting through this fight first. We'll see what happens after that."

Taken aback, she slouched onto the bench. "I'm offering you friendship. Why does it sound like you suddenly despise the idea? Why even offer to show me around London in the first place?"

Terrified eyes stared back at Melinda, startled by her words.

"No, that's not what I meant! I mean, of course I want to

spend more time with you. I just… we don't know what's going to happen," he stuttered, fighting the words coming from his mouth.

Typical seventeen year old boy, digging his hole even bigger with every word, she thought.

"Just show me around London, will you? Every second we're here, we risk getting caught." Getting up from the bench they shared, Melinda walked off. In which direction, she wasn't sure. At some point, she knew he'd catch up once he was done picking his jaw off the floor.

Wesley and Melinda spent another two hours wandering London, seeing all manner of statues, gardens, and historic buildings. Clearly this side of the Thames was nicer, given the descriptions she'd heard from Winnie's home in Bethnal Green. As their time sneaking around came to an end, the two wandered back toward the portal.

After reaching the other side, Wesley offered to spar with Melinda, though she'd quickly declined. "You upset me earlier. If we spar now, I may beat you to a pulp," she teased.

Something about his gaze made her wonder if he could sense her sarcasm.

"Joking, Wes. Calm down. Thank you for showing me around London. I really enjoyed the day," she said, offering him a warm smile.

Flushed cheeks and nervous eyes avoided her when the sound of a knocking rattled around them. He stood in attention at once, seeming to recognize that noise.

"What is it?"

"A letter arrived. Let's go!" Wesley took off running toward the front of the manor, stopping to grab the floating bit of parchment on the steps.

"It's from your family," he finally said, handing her the letter.

Nerves heated behind her cheeks, stomach fluttering with anticipation.

"At least they're not dead," she mumbled, more to herself than anything else.

Her eyes raked over the page quickly, taking in every scribble and line.

"And?" he pestered.

"They're safe for now. But…"

—•((●●))•—

WINIFRED

Upstairs sunlight slipped into Winnie's room, encompassing her in warmth just as the fire blazed on the other side. She glanced around, waking from a much-needed nap. Tara was no longer in the room, probably off to patrol London once more. Why her friend insisted on doing so alone, she couldn't fathom.

The events of the last few days ran through Winnie's mind wildly. Unable to push down the feelings that bubbled in her throat, she felt it all. Betrayal, but also guilt. She never imagined she'd speak to Ezra that way. *The look on his face when he said he'd stop seeing Thoren for me… I can't believe I let things get that far,* she thought as she sat up.

Sorrow also bugged her, thinking of the life she may have had with Thoren if she'd never chosen Samuel to begin with. The heartbreak she could've avoided for both their sakes if impatience hadn't gotten in the way. Deep down, she knew. Neither truly loved the other the way they thought. And maybe that was okay.

Dragging herself from her bed, she got dressed. Pulled on comfortable trousers and a sweater, forgoing the corset so she'd be ready to train and work on her magic. Combed her hair. Fixed it so it'd be up and out of her face. Only a single curl hung in front, a set of delicate pearl earrings in her ears. Truthfully, she felt a bit like the undead as she readied herself. Too lost in thought to fully be aware of her surroundings or what she was doing.

The sting of Ezra and Thoren brought back memory after memory. Though the events weren't nearly similar, the feelings they stirred inside her were. The same hurt she'd felt the night she ended her courtship with Samuel brought back feelings of unworthiness. The way that awful boy's words had stung her like hornets, intent on hurting her as much as physically possible. As she thought of his words, the memory of Wesley and Kane shortly after tried to surface. Though as much as she tried to remember, only nonsense came through.

Once again, she pushed at the walls in her mind. The same vague images tousled around wildly. Wesley finding her, seeing Kane's face. *He left. I'm sure of it,* she thought. The more she tried to peel back layer by layer of memories, the murkier they got.

Stepping through the doors of the sunroom, Winnie took a deep breath. The chilled air swirled shades of copper-toned leaves through the estate, the picture-perfect autumn morning. Heavy clouds lined the sky, sun peeking through and smiling down on her as a gust of wind picked up around her.

Taking a seat outside, she closed her eyes. Concentrating, she spoke to Gali. Reciting her daily prayers from when she was younger, she tried desperately to rekindle her relationship with her deity, the Goddess of Water.

Placing her hands side by side, she focused on creating the watery life inside them. Surrounding herself in blue light internally, she called on the Goddess for strength. A twinkle of her power shimmered down, a ball of water forming in the palms of her hands.

"Stop overthinking it," she heard in her mind. Gali – speaking to her at last.

Straightening her back in an instant, butterflies fluttering in her stomach with excitement. Nodding, Winnie concentrated once more. Holding out her palms, hoping for that ball of water, something else happened instead.

Up ahead, thunder sounded. Looking up, a droplet of water splashed onto her forehead. The clouds darkened, hiding the sun and turning the air icy.

Winnie walked to the center of the field as more droplets fell, little by little increasing in size. At last, the heavens opened up and poured out. With a steady hand held high, Winnie called on the water. Ordered it to stop. The connection was strong, Gali's laugh ringing through her as she successfully stalled the rain from falling.

"There you are! At last," she whispered in Winnie's mind.

Before she could think to respond to the Goddess, her blood cursed arm sent a sharp jolt of pain through her. Flinching, the control she held on the storm loosened and the shower continued. Within seconds, she stood soaking wet and cold.

"Any advice on how to stop this?" Winnie called out into the empty field, the rain beating down on her. *"Please hear me, Gali. I know you're out there."*

Only silence sat on the other end of her prayers.

Off in the distance, she heard Kane calling out her name. Motionlessly, she stood in the center of the rainstorm. All she could do was pray. Hope that they could find a cure for her blood curse and she'd regain her powers back in time to defeat the spirit that held poor Mary captive.

27

WINIFRED

Shivering in front of the fire, Winnie attempted to dry her hair of rainwater. The long awaited arrival of Horace and Mohini finally came shortly after the storm began. With the full moon passed, they had some time before the Lycans would return to their wild instincts.

She'd known her 'uncle' since she was a little girl. Though they weren't technically related, it didn't matter. Horace's first wife was like family too, until a group of ruthless hunters snagged her one night. It took years for him to recover. Years of solitude, finding himself without his other half. It wasn't until he met Mohini more recently that he was able to accept what happened and move on. Hesitantly, still, but a little less solemn.

Horace met Mohini when his worldly travels took him to India. Winnie delighted in hearing the tales of their adventures. "I'd like to visit India one day," she told Mohini when they first met the previous year.

Now, she sat watching their visitors exchange small talk before turning back to the conversation at hand: finding Boudicca's hellhounds and tracking down the abandoned factories Ezra and Tara had learned about the other night. As Horace turned away from Mohini and toward Kane once more, the shouting started again.

"How do we know it's not a trap?" Kane's voice echoed through the Library.

"We *know* it's a trap. That's why we prepare for the worst," Horace retorted. A low, Lycan growl escaped his lips as the tension between them tripled. His scarlett brown eyes glowed with anger, his face as red as his hair.

"If it's a trap, we shouldn't be going! How am I the only one thinking clearly about this?" Kane exclaimed.

His own eyes seemed to glow in anger, the same amber-toned luminescence Winnie knew came from the siren in him. *He's ready to explode,* she thought anxiously.

"You two are going to give me a headache! I understand that there's bad blood between Lycan and Sirens, but can you both please stop shouting?" Winnie called out, clutching her temples in agony.

Milicent rejoined them, placing a tray of finger sandwiches on a small table. With a huff of frustration, she looked between the two.

"You better cage your bird," Horace growled. The creases of his face folded as rage-filled eyes squinted toward the siren.

"Stop yelling, you two. Your energy is nauseating. Kane, we have to know what we're going up against. How many hellhounds there are. Horace, you know as well as I do that we can't go in blind. Stop the childish name-calling and let's come up with an actual plan!"

Winnie stood from her place in front of the fire, joining the conversation. "Kane? What if you flew up ahead of us to search the streets before we go on foot?"

Her suggestion was met with an eye roll and a grumble. "So I can be the bait? That's perfect."

"Offer a different idea then," she snapped.

"Could you apply a glamor?" Mohini asked. She'd been watching patiently, observing her husband and the young siren go head to head.

"That's an idea. We could make you look like something else that'll blend in. Something they won't notice." Her mother pondered, her voice trailing off in thought.

"How about a bloody bird?" Horace grumbled.

Kane's fists tightened, looking as though he was ready to pummel the Lycan if he said something else. Seeing his anger bubbling over, Winnie stepped between them. Reaching for his shoulders, she pulled his gaze away from his opponent and onto her.

"Combine the glamor with your talents, and you'll be fine." She squeezed in reassurance as her words hit him.

Something in his face changed, softening at the sight of her.

"This is a wonderfully *stupid* idea. One that'll just get me killed and then you shortly after," he said at last, walking toward the door to exit the Library.

"Kane, wait!"

At first, he ignored her and continued his trudge down the hallway.

"Kane!" Her voice cracked, calling out once more.

He hesitated a moment, shoulders tightening and fists clenched as his stride continued. "Not now, Winnie."

"Stop!" Her voice boomed through the hall. "What's gotten into you? The Kane I know would never dismiss me like this!"

He seemed to flinch, she noticed. Pausing in his tracks, she caught up and stood before him. At first, he refused to meet her gaze. Staring off into the distance, his mind seemed to turn. Likely thinking of all the things that could go wrong. She reached up and grabbed the side of his face, his eyes flashing nervously toward her.

"Talk to me. *Please.* Stop running away."

He reached for her hand, pulling it down. "You have to know that this plan of his is madness." A muscle in his jaw flickered, teeth grinding anxiously.

"It's not the worst plan I've heard. Tara did think it was a good idea to take Ezra to the bar with no weapons or backup..." Her voice trailed off, realizing sarcasm wasn't welcomed.

"Something's wrong with this entire situation. I can feel it." His stair dug into her skin, intense and unyielding.

"It's just a quick stakeout! We'll be fine," she said, attempting to reassure him.

Grabbing her shoulder, he pleaded. "You're not listening to me, Winnie! Something is going to happen. I can feel it in my gut. Why does he only want some of us to go? Hm? Why not the whole group. We'd be safer that way."

"You heard what he said. We have to be sneaky. The entire group would only bring more unnecessary attention to us. We can't sneak into a place with this many people."

He nodded – either agreeing or thinking, she wasn't sure.

"I don't want anything happening. To you. To any of us." His voice was soft, as though he only wanted her to hear him. His eyes wandered down the hall again, avoiding her.

"Kane, look at me." Reaching up, she grabbed his face with both hands once more. "Nothing is going to happen. We're just sneaking around and taking a peak. You'll fly ahead, glamored so they can't see you. If there's too many of them outside that could cause trouble, we'll never step foot near that factory."

"It's one thing to spy on a group of them. It's another to spy on a whole army," he added, face dropping to the ground.

"We don't know that she has an army. I promise – we'll be fine."

At last, his body seemed to settle. With a deep exhale from both of them, Winnie realized he still held her hand to his chest. Letting it go, he reached for her and pulled her in for a deep embrace.

"If something happens…" he mumbled, her face buried in his chest.

"Nothing is going to happen," she reassured once more, enjoying a few moments of comfort before returning to the others to continue making their plan.

28

WINIFRED

The day came and went, Winnie's mind racing. Kane's words swirled through her thoughts like the very element he wielded, wondering if he was right. If something was going to happen.

She wanted to spend the day training with him and Tara, keeping her mind off of Thoren and Ezra who'd hidden themselves away. And yet none of them were anywhere to be seen.

Her friend couldn't seem to keep herself off the streets of London, patrolling on her own with Cricket at her side. It was as if she were trying to make up for her mistake with Ezra. Kane stayed in his room, almost as though he avoided her as well. Even Wesley and Melinda were nowhere to be found.

The sun set and a bell rang through the house. The same one Milicent used when Winnie was younger. Her way of calling the family to the kitchen for dinner rather than having to yell through the entire manor looking for everyone.

Winnie finished readying herself for the evening. Her mother insisted that morning that everyone dress nicely for a formal dinner to welcome Horace and Mohini. Lacing the last strings of her mustard yellow gown, she looked herself over in the mirror.

It didn't fit quite like it used to when she was younger, tighter across the chest and hips. Thankfully it didn't seem to matter, the bustle at the back taking the focus away from her front and onto her rear. Layers of lace delicately accentuated the curves of her body. A few beads of pearls lay around her neck as well, more tucked into her delicate updo to match.

Admiring herself, she realized she missed dressing up like this. Wearing the same raggedy clothes day in and day out in Bethnal Green was so vastly different compared to how she grew up. *I'm here temporarily. Until things are safe again, and then I can go back to my business and my own flat. Remember that,* she thought. She felt like she was scolding herself for enjoying the simplicity of living back home again.

Exiting into the hallway, she peeked down at the lavatory where Tara readied herself. The light was still on, movement on the other side of the door. Before she knew it, she could feel a hesitant presence behind her.

"Hey you," she said, offering Kane a warm smile.

He didn't return the favor, a sentiment that hurt her more than she realized. Only a look of concern remained plastered across his face.

"I can't help but feel like you're avoiding me," she admitted, brows scrunched in concern.

"Why would I do that?" He scoffed, though his tone wasn't convincing.

"Are you still worried about tomorrow?"

"That must be it..." His eyes dropped once more. Before he could head down the stairs, he paused. When he turned back, he offered her a small smile. "You look bewitching by the way."

Reaching for her hand, he offered it a soft kiss. One that lingered on her skin for merely a moment. Small butterflies fluttered within, clutching her chest in surprise. A smirk fell across his face as he turned, leaving her speechless in the hallway waiting for Tara.

Just behind her, the redhead exited the lavatory and wandered over. Wearing a divine forest green gown, her strawberry hair lay in curls down her back. She'd taken the liberty to pin a few flowers in the creases of fabric, peeks of ruby red roses slicking out.

"Ready for dinner?" Her voice sang, locking Cricket in Winnie's room and linking arms with her as they made their way downstairs.

Entering the dining room, Winnie admired the decorations her mother worked hard to put up. They didn't spend much time in this room on the daily. Milicent saved it for dinner parties and special occasions. The kitchen was the usual location to eat. Casual and comfy, that's how they liked it.

But Winnie's mother was known for her lavishness when it came to seasonal decor. With Samhain fast approaching, an assortment of bronzed leafy decorations lined every inch of the walls, furniture, and table. Wreaths of pine cones, Chrysanthemums, and foliage were hung up. The warm yellows and rusty oranges contrasted the dark furniture, gothic floral wallpapers standing out against the frills.

A roasted chicken sat at the center of the table, rows of sides on either end. Many already sat around, eyeballing the seasoned vegetables, mashed potatoes, and assortments of meat.

Tara and Winnie took a seat at the end, opposite of Horace and Mohini. The couple was dressed to match in navy blues. Gold bangles adorned Mohini's wrists, her coal-black hair long and straight down her back. Glittering gold seemed to accentuate her in every corner of her body.

Thoren and Ezra cozied up together on the other side, hardly noticing anyone else in the world existed. They hadn't dressed too formally, merely in button down shirts, trousers, and suspenders. Ezra's attention peeled away from his newfound love momentarily, long enough to shout, "Winnie! It's you!"

Getting up from his seat, he rushed to her side. *What's he doing? Why is he acting so strange? The last time we spoke was our fight,* she thought. Pouring a glass of an unknown amber colored drink, he handed it to her.

"Are you trying to poison me?" Winnie's words were meant to be a joke, but they didn't seem to come out quite right.

"Horace brought it! It's amazing! I don't even remember what it's called." His face was incredibly flushed, voice a little higher than usual.

"It's moonshine. And I keep telling your friend to slow down," Horace barked with a roaring laugh.

Winnie took a cautious sip. Autumn flavors of apple and cinnamon exploded in her mouth as she took another.

Before Ezra resumed his seat once more, he leaned over. Placing a hand on Tara's shoulder, he attempted to softly mumble, "I forgive you, ya know."

Her face softened, eyes closed and smiling as though she'd been waiting to hear those words uttered.

Wesley and Melinda entered next, joining them around the table. Her friend tried to offer them a glass as well, though both refused. She wore one of Winnie's gowns, deep red and adorned with dark beaded lace around the edges. Strings of those same beads hung off the edge of her shoulders, paired nicely with a dainty set of pearls. Taking a seat, her eyebrows furrowed as though she'd recently been given bad news.

As Milicent and Ernest brought in the last of the plates and took a seat, Winnie realized only one last person was missing. "Where's your brother?"

Thoren's eyes drifted away from Ezra for only a moment before he finally answered. "He'll be in shortly."

"Tara – thank you for leaving that beast in Winnie's room. I swear, I've been digging fur from my mouth since you arrived!" Milicent huffed, standing at the end of the table.

She wore one of her nicer gowns, though less frills than the younger women. A simple, elegant, black dress that hung off her shoulders was temporarily covered by an apron which she swiftly removed as she took a seat.

Tara's only reply was an awkward chuckle. *Mum never liked pets of any kind,* Winnie thought.

"Let's begin!" Milicent sang with outstretched arms.

"Shouldn't we wait for Kane?" Winnie asked, looking in confusion.

A sly smile formed across her brother's face before he teased, "Why so concerned?"

She merely rolled her eyes in response.

"Did you make all of this yourself? Without the help of a servant?" Ezra asked in amazement, his glimmering eyes taking in trays full of food.

Milicent offered a modest nod before Ernest chimed in. "My beloved has been serving us feasts like this for as long as I've known her! There's never been a need for servants. Especially when the house offers as much help as it does."

Platters rotated around the table, everyone grabbing food little by little. Her mother cooked up some of the best meals she knew. After the rainstorm that morning, Winnie helped harvest an abundance of vegetables in preparation. Brussel sprouts, carrots, aubergines, cabbages, and all manner of cold-loving produce lined the plates. Some with dressings on them, some plain but well seasoned.

"Mohini and Horace brought us some more spices," she added, pointing to a few of the dishes.

At the end of the table, Ezra moaned as he ate. "I've never had anything so decadent in my life." His eyes seemed to roll back into his skull, the room chuckling. "I didn't even know I like brussel sprouts," he mumbled, gaze roaming as if he wanted seconds already.

"Do you not feed them?" Mohini asked, a small chuckle in her voice.

Milicent rolled her eyes. "I can't seem to feed them enough."

Heavy footsteps darted into the room. Kane, out of breath, stood in the archway with something wooden in hand. "Sorry I'm late! It took longer than I thought."

"Sit and eat," Thoren said, pointing to the empty chair next to him.

"Yes, one moment. First, we must celebrate someone's birthday!" He placed the box at her side with a nervous smile. "Open whenever you're ready." Finally, he sat down and served himself.

"But my birthday isn't for a few weeks," she protested.

"We know. With everything going on, we wanted to celebrate before things become too hairy. Just in case," Ernest explained, voice trailing off.

Everyone in the room seemed to know what he was trying to say. *In case we all die. In case the queen successfully kills all of us,* Winnie thought hesitantly.

"Can I open it now?" Though she hated celebrating her birthday, she adored receiving gifts. Feeling jittery, her hands itched to see what was inside.

Everyone in the room nodded. For merely a moment, Winnie felt like she could forget the impending doom looming in the air. No worries of the stakeout tomorrow night. No fears of a potential outmatched battle. Only tonight – dinner surrounded by family.

She opened the wooden crate carefully, unsure what to expect. The inside of the box was lined with black velvet, a brand new dagger sitting on top. It was ornate and intricately carved, the hilt decorated with tiny sapphires. The blade itself glittered with carved runes. With a soft gasp, Winnie removed it from the box.

"I've never seen a weapon this beautiful before!"

"One of the runes is the same as the one my family uses for protection against magic," Tara mentioned, pointing down at the dagger and then at her family's necklace.

"We all picked ones that we thought represented us best," Milicent added. "When you fight, you'll have a little bit of each of us at your side."

Wesley smiled, eagerly pointing out one of them. "This is the one I picked. It's for a clear mind so you can focus while fighting."

As she beheld the weapon's beauty, she could feel the power reverberating off of it. The energy from the runes inscribed on the blade only added to its magnificence.

"I don't know if I can fight with this. It's too beautiful," she mumbled, examining every square inch.

"It's fashioned from the strongest metal we know of. It won't yield," Kane mumbled between bites.

Winnie sat silently for a moment, unsure what to say. *Everyone around this table is here because I messed up. I'm the reason Mary was possessed. And still here they sit – celebrating my birthday of all things…*

"Thank you," was all she could muster before placing the dagger back into the wooden box.

Stalled silence fell before Ezra finally broke it. "So what are you both? Lycan, correct?"

Horace nodded with a chuckle, though Mohini simply shook her head.

"You can turn into a wolf?" His words slurred together, an almost childlike wonder to his question.

Another nod came from the Lycan.

"You have to stop asking everyone *what* they are," Milicent said with a look of disapproval.

"Aren't you going to ask me what I am?" Mohini countered with an amused chuckle.

"Not a Lycan, I presume. Some sort of half animal like the others?" A hiccup escaped Ezra nervously, as if realizing the alcohol was making him more outgoing than usual.

Mohini picked up an apple from the table, holding it up. She stared at it with extreme intensity, Winnie noticing the dark hue of her eyes turning amber in color, lightening as the apple slowly glittered. Within moments, the piece of fruit was glimmering gold and shining in the light of the chandelier above the table. Mohini handed it to Ezra, the look on his face in complete awe.

"Is it?" he began, though the words didn't form.

"Pure gold."

He continued to move the apple in his hands, turning it around and around. "May I keep it?" Mesmerized eyes scanned the fruit in its new form.

Something like that could make him a wealthy man. I wonder if he'll keep it or sell it when we go back to our old life, Winnie thought.

"Of course," she said with a soft smile.

"Can you do that to anything? Even people?" His question seemed strange, nervously examining her.

"It's a bit more difficult, but yes. If need be."

A layer of suspicion hid in his voice as he asked, "How do you control it?"

"Probably the same way your siren controls his powers. You make the choice to use your gifts the right way," she explained.

A few moments passed, pockets of conversation forming before Melinda interjected to the entire group. "I finally heard back from my family."

All eyes in the room turned toward her, curiously. Her face was stern, as though she didn't like the answers she'd received from them.

"If they answered, they're alive. Why do you seem so upset?" Winnie asked curiously.

"Chicago is overrun by hellhounds. I need to go back."

"Melinda, you can't leave just yet. It's not safe," Milicent began.

"My family is sheltered for now, but running out of supplies. They'll die if I don't go back," she insisted. "I'm not a prisoner here. I can leave whenever I want, right?"

"I suggested we send supplies to them," Wesley interrupted.

"Of course you're not a prisoner, Melinda, but we do want to keep you safe. I wouldn't advise leaving the estate at all," Ernest said softly. "We can send food, water, and protection until we can make it back there to begin working on the hound problem."

Melinda's eyes jutted toward Wesley in accusation. Winnie couldn't quite tell what she seemed so upset about. Clearly her brother had done something.

"How will I know you actually sent supplies like you're promising?"

For a moment, Milicent stared at the young woman perplexed. "Have we given you any reason to suspect we wouldn't keep our word?"

Wesley grabbed her hand. "I'll ensure they get what they need. With everyone here, we can create a new portal. I'll go myself and ensure they're taken care of. Boudicca isn't looking for me, so I should get in and out quickly."

Winnie watched curiously as Milicent's face flashed in a panic.

"One of us should go with you. Safety in numbers," Kane added.

Melinda quietly nodded, lips sealed tightly and eyes avoiding Ernest and Milicent.

"First the stakeout." Horace's tone was equally as serious, reminding everyone of the planned mission tomorrow. "We can't do anything about this queen unless we know how many we're up against. I'll have my pack here soon, but there are only so many of us. We're not a trained, organized army."

A tight frown sat across the young woman's face. "Immediately after then."

With a nod, Horace turned back down to his food.

"Judging by the letter, they should have enough supplies to last them a few more days," Wesley added with a hopeful nod.

"I know what the letter said. I think I need some time alone." Standing from her seat, her gaze rested back on Milicent. "Thank you for the food. It was delicious."

Winnie looked at her plate, noticing that it sat completely untouched.

Dinner ended with a decorated cake brought out, cut and served to each member. Almost everyone retired to the bar to wind down for the evening, though Winnie sat with Tara discussing the latest book they read together. It wasn't until Kane entered that her friend smiled, stood, and excused herself to quickly care for Cricket.

Winnie watched as her childhood best friend walked past her and into the sitting room. Taking a seat on the loveseat alone, she eventually followed after him.

"Is everything alright? You've been acting so strange." Taking a seat beside him, he only offered her a half-hearted smile.

"Of course," he said with a sigh.

"This was your idea, wasn't it?" A smile graced her lips as she asked, nudging him playfully.

Kane slouched back, hand over his own mouth seeming to hide a small smirk. "Only the dagger. Tara thought to add the runes. The celebration itself was Wesley's idea. He insisted on celebrating now instead of waiting." Leaning forward, he took the blade from the box to look it over once more.

"Which rune is yours?"

Kane pointed down to one of them.

"What does it mean?"

"It's not technically a rune. It's actually the symbol for the Falke family. That way you'd always have me with you to protect you." A half smile formed, dropping the same time as his eyes.

She examined it carefully. The letter 'F' was surrounded by delicate swirls resembling the air element signs. Those same butterflies reappeared in her chest as she grabbed the dagger from his hands, fingers brushing against each other for a mere second. He looked back up at her and suddenly she realized: *He's never looked at me like that before.*

"You've seemed different the last few days," she added, placing the dagger in the box once more.

"Being here just makes me realize how different things are now." His voice seemed sad, she realized.

"Different how?"

"It doesn't matter," he began.

She nudged him once more, trying to draw out the playfulness she loved so dearly.

A sheepish sigh escaped his lips before continuing. "Fine… I regret what I did two years ago. It took me away from you for longer than I wanted. Being here, spending time with you again, it's made me realize how much I've missed you."

She examined him curiously. "Still won't tell me what you did?"

He shook his head with a sigh. "I don't want you to think of me differently."

"You underestimate me, Kane. One mistake won't make me suddenly hate you. I've done things I'm not proud of. We all have."

"Maybe if we survive this whole ordeal with Boudicca, I'll tell you." A full smile sat across his face at last. Not a half hearted one, but a true smile.

Her grin ceased, worry replacing it. "You think we'll survive this?"

"We don't have a choice. One way or another, we have to make it."

Winnie sat back in silence, unsure what to say.

Carefully, hesitantly, he grabbed her hand. "You know I'll always protect you, Winnie. Even if it's the last thing I ever do."

Again, she didn't know how to respond. Her cheeks flushed, unsure if she should pull away from his touch or not. "I know. I hope you know I'll always have your back as well," she added at last.

"I saw something…strange. The night of the healing circle. Perhaps that's why I've been so unusual." A nervous chuckle echoed through her as he nervously rubbed his forehead.

"And? What was it? Tell me!" Excitedly, she scooted in closer beside him.

He opened his mouth to answer, though closed it as if unsure he should even say. "It's hard to explain. It was very…emotional. I don't know if I can really describe it," he confessed, examining the fire past Winnie.

"Just tell me!" she badgered playfully, grabbing his hand in her own to regain his attention.

"Well, I saw you. When I opened my eyes, you were glowing. Like a…rare treasure." The words tumbled from him, low and soft. If she hadn't been sitting so close, she likely wouldn't have heard him.

"What does that even mean?" she giggled, scooting back a moment.

A huff of laughter followed before he admitted, "I have no idea. But I've spent all this time trying to figure it out." Tilting his head to the side, a smirk fell across his lips as his eyes seemed to wander. "Things just feel different now. I can't explain it."

Unsure what to say, Winnie examined him. Noted the features of his face, both delicate and gruff. The way his long dark lashes fluttered over his nervous hazels when he looked at her. The hair that fell across his face as if avoiding her gaze. Noticing so many little details she never saw before, she couldn't help but sit in blushing silence.

"Come," he said at last, pulling her from her admiring trance. Getting up, he stretched his hand out toward her. "We should join the others in the bar. We're celebrating *you* after all."

Following Kane with her hand in his, energetic music sounded through the house ushering them toward the celebration. Stepping through the doors, Ezra and Tara danced in the center of the room with linked arms and spinning in circles.

"The birthday girl!" Ezra cheered.

Winnie rushed to join them at the center, momentarily forgetting about the heartbreak of the previous days.

Late into the evening, almost everyone excused themselves to rest and prepare for tomorrow's stakeout. Winnie was too focused on trying to keep her mind *off* of the potential fight ahead. Instead, she remained in the bar well past midnight with her friends.

In the corner, Ezra lay on a bench asleep. Between the

moonshine and the late hour, he was tuckered out. His head lay cradled in Thoren's lap as the siren watched Tara and Winnie dance together in front of a simmering fire, attempting not to fall asleep himself.

Carefully, Winnie snuck over to him. "Think you can get up without waking him?"

Delicately, Thoren moved Ezra's head aside and stood. "What now?"

With a giggle, Winnie grabbed his hand and pulled him to dance. The music changed, slowing to a pace where the two could talk as they swayed. He seemed a little uncomfortable at first, eventually settling in.

"I wanted to talk to you. Alone."

Thoren's brows furrowed. He didn't say a word as they continued to sway.

"I'm sorry for everything. Especially the way I acted when I found out about…" she said, her voice trailing off. "I didn't mean for either of you to feel ostracized because of me. The last thing I want is for either of you to think I don't accept you."

"I'm sorry, too. I should have been honest with you the moment I realized there was something between us," he admitted, his voice soft.

"I think we both could have been honest. I clung to the idea of us for so long. I wonder if things would've been different for us if I'd apologized a long time ago."

"The past is just that… the past. We can't change it. Only move forward. Just don't think too much. That's what got us in trouble."

The conversation stalled, the song nearing its end.

"It's amazing to see you two together. I've known him a whole year and I've never seen his smile beaming like that. Or yours. You two seem so…content."

"He's incredible," Thoren whispered, barely audible. A glimmer of the friendship they'd shared long ago seemed to showcase itself as he giggled with childlike whimsy. The music came to an end as he bowed before her, half formal and half sarcastic.

She held out her pinky toward him. "No more awkwardness. No more heartache. Only friendship. Swear it?"

He nodded, linking his pinky in hers. "I swear." Heading back toward his newfound love, Thoren moaned. "He's going to feel like hell in the morning."

Winnie chuckled as he helped Ezra up and out the door for bed. Glancing around, her eyes settled on Kane. He waited at the door, motioning to go upstairs.

"We should go to bed. Big day tomorrow," he reminded wryly.

She chuckled, linking her arm in his once more as they wandered upstairs. "Are you going to drunkenly dance with me in the hallway again?" She giggled as his eyes seemed to roll into the back of his head.

"You're not going to let me live that down are you?"

"Nope." A feline smile fell across her face, walking up the stairs and toward their rooms.

"I noticed you dancing with my brother. All is well, I take it?"

She nodded cheerfully. "I think we're finally moving past everything."

"I'm glad." Stopping outside her door, he turned. His gaze down at her felt piercing. Those hazel eyes seemed to plead with her, though she didn't know what for.

"Thank you," she said, reaching out and placing a hand on his chest.

His eyes trailed her every movement, landing back on her face.

"For everything. The gift especially."

Winnie reached in, pulling Kane toward her for an embrace. Her heart fluttered, throat bobbing, palms sweating. They'd shared a million hugs but never one that felt like this.

She pulled back, still in his arms, looking at him. She couldn't help but notice as his gaze seemed to flicker from her lips back to her eyes. His breath quickened beneath her touch, both lingering for a moment.

"Anything for you, Winifred."

She fought back the urge to smile or giggle. Anything. But somehow she couldn't seem to move from that spot. Nerves tickled her throat and clouded her vision, but she couldn't think to speak or say anything.

"Good night, Kane." Her voice fell soft and low, pulling away slowly. Unsaid words and unidentifiable emotions waited for her to explore them, but all she could do was wish him a good evening.

"Good night, love," he whispered, grasping her arm with delicate grace. His fingers trailed down her skin before supple lips planted on top of her hand. At last, he turned and headed toward his room with careful steps.

29

⊷•(((●●●)))•⊶

WINIFRED

Sunset streaked across the sky, the streets of London cool with an autumn breeze flowing through rows of buildings. Their target location wasn't too far away, a few blocks to walk. South of Bethnal Green sat a row of abandoned factories. *Any one of them could be housing her beasts,* Winnie thought, pulling her coat around her to brace from the nipping wind.

Tara clung to her, equally shivering and ready to get the night over with. Kane and Horace spent the morning going head to head once more, the tension between them only growing. Bit by bit, they agreed even less as the arguments raged on. At last, the Lycan won thanks to her father intervening.

Both men stepped through the portal, glaring at each other as their feet met the pavement. Kane stalked toward her, shoulders tense and scowling. *He's been so grumpy all day,* she thought glumly. Handing him his onyx pendant she'd borrowed for the day, she couldn't help but notice the nervous ticks. He couldn't seem to stand still, fidgeting and fussing over everything.

"You're sure it'll work? The last thing I want is to be shot down."

As the pendant made contact with his skin, a small glow surrounded the tiny gem.

"I spent all afternoon assuring it would. My mum watched me every step of the way. Thoren tested it out for us. But please, be careful regardless. Don't get too close. It only works if you're high up. When you're in the sky, they *should* only see the stars and nothing else."

With a shrug of his shoulders, Kane's wings expanded behind him. They were almost identical to Thoren's, slightly lighter in color. Containing more speckles of white, Kane's wings were identical to a hawk's. Small frosty bands sat on the tips of each quill. As his wings ruffled behind him, his dark eyes brightened to tawny yellow that gleamed in the moonlight.

"I always forget how beautiful they are," she whispered shyly, running a hand over the edge of his wing.

"No time for flattery," he half-heartedly joked.

He stared at her a moment, as if unsure what to do or say. Before she knew it, he was reaching for her. Pulling her in until they were forehead to forehead. His breath quickened just as her heartbeat did.

"I still think this is a bad idea," he whispered.

Tara and Horace stood a few feet away, focused down the road on watch.

Winnie didn't know what to say. Squeezing her eyes closed, she prayed. Hoped that his gut feeling wasn't true and they'd be okay. That they'd live to see another day. Her heart felt like it was pounding in her stomach as his fingers wrapped around her cheek.

At last, he broke the silence. "Watch your back, love. Stay vigilant."

Kane stepped back, examining her one last time before shooting up into the sky. Hovering above them for a moment, Winnie gave him a thumbs up that the glamor worked. His body disappeared into the night sky at last, only stars staring back at them.

"Goodbye pigeon," Horace called out as Kane exited from their view.

"That'll light a spark under him," Tara teased, eyes searching the night sky for the siren.

KANE

Kane's stomach was in knots as he flew over London. He monitored the area carefully, an eerie silence spread across each alleyway and street. He couldn't help but notice there were no pedestrians walking about. No one wandered from the bars and establishments. No musicians played to make extra cash. No one took an evening stroll. It was as if everyone had simply vanished. He didn't notice any hellhounds either. *It's like the damned apocalypse,* he thought as he continued his flight.

He eyed one of the factories not far ahead, the windows glowing with life inside as if it were the last place left on Earth. He circled the building, attempting to see inside. It was certainly abandoned at one point, the walls crumbling. Cracks lined the sides, barely standing up. Thick foliage wrapped around the base.

From afar, he couldn't make out any details. Couldn't see far enough inside to tell if this was the right place. He flew in a little closer, squinting in the darkness. *Still nothing. Damn it!* Flying in a little closer, at last he saw them.

Not dozens.

Hundreds.

Beasts roamed the building, laughing inside as though they were throwing a massive social gathering. Flying room to room, he watched in horror. Humans and other magical creatures were strewn about, tied up for the hounds' amusement.

Rage bubbled inside him, knowing their torment would be unending unless he put a stop to it. It took a moment to gather his wits before realizing that wasn't an option. Even in a single room, there were too many hounds to risk a solo ambush.

"Caelus, forgive me. I can't save them. Send them strength as they endure such atrocities," he prayed to the God of Air. A small breeze greeted his prayer, a sign from the deity himself.

Idly, he hovered outside one of the windows. Desperately, he tried to count them all. Make sense of what he was seeing. Trying to get some idea of how many there truly were to report back to the others.

A feeling of being watched suddenly washed over him, the hair on his arms standing. He peered around, remembering Winnie's warning. Below, a voice echoed up to him.

"Do I see a little birdie peeping through my windows?"

Beneath him, a pack of hounds waited. Panic spread through his body as the electric-eyed man smirked at him.

"Alaric, we meet at last," he called down.

Within moments, a shrill tenor note burst free from his throat, turning and darting back toward the portal. The beasts fell to their knees clutching their ears in pain as he flew ahead. *I have to warn them! There's too many! They need to get back to the...*

Before he could finish his thought, a loud *'pang'* sounded through the air. A sharp pain jolted through his left wing before he tumbled toward the streets of London, Boudicca's beasts waiting for him.

━◦‹‹●●●››◦━

WINIFRED

Winnie took a seat next to Horace, wondering where all of London was. Butch's pub was known for its noisy chaos. Tonight there was only silence echoing along the cobblestone. Sitting there, she realized she missed it.

Tara slumped next to her. Winnie anxiously lay her head on her friend's shoulder, a loud huff escaping her lips.

"I hope everything's alright. I have a bad feeling about this..."

"I'm sure your pigeon is fine," Horace grumbled. "He's perfectly capable. Most sirens are."

"Why did you pick us?" Winnie asked in suspicious curiosity, remembering Kane's concerns.

"You three seemed to be the most sneaky," he replied with a

shrug. "I didn't expect you to talk this much."

"I remember you being a lot nicer when I was younger." Her brows furrowed in frustration at the man she'd considered an uncle growing up.

"You must not be remembering me very well," he laughed, deep and guttural.

Down the street, she heard it immediately. The *'crack'* of a bullet shattering the air. Her mind raced as she shot to her feet, hounds howling in the night. Turning the corner, she saw him.

Eyes wild and feet racing with a pack of hounds hot on his heels. One of his wings drooping, the inner white feathers covered in blood.

"Go!" His voice echoed through the street. "Go home!" A desperation hid within his tone, eyes pleading and mouth panting as he pushed himself harder and harder to run.

Ignoring his orders, Winnie ran toward him.

"Gali, I need you!" she called out in her mind.

She pulled on every ounce of strength she had within. As her feet continued to pound, she imagined the flow of glowing azure light around her. Tapping into the well of family magic she had inside, she prepared.

Shooting her hands out in front of her, a wall of water sprang free like wild horses. Crashing into the hounds, narrowly avoiding Kane, the water brought them to a screeching halt. His feet continued to sprint as the hounds paced behind the temporary waterlogged blockade.

With reaching hands, Kane grabbed her and tugged at her to run. She could feel her magic slipping. Every second the water flowed through the air, she felt the sting of her blood cursed hand. The pain intensified, heat radiating through her.

"I can't keep it up much longer! Boudicca's curse – it doesn't like me using my element," she cried. The navy lines around her arm glowed, shimmering just as Kane's eyes did.

He paused. "Drop it! I can hold them off."

If he uses his voice, it'll impact us all. What is he thinking? But it was too late. Without even trying, her forcefield saturated the streets, falling away and allowing the beasts through once more.

Kane turned, taking a deep breath. Winnie clutched her ears, expecting the worst. He expanded his arms and wings around himself, a barrier of air forming between the two of them. Beyond it, she couldn't hear anything. She watched as the beasts crumbled to the floor, twitching and shivering as Death awaited their souls.

I didn't know he could do that, she thought in wonderment, curious as to what the maddening cries of the siren sounded like.

As the hounds fell, Kane turned. The forcefield between them faded, his eyes darting back toward the portal. "Let's go!" His voice rang through her, the seductive siren song still lingering.

Snagging her hand, he pulled her toward the alley. A few strong-willed hounds resumed their fighting positions, paws barreling toward them once more. Closer and closer the portal got, but seconds felt like a lifetime as they rounded the corner. Only moments behind Kane, Winnie pushed and pushed, trying to keep up.

Tara and Horace waited for them at the edge.

They saw them near, Kane shouting once more. "Go!"

The two hurried through, followed by the siren. As his feet entered the portal and his body disappeared behind the veil, Winnie felt her fingers slip from his and a tug on her body.

Behind her, Boudicca stood with her hand held out toward Winnie. Caught in her telekinetic grasp, Winnie struggled to free herself. Her blood cursed arm seemed to vibrate in excitement at the queen's presence.

He's safely through. I know what I have to do. Without thinking twice, she pulled on magic she didn't even know she had. *I won't let her anywhere near them.*

Closing the portal, her heart felt a rip as the connection to her home severed. "No way out. It's just me and you," she spat, turning toward the crimson queen.

30

KANE

Just as Kane's feet touched the portal, he turned. Saw her. Saw the red hair and the blazing eyes of their enemy. As his body shot through the portal and landed on the other side at Fox Manor, he felt Winnie's fingers slip through his. Taking his heart with her.

He blinked. Heart racing, stomach twisting. Mind replaying those moments in a loop.

"No!" Rubbing the onyx pendant, he envisioned London once more. No matter how hard he tried, he couldn't seem to open the portal back up.

"Where's Winnie?" Tara screamed.

"She was right behind me. Boudicca got her right as we were about to leave," he cried frantically. "Tara, try yours!"

She reached for her own necklace, standing in front of the portal squinting in concentration. "It's not working! It's like it's closed or something! We have to get back to her!" Tears welled in Tara's eyes as she cried out.

Off to the side, Winnie's parents ran out followed by Mohini. Horace paced in circles, rubbing his temples feverishly.

"That wasn't supposed to happen," he muttered in a panic.

Kane's attention snapped toward him.

"Where's Winnie?" Ernest asked, eyes flashing between the three. "Where's my daughter?"

"Horace likely got her killed with his ridiculous plan!" Kane shouted, rushing toward the Lycan.

Horace returned his accusations with a growl. "Maybe if you hadn't led those damned things right to us, she would've gotten back safely!"

"That's it. I'm done with you, mutt," Kane bellowed.

Lunging toward the man, enraged siren songs escaped him once more. Reaching for the Lycan's throat, he pummeled him into the ground. As the vibrations reached Horace's ears, his face shook and eyes rolled back into his head.

Kane's song continued to infiltrate Horace's mind, feeling the snap of a vine reach for his body. Thrust into the air, they held him high. Milicent stood in front of him, eyes panicked and seeming to search for answers.

"That's enough! We've been through this before, Kane! Stop acting childish and help me open this damn portal! I won't let my daughter die!"

The siren shook his head, ceasing his songs at last. Horace cleared his throat, taking a seat as Mohini rushed to her husband's side.

He lowered onto the ground, the vines retreating back into the earth. Following behind Milicent to the altar, anxious rage only built.

"Let's pray she can hang on long enough for us to get through," she said at last.

—•((●●●))•—

WINIFRED

Winnie's feet hung in the air, upside down as if she were cattle ready for slaughter. The blood in her body rushed to her face, her head heavy and dizzy. *If I hang upside down any longer, I might be sick,* she thought with a shudder.

"Winifred," Boudicca sang. A group of hellhounds huddled underneath Winnie's body, jumping and snapping at her as if she were a snack.

"Cut it out, mutts! Leave us," Boudicca scolded.

Obeying their queen, they filed out of the alley leaving her alone with the deranged woman.

"I've learned a few things from our chats," Boudicca began, circling Winnie as though she stalked prey. "My blood coursing through your veins allows me to gather all sorts of wonderful information."

"Let me down!" Winnie shouted through gritted teeth.

"I began to wonder," she continued, ignoring the request. "What would happen if I got some of your blood? We've been having an awfully hard time penetrating the walls surrounding your lands. Every time we think we're close, the location seems to slip through our fingers."

Winnie's face went pale, despite the blood rush, thinking of the carnage that would happen if Boudicca and her beasts managed to get onto their estate.

The queen took a dagger from its sheath and prowled toward Winnie. She trembled as the cool blade rested on the tender skin of her throat. Her heart sounded thunderous beats through her body as the metal dug into her skin. Not enough to kill but enough to intimidate.

"Better not do away with you just yet…In case I need you again," Boudicca mumbled. "Something small perhaps?"

Her eyes landed on Winnie's scarred forearm from the initial injury. The midnight blue swirls surrounding it slithered away, fleeing the blade as Boudicca moved toward it. With a purposeful stroke, Winnie's blood ran freely. The queen laid the dagger onto her own arm, a twin wound sliced before holding their forearms together.

When the woman's blood touched Winnie's skin, a spine-chilling cry escaped her, so loud she wondered if they'd be able to hear her through the closed portal.

Centuries of rage coursed through her veins, every image

Boudicca had ever seen flashing through her mind. Tears welled in her eyes. She'd felt what the mother felt when she was given the visions of the battle. Then the attack. But to see it all… Her entire life in mere seconds. The pain was too much to bear. Strangely, the queen seemed to weep as well.

"You've lived a great life. Your sacrifice will not be in vain," Boudicca whispered, holding the blade back up to her throat.

Still reeling from the memories, the pain, something inside Winnie stirred. No, *burned.* All those years watching General Paulinus's lineage from Oblivion, waiting for the final call she needed, Boudicca's anger festered. Putrefied into something inhuman. Winnie felt the power inside her charging, ready to explode.

A violent cry sounded, echoing through the streets once more as a wave of flames emanated from her body. The walls singed, a blast of fire catching the queen off guard long enough for Winnie to tumble to the ground.

Moments of confusion gave her what she needed to make a run for it. Reaching the portal, it opened just in time. *I don't know if I did that or if my family back home reopened it.*

She leapt through, the jump feeling different this time. The second her feet hit the grass of Fox Manor, she turned to close the portal, though she realized it had never opened to begin with.

Seeing the familiar sight of her family home, the weight of pain and anguish fell heavy on her, tumbling to the ground and falling into darkness.

KANE

The group stood around the altar, attempting to summon another portal.

"This is taking too long!" His words shot at Milicent. "I can see you're trying, but it's useless. Damn coven magic requires all participants. You and I both know that you can't reopen it without Winnie."

Milicent stood at the center of the altar, eyes watering.

Ernest rushed to her side as she rubbed her head breathlessly. Sharing a quick, quiet conversation, the two seemed to scheme ways to get it back open without their daughter. Wesley approached the two, adding to their muted conversation.

At once, the hair on Kane's arms stood up, a strange feeling washing over him. A sense of familiarity, a closeness that surprised him. He turned, a curiosity pulling him toward the front of the house.

Darting, he rounded the corner. Just as he turned, he saw her. Winnie, he thought gratefully. *She's alive. Thank every God and Goddess in this and every universe, she's okay!* She stumbled, falling to the ground as his feet pounded on the dirt leading to her.

Not far behind, the rest followed suit. Sliding next to her, Kane reached out and pulled her into his arms. She seemed weak, but alive. Her pulse strong – too strong it seemed. He could feel her racing heartbeat through her skin.

"You're burning up," he mumbled, placing the inner part of his wrist on her forehead. Grabbing her decorated arm, he realized it wasn't the familiar slithering navy veins that printed patterns on her skin. Instead, it was crimson and glowing.

Softly, he called out her name.

"She…has my blood." Her words were barely audible, a vacant stare searching the sky.

"Winnie?"

As her name escaped his lips, the wound on her arm sealed itself. Celtic swirls inked themselves into her skin, permanent and unyielding. Intricate and deadly beautiful, they no longer moved. Instead, they glowed like embers. Ready.

Milicent swooped beside him, examining her daughter. Ernest crouched on the other side.

"She did it… Boudicca joined their souls." Milicent's words

struggled to come out, hand hovering over her daughter's body. "I can feel her soul tied to our magic. Eventually she'll figure out how to get past our barriers here. We're no longer safe at the manor."

"I closed it… the portal. It's closed," Winnie said weakly. She struggled to sit up, though only fell back once more into Kane's arms.

"I'm not sure that's something she can do on her own…" Milicent mumbled more to herself than anyone else.

"We should get her inside," Ernest mumbled. His eyes avoided his daughter as he spoke.

"What of the blood curse? We need to fix this!" Kane's tone matched his accusatory glare.

"There's nothing we can do now." Milicent's words were barely audible over the sounds of Kane's heavy breathing.

Rage fired inside him once more. "What do you mean we can't do anything? We can always do something! We have to at least try!"

"I'm sorry, Kane. It's done. Their souls are eternally tied."

Her mother placed one hand on the siren's shoulder, the other on Winnie. Together they sat in solemn silence as if each waited for someone to break the stillness.

At last, he tucked away the anger within and picked Winnie up. Hanging on to that rage, he saved it. Hid it away knowing they'd need it in the coming days.

Passing Horace on the way in, he grumbled. "You're lucky she's still alive. You do something like that again, I'll finish what I started."

A spark of guilt flaring in the Lycan's eyes as he looked away.

"Stop that," Milicent scolded, pulling him inside. Leading him up the stairs, she added, "I'll get something for your wing. Take her to her room. I'll be right there."

I almost forgot about myself in all this, he thought. The realization brought a sharp string, adrenaline wearing off slowly as his heart slowed to a normal pace.

He laid Winnie down on her bed as she mumbled unintelligible words. Looking her over, he realized with great relief that there were no injuries anywhere else on her. Aside from the curse, she was in one piece.

Milicent entered once more, pointing to Tara's twin bed without a word. They sat in silence for several moments while she worked on healing his wing before she finally spoke.

"What you did to Horace was childish. You know as well as I do that those kinds of behaviors are what got you in trouble the last time. We can't turn on each other right now. His Lycan are all we have."

"I'm sorry," he said at last. Memories of the night Winnie came back with a bruised cheek and tear-stained eyes reminded him of the hurt he felt the night he and Thoren were banished. "He almost got your daughter killed tonight," he reminded.

Milicent released a sigh. "I know."

As she continued tending to his bullet wound, he told her what he saw. His voice shook as he described the sheer number of hounds lurking with the factory.

In disbelief, a tear escaped Milicent. "Afissa said they can't help us right now. She wouldn't tell me why. But it sounds like our only survival relies on her army. Ernest and I need to pay them a visit ourselves. Try to convince them to help us."

Kane nodded as she finished applying the last layer of healing ointments.

"Try to get some rest. Don't mess with the wound. The bullet cleared straight through so it should heal up quickly. It shouldn't impact your flight once it's restored."

He offered her small thanks before she left.

That night, Kane stayed with Winnie the entire time. *I can't leave her. I don't want to take my eyes off her for a single second. I have to know she's okay,* he thought. Belly down, he laid on the bed beside her. His wing would likely be healed by morning, the siren blood coursing through his veins allowing for quickened recovery.

Hours passed and sleep continued to evade him. All he could do was wonder.

What if she hadn't made it back? It would ruin him, he realized. I don't want to live in this world without her…

A few hours before sunrise, he was able to turn onto his side and move his wings just enough to lay comfortably. Scooting under the blankets, he pulled her in close. A silent tear escaped him as he held her.

Facing him, she seemed to nuzzle into his chest for comfort. *I don't think she even realizes how I feel about her,* he thought with devastating realization. Regardless, he could only thank the universe and everything in it that they were spared for at least one more day.

31

WINIFRED

*W*innie *looked around. Where am I? The place looked familiar, but somehow felt like a distant memory.*

The answers just barely out of reach. She blinked her eyes... tried rubbing them. Everything around her was blurry. Like looking through a telescope out of focus.

She examined the landscape. Tree line, burning leaves falling from the sky. Those same leaves drifting into pools of blood. Water–the lake, only the wrong color. Crimson, she realized, like the puddles she saw laying about.

Behind her, a house. Set ablaze. Silently, the flames consumed it.

My home, *she thought.* This was my home.

She walked to a pool of blood and touched the glistening surface. A face peered through the puddle, the features indistinguishable. Slowly, it became twisted and distorted – crying out in pain.

She didn't know this one.

Moving on to the next, she found another faceless, unnamed body. She didn't recognize that one either. And another, and another. She came across one, the body of a wolf, the soul of a human. This one belonged to Boudicca.

Hearing a branch snap behind her, she turned quickly in fear. Ezra and Wesley stood close by, their faces twisted in terror and pain. Beneath their unusually pale skin sat darkened skulls, as if stamped for Death. They reached to her, though she was too afraid to take their hand. Too afraid to know what was to come.

"Winnie," she heard softly behind her. The voice was familiar and pleading.

She turned, only to see Kane lying on the ground. His wings were torn to shreds, a heaping pile of flesh and blood.

Thoren stood next to him, looking at her. He was emotionless, merely pointing at his brother, then to her. She felt an invisible spear of blame come her way. Attempting to run to Kane's side to check on him, her feet were stuck in mud.

Not mud, she noticed.

Looking down, her feet sunk into the ground. Hands grasped her ankles, pulling her into the earth. Who's hands, she wasn't sure. Just those of the dead. She could feel the pain they'd suffered course through her as if it were her own.

Attempting a scream, nothing escaped her lips. Wesley and Ezra snapped to her in attention.

"You can save us," Ezra rasped softly.

The hands dragged her further and further beneath the earth as she listened to his words. Blood pooled around her, ready to drown her in her own guilt.

"How?" she mustered, gasping for air and attempting to free herself of the vicious hands that held her.

Ezra opened his mouth to answer, but at last the hands pulled her in with one more swift motion. The last thing she heard was the menacing cackle of Boudicca as she drowned in the blood of those she couldn't save.

Winnie's eyes jutted open, looking around in a panic. *I'm in my room… I'm alive.*

For what seemed like an unlikely moment, all was calm around her. Arms wrapped around her waist, though she didn't feel trapped. A walnut wing draped over her, a reminder that it was just Kane.

Gently, she ran a curious hand over his feathers. The small

touch on his wings woke him in what seemed like a frenzy. "Winnie?" he muttered, blinking wildly trying to force himself awake faster than his body would allow.

"I'm here," she whispered softly as she turned toward him.

"Good morning," he sighed, settling as her amber eyes met his.

"I've never seen them like this before," she said, still carefully caressing the wing draped over her.

"It's not normal to have them out unless fighting," he admitted. "Sirens see them as a weapon after all."

She pulled him in tightly, bodies pressed together as she lay thinking about her dream. It didn't feel like just any random barrage of images. She knew what that was. She'd had nightmares like that before – messages sent straight from Death. A strange side effect to her sensitivity to the spirit realm.

"How could you do that to me?" Kane's voice ripped her from her thoughts.

She scooted back a little to see him better. "Do what?"

"You sent me back. Without you. I couldn't get to you," he began, trailing off.

"I couldn't stand to see you hurt," she murmured, reaching up and cupping his cheek softly.

It felt so strange – such an intimate touch. And yet so normal at the same time. Like it was always meant to be this way. He closed his eyes with a scowl, leaning into her palm in comfort.

"I thought I lost you…"

Curious fingers left the sides of his face and ran through his hair. His eyes examined her curiously, as if unsure what she was doing. Quickly, she withdrew her hand from the silken strands, softer than she'd expected them to be.

"I'm sorry," she said with a small nervous huff.

Rather than let her touch escape, Kane grasped her hand. Bringing it to his chest, he scooted onto his elbow with glittering eyes that beamed down on her. The butterflies in her chest sank to burning embers, her core heating and threatening to engulf her entirely.

He peered down to her lips. In an instant, his gaze returned back up and she could feel the draw. The pull. He leaned down slightly, mere inches away from what seemed like a kiss. Time stalled, her heart pounding in her chest. In a moment that she'd regret for years to come, she turned her face to examine him more carefully. Not fully comprehending what he was doing or how badly she wanted him to fully plant his plump lips across her own.

Hurt stung his eyes, shooting back away from her. "I shouldn't have…" he stuttered, pulling himself free of the blankets that held them closer together. Jumping from the bed, he darted for the door.

"Wait!" She cried out, trying to untangle herself from the sheets.

He paused, though couldn't seem to bring himself to turn. At last, she stood before him once more. Her chest ached to feel the warmth of his body against hers, her brain fighting the realization she knew deep down but hadn't come to accept.

"What was that? Were you about to…"

"No," he nervously chuckled, cheeks flushed. "That's not what I was going to do. You should get some more rest." He fumbled with his words, body antsy to escape.

"Kane, what's going on? You're been so strange the last few days." Looking back on this moment years from now, Winnie would recognize her naivety in the situation. But for now, her mind only clung to the idea of their childhood friendship and the reminder from past loves that she was unworthy of anything more than a simple companion.

"I was really worried about you. That's all." Nervous eyes avoided her gaze as he rubbed the back of his head.

"Do you…have feelings for me?" At last, the words she'd been thinking came out.

"You know that I care about you, yes, but…" Once more, he tripped over his own tongue. Unable to speak and flustered, his face only reddened more.

"Care about me *how?*" Her tone was insistent. Deep down, it was obvious. But she couldn't fathom why he would possibly feel that way about her of all people.

"I need to go…"

Pushing past her, Kane stormed off.

"Wait!" She called out to him once more, but before she could say another word, the door was already shut. Left alone in her room, the emptiness weighed her down. Made her realize just how lonely she suddenly felt without him near.

KANE

*Y*ou *idiot!* He scolded himself internally, rushing down the hall. *She's one of your best friends! How could you do that? What if you ruined it all?*

He wasn't sure where he was going. It wasn't until his feet dragged him into the kitchen that he realized he was hungry. *I felt something there. I think she did too… Maybe I didn't ruin anything.* Trying to reassure himself, he heard the sounds of Ernest and Milicent's voices coming from the sunroom.

"Good morning, dear. Is she awake?" Milicent's tone was cheerful, though her eyes revealed anxious fear.

He nodded, unsure what to say.

"Let's take a look at that wing of yours." She offered him a warm smile as she rounded toward his back. "Incredible! I'm always so fascinated by siren healing. The wound is completely gone!"

He offered her soft thanks, avoiding her gaze. *You can never trust a clairvoyant when you're trying to hide something,* he thought.

"Give her some time," she began, placing an encouraging hand on his shoulder. "She doesn't see it yet, but I do. She's still too clouded by what happened with Samuel and Beatrix to realize the truth."

"I'm not sure what you mean."

"Yes you do." A soft chuckle followed her sure words. "You forget I see it all, Kane. I'm aware of so much more than people realize. Much to my dismay."

Looking past her in an attempt to avoid her all-knowing stare, he examined the gear sitting on the coffee table. It took a moment before he recognized what it was.

"Is this the breathing equipment you've always talked about?" He directed his question to Ernest who stood silently looking out over the lake.

"Mhm," he mumbled. "I'm hoping it still works. We haven't used 'em in several years."

"You're headed to Marvivia then?" Kane asked, running a hand down the sides of the rim.

Two sets of golden breathing apparatuses sat on the table. The lines of the dommed, clear helmets were intricately carved with runes and symbols. Magic embedded the metal, he could feel it. Just placing a hand on it, the familiar feel of Caelus and his air element whispered to him. A set of singular fins sat next to the breathing gear, floppy material crafted to aid in faster travel.

"We have to convince Afissa's army to help us. It's our only chance." Milicent nibbled at her cuticles nervously.

"Will it be dangerous? Do you need help?" he questioned, sensing the tension between them.

"More than likely. They have a hefty selkie problem. Plus her husband is one of the most unreasonable creatures I've ever met in my life. But we only have breathing gear for two. They're rather private and don't like strangers. It's best if the two of us go."

Both pulled on tightly fitted one-piece suits, shimmering just as Afissa's corsets always did. Similar in color to abalone seashells, the clothing glittered in the morning sun

"Keep an eye out for everyone while we're gone, will you?" Milicent asked, offering him a pat on the arm.

He nodded carefully. "Aren't you afraid Boudicca will strike now that she has Winnie's blood?"

"I've seen what happens. We still have some time left."

"Care to share your visions with the rest of us? It could help us prepare better." Kane scoffed a little.

"It won't change the events either way. Plus, some things Fate won't allow me to share. Just keep training. And be sure no one kills anyone while we're gone."

Grabbing the remaining gear, Milicent and her husband trudged toward the family lake. Kane knew the portal was located down there. *I don't remember how many times Thoren, Wesley, and I tried to swim down and go through that stupid thing,* he thought. A small chuckle escaped him, remembering how wonderfully stupid they'd been as young teens.

The thought of his brother triggered an instant panic. Remembering how betrayed Winnie felt about Thoren and Ezra, he wondered if his brother would be just as upset with him. Trudging back up the stairs toward their room, Kane's mind only raced.

32

EZRA

Panicked knocks sounded outside Thoren's door. Ezra lay curled up beside him in bed, sharing tender kisses as the morning sun beckoned them to get up.

"I never want to leave this spot," Ezra whispered, heat flushing his cheeks and warming his insides.

Thoren's hands stopped exploring beneath the covers, grumbling as the knocking continued. "Go away!"

"Brother! I need to talk to you!" Kane's voice sounded from the other side of the door.

"Can't it wait? We're…busy."

Ezra leaned back, watching as Thoren's eyes darted between him and the door. Teasing fingers ran along the siren's body, eagerly waiting for his older brother to leave them be.

"Oh…um, well. It's rather important. I guess I can come back…"

With a heavy sigh, Ezra motioned for Thoren to get the door. "I'll still be here when you get back."

His lips hovered over Thoren's, each word another temptation to stay. Ezra offered a swift kiss and a gentle nudge before the siren groaned and finally got out of bed. Euphoric bliss spread over him as he watched his lover dress quickly.

As Thoren opened the door, Kane pushed past him. His eyes seemed wild, darting around anxiously. Landing on Ezra as he pulled a sweater over himself, the older brother's face blushed.

"Oh…busy. I didn't think… I don't know why I assumed…" He shook his head.

"This is the most I've ever been embarrassed for someone else. What the hell's gotten into you?" Ezra asked, examining the siren carefully.

"Did you think we were studying in here? What do you want, Kane?" Thoren's arms crossed over his chest, foot tapping impatiently.

"I need to talk to you about something important. Alone." His eyes flickered toward Ezra in bed.

A lull passed before he finally got up. "I needed to go see Winnie, anyway. I'll see you outside?"

As he passed, Thoren nodded his head. Moments later his eyes returned to his brother in annoyance as Ezra closed the door behind him. He stood for a second outside, unabashedly eavesdropping. Though Kane's voice was low and mumbling, he could make out a few words. Winnie's name was the first thing he heard. Then a sharp laugh from his love.

"It took you this long to realize?" Thoren's voice echoed into the hallway, Kane shushing him swiftly.

I know exactly what he's talking to his brother about, Ezra thought with a chuckle, heading toward Winnie's room.

He knocked carefully, the sounds of shuffling on the other side. Winnie opened the door, her eyes seeming to drop realizing it was him.

"Expecting someone else?" Ezra mused.

Her eyes met his once more, her face softening. Suddenly, she leaped forward and pulled him in for a close hug. Tears streamed down her face as she embraced him.

"Hey, calm down! What's wrong?"

She pulled him into her room, closed the door, and then once again snatched him as if her life depended on that hug.

"I'm so sorry, Ez!" Every sob echoed through the room.

"Why? What are you sorry for?" He pulled away, grasping her

by the shoulders to meet her gaze.

"I was so cruel to you. And Thoren. I…" Waves of sadness drifted off of her, eyes red and face glittering with tears.

His gut turned in knots, never having seen her so distraught.

"Winnie, take a deep breath. There's no need to be sorry. You were in shock and reacted. That's all. I said things I regret, too," he mumbled, pulling her back into his arms.

Gently, he squeezed her. Softly shushing, he waited for her tears to cease until only small sharp inhales came from her mouth.

"I heard about the mission from Tara. About the blood curse. Are you okay?"

"I can feel her slithering around inside me. The curse…it draws out all the worst parts of me." She pulled away, taking a seat in front of the fire and gazing toward it. Stretching her arm out, the navy lines on her cursed arm glowed like the coals in the fireplace.

He took a seat next to her, examining it and unsure what to say. "Well, on the bright side, it looks truly badass. Though I doubt your mother approves of her perfect daughter having some ink."

She didn't return his smile or chuckle, only seemed to stare right past him.

"There are no 'worst parts' of you to draw out, Winnie. You're in your head too much."

"You're wrong, Ez. There's so much darkness inside me, I feel like it'll eat me up some days. I'm not a good person…"

His heart sank. A long sigh escaped his lips before speaking again. "We all have darkness. We all say and do things we don't mean. That doesn't make us bad people. Hell, even Boudicca had her reasons. I'm sure, deep down, she was once a good person, too." He placed an encouraging hand on her shoulder, unsure if he should pull her in once more or give her space.

"I don't deserve any of you… Every last one of you loves me more than I've earned." Her head dropped to the fiddling fingers in her lap.

"Don't you dare say that." He grabbed her face, forcing her to look at him. "Look at me and *hear me*. Your brain is playing tricks on you. I know where this is coming from – and none of it's true."

She scoffed, pulling away.

"What you're feeling is regret and shame. I know it all too well. Somewhere along the way, someone told us we shouldn't be ourselves and we took it to heart. And now, we think that every little mistake is the end of the world and that we're only proving that person correct. But you have to realize that your mistakes don't define you."

Another tear rolled down her cheek.

"I'm not someone capable of being loved. Fate has proven that over and over. First Samuel, then Bea. Even my own friends. I just hurt people. The seance, the attacks, all of this. It's my fault! You getting hurt. *My fault!*" Her gaze shot to the ceiling as if trying to find the answers from the heavens.

"You are the farthest thing from unlovable. You have an entire family downstairs, myself included, that's ready to go to war with you. For you." The conversation came to a halt, Ezra peering over her curiously. "Besides, the seance wasn't your fault either. If you remember, you didn't want to do the ceremony. You only did it because I insisted. So blame me. I'd rather you do that than continue to let this eat away at you."

She turned back toward him, eyes softening. *I'm getting through that thick skull of hers,* he thought.

"I don't want any of you risking yourselves for me. It's not fair to any of you."

"You don't get to make that call. No one is forcing us to be here with you. Face it, Winnie. We're ready to go to hell and back because we love you. Kane more than any of us."

Her eyes sparked at the mention of that name. "I just feel so guilty…"

"Well stop. Accept it – you're stuck with us. Just because some asshole told you that you weren't worthy of love doesn't mean you have to believe it. Eventually you have to learn to forgive."

Her gaze dropped away from him once more. "I'll never forgive him."

"I didn't mean Samuel. Or Beatrix for that matter. I mean *yourself.* I've watched you, every day, beat yourself up over every little thing. You seem to think everything is your fault. You put way too much pressure on yourself, keeping everyone at an arm's length because you're too afraid to let in any true emotions. At some point you have to realize that you didn't do anything wrong."

"Why does it sound like you're speaking from experience?" Wiping away a tear, a small smile finally formed on her face.

"I felt the same way for a long time. Still do on occasion. But ever since that healing circle, things have just made sense. Something clicked." He released a lazy shrug.

"I'm sorry I didn't see it. Didn't see how badly you were hurting. I should've paid better attention."

"There you go again – blaming yourself." A small chuckle fell from both of them. "Everything happens the way it's supposed to. There's no use dwelling on it."

"I think Kane has feelings for me…" she seemed to blurt.

"You think?"

She whipped a tear away, smile dropping as she looked at him in disbelief. "What does that mean?"

"If it's taken you this long to realize that, then you're blind. I could tell from the moment I saw you two together."

"Can I be honest?" Her voice was merely a whisper as she leaned in close.

He nodded, crouching down to meet her face to face as she revealed her truth.

"I think I have feelings for him too. But…why does it feel so wrong?"

He chuckled. *She must really be blind to love to only realize all of this now.* "For the same reason you blame yourself. There's nothing wrong with the feelings you have. Again, forgive. You don't have to forget, but you do have to let go."

She nodded. "I'm really happy you're here. And I'm so happy you found Thoren."

"I didn't know it was possible to be this happy." A dimpled smile spread, his heart fluttering and cheeks blushing a little as he thought of his newfound love.

"When I see you two together, it's like you're made for each other. You've seemed different since the circle. Just in general. More content and at ease."

"I had the strangest dream while I was unconscious. I think I actually died for a minute there. I could feel my heart stop. But I saw a woman who brought me back. She was made of tiny creatures and greenery. When I saw her, it felt like the heat of the sun fell on me. It felt like I was finally home. Like I'd found my purpose."

As he explained, Winnie's brows furrowed in confusion. "It sounds like you met Ina." A look of curiosity spread across her face as she examined him. "Have you felt different in any other ways since you've come back?"

"No, not that I can tell. I feel less anguish, of course. But other than that, I'm still just me." He shrugged, taking a stand to pace. His mind raced back to the woman he'd seen, remembering her serene beauty.

"If that changes, tell me. It's a rare occasion to meet the Gods themselves." She stood to pull on a jacket over her trousers and sweater, lacing up a pair of boots.

"Are you going out to train?"

She nodded. "My mother left me a note that said to keep practicing. I have to figure out how this blood curse will impact my powers now that Boudicca is permanently attached."

He nodded, escorting her out of the room. As they walked silently down the hall, they could hear the sounds of an argument coming from downstairs. They looked at one another in confusion before following the sounds of shouting.

"That's the dumbest thing you've said to me, Tara. Even dumber than your little stunt with the bar," Thoren spat.

The redhead stood in front of him, arms crossed over her chest and Cricket seated before her, growling. The hair on the mutt's back stood straight, reacting to his owner's frustration.

"I saved you! How are you going to turn on me?" Thoren peered down at Cricket, placing a gentle hand on the dog's head as he shushed him.

"Everything okay in here?" Ezra asked, wandering to Thoren's side.

"This one wants to celebrate Samhain." An accusing finger pointed at Tara.

"I think it's a brilliant idea! We're going to have a few dozen Lycan running around. They'll need entertainment." As she argued, the reds of her cheeks flushed in anger.

"What's wrong with celebrating Samhain?" Winnie asked innocently, taking her friend's side.

Thoren scoffed. "We can't throw a party knowing Boudicca could burst through the wards at any moment."

"Kane just said…" Tara's eyes flared in anger as she was swiftly interrupted.

"I know what he said! Milicent says we have time," he mimicked with a grumble.

"Then it's settled. We ensure everyone is armed just in case, and celebrate!" Winnie's smile finally returned, the anxious negativity in her stomach simmering away and replaced by excitement.

Thoren only seemed to growl in disapproval as the group wandered toward the sunroom exit. Outside, she could see Kane and Melinda sparring. Horace, Mohini, and Wesley stood to the side, watching and laughing as she knocked him to his butt.

"They've been going at it for a while now. I don't know who trained her but she's one of the best fighters I've seen in a long time," Tara said, hooking Winnie's arm with her own and leading her outside.

Winnie exited with the others just as Kane and Melinda started another round. She took a seat with her friends, watching. As her eyes met with the siren's, another swift kick to the jaw brought him back down to his knees. She winced, thinking to herself: *I think I may have distracted him…*

Melinda took a cocky bow before helping him up.

"I want it notated that chivalry is, in fact, not dead…" he said through exasperated breaths. He walked toward Winnie, taking a defeated seat next to her on the ground. Panting, he offered her a smile as he nursed his sore cheek.

"Who wants to go against me next?" Melinda asked, arms outstretched and gesturing for the others to come up to her. Her breath was heavy, but she looked ready regardless.

She pointed toward Wesley who quickly declined with a laugh.

"I'll go," Tara said, jumping with excitement.

"We're in for a treat. Of all the people I know, Tara is ruthless when it comes to sparring," Winnie mumbled to Kane.

"I'll go easy on you," Melinda mocked, circling the redhead.

"As will I." She flicked her long braid over her shoulder, tightening her jacket to ensure it didn't get in the way.

Back with Winnie, Cricket fidgeted in his seat. She shushed him softly, trying to calm the shuck as he watched his owner prepare for a fight.

Melinda's eager fists lunged forward, a low growl escaping her lips. Tara held her distance, guiding the girl's fist away from her. Melinda received a swift punch to the jaw, and Winnie could tell Tara hadn't put her full weight behind it. The girl didn't back down however, swinging once more.

The redhead grabbed hold of Melinda's arm, placing a firm hand behind her stretched elbow. "If I were to push right now, your bone would shatter. Don't be so eager to charge," Tara coached.

Melinda snatched her arm back, shaking her body as if to clear herself from the small embarrassment.

"Again," the redhead barked.

"I haven't seen warrior-Tara in a long time," Winnie mumbled to Kane.

Melinda circled around her, the two looking each other up and down as if trying to anticipate the other's next move. As Tara's fist raised to strike, Melinda successfully dodged. She swung around back, kicking at the redhead's knees. With a grunt, Tara returned to her feet instantly.

Impatience grew in the young woman's eyes as she waited for Tara to strike. Unable to wait any longer, she distracted the redhead with a false punch, only to land a swift kick in the center of her opponent's chest. The group watching let out soft gasps, knowing the hit had to hurt.

A few more rounds of punching, blocking, and dodging continued. Their abilities seemed evenly matched, Melinda and Tara both skilled and fierce. Unwilling to yield.

"Who do you think will win?" Winnie leaned down once more to Kane.

His eyes met with hers, a wry smile greeting her. "My money's on Tara."

Winnie looked at the two fighting, each throwing blow after blow.

"I don't know. I've never seen Tara take so many hits. Melinda could win," she said softly.

"Loser has to make dinner for everyone tonight," he wagered.

They both nodded in agreement, turning their attention back to the two women fighting. Tara threw a leg up once more to strike, though it was swiftly snatched. Melinda grasped her firmly, tossing her onto her back. Cricket watched as his owner lost her balance and landed with a heavy thud.

"I think you're making dinner," Winnie teased quietly.

"Not so fast…" Kane mumbled, eyes fixed on them.

Melinda turned, arms outstretched in victory. The fight seemed over until Tara smirked and swung her leg under the girl. Only moments passed before both regained their positions. Tara lunged, her shoulder meeting Melinda's ribcage. She released a slight moan of pain and readied herself once more.

She swung her leg high and kicked Tara in the side of the face. It took the redhead a moment to recuperate before landing two swift kicks to Melinda's gut then nose. It only seemed to anger the girl.

Swiftly, Tara rolled over to where a baton lay on the ground. Melinda seemed to egg her on, a look in her eyes that screamed, *'I don't need a weapon to defeat you.'*

Tara lunged at her, baton outstretched and ready to strike. The girl dodged, grabbing a hold of the stick and swinging the redhead's body toward her so that the baton lay flat across Tara's neck. Attempting to pull away, Melinda's grasp on the weapon was too tight.

Placing her foot on the edge of Tara's knees, she taunted. "If I were to strike you like this, you'd never walk again."

Instead of releasing what would have been a devastating blow, she snatched the baton from Tara's hands and whacked her on her upper back. Finally giving up and laying on the ground, the redhead looked to the sky in defeat with a smirk on her face.

"You know what you're cooking?" Winnie mused. Kane merely sneered at her.

Though Tara was down, she was determined to get one last shot in. Swinging her legs under Melinda, she knocked the girl onto her back with a wicked laugh.

"Damn lass, you're tough." Belly laughs escaped Winnie's friend as she peered toward their guest.

Melinda chuckled, turning to her side. She helped Tara up, both looking each other up and down to ensure no serious damage was caused.

"Technically they both lost so I think you should help me," he whispered to Winnie.

"I'd rather watch you scramble on your own," she joked, thinking back to his lack of skill when they were younger. "Also, don't tell Tara I bet against her."

His eyes lit up in playful wonder, just as they did when they were kids.

33

WINIFRED

Later that day, the sky set leaving only the pale moon in its wake. Each member of the house retired following an afternoon filled with training and combinations, eager to clean up. Winnie took a swift bath, excited for the evening ahead.

Dressing herself in a casual sky blue dress, she laced her corset tight and pinned her hair up as usual. *I don't want to seem too eager,* she thought as she examined her outfit. Thinking back on the more recent days spent with Kane, she could see it suddenly. The way they spoke to one another, like their souls knew each other from eons ago. More than friends, but never having given anything a chance due to troubles of the past.

She exited her room, passing his on her way down. The lights were off and she could hear clattering from the kitchen below. Entering, she noticed the variety of ingredients strewn about. He paced back and forth between bundles of potatoes, carrots, broths, flour, bread, and seafood. The siren's eyes jumped from one thing to the other as if trying to rack his brain.

"I know I said you're on your own, but you already look lost," Winnie teased as she took a seat across from him at the bar.

"My savior! Here to do more than just make fun of me, I hope." A wry smile sat across his face, pointing to the potatoes. Handing her a cutting board and knife, he added, "You start peeling and chopping. I'll prepare the rest."

She looked over the ingredients once more, carefully gliding the blade along the skins of the potatoes. "Is this the same stew your mum used to make? The one your father's mother taught her after they got married?"

Winnie's mind thought back to the times she visited. A kind woman, Mrs. Falke was usually the loudest in the room and yet somehow the smallest. With a presence that commanded attention, she was the picture of siren beauty. Winnie remembered her thick, dark hair fondly, and deep russet eyes that seemed to analyze everyone so deeply when interacting.

There was a time when Kane's mother never missed a visit. Until she fell ill and the portal took too great a tax on her health. Memories of trying anything and everything to heal her strange illness pelted Winnie's mind, heat bubbling in her throat as she fought the sadness that threatened tears.

Kane flashed her a thoughtful smile. "You remember?"

"Of course. Your mum's cooking was incredible. She was the one that taught my British mother how to properly season food," she said, both chuckling softly.

Even in laughter, the word 'was' seemed to hit him like a punch in the face. He lowered his eyes, stopping a moment. "There's days where I don't think about my parents and the grief feels manageable. And even years later, there are days where I feel everything could come crashing down around me without them here." His smile faded, a slight gloomy scowl replacing it.

She recognized that feeling all too well. It was one of the reasons she'd wanted to host seances in the first place. A small spark or message from the other side was sometimes enough to ease that pain. Unsure what to say, she walked toward the music box at the side of the room. She turned on the song they always listened to as a kid, nostalgia chipping away at both their walls.

"I still love this melody," he mumbled, helping her peel more potatoes as his lips playfully hummed along.

"Me too…"

Their eyes met across the counter. He held her gaze for a few moments before she finally refocused on the vegetables in front of her. With a sheepish grin, she realized the true meaning behind the way he studied her so carefully.

They'd spent plenty of time around other young ladies during their earlier years for her to recognize his fascination now. But it wasn't the same as it was back then. The connection they shared, rooted in affection and pure adoration, went deeper than mere curiosity. And the warmth that spread through her made Winnie realize she shared similar sentiments.

"I've been meaning to ask," he began. She watched as his breathing quickened, creeks flushing a little. "I'd like to…court you. Formally. When all of this is over. With your mother and father's permission of course." Nervously, he looked back at her with shifting, fidgety feet. He seemed to hold his breath awaiting her answer.

Butterflies fluttered in her stomach as her own cheeks reddened and an uncontrollable grin formed. "I'd like that."

The tension in his chest seemed to ease as he sighed in relief. Before turning away from her, all he could do was offer her a feline grin. Then, he worked to coat a piece of fish in seasoned flour.

"The potatoes are ready," she said, taking a stand next to him in front of a large stock pot on the gas stove. She noted his hesitation for a moment, eyes fixed on the fish before him.

"Come look at this for me. Does anything seem odd to you?" Curious fingers pointed down at the filets coated in flour.

She peered around, sniffed quickly. Examined carefully for any strange colors or textures. "I don't see anything amiss," she started to say.

Just as she looked toward him, he smeared a line of sticky flour across the front of her face. Stumbling back, a shrill squeal escaped her lips as he clutched his sides in laughter.

"You have fish fingers!" Grabbing a handful of flour, she chucked it at him.

The white powder smacked him in the face, coating his stubble and lashes. "I think you got some in my ear," he laughed, reaching past her for a towel.

She snatched it, holding it away from him. His laughs lowered, reverberating through her and heating her to the core. *Goofing off with him feels like healing,* she thought to herself, still holding the towel away. As he reached again, she realized he was mere inches from her. Pinned between the counter and the man in front, she had nowhere to go.

Flour coated lips curved into another sly smile as his eyes landed on her mouth once more. Leaning in, she was ready to tiptoe her way toward him. *God, just kiss me already,* she thought as he slowly leaned down. His hand braced on one side of the counter, the other reaching for her side.

Time seemed to stall and all she could do was count the heartbeats in her chest, insides burning and mind stilling. As his hand gripped her waist, her breath quickened while his seemed to slow. Just as their lips sat inches apart, footsteps thumped down the hallway.

He jumped back, turning to see his brother standing in the doorway.

"What the hell are you two doing? I'm not cleaning this mess up like when we were younger!" Thoren scolded, pointing at the flour strewn about.

Winnie let out a heavy sigh.

"We'll clean up, don't worry little brother." Kane nervously chuckled, eyes resting on Winnie again. A longing sat behind them as he playfully snatched the towel from her at last.

Thoren took a seat at the windows, a book in hand as a pot of tea appeared in front of him. "Any word from your parents?"

"Not yet. They should finish with their meeting shortly. My mother promised to write as soon as they know for sure."

Winnie hopped on the counter next to the stove, watching as Kane shuffled around. As he worked, she watched him curiously. Counting the newly beloved details of his face, she memorized every detail. The small scar on his forehead, the slight creases around his eyes when smiling. The way his hands moved carefully, navigating the kitchen with greater ease than she'd expected.

"Make yourself useful, love, and cut up some bread," he teased, shooing her out of his way.

She giggled, hopping off and taking a seat at the bar once more. The nickname 'love' heated her insides once more. By now, he'd called her that a million times, but never had she clung to that word so carefully, wondering if he also called others by the name.

As he continued to work, others from the house eventually joined. Tara took a seat beside her, sniffing the air carefully.

"That smells incredible. Didn't think you had it in you to cook a decent meal." Her tone seemed harsher than expected, Kane glaring at her as he worked.

A small knock echoed through the kitchen. She knew that sound. Her heart raced as a cloud appeared in the center of the room, a letter floating inside. Tentative steps inched toward it, reaching with hopeful hands. Tearing the paper open, her eyes skimmed the page. No one said a word as she looked toward them glumly.

"Not good news, then?" Kane seemed to read her mind.

She shook her head. Fighting back tears, her throat burned. "They're alive and well. They've survived several Selkie attacks. But… Afissa's people can't help. They're too busy fighting their own war."

As she spoke, Wesley and Melinda entered from the side.

"What does that mean?" Her brother's voice faltered, glancing to Melinda in concern.

"It means we're outnumbered. And we don't have an army to help us…" Winnie felt like she'd choke on the words coming from her mouth. "I don't know why I was so naive to think they'd be the answer to our problems."

"So all we have is a few dozen Lycan?" Ezra asked, catching up with the conversation. He took a stand behind Thoren, bracing himself on the man's shoulders.

"And us…" Her words fell, the room stilling.

"We'll…" Kane began, though he didn't seem to know where he was going with his statement. "We'll figure it out. We have to."

"All of this for me," Melinda mumbled, grabbing a hold of the counter to ground herself.

"We'll protect you. Till our dying breath," Wesley whispered, placing a hand on her back.

A small nod followed from the rest of the group, though Winnie's eyes connected with Kane's. The night of Boudicca's visions reminded her what she'd said to him: *Maybe we should give her over.* As if reading her mind, he gently shook his head. Taking a stand next to her, he pulled her in for a tight hug.

"We'll make it through this." Only she could hear his words as strapping arms wrapped around her with a squeeze of reassurance.

34

WINIFRED

"I'm coming with you," Winnie insisted, glaring at Wesley and Kane. Their bags were packed, supplies ready and weapons in hand.

"No you're not. You have to stay here," Wesley commanded.

"Since when do you tell me what to do, *little* brother?" she scoffed.

Behind him, Ernest and Milicent paced back and forth. They seemed to be off in their own worlds since returning from Marvivia without an army. Horace's Lycans arrived not long after, settling into tents in front of Fox Manor. Standing on the family's stone slab altar, the sounds of a small militia training were heard. The clanking of practicing swordsmen reverberated to the back of the house. It wasn't much, but it was better than nothing.

"If Chicago is truly overrun, you're going to need an extra set of hands and eyes looking out for hellhounds. It's safer if I come," she retorted, her hands balled into fists. Slowly, the small sliver of Boudicca's attached soul riled up. The navy lines of her arm gleamed in the evening light, the glowing embers matching her temper.

"I can't explain how, but I know we'll make it back alright," Wesley tried to explain, though she had no intention of letting him win this argument.

To the side, Kane's eyes darted toward her glowing arm, at last finally joining the conversation. "We'll be in and out quickly. No need for backup. Melinda showed me her memories earlier – I know exactly where to go when we get there. Any sign of trouble, I can fly the two of us back to the portal." He placed a reassuring hand on her shoulder.

"The last time we said we didn't need backup, we ended up *needing* backup. We have to stop underestimating Boudicca's hellhounds."

"We'll have the cover of darkness, and Kane still has the glamor on his necklace from you. It worked well enough in London until he got too close. If we need to, we can fly overhead," her brother added.

Kane nodded, as if remembering the necklace still had that extra boost. He patted Wesley on the back, eyes pleading with her to understand.

"Remember how you felt when Horace wouldn't listen to you about his plan? This is what that feels like now," she muttered.

Kane's eyebrows furrowed before Wesley interjected once more.

"Mum shared some of her visions with me. I know we'll be fine…"

Her attention snapped onto her little brother. Before she could pester him further, their parents pulled their attention toward the ritual. Taking their usual places, each member of the Fox family played their role as the Falke brothers hummed their siren songs on the outside.

Winnie drew on Gali as usual, though she felt the struggle internally far greater this time. The Goddess's voice was with her, but muffled. Any use of her water element caused seething pain through her tattooed arm.

Boudicca's soul doesn't want me using my element. Doesn't want me at my full strength, she thought as she pushed past the agony. Each laid their offerings on the altar one at a time as the portal opened cautiously. Envisioning Chicago was easier this time, she realized. Having seen the place herself, she didn't have to wade through memories of drawings and photographs to see their destination.

Just as the portal opened, she glanced back toward the sunroom. Melinda stood at the door, her hand placed on the glass in worry. Behind her, Tara attempted to pull her away with a reassuring pat on the back. The girl could only stare, watching as Wesley and Kane prepared themselves to step through the shimmering light of the passageway.

Grabbing the bags of supplies, the siren's gaze landed back on Winnie once more, eyes locking together. As though he wanted to say something before he left, he couldn't seem to find the words. Hesitancy followed his stare back onto the portal.

At last, he turned toward Wesley. "Ready?"

Her brother nodded, fastening a pistol at his side. His face screamed of stress, but Winnie could tell he was doing everything in his power to hide it. A tight frown was joined by weary eyes that flashed between each family member.

As the two stepped through the portal, Winnie leaped forward – an act of impulse. She snagged onto Kane's shoulder, traveling behind him through the passageway to Chicago. As they reached the other side, he reeled around, his glare wicked.

"Are you out of your *fucking* mind?" His voice boomed through the street, reverberating through Winnie.

A small drop of hurt sat in the back of her throat, shocked by his outburst.

"I said I was coming with you!" She shouted toward him, Wesley shushing them both as he ran to the end of the alleyway. The buildings that stood previously now law in rubble around them, charred and crumbling.

Kane's temper matched her own as he glanced between her and the portal. When he didn't say anything, she glanced behind herself in confusion. Opening her mouth to speak, he silenced her with a lunge. Barreling into her, he scooped Winnie up over his shoulder.

"You're going home," he insisted as she thrashed.

"Put me down! You and I both know I can get out of this, but not without hurting you in the process!"

Just before the exit, knowing she was about to be sent home, she wrapped her forearm under his chin. Squeezing, she didn't put her full force behind it just yet.

"Winnie," he grumbled while the hold still held loose around his throat.

"Let me go or I'll start pressing harder," she ordered.

When he still didn't cease, her grip around his neck tightened making him drop to his knees. He fell on top of her, pinning her to the ground. Wrapping her legs around him, she thrust her hips forward and threw him off. Landing on his back, he clutched his chest and throat in surprise.

"Seriously Winnie? Why are you so damn stubborn?" he managed to choke out.

She scooted next to him, checking for a moment to ensure she didn't cause too much damage. "I told you, I'm staying. Even if you had gotten me through that portal, I would've just come straight back."

She got to her feet, helping him up as he continued to rub at his throat.

"I normally admire your strong will, but when it puts your life in danger it makes me want to murder you myself." Though he spoke through gritted teeth, she couldn't help but notice the crinkle around his eyes, hiding what would be a smirk if he weren't so angry.

"We have a job to do, remember?" she sneered.

She walked past him toward Wesley who still stood on lookout. Chicago seemed awfully quiet, the streets full of mere rubble and not a living soul in sight. When Kane didn't follow her, she turned. Realizing he was watching her as she walked away, she couldn't help but blush.

Mischievously, she sauntered toward him again and pulled at

his arm. "Watching me are you?"

"Always." With a smirk, he followed behind at last. "Don't think I'm not still mad at you for jumping the portal."

"Quiet you two," Wesley scolded.

Far off, howls echoed through the streets. As she glanced toward the racket, peering from one ramshackle building to the other, she noticed them suddenly. Faces, looking back at her. Souls standing in the remains of the burned structures. *The people we couldn't save,* she mourned.

"Shit," Kane whispered, the hounds getting closer. "The plan was to fly there with Wes, but of course you had to pull your little stunt."

A part of her took his blame like spears through the chest. She stepped back a little, her hurt visible on her face.

He shook his head apologetically as he realized. "I didn't mean…"

"You two go ahead. I'll hold them off." Straightening her back, she prepared for a fight. Reaching under her jacket, she pulled out a pistol and the dagger they'd gifted her as a birthday present.

A huff of laughter escaped Kane as he watched her prepare. "Of course you brought weapons."

"Would you expect anything less from her?" Wesley asked, his tone almost accusatory.

"I don't feel right leaving you here by yourself. We don't know how many there are," he added, grabbing her hand anxiously.

"Go. Get Melinda's family the supplies and protection they need. But hurry. I'll hold them off as long as I can. If things look too hairy, I'll go back through the portal."

Hesitantly, he nodded. "Give 'em hell, love."

A mere second passed as his eyes locked with hers once more. For a moment, the sounds around them faded. Her heartbeat stalled, breath slowing. *I should just do it… What if something happens? Just do it,* she coaxed herself. And yet, she could only offer him a nervous smile. Unable to summon the courage to do what she really wanted.

Glowing bronze eyes gleamed at her as his wings expanded behind his back. Before letting her hand drop, he offered it a gentlemanly kiss as if to say goodbye. Holding onto Wesley, the two took off into the sky toward Melinda's house. Before the glamor kicked into effect, she watched as he turned toward the howls of approaching hounds.

"Where are you going?" She shouted toward the sky as the two disappeared behind a cloud of magic. Only the stars glimmered back at her.

Down the street, she could hear the echoes of his siren song. Peeking past the buildings, she watched as the group of hounds huddled on the ground, some in wolf form and others still human. All clutched their ears, crying out in pain as his deafening melody took hold of their brains. When the pain wore off, a few turned their attention to one another and snapped wildly at their own pack members. *He's making them fight themselves, she thought. I didn't know he could do that...*

She heard the sounds of flapping wings zip by toward the opposite direction, knowing they were off. Inching her way behind rubble and debris in the street, she snuck up on the unsuspecting beasts. Too busy fighting each other, she got as close as possible.

"What the hell is wrong with them?" One of the females cried out to others in human form just as her own comrade lunged on top of her, ripping at her throat.

A group of two stood with their backs toward Winnie, eyes panicked and fixed on the deranged wolves. Targeting the biggest one first, she reached for her dagger. Carefully, she slithered behind him. A swift flick of her wrist and the man crumbled to the ground, the backs of his achilles tendon sliced. As he fell, the sharp end of her blade glided across the front of his neck.

The man next to him turned in shock, seeing her and baring his teeth. Though still in human form, his canines lengthened as he prepared for the turn. Calling on Gali to aid her, she envisioned a ball of water. Thrusting it toward him, she managed to create a bubble big enough to cover his mouth and nose. He writhed in place, digging at the water attempting to drown him. Thrusting the knife into his gut, Winnie ripped until his insides met the ground.

Releasing the ball of liquid gave way to such relief she wasn't expecting. Every ounce of water magic she conjured drew on her energy more and more. As if draining her, the use of Gali's gifts felt wrong now.

The last of the possessed hounds met their demise, the remaining survivors turning and noticing Winnie's presence. A female beast lunged toward her, arms reaching under Winnie and slamming her to the ground. As the attacker attempted to pummel her, Winnie snagged a handful of dirt and thrust it into the woman's eyes. The delay was just enough for her to reach for the pistol at her side, firing a round through the hound's skull.

Stumbling onto shaky feet, she let loose another round of shots. She'd never been one to prefer bullets over blades but with this many hounds, she couldn't be too picky. Beasts dropped to the ground before her as the bullets finally ran out.

A group of three more in wolf form stood ahead of her. One lunged toward Winnie, though she blocked it with a wall of water. The act alone burned her internally. *I can't keep using my element. I think it's killing me,* she panicked. Feeling the strain it put on her, Gali no longer answered her cries.

Before she could stop to think, the next was already on its way toward her. Leaping out of its way, Winnie struck from behind. Digging the blade of her dagger into the beast's skull, she ripped it out only to begin slicing toward the third. Yelps of pain escaped the hound's muzzle as she stabbed wildly.

Unphased by her slashing, the hound chomp at the length of her blade. Kicking at her opponent, just enough space formed between them for a final thrust of the dagger through its throat. The sounds of gurgling echoed through her mind, an uneasy feeling bubbling in her stomach.

I hate having to fight like this, she thought. Though something deep down seemed to revel in it.

Another set pounced toward Winnie simultaneously. As she evaded one, the other barreled into her. With lost balance, she fell to the ground. Both beasts morphed back to their human forms, grabbing ahold of her. She slashed at the wrists of one just as the other snatched her neck. He knocked her head back into the ground, the dagger falling from her hands.

For a moment, dark spots clouded her vision. Firm palms pushed down on her throat, cutting off her oxygen. She reached up, hooking her fingers around the backs of his ears. Driving her fingers into his eye sockets, the man screamed out in pain. The grip around her neck loosened as she arched her back and kicked him off.

Rolling, Winnie reached for her dagger. Her other opponent kicked it away, wrist bleeding and eyes filled with rage. Before a single thought could cross her mind, the tip of his boot met the side of her face. Forehead firmly pressed into the dirt, a broiling vengeance bubbled inside her. She gasped as another kick landed on her side, air alluding her.

Winnie could feel the skin of her tattooed arm burning, her jacket singing just below the surface. The hellhound reared once more to land another kick as she snagged his ankle. Pulling on every ounce of strength she had left, she shoved his leg toward him, landing on his back in an instant. Ripping her jacket off, Winnie realized why her arm felt so hot. A bubbling, molten heat burned from her tattoo.

Deep inside, she could hear a voice echoing.

"Do it…"

An unknown male voice boomed, the temptation to use the molten gifts overwhelming.

"Do it. Set yourself free. Use my gifts to save yourself…"

She could feel the deity slithering inside her mind. Like a nagging itch, his voice pestered. The heat fired in the palm of her hands, begging to be set free.

At last, she realized whose voice she was hearing. One she'd never heard before. A voice she'd only heard about from her brother and Thoren.

Aelius. God of Fire.

"I've been waiting for you," he purred.

35

KANE

Flying up ahead, his eyes continued to glance back. Eventually she was out of sight and Kane couldn't tell whether or not she was okay. *She's been training her whole life. She'll be fine,* he tried to reassure himself. Still, he hated the idea of leaving her to fight on her own. Worried he'd lose her like he lost so many other important people in his life.

His stomach churned anxiously as they approached the familiar sight of Melinda's street. She'd allowed him to use his siren song to see into her mind earlier in the day, though breaking through the young woman's mental walls was a greater feat than he'd expected. It took an extremely strong will to withstand siren magic.

Approaching a massive brick building, Wesley's eyes darted at him in confusion. "Are you sure this is the right place?"

Kane nodded. "This is the building she showed me."

Following the confused gaze, he realized why Wesley seemed so perplexed. A sign stood out front: Chicago Orphan Asylum.

"She mentioned she didn't have any family by blood. I didn't realize she lived at an orphanage," he muttered sadly.

The siren motioned forward with his chin, in a hurry to get back. Four stories high with several sets of windows out front, the brick building was truly enormous. It stood tall and strong, the buildings a few blocks away scorched from the treacherous fire that thankfully never reached the orphanage.

Carefully, Wesley knocked on the door. Not a single sound was heard from the other side, though a slight glimpse of movement was seen. Wesley peeked through the large windows before calling out.

"Anyone in there? Miss Leona? We're here to help! Melinda sent us!"

Kane shushed him quickly, worried more hellhounds could be lurking nearby. Though the entire block seemed lifeless, the shadows had a way of hiding evil.

The lock to the door opened swiftly, a hand reaching for Wesley's shirt and tugging him. The arm reached again, grabbing Kane and bringing him inside as well as a woman locked the door behind them. She was much older, her hair graying and eyes tired from stress. Wearing a modest nightgown and robe, Kane noticed a large cross around her neck.

"Praise God! You're here," she cried, reaching out to the two men and embracing them. As she reached out, she brushed up against Kane's wings. Backing up in a panic, her gaze appeared petrified. "A living…*angel.*" Her words choked out of her mouth as though she didn't believe what she was seeing.

"Not quite," he rushed. "We don't have much time. Wesley – fill her in. I'll start placing wards."

"What is he doing?" she asked, looking to Wesley for answers.

He tried to offer her an encouraging smile though her worry superseded his charm. "Melinda sent us. We bring supplies and protection," he explained, handing her an enchanted bag.

"This bag is…small. This is all you brought? Do you know how many men, women, and children have been living here since the fire?" The woman's voice crackled in distress.

Kane scoffed, entering the next room to begin his work. As he applied runes, he heard bits and pieces of their conversations in the foyer.

A low gasp came from the woman as the siren stopped, peering over in the hall. He chuckled, seeing Wesley try and explain the aspects of magic that allowed a month's worth of food for hundreds of people to be stored in such a small tote. Bringing out handful after handful of food, the woman looked like she could faint.

"And what is he doing?" She rushed into the room Kane worked, disapproving huffs following behind almost every word.

Before Wesley could try to explain, she shouted at the siren.

"Get down this instant! I cannot allow witchcraft in this Asylum! If the Matron were to find out, I'd be thrown to the streets for sure!"

"We don't have time for this," he grumbled. Glancing toward Wesley, the boy instantly seemed to know what he was thinking.

"Follow me, ma'am," he said, grasping her arm carefully.

Guiding her back to the foyer, her skittish breath slowed and seemed to calm. The siren sighed in relief, continuing to apply symbols along the walls.

Gently, Winnie's little brother explained the wards to the woman. "It's only some prayers," he explained, guiding her to have a seat.

"And this will protect us?" she asked sweetly, her tone entirely different.

Wesley nodded.

"So kind of you two boys to come all the way here and offer us protection and supplies." The anger in her face dissipated, replaced only by relaxed euphoria.

Kane finished the last of the wards above the windows at the front before heading to the room on the other side of the foyer.

"What's your name dear?"

"Wesley. And that's Kane," he mumbled as the siren walked by.

"It's a pleasure to meet you nice boys." Her sweet tone matched the fluttering of her eyes as she carefully crossed her arms over her lap.

Finishing the last of the wards, a burst of power emanated through the entire building. Kane re-entered, watching as the older woman wandered up the stairs and toward the sounds of snores.

"How long will that trance last? We can't leave her blissfully unaware of the dangers outside." Kane's nervous feet tapped, anxious to leave.

"It'll fade the second we're out the door. She won't remember the wards at all. Only the supplies."

"Good," was all he replied as he pulled Wesley from the orphanage.

Snagging his wrist, the siren pulled them back into the sky. Howls and cries reverberated from down the street, though Kane couldn't tell whose they were. As they bounded toward Winnie's location, he watched in horror as swirls of fire danced and rained down upon the hellhounds of Chicago.

—•‹‹●●●›)•—

WINIFRED

Pulling on her water element had been like running with strained muscles in recent weeks. Gali's voice muffled through her mind, the relationship between them strained. A year of inconsistent practice, time spent away from her family, and it felt like the water goddess had given up on her.

The sound of Aelius's voice through her mind melted into her subconscious like butter, the power of fire tempting her. Ready to explode, she felt lava coursing through her veins as the God of Fire coaxed her to use her newfound magic. Whether these new gifts came from the deity or Boudicca, she didn't have time to contemplate as more and more beasts attacked.

Another small group of hellhounds joined, the last of the previous batch writhing in pain on the ground. Flames burned behind Winnie's pupils, a living torch ready for a fight. A hound leapt toward her, though the mere touch of her hand landed the beast yowling in pain as it reduced to nothing more than ash.

The strain of using such potent fire magic drained her instantly, but the fury of Boudicca's spirit didn't seem to care. That same nagging vengeance danced on her tongue as she released a blood curdling cry – a ring of flames shooting from her body and encompassing the beasts before her.

One stood in human form, blocking the wall of fire with a shield made of air. As their magic met, her flames only burned brighter and hotter, pulling on the beast's magic. *That's the first hellhound I've seen with elemental magic. I didn't know that was even possible,* she thought.

Only one hound stood between her and that final victory. The man twirled his wrists before him, a swirl of funneling storm clouds forming above her. Winnie could feel herself lifting into the air, her attacker waiting below to end her. Struggling against the force of the wind that carried her, Winnie couldn't seem to free herself.

Drawing deep within, knowing this was the last hound left, she drew on the well of powers inside herself. The shared magic between her family members. With a blink and a strange all-over tingling sensation, she was suddenly no longer in the air. Instead, she stood behind him. Too confused to understand how she got there, she reached out. As her flaming tattooed arm touched his shoulder, he too reduced to ash in seconds.

She rubbed her temples, confusion washing over her. *I was in the sky one second, then behind him the next. I've never been able to teleport like that. What's happening to me?*

Behind her, the sound of feet thudded on the ground. Turning wildly in a panic, she shot a ball of fire before realizing it was Kane and Wesley. The siren placed a shield between them, blocking the attack just in time. Her heart sank as she watched her uncontrollable magic almost kill two people she cared about, feeling like she could pass out realizing it was done.

"Winnie! Are you okay?" Kane rushed to her side, examining her. Grabbing the side of her face to examine her bruised neck, he retreated immediately as though he'd stuck his hand in a furnace.

"They got a few good hits in, but I took care of it." She felt like the flames still burned inside her, anxious rage festering.

His eyes darted around, seeing the mangled bodies of hellhounds strewn about the street. Those same hazel gems then landed on her forearm, still glimmering like embers waiting to cool down.

"I don't know why I was worried about you," he joked.

Hesitantly, he touched the skin of her arm. His overall calm wore off on her, the bubbling temper inside simmering until her body was merely warm to the touch, no longer molten. At last, he pulled her in for a tight embrace, cradling the back of her head tight to his chest.

"Let's go home," she whispered, pushing toward the portal. She clutched at her ribs in pain, realizing they'd done greater damage than she initially thought.

Far off, another wave of hellhound howls sounded.

"We need to hurry," Wesley urged.

The three of them sprinted toward the portal, Winnie wincing in pain as she stumbled home. Leaping through, they once again stood on the stone of the Fox family's altar. Swiftly, each member got into position to close the portal.

"I cannot believe you would do such a reckless thing!" Milicent scolded after the passageway closed, grasping her daughter's elbow firmly. As her mother's arm touched her skin, a look of alarm darted toward her tattooed forearm.

"I know it was reckless, but I don't really care. Melinda's family is safe and we all got back in one piece," Winnie retorted, pulling from her mother's grasp.

Limping toward the house, she ignored the voice in her head. The sound of Aelius applauding her for her victory. The words of a darker deity than she'd ever worked with before. Though her water magic was powerful, it wasn't explosive. Never had she been so consumed by destructive energy.

As she walked, her eyes landed on the woodline. The usual mass of fluttering tiny fae didn't glitter like they normally did. Stumbling around as if they were drunk, their lights faded in and out. *This is my fault. I used dark magic, and now the land is paying the price. What will this do to me when all of this is over?*

36

KANE

Winnie's zombie-like movements toward her room caught Kane off guard. He'd seen the bruises around her neck, the way she clutched her sides in agony. *She can handle herself, but someone got a few good swings at her,* he thought as he cautiously followed her upstairs at a distance.

Standing outside her door, he waited a few moments. *Do I knock? Go inside? She knows I can heal her...* A few stalled seconds passed when a careful fist rapped on the door. It creaked open, Winnie's amber eyes peering through the slit. They seemed to soften when she saw him.

"I'm fine," she muttered, attempting to close the door.

Placing his hand in the small gap, he pushed his way into her room. She'd removed her corset, wearing only her trousers and a loose shirt over her upper body. The whites of her blouse were covered in soot and blood, though he wasn't sure whose it truly was.

"Let me see," he said gently, lifting her shirt with careful fingers.

She flinched as the fabric moved aside, revealing purple bruises along her ribs.

"Have a seat, I'm going to heal you." He attempted to guide her toward the twin bed in front of the fire, though she pulled back.

"No." Her face was in a tight frown, stubborn as ever.

"What do you mean no? You need healing!"

"I deserve these wounds. They should heal on their own time."

Walking to her armoire, Winnie removed her family pendant and earrings, unfurling her dark curls.

Kane scoffed. "Deserve them? What are you talking about?"

"I used dark magic tonight. I think I tapped into Boudicca's powers. When I did, I felt Aelius revel inside my mind. I did exactly what they wanted me to do."

"I saw you using fire magic, but that doesn't make it bad. Thoren and Wes both use fire, and they're not evil. It's just an element. It isn't darker than the other three," he tried to explain, but it seemed to fall on deaf ears.

"You've never wielded fire. It consumed me. Until I had nothing left to give."

He took a stand behind her, hands placed gently on her shoulders. Looking at her through the mirror, he watched as her eyes avoided his.

"You don't deserve to spend the next few weeks in agony when we know the queen could attack at any moment. Let me heal you." His voice faded softly as she turned toward him.

Those auburn irises gazed up at him and he felt his heart could explode. Deep within, he felt the burning need. Wanting to reach out and kiss her so badly, he held himself back. If only to focus on healing her.

When she didn't answer, he made the decision for her. Pulling her in close, he wrapped his arms around her. Humming their favorite song, the tenor notes reverberated through Winnie. As the healing started, she clutched at the fabric of his shirt. *Healing broken bones isn't painless,* he reminded himself when worry threatened to take over.

As the song finished, a thankful smile fluttered back up to him. The bruising on her neck faded, her stance easing. Only blood and soot covered clothing remained as a reminder she'd been in a fight at all. Time slowed as their eyes connected. Her hands lay delicately on his chest now, mere inches separating them.

Kane's breaths matched her own, slow and deep. Nervous

flutters beat in his chest, mimicking the strange sensation he felt when flying straight down toward the ground. Almost as though he were falling. Pure adoration washed over him in waves as he watched those heavenly eyes roam his features. First they darted to his lips carefully, then examined the rest of his face before meeting his gaze once more.

Gently, he reached toward her. Placing a strong hand on the side of her face, his thumb carefully caressed the cheek that was no longer bruised. She closed her eyes, leaning into his touch as her breath quickened once more.

"Every moment we spend apart, I can only think of getting back to you. Your smile. Your laugh," he began, brushing his thumb across her lips as they quivered. "Even if you're just in the other room. I've never known a single person who makes me lightheaded with nerves. No one's ever seemed worth it. Two years away were far too many. I don't intend to leave you ever again."

Grabbing a hold of the hands that braced herself against his chest, he brought them to his lips. Offering a soft, tender kiss to each, she broke free of his grasp to place her hands around the back of his neck. He felt he could stop breathing all together as the beats of his heart intensified, her grip firm and pulling him closer toward her face.

Foreheads pressed together, he could feel her breath on his skin as their noses touched. She nudged him softly at first, as if asking permission to give into the desire that had been slowly building. He wanted desperately to surrender to the magnetic energy that pulled them together.

"I should go," he muttered, though he couldn't bring himself to move.

"Please…stay." Her eyes squeezed shut as if trying to trap him in her mind. Exploring hands glided through his hair just as they had the other morning. Curious and gentle, they searched for something he wasn't sure of.

"If I stay, we can never go back to what we once were," he

whispered.

Her face turned to a scowl, her grip only holding him fast against her. "I don't want you to go."

"Trust me, I can't fathom why I would. I don't think I can ever go back to pretending I'm not brazenly in love with you."

"Just kiss me already," she mumbled with a huff of needy frustration. Her eyes flashed open in an instant, guiding his lips to her own. At once, they slammed together. Heat burned within as her tongue danced with his, a ferocity he hadn't expected. Like she'd been longing for him just as much as he'd craved her.

Reaching around her waist, he pulled her into his arms. Effortlessly, they seemed to fit perfectly against one another. Guiding her toward the armoire, he placed her on top with a light thud. Nicknacks fell to the floor as she shoved them away, her other hand gripping his hair firmly. Their heartbeats synced, bodies pressed together when her legs wrapped around his midsection. Exploring hands grazed his muscled body, his own hands exploring beneath her loose blouse.

Winnie pulled away for a moment, the inches apart feeling like miles. Hopeless longing pulled him toward her again as he craved her lips on his own, watching as they curved into a feline smile that threatened to engulf him entirely.

"You cannot comprehend how long I've been wanting to do this," he whispered, planting another peck on her cheek.

Slowly, his kisses trailed down her neck and over her collarbone as soft whimpers escaped her. At last, the sound of his name on her lips drove him mad with longing.

"We should stop…" Cradling the back of her head, he pulled her in for another kiss. Softer this time. Long and drawn out, he didn't want to part from her.

As if reading his mind, she mumbled softly, "Please don't go."

"We should do this the proper way. I am, first and foremost, a gentleman." A teasing lilt sat in his voice, enjoying seeing her squirm a little as he pulled away.

Pleading eyes begged him to stay, her hands still interlocked with his as he backed toward the door. A coy smile sat across his face, playful and flirtatious.

Hopping off her armoire, she moved to stand between him and the exit. "You're going to leave now? Just like that?" Her brows furrowed in frustration.

"Oh, I rather like seeing you like this," he teased with a chuckle, twirling a stray curl around his finger. "I'll see you in the morning, Winifred." Grabbing her hand gently, he offered her one last kiss before turning to leave.

A long, deep sigh of frustration escaped her as he stood in the doorway for a moment, memorizing the wild ringlets that hung down her back and the glittering light of the fire reflected in her amber eyes. The small smirk she tried to hide on her face as she watched him made Kane question every decision to leave.

"Please stay." This time her words were less of a plea and more of an order. Still, he resisted.

"Goodnight, love." As his feet exited the room, he felt his heart rip apart. As if left behind with her, he no longer felt whole without her pressed against him. How he'd managed to hide these feelings deep down all these years, he wasn't sure. But seeing her yearn for him settled his mind enough to know that at least his love was well-placed, guarded by one of the fiercest women he'd ever come to know.

WINIFRED

Waking the next morning, she felt like she was stepping into a new world. Never in a million years had she imagined she'd be falling for one of her dearest friends. She found herself lying in bed, reliving that kiss, fingers pressed against her lips as if to feel the warmth of him again. Her body and soul ached, knowing he was only a room away and yet he wasn't there with her.

As she dressed herself in a casual gown of earthy greens and browns, the sounds of her favorite song – their favorite song – drifted toward her. Only different than she'd previously heard. An occasional sour note snagged her attention, wondering what on earth was going on.

Her curls bounced down her back as she followed the sounds toward Kane's room, a curiously nosey ear listening in. A note or two sounded just as the recording did, followed by clumsy hands that didn't get the notes quite right.

The door creaked open as she peeked inside, witnessing him in front of the window hunched over a piano that looked like it'd never been touched before.

"Since when do you play?" Her words startled him as she stepped inside carefully, shutting the door behind her.

Panicked eyes settled when he realized it was Winnie. "I don't know that you can call what I'm doing 'playing' but nonetheless I try."

As he chuckled, the sounds echoed through her and her heart swelled. She walked to his side with careful steps, almost as if she didn't want to get caught in his room.

"Ironic, isn't it? A siren with no musical talent. During our time apart, I tried to learn our song. But these damned fingers don't seem to work the way I want them!"

Our, she thought. *Not his or simply mine. But one we share.* Butterflies fluttered in her chest once more and her mind stilled. Any company she'd taken since Samuel had only ever left her shaken and unbalanced. Even Beatrix, who'd seemed like a kind and gentle soul until her betrayal, had never had the same effect. But he was her peace, she realized. Even since they were children. He was the breeze on a summer's day. The wind picking up her favorite autumn leaves. The calm after the storm.

"I'm sure your fingers work just fine," she said with a playful smirk.

Something in his eyes darkened at the sentiment. He reached

for her, pulling Winnie into his lap as they sat before the piano. Mere inches apart, she could feel his heart pounding beneath his chest as her hands lay delicately on him.

"Did you sleep well, my love?" he asked, planting a soft kiss on her cheek.

She closed her eyes, a huff of tension escaping her lips before reconnecting with his gaze.

"I thought of you all night," she whispered softly, hovering over his mouth if only to tease him.

"Dream of me, did you?" His words were taunting and playful as one of his hands reached up and coiled a few stray curls.

As he spoke, the nightmares she'd had the night before pelted her. Tore her away from his touch. Reminded her of the pesky messages from Death she shouldn't ignore.

"Kane, I think Boudicca's close…"

Her words pulled him from his trance. Though he'd previously been enamored by the sight of her rosy lips, he now furrowed his brows in confusion.

"We knew she'd make it through the wards eventually."

"I think," she began, unsure how to confess. "I think something's going to happen to you. In this fight. I saw you…"

He cut her off immediately. "Nothing's going to happen to me."

She wasn't sure who he was trying to convince. Though he spoke confidently, his eyes revealed a hidden sadness she probably would never have noticed if she weren't sitting so near.

"Please don't ignore my visions," she pleaded.

"I'm not. I've noted them in my mind. When the fighting starts, I'll be extra careful. But if I have you at my side, no one can stop me. Not Bouddica. Not her hellhounds. No one." A sad smile sat on his lips.

Leaning in, she cupped the side of his face. His heart still beat thunderously beneath his chest, but as their lips met it seemed to slow. Steadily, he calmed beneath her touch. When she finally backed away, a deep long sigh escaped her.

"I suppose my visions aren't like my mum's. Perhaps Death is trying to warn me so that I can actually stop it," she mumbled.

Moments passed before they wandered downstairs to get breakfast. Arm in arm, the two giggled discussing anything and nothing all at the same time. Most still slept soundly in their beds, or so it seemed. A pot of tea sat on the kitchen counter as they entered, waiting for someone.

She poured two cups, Kane standing close behind. As he guided her dark locks away from her neck, the mere touch of his breath on her skin set her ablaze. Fighting every instinct to turn around and wrap herself around him once more, she merely poured the tea.

"That was supposed to be for Ezra and I," Thoren said, entering from the sunroom, his voice playfully chipper for so early in the morning.

Winnie jumped aside, away from Kane. Oh my, in all of this I haven't even thought about Thoren. *I made such a fuss about him and Ezra. What is he going to think when he finds out?*

Trying to hide a smirk, Thoren sauntered toward them both. With a playful nudge, he pushed the two together. He let out a sigh before saying, "No need to hide your closeness around me. I think I knew before you did." Stealing the cups she'd poured, he left through the sunroom once more.

"I told him what I saw in the circle," Kane confessed. "After I realized how I felt, I confronted him. Told him of my feelings. He merely laughed at me and proceeded to call me all sorts of names, insinuating my daftness."

"Ezra said he noticed it, too. How did they see it before we did?" She scoffed, grabbing two new mugs for them.

"It doesn't matter. All that matters is now."

He jutted his chin toward the outside, ready to join his brother and Ezra. As they stepped through the doors, Winnie was reminded they'd invited a few dozen Lycan to stay on their property. She heard the sounds of their muffled voices long before she ever saw the first ray of sunshine across her face.

The sight was jarring – dozens of fighters training early in the morning. At the front of the house sat rows of tents, fires simmering and breakfast in large stock pots. At the back, they trained. Readying themselves for an outnumbered fight. Though the Lycan were no army, they were no strangers to a brawl.

Thoren and Ezra sat with Tara outside, watching as the Lycan trained. Cricket ran wild laps around the yard, letting off some early morning steam and howling with the Lycans.

"Did you make your own tea this morning?" she asked, taking a seat at the table next to Ezra.

Without enough seating, Kane plopped down in front of her on the ground.

"I think the house is a bit stretched thin. It didn't respond when we asked, so I did the mundane thing for once and made it myself," Thoren muttered with a slight grumble.

Tara pulled her attention away from the training Lycan when she realized her friend had joined. "We're going to get ourselves in trouble tonight, Win." A feline grin sat on her face, ready to blow off some steam just like her dog.

"*You* can get yourself in all the trouble you want."

Her friend turned, noting the closeness of Winnie and Kane with wide eyes. A happy squeal sounded as she clapped in delight.

"Shouldn't they be conserving their energy?" Ezra questioned, a scowl on his face.

"They're warriors, moró mou. Not everyone tires as quickly as you," Thoren teased, offering him a wry smile.

"What did you just call me?" Ezra scoffed.

"I called you a giant baby," Thoren retorted with a smirk.

"Don't let him fool you, Ez. He's a big lush. That's the same nickname our mother used to call our father. It's actually quite sweet in Greek," Kane explained, settling Ezra's mind.

Taking a sip of Thoren's brewed tea, the man's face turned to a grimace. "You're truly terrible at brewing this stuff. I've tasted Bethnal Green water that was better than this."

"You can't be bad at brewing tea. It's water and leaves!" Thoren rolled his eyes, taking the cup and chugging it down himself.

"What's happening tonight?" Winnie asked, directing her attention back to the redhead. She took a sip of the tea as well, making an equally puckered face before handing her cup to Thoren to finish.

Kane chuckled, his brother making eye contact with him as if to say, *'Can you believe these two?'*

"Winifred Lucille Fox! How could you forget? Tonight we begin our Samhain celebrations! It's fire night!"

"I still think celebrating when Boudicca is just around the corner is a bad idea," Thoren interjected.

Kane nodded in agreement, Winnie's eyes lowering sadly. The images of her dream reminded her that they were not safe – no matter how hard she tried to tell herself they were.

"I hate to admit it, but he's right. I can feel that Boudicca is close. She could come through any moment." Winnie silently pleaded with Tara to have some sense.

"I don't care where this bloody queen is! I want to celebrate. These Lycan need entertainment. We owe it to them to have some semblance of normalcy. I will not let her take that from us," she argued, her Irish accent getting thicker as she became more riled up.

"Can we not do both?" Ezra suggested, the group turning to look at him. "We celebrate, but we're also ready for her. Everyone is mindful of how much they drink – careful not to go wild. We keep weapons on us. If she strikes, we'll be fine."

Thoren grumbled. "If we must…but it seems reckless regardless."

"Don't be such a downer, little bird. And make sure you have a costume and mask ready," Tara teased. Her hands clapped in delight once more, eyes returning to watch the Lycan train.

There was a moment of pause before Thoren finally spoke again. "Perhaps there's a way to ensure our safety in all of this."

The group turned to him in confusion, unsure where he was going with his statement. It took a minute before he finally explained, letting the group in on his plan.

37

WINIFRED

"**B**efore anyone says a word, I need everyone to just let me explain," Thoren began, placing a steady hand on the kitchen countertops.

The rest of the Fox family and their guests stood around, some seated and some pacing. Winnie sat on a barstool, Kane at her side, the two exchanging careful glances as his brother schemed.

"You're going to want to argue with me. But just let me explain first," he continued, his eyes locked specifically on Kane.

"Well spit it out already!" he scolded in typical brotherly fashion.

"As ridiculous as celebrating Samhain sounds," Thoren began. Tara moved to interrupt, but he held his hand up and rushed to grumble, "I also understand it's important to some of you."

The redhead offered him an approving nod, her arms crossed over her chest as though she were ready to argue at any moment.

"We have to accept that we are in danger, however. Celebrating without knowing where the queen is, is reckless. It's asking for trouble. We may as well hand Melinda over and call it a day if that's the plan."

Melinda shifted nervously from one foot to the other, taking a seat alongside Winnie who merely offered her a sympathetic pat on the back.

"We won't let anything happen to you," she reminded the young woman, who returned the favor with a soft, quick smile.

"So what do you suggest?" Ezra asked.

"Winnie – you and Boudicca have been connected since the beginning. You're the reason she's here; the reason she possessed that woman in the first place," Thoren reminded.

"Yes, please rub it in, why don't you?" she grumbled.

"No *arguing* until I'm done!" he hissed. "This connection. Surely there's a way you can use it to our advantage."

Milicent stepped in immediately, cheeks flared in motherly worry. "She cannot rely on this connection! The blood curse is already strong between them. Should she try to reach out to the queen, it may only make their link more powerful."

With a slight growl, Thoren continued. "We cannot sit here and do *nothing*. Winnie has the ability to see where Boudicca is."

"I don't think I can do that. She's always been the one to reach out to me," she reminded, feeling utterly useless.

"She's come to you in dreams," Kane reminded. "Was there anything special or different about what you saw?"

"They weren't dreams, technically. She always met me in Oblivion. It's where I sometimes go during seances when I want to talk to the dead," Winnie explained.

"The fact that you entertained this woman to begin with is precisely the reason we're in this mess," Milicent countered, arms crossed and pacing. Her eyes couldn't settle anywhere in the room, darting from one member to the other.

"If you've met her in Oblivion before, you can do it again," Thoren suggested.

Frustration brewed inside, Winnie's tattooed arm blazing. "And what am I going to do? Ask her nicely not to come kill us so we can have the night off? That's not going to work!"

"Can you, for one second, just try to make this work rather than shoot down every idea I have?" Thoren clenched one fist on the counter, back hunched and rubbing his temples.

"Is there no magical way to simply spy on her?" Tara asked, stepping forward at last.

"How did you find out about Melinda? I saw you and your mother performing some ritual the day after I got here," Ezra asked, moving to Winnie's side as though merely his presence would reassure her.

"Mother – you were trying to have a vision. I just happened to speak to Mary's spirit. I doubt Boudicca will let her leave again like last time."

"Can you try to have a vision again? So Winnie doesn't have to rely on the blood curse?" Kane asked, directing his attention to Milicent.

Her face was twisted in a tight frown. "I've already tried. Fate has already given me all they're willing to regarding this situation."

"Why is everyone acting like this blood curse is the end of the world?" Horace chimed in, stepping in from the sunroom with Mohini just behind him. "Pardon our intrusion, we're just catching the end of your conversation."

"It's called a curse for a reason. It's literally rendered me useless with my element," Winnie reminded.

"False. The way I see it, you've simply traded. Rather than water, a more passive element, you've gained fire which is destructive and powerful. That seems like a bonus to me. You're pretending that this thing with Boudicca will destroy you when in reality it's only made you stronger," he finished.

"Maybe I don't want to be destructive. I liked using water. It was familiar," Winnie retorted with an eye roll.

"Let's face it. Boudicca has been spying on you for weeks. It's time to return the favor. If you want the upper hand in this fight, which we're outnumbered for, you're going to have to play the game just like her," Horace finished saying.

"We could turn the tables – have the upper hand. Know what to expect," Thoren agreed, nodding alongside the Lycan.

"Have you ever tried astral projection? It would allow you to see where she is," Mohini added, walking to the edge of the counter alongside everyone else.

Winnie shook her head. "It's not a skill I was born with. I can only speak to spirits."

"This is not something one needs to inherit. It's a skill you learn. I've been able to astral project for years now. With your ability to transport yourself into Oblivion, this should come as second nature," she explained.

"There's too many risks associated with astral projection," Ernest chimed in at last. "I've seen what it can do to those that don't know how to come out of the trance. They become vegetables!"

"I think you should do it."

The group turned in shock toward Milicent, who at last began to side with the others. Even her father's face stood still as a statue, examining his wife as though she were someone he'd never met before.

"It's not something she has to do alone," Mohini noted, directing her gaze toward Ernest. "I can travel with her, guiding her and ensuring she comes back safely."

"I don't know about this…" Winnie mumbled, burying her head in her hands. "This all feels like it's resting on me. If I fail…"

"You won't fail. You can do anything you put your mind to," Thoren retorted, placing his hand on top of Winnie's.

"Wow, that was actually rather encouraging," she chuckled.

"Thanks. It sounded like something Ezra would say. Figured it would help a little." Thoren offered his love a wry smile that was returned with a smirk and slight disapproving stare.

"No one is forcing you to do this," Kane reminded, placing a loving hand on her back. "This is your choice. If you don't feel comfortable, then don't do it."

Thoren shot his brother a glare, though Kane merely ignored him.

"I'll try. For everyone's sake." At last, Winnie nodded before taking a stand. "Let's get this over with."

The rest of the house retired to various pockets, some joining the Lycan outside to train and some retiring to their rooms for relaxation. Winnie and Mohini prepared the family library for the attempted astral projection, pulling the curtains low to block out as much light as possible.

Knowing that she needed a place to lay down where she'd feel the most comfortable, Winnie pulled her reading hammock to the center of the room before the fireplace. Surrounding the chair, Mohini placed frosty crystals of selenite and clear quartz to aid in concentration. At last, it was time to begin.

The other members were instructed to remain outside, given that Winnie needed her full concentration to pull off such a large jump. Though she'd technically astral projected many times to Oblivion, she'd never chosen her location. She'd only ever been guided by Death to the place between, where spirits awaited her. This would be a much greater feat, requiring her body and mind to be in a state of complete euphoric relaxation.

"Remember, I'm right here. Should you need something, follow the sound of my voice and the tether to your soul," Mohini explained before they began.

Laying down in the hammock, Winnie placed her palms over her heart. Outside of the circle, the woman's soft voice soothed her, lulling her to a near state of unconsciousness.

"I want you to picture a glowing white light. Imagine this light surrounding each part of your body individually, inviting relaxation and content."

Winnie did as she said, beginning with her toes and working her way up to her head. Just as Mohini's words soothed her, she felt her body slowly turn weightless in response. With each second that passed, she faded into a state of higher and higher relaxation, until she could no longer feel her body.

"Open your eyes," Mohini whispered.

As she did, Winnie realized she was no longer in the hammock. Instead, she watched as the woman stood outside of the circle, her body cradled in the fabric. Looking down at her body, she realized she had none. Only a shimmering outline of her essence, floating above the ground and free to move about however she pleased.

Turning to exit the library, Winnie stuck her head into the hallway. Outside, Ernest and Kane paced anxiously awaiting good news.

"Don't stray too far. You need to focus. You can explore later." Mohini's voice rang through her mind, pulling her back into the library.

Winnie opened her mouth to ask a question, though nothing came out. And yet, the woman still managed to respond.

"To find Boudicca, focus on your connection. You two share the same blood now. If you follow her essence, you'll find her."

Winnie glanced back down at her body, noticing a silver tether that connected her floating spirit to the figure laying in the hammock. Concentrating on the queen, another chain formed, glowing golden like the sun. It led away from the library, through the walls and into the unknown.

"Yes, follow that," Mohini coached.

With a nod, Winnie did as instructed. Following the golden glow, she felt her essence part farther and farther from her body. Seconds passed, but it felt like a lifetime following that strand. Across expansive bodies of water, Winnie finally landed back on land, though her soul continued to trek forward.

At last, she found herself surrounded by the familiar rubble of Chicago. Glancing around, she realized the tether still had some ways to go. Past Chicago and into the surrounding woods, Winnie followed the line until she found herself surrounded by hundreds of tents.

Camp fires were strewn about, all manner of hellhounds seated around and chatting as casually as the Lycan did at her own estate. Some sat around, cooking food for the masses while others gathered supplies in the surrounding wilderness. A few practiced their sparring, even fewer working to conquer gifts given by the elements. Just past them, she found herself entering an altar that nearly mimicked her family's.

Though it wasn't made of stone, the dirt of the forest floor was packed down and carved to match many of the symbols of the Fox family. *She's definitely working with a coven,* Winnie thought as she examined the intricacies. Just beyond her, Alaric appeared from his tent, walking to the center of the circle with a deep blue aura surrounding him.

Quickly, Winnie retreated behind a tent. It took a few moments before she remembered he couldn't see her. From inside the tent that she hid behind, another young woman exited. Winnie couldn't see her face, only noted the long raven strands that hung down her back, similar in color to Alaric's. A kindred aura glowed around her, deep purple and haunting.

The glimmering tether to Boudicca suddenly glittered brighter, the queen rounding the corner and joining Alaric and the mystery woman. As the queen's feet met their altar, her attention snapped to Winnie.

"Do I sense a spy in my midst?" Boudicca sang.

Though their eyes seemed locked, Winnie couldn't tell if she could actually see her.

"Who is it?" Alaric growled, looking around the campsite in anticipation.

"I sense her. Winifred. She's watching us. Clever little girl, that one."

As Boudicca searched around, Winnie's stomach stirred anxiously.

"Come on out dear. There's no need to hide. You could join us, you know. We're going to do incredible things!"

"Get rid of her!" the mystery woman shouted. "We can't risk them finding us. We need to find them first!"

As Boudicca's gaze continued to rake over the campsite, Winnie felt a tug on her own silver laced tether. Mohini's voice was muffled, inaudible from where she was. Knowing her time was likely running out, she turned to head back toward the manor.

From behind, she felt a strange presence all at once. Turning one last time, she noticed her. Boudicca, though not in her physical form. Her astral form, staring directly at her.

"And where are you off to?" she mused, head cocking to the side in playful fierceness.

Winnie opened her mouth to respond, though once again nothing came out.

"Haven't quite figured out how to do all of this, have you?" the queen asked with a chuckle. "You'll learn. In time. I hate to admit it, but I've grown fond of you during our time connected. You should join us. We'd love to have another witch in our coven."

Boudicca motioned toward Alaric and the mystery woman, standing around Mary's unconscious body. Winnie shook her head, turning and ready to dart away from the queen. As she did, the feeling of the woman's essence hot on her tail singed her. Pulling as hard as she could, Winnie pushed harder and harder to make it back to her body before the queen could catch up.

At last, Mohini's voice came through in her mind. "Kick her out! Stop focusing on the link so she can't follow you back!"

Unsure how to do that, Winnie tried to break the connection. The golden glow to Boudicca's tether lightened, but didn't fully dissipate. As her soul crossed back into the safety of her warded home, she stopped just on the other side. There, the queen's spirit floated. Watching her through the wards that surrounded the family's estate, she merely waited.

Winnie shuddered, turning back toward the library. More than ready to be reunited with her physical flesh, she trudged as fast as she could toward the hammock where she lay. At last, she saw herself. With a deep sigh, listening to Mohini coach her, she opened her eyes once more as anxious hands touched her physical form, thankful she'd made it back in one piece.

38

WINIFRED

Throughout the house and estate, everyone prepared. After Winnie's successful astral projection, the Fox family felt it was safe to celebrate for at least one night. They weren't blind to the fact that Boudicca was close, however. Tomorrow, the actual night of Samhain, the veils between worlds would be at its thinnest. They would lower the wards then, on their terms, to end things once and for all. But for this last night, they could celebrate.

The announcement of Samhain brought everyone to cheer, from the members of Fox Manor to Horace and Mohini's Lycan. The thought of spending a joyous evening celebrating properly was a welcomed distraction. However, everyone was instructed to stay armed and ready, just in case.

Upstairs, Winnie attempted to get ready for the evening's celebrations.

"Go!" Tara shouted, ordering Kane to leave the room. He stood in the open doorway, bracing against the frame with his arms across his chest. "I understand you're both annoyingly cute and in love now, but we have costumes to prepare!"

Winnie chuckled as her friend fiddled with some jewelry near the armoire. She glanced back at him before adding, "You heard her. Off with you!"

He leaned in closely, whispering, "You should send her away. I'm feeling less gentlemanly and the thought of you is driving me mad." He bit his lip playfully as he stared down at her.

"Go! I want my costume to surprise you!" She jokingly scolded him, pushing him through the frame.

"Get out before I throw your ass outside to be feasted on by Lycan!" Tara shoved him into the hall before closing the door swiftly.

In the hallway, Kane sighed loud enough that Winnie heard him even through the door.

"Men," Tara grumbled before returning to the mirror to finish applying tinted lip salves and a clear coating of rice powder that sadly hid her freckles.

"I forgot how serious you are about your holidays," Winnie chuckled.

Tales of the Quinn family celebrating in Ireland reminded her that tonight was quite sacred for her friend. Stories of large bonfires; getting lost in song, dance, and costumes. It had always seemed so magical to Winnie. A night to let loose and be free for even a small moment. These were only a few of many reasons Samhain was one of her favorite celebrations.

The group agreed that dressing as their elements would be the best way to honor their deities. Though Tara didn't technically have one of her own, she'd chosen Earth. The greens and browns of her gown matched her red hair splendidly. Flowing, whimsical sleeves hung off her shoulders and accentuated her chest and collarbones. The skirt was equally as mischievous, falling magnificently around her waist with a large slit up the side of her leg.

Lines of ivy trailed down the sides, a bustle of flowers at the back. Her arms and neck were adorned with gold and emerald jewelry which matched the headpiece she wore. At the center were two small deer antlers surrounded by leaves and flowers. A dainty white lace mask adorned her face, ready to hide her from the spirits lurking on this mystical night. She looked like a wood nymph that walked straight from the forest.

"Where on earth are you going to hide a weapon on that tiny little costume?" Winnie teased.

"There's always room for a dagger and a pistol at my side," she smirked, pulling the fabric of her bustled skirt back to reveal both weapons.

"Tara, you're barefoot! At least wear shoes!"

"No! I have to remain grounded during Samhain. Stop pressuring me to conform!" Her friend twirled a few stray strands of hair around the heated tongs, leaving behind perfect ringlets.

Winnie ignored the instincts that attempted to talk some sense into her friend before turning to examine her own outfit. She'd of course picked her own element – water. Though some part of her wondered if she should've picked fire instead. She hadn't heard Gali's voice since using Aelius's gifts to defeat Boudicca's hellhounds.

Her dress was simpler than Tara's. Not as extravagant, but equally decorative. The heart-shaped neckline glittered with small gems that faded from deep navy to shimmering silver. The sapphires made it look like small puddles of water pooled around her shoulders in particular, lining the mesh that covered her collar bone. Small inky blue gems adorned her ears, her hair loose and curled, bouncing around wildly for the night.

Lastly, she placed a silver mask across her face. Shimmering scales lined the majority of the piece, leading to fanned fins on either side. A small seashell sat at the center of the mask, a few navy gems surrounding it.

My mother is going to call us both harlots when she sees us, she thought with a slight chuckle.

"And you, madam? Where are you hiding your weapons?" Tara's accusatory tone faded to reveal playfulness.

"My weapons are mostly here," Winnie began, holding up her hands. "But I also have my dagger fastened under my dress." Lifting the hem of her skirt, she revealed her leg, weapon strapped to it and ready.

"Kane's a lucky man," Tara said with a deep sigh and admiring eyes.

The sounds of drum beats echoed from outside, a sign it was time to begin the celebration.

"I imagine the Lycan will go feral when they see you." Winnie smirked as Tara continued to twirl around the room.

Tara offered her a quick wink before adding, "It's a shame you're committed now. We could've broken some hearts tonight."

"I'm not technically committed. We haven't officially begun our courtship. But regardless – all the more for you." A small shrug followed her words.

"The second he sees you, he'll be down on one knee and ready to propose!" Tara waved her hand as if to indicate she was overheating.

Panic stirred in Winnie's chest, realizing she was more nervous than she'd anticipated.

Peeking her head into the hall, Tara called down. "I hope you're ready for our big reveal! I expect loud, audible 'ohs' and 'ahs' as we're walkin' down the stairs!"

Winnie could hear the sound of the men laughing softly, waiting for the ladies to join. Tara turned, looking at Cricket who sat eagerly by the door. A small wreath of leaves sat around the hound's neck, ready to enjoy the festivities himself.

"Well hurry up then! You insist this is the best holiday ever, and yet we're still waiting around for you to exit your room!" Ezra's impatient words echoed toward them.

Tara joined them first, Cricket darting to the bottom of the stairs. Her giggles sounded through the hall as the gentleman downstairs did as she asked. Applauding her costume, they offered soft praises.

"You put my costume to shame," Ezra praised.

Winnie waited in her doorway, her heart sitting in her throat and bobbing as if unable to breath. Finally, tentative steps guided her down the stairs. At the bottom, they waited. And Kane, standing with his hand clutching his chest in awe, grinned from ear to ear seeing her.

He bowed before her as she admired him. Dressed in his element of air, he wore a deep, inky blue suit with a waistcoat decorated in golden swirled feathers. He'd rolled the sleeves of his dress shirt up, revealing the inked art decorating his skin. His mask was also navy, simple and with very few frills. A delicate pattern matching his waistcoat was painted across the bridge of his nose, though otherwise it remained rather plain.

Beside him, Thoren sported his element of fire. His black button down was topped by a maroon waistcoat. The most extravagant part of his outfit was his mask, a mix of reds, oranges, and yellows to mimic the bonfires waiting for them outside.

Peeking next to him stood Ezra, who'd curiously chosen Earth for the evening. He wore a moody emerald suit with a golden waistcoat beneath. His mask matched many of the trees outside, the outer texture mimicking bark. Small branches led way to leaves along the top, a few small blossoms strewn about. The colors matched his ashy hair well, blue eyes glittering by the light of the gas lamps.

"Stunning," he gleamed, offering Winnie a quick twirl before returning to Thoren.

The group exited, leaving Kane and Winnie behind. As the door outside opened and shut, the sounds of lively music and drumbeats came and went. The low thumping could still be heard through the walls of the house.

She turned, seeing Kane still waiting for her. His hand remained on his chest, a deep smile plastered across his face. Reaching out, he offered her hand a delicate kiss.

"Just when I decide you couldn't be any more radiant, you surprise me still."

"You look quite dapper yourself," she said with a smirk, offering a quaint ladylike curtsy.

"Be my date tonight?" He pulled her in close, brushing the curls off her shoulder and offering it a delicate kiss before placing another on her cheek.

Her face turned to a scowl. "I assumed I already was."

"You can be my date from here until the end of time, my love." His words reassured her, placing his plump lips on her own with intention before linking their arms and pulling her outside.

The scowl on her face dropped as a small squeal escaped her, excited to rejoin the others. Exiting the manor, the Samhain celebration awaited. Tents were moved farther out to make room for the large bonfires at the center. Rows of drummers and other instruments sat along the outskirts, playing boisterous music as the Lycan danced.

Tables offering food and drink stood throughout, accompanied by the occasional tarot or tea reader. Lines of carved pumpkins, turnips, and other root vegetables lead from the house to the celebration just beyond, welcoming them to the festivities.

The rhythm of the melodies escaping the musicians' instruments pounded through Winnie's chest. She could feel it all – the energy of the crowd, the intoxicating pull of the party. It'd been a long time since she'd celebrated like this.

As Winnie and Kane joined the others, Wesley and Melinda sprinted from the side. She was shocked to see her brother dressed up. Though not wearing anything too unusual compared to his everyday clothes, he'd at least worn a burgundy jacket and matching red mask. *He's never wanted to dress up. I'm not surprised he didn't do much tonight,* she thought.

Melinda, on the other hand, was splendidly dressed. She wore white silk trousers decorated with fanciful frills along the sides. A golden, lacey corset sat atop a flowing cream blouse, her shoulders exposed and covered in feathers and glitter. White roses and greenery were woven into her thick braids, the embodiment of heavenly clouds. The mask she wore matched her outfit, glimmering golden with small white feathers protruding from the top. *She must've chosen air,* Winnie thought.

Looking around, she realized many of the Lycan hadn't chosen to dress up. Given that they'd been surprised by the news, it made sense. Still, many fashioned makeshift masks out of supplies to partake in some of the celebration regardless. A range of spooky and beautifully intricate disguises peered back at the group,their guests enjoying their evening.

"I'll get us some drinks," Kane shouted over the thumping live music.

Winnie nodded as Tara dragged her toward the center where people danced. Even her brother, who was usually too shy to do anything but hide, danced with arms linked. Hopping from person to person, he seemed to delight in the evening.

His sister joined, linking arms with him as they spun in a circle.

"You seem to be having a good time!" Her voice was barely audible over the drums.

"Who knows how much longer we have. Might as well make the most of it!" He skipped off, linking arms with Melinda once more.

Winnie's heart sank a little. Somehow in the excitement of it all, she'd forgotten. The lively music faded for a moment, her vision tunneling to focus only on the friends who stood near her. It took a few moments before her senses finally returned.

She turned, looking for Tara in the crowd. Her friend was surrounded by a group of Lycan, male and female, dancing flirtatiously around them. A hand grasped at Winnie's waist, sloppily and with more force than she'd expected. Turning, expecting to see Kane, she realized it was someone else.

Jumping back in surprise, a devilish drunken smile waited for her. She backed away, not recognizing the Lycan before her. As he reached toward her again, insisting on a dance, Winnie swatted at him.

"Not interested! Move on you drunken fool!"

"Oh come on! It's just a dance." His words slurred as he spoke.

"Clearly you didn't hear the rule about not drinking too much!" she scolded.

Once again, she felt a presence behind her. This one familiar, at least. She glanced back, seeing Kane. A welcomed sight, one that calmed her as the drunken Lycan waved before her still waiting for that dance.

"You heard her – move on."

The Lycan rolled his eyes lazily, sauntering over to a new group of ladies.

"Was he bothering you?" Kane asked, handing her a cup of cider. Fire burned behind his pupils, tracking every movement the young fool made.

"I could've taken care of him," she reminded with a sly smile.

Kane merely chuckled, his smirk waiting above the rim of his cup.

"I worry they're not listening to our rules. Half of them seem drunk already."

"I thought you said Boudicca was in Chicago?" he countered.

"I did, but…"

He cut her off swiftly. "It'll be okay, Winnie. Just enjoy the night. Care to dance?"

"I thought you hated dancing?" she asked, though she happily obliged.

With her drink in one hand and the other placed on his shoulder, the two enjoyed the music as the evening continued.

EZRA

Along the outskirts, Thoren and Ezra sat with a Lycan as she read their tarot cards. After just finishing a tea leaf reading, she'd talked them into more of her services.

"This all seems so strange. If my mother could only see me now, she'd tell me that I'm going to hell for sure," Ezra mumbled. Though his words came out playful, there was a bitterness to them.

"Forget about her and just enjoy the festival, moró mou," Thoren teased, planting a delicate kiss on his love's cheek.

"How can some drawings on cards tell you anything?" he questioned skeptically.

Thoren shushed him with a smirk, pointing to the woman as she examined the spread before her.

"I see," she began, holding a few cards up to the light from the fire. "The lovers. You have recently found great happiness."

Ezra's eyes flashed to Thoren as giddy flutters formed in his stomach.

"I also see…" There was a long pause. For a moment, she seemed to eye the siren with suspicion, analyzing every detail. "The tower. You may find yourself going through significant changes right now or in the near future. It might feel like your whole world is falling apart, but sometimes this can be for our greater good. Paired with the seven of swords, however, you're warned to be very careful who you trust. Be sure to listen to your intuition. It'll know what's best for you."

Ezra wracked his mind, wondering who she could be referring to in his reading.

"Your turn," she said, eyes landing on Thoren next.

"No thanks, ma'am. I just wanted him to experience this. It's his first Samhain celebration."

"If I had to do it, so do you!" Ezra insisted.

Hesitantly, he nodded as she shuffled the cards. Pulling out three of them, her eyebrows scrunched in confusion as she once again took in the meanings behind each one. "Do you feel like time is running out for something?"

"What do you mean?" Thoren inched forward anxiously, surveying the three cards she laid in front of her.

"Your spread is…concerning. First, you have the devil. It indicates a need to allow certain negative thoughts or behaviors to end. For your own sake." For a moment, she peered back over toward Ezra. "You also have the five of wands and the ten of swords. You may experience an immense amount of conflict or pain. It usually means something is coming to an end."

"Well what is it? What's going to happen?" Thoren's chest began to heave, anger bubbling toward the surface.

"It's hard to say. I can try to pull some more cards to find out. I didn't mean to upset you! It's all up for interpretation. Maybe I read them wrong," she tried to explain, though her hands fumbled nervously.

"They're just cards, Thoren. What's wrong?" Ezra tried to say, though the siren ignored him as he took a stand.

"Don't bother. This is all mere trickery. You've gotten enough coins out of us for one night. Let's go, Ezra," he grumbled.

Dragged back to the dancing near the fire, Ezra attempted to ask him what was wrong one more time. He merely ignored the questions, focusing on the music instead.

—•((●●●))•—

WINIFRED

Hours passed and the celebration raged on. As the night grew later, Winnie's nerves only amplified. They'd taken a seat near a small fire along the outskirts of the party, sitting and talking to one another. With the first night of Samhain coming to a close, they each took turns telling tales from previous years as they carved more pumpkins and turnips of their own.

Tara eventually wandered off, leaving Cricket with the others and making eye contact with one of the Lycan she'd danced with earlier in the night. She'd offered Winnie a quick wink before meeting up with the dark haired beauty behind a tent.

Curled up in a chair, Winnie floated in and out of consciousness. Unsure what time it was, she was sure it was well past midnight. While Kane told tales of his shenanigans with his brother, the others laughed and listened.

It wasn't until a low, soft mumbling startled Winnie that she awoke again. It wasn't the sounds of her friends, no. It was different. The sounds she knew all too well – Death, whispering to her. Sitting up abruptly, her eyes flashed around in a panic.

"Winnie?" Kane asked, placing a hand on her back.

She ignored him for a moment, trying to piece together the voices she heard. The mumbles changed slowly, morphing into two voices she knew she'd heard before. At once it clicked.

The siren attempted to get her attention once more, though she simply swatted at his hands trying to concentrate. Their voices were there, though barely audible.

"Girls?" she called out, trying to draw them closer. Removing her mask, she continued her search.

"Winnie, what is it?" Kane tried to get her attention once more, breaking her trance.

"I hear them," she began. "Boudicca's daughters, I need to find them."

She followed the sound of their voices, running past a few tents. Reaching under her dress, she pulled out her dagger. Kane chased after her, wings freeing when his eyes met with her weapon. Pulling a sword from a nearby tent, he removed his jacket and prepared for a fight.

"Girls?" Winnie shouted once more through the camp, running straight into the forest.

Around her, voices slithered in the dark. Barely any light reached the woods, densely populated by trees. The small fae creatures were nowhere to be seen – only darkness waiting for her.

"She's coming," she could hear, a whisper just outside of her reach. The sound seemed to circle around her as though she were prey.

"How did she find us?"

"You led her right to you…" The soft murmurs of Boudicca's daughters continued to surround her. "Our mother will be here soon. You must stop her."

"Will you help me?" Winnie asked, sensing the daughters near.

At once, both appeared in front of her. Nodding, they did not say a word.

"Where is she?"

Though it was dark, she could just barely make out the girls' figures from the distant light emanating from the bonfires. They turned to the darkness with their backs to Winnie, pointing out toward the nothingness that lay before them.

39

Breaking away from the group, Tara chased after one of Horace's Lycan she'd met dancing. They sat around a fire pit, just the two of them. The young woman's icy blue eyes glittered by the flickering light of the flames, though Tara quickly realized they had little in common.

It's just one night. I don't need to have a strong connection with her to enjoy myself, Tara thought. "What's your name?" At last, she'd asked the question she probably should've started with.

"Augustine," the Lycan hummed, fingers playfully dancing across the redhead's skin.

The conversation came to a stall, realizing they were both done talking. Tara ran curious fingers through her silken curls before pulling the woman in closely. Passion ignited between them, Augustine snatching her hand and pulling her away from the crowd.

Clumsily, they walked in the shadows behind Fox Manor. The Lycan's hands ran over her body, removing bits and pieces of her costume. With Tara pushed up against the cold brick of the house, Augustine's exploring hands reached up under her dress. Supple lips trailed down her body, Tara's eyes fixed on the sky as pleasure washed over her.

The sounds of slower, less lively music still echoed through the fields. Most of the estate either slept or quietly enjoyed the remaining hours of the first night of Samhain. With her eyes still shut enjoying the tenacity of the Lycan, she felt Augustine's body tense. Her hands stopped moving when a loud *thud* drew Tara's attention away from the sky. The pendant around her neck glowed in the darkness, an untimely warning.

Behind Augustine, a figure appeared as she fell to the ground. The glint of metal reflected from far off fire light as her body tumbled forward.

"I hate to kill a lover before they've enjoyed their last meal," the voice purred.

Tara stifled a cry, reaching at her side for her blade. The man lunged forward, pinning her arms to the brick behind her. The final gargles of Augustine echoed through her mind, realizing the woman was gone.

"Take it easy, little fawn. I need something from you," he hummed, a playful finger poking at the antlers mounted to her decorative headpiece. A glimmer of moonlight illuminated his face, revealing a disastrously handsome physique. Electric blue eyes examined her, a scar running down the side of his face.

Taking both hands and fixing them above her head, he reached out toward her neck. The more she struggled, the harder he held her. When his skin made contact with the Quinn family necklace, the pendant released a burst of power. As he pulled back with a gasp, skin bubbling from the burn, she made her move.

With just enough space to finally fight back, she snagged his middle finger and bent it until she heard a snap. Offering him a final kick to the groin, he fell to the ground groaning before a deep, haunting laugh seemed to chase her as she ran. Grabbing the pistol at her hip, she turned ready to fire.

Only his figure no longer loomed behind her. As if he disappeared entirely, only Augustine's body remained. Fastening the gun back on her hip, she hauled the Lycan over her shoulder.

Stumbling, she carried the woman as a small tear ran down her cheek. The music around the estate ceased in an instant, masses of Lycan running from tent to tent waking others up and grabbing weapons. She laid Augustine's body down carefully near one of the tents, covering her with a sheet when she was sure there was no saving the woman.

Seeing Winnie up ahead, she cried out to her friend. "They're here!"

"I know, I can sense it." Winnie's eyes never met Tara's, searching the estate's woodline.

"I'm wearing feckin' antlers on my head! And you mean to tell me the queen's army is here? I thought we were safe?" A wild gaze fell over her friend.

"I don't know what happened. Her daughters said that I led her here. I just don't know how." Winnie rubbed her forehead, pacing before wandering off to prepare.

With a shrill whistle, Cricket came running from the center of the party. Clicking a command, the mutt's ears pinned back and his hackles raised. His tawny yellow eyes shifted, turning to ruby red and ready for a fight.

Tearing at the skirts of her dress, Tara removed bits of her costume and headpiece to ensure she could move freely. Snagging a pair of boots she'd laid by the sunroom door just in case, she laced them swiftly before picking up a spear and checking on her other two weapons at her side.

With a pat on Cricket's head, she said, "We've survived plenty of fights, haven't we? This one will be no different."

———•((●●●))•———

WINIFRED

Glancing to her side, she watched as Kane and Thoren's wings both expanded across their backs. The picture of angelic siren beauty, they stood ready. She'd slipped a pair of pants under her large skirt, removing it in order to fight.

Seeing Kane standing there, images from her dream flashed in her mind. Desperately, she tried to remind herself that it had been a warning, not an omen. Death surely wished to forewarn her so she could stop it. That was all she could hope for.

Her eyes landed on Ezra next, pacing with a pistol at his side and sword in hand. She lunged toward him, grasping him tightly in an embrace.

"It's not too late to go inside. No one would judge you for it." Her voice was low and hushed, his eyes softening at her words.

"Not a chance in hell. You think I'd let you fight this alone?" Though his voice cracked, he straightened his posture and took a deep long breath.

The sirens flew up ahead, alerting any Lycan that weren't already awake. Many slept soundly in their tents or sat drunkenly by the fires. She thought she'd made herself very clear with Horace when explaining the stipulations. Apparently her instructions had fallen on deaf ears.

Around the estate, it seemed quiet. Too quiet. Shadows fell over the manor, seeming to lurk toward the tents and bonfires. Up ahead, the sirens let out soft baritone notes. A message to everyone, she realized. As she heard the seductive tones of their songs, her mind could only focus on one thing: the fight ahead.

Tara and Cricket joined at her side, the redhead offering her a quick hug.

"Please be careful. Stay together and watch each other's backs," Winnie ordered, though she knew her friend didn't need the reminder. At her other side, she felt a gentle hand grasp her shoulder.

"Be my date?" Kane asked as she turned toward him.

With a nod, he pulled her in. His eyes peered down at her, his smile dropping with a solemn look. His mouth began to move, though no words seemed to come out. Like he couldn't think what to say or couldn't verbalize it correctly. When words failed, he leaned down and merely kissed her.

Such passion she'd never felt before coursed through her veins.

Centuries of souls living and longing for one another seemed to crash into her being, recognizing this kiss as one many shared before their final goodbye. Her tattooed arm flared red hot as her insides heated to molten lava. She tugged at him, trying to bring him in closer and unwilling to let go.

"We have to make it," she mumbled helplessly as their lips parted.

"If something happens," he began, pulling away and grabbing Winnie's face.

"Don't you dare finish that sentence. No one is allowed to say goodbye," Winnie scolded, cupping his cheek and pulling him in for another kiss. "We will make it."

He nodded hesitantly. Still, unsaid words seemed to dance on his lips. Moments passed when the hair on Winnie's arms stood tall. The back of her neck felt a tingle, her stomach twisting. Deep within the forest, she knew the queen was coming.

Mere seconds passed and the wards shattered. Like broken glass, the pieces of her family's magic dropped as her inside twisted. Every hellhound that breached the estate felt like another thunderous heartbeat tattering her insides.

From behind, Milicent called to her daughter. "We have to seal it! We can't risk anyone getting inside!" She pointed toward the manor, ushering Winnie to help. Pulling out a knife, her mother sliced into her hand. Placing it on the door, she offered the blade to her daughter.

"She has my blood. She'll be able to get through if I do it," Winnie muttered, handing the blade back.

Milicent's eyes lowered, realizing it too.

"I'll do it. I'll help seal the house." Kane said, stretching his hand out as Milicent nodded and sliced swiftly.

Placing both their hands on the door, she chanted soft prayers to the Gods, a wave of energy covering the house in protection. Glancing through the windows, Winnie saw the figure of someone sitting on the couch in the entry parlor.

"Is that…Melinda?" She squinted, trying to make out who it was. Ready to go inside and warn her, she felt someone snag her arm.

Turning, Wesley waited. "Leave her inside. I put her under a trance."

"You can't do that, Wes. She'd want to fight! You know how strong she is. She's an asset to us. We need her!" Winnie's eyes pleaded with her brother. As his hands still lay on her arm, she knew he could persuade her even without words.

"I have to keep her safe. I can't risk anything happening to her. She can hate me when all of this is over, but I won't risk her life." Sad eyes lowered to the ground, avoiding his sister's gaze.

In the distance, deafening howls broke through. Seconds passed and they only grew louder, more intense. A flutter of flaming light glowed through the woodline, the sounds of Boudicca's orders bellowing throughout. They had mere seconds before the queen's hellhounds would meet them. Unprepared, outnumbered. Their only hope was that by some sort of miracle, they'd make it out alive.

40

WINIFRED

Winnie took a deep breath in. She could see the hellhounds, mouths snapping and frothing. They were bloodthirsty and ready to kill. Her body shivered, afraid of what was to come. As her mind ceased its thoughts, the first wave of beasts dashed from the woodline, face to face with the Lycan.

Gun fire pulsated through her whole body, watching as Horace's small force fired away at the beasts. Bullets seemed to do little good, only slowing them down momentarily unless the shot was clear to the head. Each side carried swords and spears as well, ready for any fight necessary.

A few of the Lycan possessed various elemental gifts, she realized. Swirls of tornado winds knocked into attacking hounds, blasts of fire setting others ablaze. Very few Lycan appeared to harness water or earth, but the occasional icy spear or shooting vine materialized in the crowd.

Boudicca was not far behind, riding a chariot of flames. She neared the lines of Lycan without ceasing momentum. Barreling through anyone that stood in her way, even her own fighters, she searched for her target: Melinda.

A trail of fire burned behind her, the woods set ablaze. As the mass of hellhounds arrived, Winnie realized they hadn't brought nearly as many as expected. *She has hundreds. Why did she not bring them all?*

Panicked eyes searched around the field. The hellhounds were getting close. She needed to begin her flight. *I've trained my whole life. Why can't I move?* Her wits faltered, the first beast lunging toward her with a snapping muzzle. Kane slammed a shield of air between her and the beast before his sword beheaded the wolf.

Shouting at her, she couldn't make out what he was saying. The feeling of being underwater – drowning – overwhelmed her. The muffled noises of water-logged ears. Panic ripped through her, causing her feet to cement into place and eyes fasten to the ground. She held her dagger in hand, ready to fight. And yet she couldn't move.

Kane grabbed her by the shoulders, shaking her violently as he pleaded for her to come to her senses. Finally, something grabbed her attention.

"Stop her," a voice sounded through her head. Not a voice. Two. Boudicca's daughters, ready to bring their mother back to the afterlife.

At last, her eyes met with Kane's. Scowling in concentration, she shook her head. Winnie witnessed the carnage already forming around her. The smell of Death clung to the air, the siren jerking her around to avoid an on-coming spear from one of their enemies.

"Winnie – get yourself together or die!" His voice begged her, eyes equally as imploring.

She nodded, grasping firmly at her dagger. Her tattooed arm glowed. Throwing a fist down, a ball of fire encompassed her hand.

Across the field, Winnie made eye contact with the queen. Boudicca's gaze flicked from her to Kane, burning with the intent to kill. A smile formed across her lips as she looked back at Winnie. Ceasing her merciless attacks on nearby Lycan, she moved. Carefree, as if she didn't think anyone could touch her.

Kane glanced between the queen and Winnie, as if seeing the unspoken tether between them. The vengeful spirit plowed toward the lake-side of the house, beckoning her to follow. A mass of hellhounds stood between them, but that wouldn't stop her.

Rounding the corner, a group of shifted beasts stood with

weapons ready to fire. A gun held tight to her head, Winnie's heart sank. Without thinking, she smacked the flat end of her dagger across the man's wrist. As he dropped the gun, she plunged the blade into his gut. Snagging his pistol off the ground, she turned the barrel on the other three that stood ready to attack.

Instinct took hold of her. Several rounds fired. Blood dripped from their wounds as they fell to the ground, lifeless at once. At her side, Kane fought his own battle, Winnie ending it in moments with a single shot. With the few remaining bullets, she fired at nearby hounds, taking out as many as she could before striking an oncoming hound with the blunt end of the weapon. Dragging her dagger across his chest, she ended him at last.

Behind her, another came running. A woman, dagger in hand, ready to strike. Kane moved Winnie to the side, thrusting his sword through her stomach. She clutched at herself as she fell to the ground, blood pooling around her. Winnie turned, swinging at another hound at their backs. Yelps howled through the estate as they took out as many as possible, though they seemed to come from every direction.

Another group of hounds bounded toward them. Drawing on her internal strength, she pulled on Aelius's powers. Forming a ball of fire before her, she shot the flames toward those that attacked them. Kane added his air element, enhancing the power of her darting deathly blaze. The two had just enough time to make it a few feet toward the Queen when they were met with another group of beasts.

WESLEY

Tara, Cricket, and Wesley stood side by side, partnered for the battle. In front of them, they could see a group of four. Each in human form, weapons in hand. A dagger, a spear, and two swords. *Easy,* Wesley thought confidently. Tara clutched a spear, using the length to her advantage. Cricket's bloodthirsty jaws snapped and barked toward their opponents, ready to protect.

Fighting was a tricky business for Wesley. Given that he had no active fire powers outside of rituals, he relied heavily on his empathic nature. If he was close enough to touch an attacker, he could easily lull them to sleep. Getting within a safe range was a tricky feat, however.

Looking over his shoulder, Wesley realized Tara and Cricket were handling themselves well in the fight. They took turns, distracting the hounds and lunging strike after strike. The two worked as an unstoppable team, each watching the other's back.

Two hounds in front of him morphed back into their wolf forms, jaws snapping and frothing as they inched toward him. One rounded behind him, trying to distract from the other in front. Wesley gripped his sword, ready to strike.

The beast behind lunged, though Wesley dodged just in time for it to miss him. The two hounds continued their feverish swatting as he dove forward. One dodged, the other receiving an injury as his sword sliced through the pads of its paws. It yelped, stepping back as the other struck again.

Wesley crouched down, sword lifted, slicing into the beast's stomach. The injured creature turned as if to run when Wesley came up behind fast and sliced through its stomach swiftly. Before he could think, he had another attacker behind him, grabbing hold of him with a forearm across the neck.

Big mistake for you, he thought with a grin. Calling on his empathic abilities, he sent the man radiating waves of calm. He fell to the ground, asleep in seconds, before Wesley plunged his sword into the man's gut.

Turning, he watched as Tara's opponents swung swords at her. She skillfully ducked, thrusting her spear into one of the women's stomachs. Cricket ripped at the arm of another before Wesley joined. He kept the hound busy as she grasped for the pistol at her side. A loud *'pang'* of the bullet sounded and at once the beast was down on the ground. Only moments passed before they moved on to the next pair.

⸺•‹‹●●●››•⸺
THOREN

Ezra and Thoren were at the side of the house, closer to the back of the action. The siren's mind raced, unable to think of anything but protecting Ezra. *I only just found him. I'm not willing to lose this love now,* he thought.

They'd positioned themselves with the house at their backs, hoping it would keep some of the fight at bay. Ezra held a shield in one hand and a sword in the other, a gun on his hip just in case. Thoren used a variety of assets: fire, siren songs, and a dagger.

Three hounds stood before them, one in wolf form and the other two human. Carrying pistols at their side, they smirked thinking they had the upper hand. The wolf leaped forward first, Thoren catching it mid-air and slamming it to the ground, plunging the dagger into the beast's chest. It yelped in pain, blood pooling around it. The other two reached for their pistols at once, pointing at the two men.

At first, Thoren put his hands up as if to concede. Ezra dropped his weapons and inched forward, just as they'd practiced. Thoren let out a small hum, the beast in front of him beginning to twitch from the maddening songs. The other looked at his friend in confusion. Just as he looked away, Ezra grabbed the end of the pistol with one hand and smacked at his elbow with the other. Turning the gun, he pointed it directly at their attacker's head.

A split second of hesitation stalled the attack. When the hellhound lunged for him once more, he finally fired. Thoren watched as his violent blinks brought him back to reality. He aimed toward the hound in front of Thoren, shooting a second round.

"It was you or him," the siren reminded.

He nodded, wiping away a bead of sweat forming on his brows.

Ezra peered wildly around the estate, in shock.

"Hey, first kills are hard. You did good," Thoren reminded, grabbing Ezra and offering him a reassuring squeeze before they readied themselves for the next round of attackers.

Noticing the gunshots, a swarm of hounds came running. Five or so surrounded them in a semicircle, both men's backs still toward the house.

Ezra had a few bullets left, though his aim wasn't perfect. He fired a few times, hitting two. One in the shoulder, one in the chest causing her to fall to the ground. The hound with the shoulder wound transformed back into a wolf, enraged.

The others swarmed Thoren, isolating Ezra with two of the others. Firing panicked shots, he eventually ran out of bullets. Grabbing his swords, he swung wildly at the hounds in front of him. Thoren watched from afar, trying to keep an eye on his love as he faced the hounds in front of him.

Before he could begin his siren song, one of the wolves tackled him to the ground. Reaching up, he grabbed for the beast's eyes and dug deep. The hound squealed as it attempted to jump away. At once, he dug the dagger deep into its side.

The second spared no time leaping into the other's place, turning into human form once on top. She instantly punched Thoren in the throat as he opened his mouth, ready to use his siren song. He gagged, gripping his throat tightly, seeing stars. She snatched his dagger from his hands, ready to plunge it into his chest.

To the side, Ezra noticed Thoren on the ground. Their eyes connected and a swift punch landed him on the ground. The siren collected himself, knowing they needed to think clearly to make it out alive. Drawing on Aelius, he released a ball of fire from around him. Igniting the beasts that held him down, they ran away engulfed in flames. As he recollected himself, two more hounds circled Ezra.

He backed away in a panic, running around the side of the

house.

"No! We need to stick together!" Thoren called out.

The siren's mind raced, unable to see him. Finally getting to his feet, he turned to go after his love. But before he could, four more hounds whirled around him, snapping viciously.

41

WINIFRED

Around the side of the house, Winnie and Kane continued to work their way toward Boudicca. Milicent and Ernest stood on the front porch, using their magic from afar to assist the Lycans. Swirls of the elements surrounded the front line, still trying to stop wave after wave of hounds from Boudicca's army. Though their enemies were less than expected, they were still outnumbered.

The pair used the elements to their advantage. Vines sprung from the ground, disarming their enemies or striking through their chests. Blasts of air knocked back attackers, slamming them into nearby trees or boulders.

Winnie's parents always relied more heavily on magic than the others. Given they were the leaders of the Fox family coven, their power was far greater than Winnie and her brother. Though they could wield weapons, they often found they didn't need to. They worked as a perfect pair. When one felt the sting of burnout, the other took over allowing their partner to rest.

The fight itself seemed to make little impact on the hoards that attacked. Bodies from both sides were strewn about the ground like fallen leaves, their numbers dwindling. Another mass leaked through the edge of the woodline, a few dozen more hellhounds joining the fight.

Winnie heard as her mother shouted to Kane.

"We need something big!" She pointed at her throat, the

sounds of the battlefield threatening to drown out her words.

He nodded, taking to the sky. Ernest prepared shields around the Lycan and family, awaiting the maddening cries of the siren above. She watched as he inhaled deeply, releasing a low baritone hum at first, then turned sharp countertenor high notes. Any beasts nearby shriveled, their eyes bleeding and throats gagging as the tunes continued.

As he finished his song, the beasts scratched wildly at their heads like their brains were on fire and they couldn't get to them fast enough. Dozens of hounds dropped to the battlefield, dead within moments from either the song or self-inflicted wounds. It was just enough of a break for their militia to reload their weapons, take a quick breath, and prepare for the next round.

WESLEY

Tara, Cricket, and Wesley enjoyed a small moment of peace as the hounds in front of them dropped like flies. A few of the stronger ones resisted, finally finished off by their weapons. He looked over to check on those around him, noticing that Thoren was at the bottom of a pileup, pinned to the ground. As the beasts resisted the maddening cries of his brother, their grip on him only grew stronger.

"I'll be back," Wesley told Tara, knowing she could handle herself as she waited for the next round of hounds to get to them.

He ran to the side of the house, lunging toward the beasts on top of Thoren, knocking them to the side as they continued to writhe in pain. Getting off the ground, the siren finished them off with his dagger before noticing the next swarm quickly headed their way.

"I can handle this out here. Go help Ezra! He's around the back," he shouted, wiping smears of blood from the blade. He panted, trying to regain himself. A large bite caused his shoulder to bleed crimson.

Reluctantly, Wesley nodded. Rounding the corner of the house, his heart beat skyrocketed. A stone sat in the pit of his stomach, a familiar feeling washing over him. One he hadn't expected. Then, seeing a body on the ground, he slowed. Examining it, a sigh of relief escaped him realizing it wasn't Ezra. Pressing on, he searched for their friend.

Hearing a scream farther back, he ran swiftly toward the noise. Anxious eyes jutted around, looking for the source amidst the darkness. Ezra thrashed on the ground, arms pinned with a salivating beast chomping toward his neck.

"No!" Wesley cried, leaping toward the hellhound.

He ran to aid his friend, digging his sword into the hellhound's back. The attacker let out a pained yelp, falling to the side though the adrenaline made it thrash violently. The beast, with claws outstretched, swung toward both men in a fit of desperation, trying to survive the encounter.

EZRA

Ezra turned, reaching for his sword as the beast's attention was on Wesley. They were face to face as he kicked toward the hound, his weapon digging into its side once again. Jumping to his feet, he finished the beats off with a final stab through the skull. His eyes met Wesley's, thankful for the assist.

"Thanks, Wes. You really saved my ass." Ezra reached out, ready to help him come to a stand.

A small smile sat across the boy's face, kneeling on the ground as he dropped his sword. He didn't seem to move from his place, eyes welling and lips quivering.

"Wes?" His words were soft at first, unsure what was going on.

The boy coughed, blood spilling from his mouth. The center of his white shirt darkened, crimson spilling from a wound Ezra hadn't noticed yet.

"Wes!" he screamed again, looking around for help.

At the side of the house, no one could hear them over the sound of the battle. He continued to scream, the events unfolding in his head once more.

"No, please no! This is my fault! I should've fought harder. Protected you!"

Wesley's body shook in his arms, searching around wildly with a small smile on his face.

"Take care of them, will you?" Wesley muttered, blood spilling from his lips. He lay delicately in Ezra's arms, reaching up for his face.

"No, no, *no!*" he screamed, focusing on the sky and unwilling to look back down from fear of what he might see.

"I always knew this day would come. The minute I saw you," he began, coughing once more. "The moment Winnie introduced you, I knew this would happen."

"What are you talking about?" he cried, cradling Wesley and attempting to apply pressure to the wound. "You have to hang on, Wes! Stay with me! I only just met you. Only just got to know you. Stay with us!"

With each passing second, his life faded more and more. Slowly, the skin of his face paled, expression more stoic than before.

"I wouldn't have it any other way, brother," Wesley said, his small smile fading as his face went blank.

Ezra shook him violently, pulling him in and beginning to scream.

Heavy footsteps sounded from around the corner, Thoren following the sounds of Ezra's cries.

"Ez? Wes?" The siren landed next to him, examining Winnie's little brother.

At once, he emitted soft hums, trying to call on the siren magic within him to heal the boy. He tried and tried, though it was no use. Wesley's eyes stared blankly at the sky, a small tear streaming down his face. Thoren shook him as if trying to wake him up.

"We need to get him to Milicent," he muttered. "You take him. I'll hold off anyone that tries to fuck with us." Thoren's voice was cold, commanding.

Ezra wondered if he would blame him for the death of their dear friend.

Cradling Wesley in his arms, he followed behind the murderous siren. Any hounds that dared near them were instantly met with deadly strikes to the neck, gut, throat, knees, or achilles tendon. They neared the porch, Ernest turning to look first. He dropped his hands at once, his magic ceasing.

It was only moments before Milicent noticed it too.

Her son.

Dead, in the arms of Ezra. Carried delicately like the most priceless of porcelains, ready to shatter at any second. She dropped to her knees, screams shattering the sky.

He set Wesley on the floor of the porch gently, stepping away in guilt. Everything inside roiled with pain, dread, fear, hate. He didn't know if he'd be able to let go of the regret building inside.

Milicent stood, her eyes lit with fire. One look and it was clear: her rage matched that of the queen's. Ezra peered down at Wesley once more, noticing his features slowly morphing. His already pale skin grew a shade stranger, soft and almost sage in hue.

His stomach churned, an uneasy feeling washing over him. The features of Wesley's face seemed to melt away for a split second. Milicent's eyes widened at the sight of him, just as surprised as Ezra. Carefully, she approached him. Ready to place a curious hand on him, his features snapped back to the face they all knew. Milicent jumped back in shock, though her fear seemed to settle.

"Stay with my son," she ordered Ezra. As she stepped onto the ground of the estate's warzone, the entire earth shook in contempt.

42

MILICENT

Loss. Milicent had expected this. Knew it would come one day. The visions had shown her this would happen ten years ago. And yet nothing could've prepared her. As she stalked toward the queen, her mind raced thinking of all the firsts she'd miss. The lasts she'd taken for granted.

I'll never see him marry. Never see him become a father. Become the man he could've been. Never see him grow old. He'll always be seventeen. I'll never be able to make pancakes with him again. Smear the batter across the bridge of his nose. Never see him and Winnie swimming out on the lake. Sneak off through the portal he thought I didn't know about. Never again. Forever. For the rest of my days, there will only ever be nothingness.

The earth beneath her rumbled, Ina's power coursing through her veins. Drawing on every ounce of energy she had, the ground below split. An earthquake of chaos spread over the estate, hounds falling to their deaths below the surface. Any beast that tried to escape was met with a sharp edged vine, spearing them through the chest and dragging them to hell.

Milicent's rage took out dozens. Torn in half. Mutilated. The cries of hounds echoed through her mind. But she didn't care. *They took my son. They will pay,* she vowed.

"Mum?"

Winnie's soft voice broke her concentration. Milicent's eyes connected with her daughter before she realized. Saw what was happening. Saw the body of her brother laying on the porch. Lifeless. So still. And simply gone.

Her daughter's cries for her brother broke her. The visions never showed her this pain. Didn't prepare her for everyone's reactions. She told Wesley long ago what would happen but never dared to utter a word to anyone else. Not even her husband. It was a guilt she'd live with for the rest of her life.

WINIFRED

"Is that… Is that Wesley?" she cried out to no one in particular. She'd worked her way closer and closer to the queen, only to turn back.

Guilt swirled around in her mind as her sobs sounded over the cries of battle. An unnoticed hound prowled behind her as she ran toward the porch. Leaping at her, the beast's talons sunk deep into her shoulder. Fiery panic coursed through her as she fell and swung her blade toward her opponent's midsection.

Anticipating the attack, a heavy paw blocked her attempts to save herself. Deep within, she called forth Aelius though the powers seemed weakened. The God's voice in her mind barely audible, feeling helpless. Death's call, grief, drowned out the empowering voice of the fire god.

As she pushed the hound's face away, Kane's sturdy foot slammed into its side. The beast rounded, recollecting itself and backing away before fatal eyes locked in on the siren. Kane lured the beast away from Winnie, ready yet unaware of more danger lurking behind him.

Seconds passed.

Years, they felt like.

She saw it all in an instant.

Her dream.

The events about to happen.

Death lurked not far away, she could smell it. Drawn to the carnage around them, it waited for Kane.

A heartbeat sounded through her chest. The beasts both leaped. The images of Kane's torn and mangled body flooded her vision and panic threatened to take control of her body. Another *'thump thump'* of her heart and seconds passed. Only moments separated her dream from reality.

She screamed his name – pointing behind him. His eyes landed on her as she panicked. Trying to get up, her feet slipped on the bloodied mud beneath her. *Don't look at me! Look behind you!* The words flowed in her mind but wouldn't escape her lips.

I need to get to him. Need to be right there. If I could just…

Only a moment passed when she blinked. That sharp zap she'd felt in Chicago hit her. Confusion washed over her. As though time skipped a beat just as her anxious heart did, she stood in front of Kane in an instant. The beasts were about to collide into him. Given her vicinity, she was in line to be pummeled as well.

He nodded toward her, arms outstretched behind her head. She did the same. Covering his back, a wall of ice blocked the beast's path. A forcefield of air formed behind her. Encompassed in ice and cyclonic winds, Kane and Winnie were safe for the moment.

A long sigh escaped her lips, realizing she'd been holding her breath for who knows how long. Glancing past him, she marveled at the wall of ice. She hadn't been able to conjure that much power since Beatrix's mob attacked her.

"I…almost died. They almost had me. How did you get over here so quickly?" Kane asked, offering her a quick embrace. Worried eyes examined her injured shoulder, no time to heal.

"I don't know," she admitted. "One second I was here, the next I needed to be with you."

The shields around them fell at last, Kane plunging his sword through one of the beasts and Winnie driving her dagger into the other.

Her eyes shot to her mother, realizing she was recklessly headed toward the queen. She glanced back at the porch, internally battling herself. Crying out, she pleaded for her mother to stop and listen. But she persisted. Gaze fixed at the edge of the lake, her mother raged on toward the queen.

•((●●●))•

MELINDA

Fluttering eyes opened carefully, head heavy. She rubbed her temples, realizing she was inside. *The last thing I remember is dancing around the bonfire with Wes. What am I doing inside? Did I fall asleep?*

Her attention snapped to the sound of gunshots outside, instantly knowing something terrible was going on. The realization hit her immediately: Wesley. *He used his magic on me, I bet. I'm going to find him and kill him myself,* she grumbled.

Ensuring her pistol was loaded, dagger fastened at her side, and spear ready, she exited the house. Anger riled her up, ready to find him and tell him how she truly felt. As her feet hit the front porch of the manor, her eyes landed on him. Lying there. So still…

"Wesley?"

Ezra sat with his back to the door, eyes red with sorrow. He turned, surprised to see her.

"Is he…" Melinda asked, bending down to check on the young man.

Reaching for his neck, she felt for a pulse. Nothing. When her fingers retreated, she saw him suddenly. The boy she'd known. The real one.

Delicately soft features sat beneath whatever glamor was over him. She could see him now for who he truly was. Tall and lean, like a string bean on a vine. The minty green skin of some creature she's never laid eyes on before. She'd caught glimpses before, but never this clear.

The anger inside her melted, if only for a moment. Falling to her knees before the young man, her eyes watered. "You promised…" she cried out to him. "Promised you'd never use your powers on me again! You swore!"

A part of her wanted to hit him. Anything was better than feeling the torment of grief that threatened to destroy her.

Laying across his body, she whispered. "I could've saved you. If you'd just let me… I could've stopped them from doing this to you. Damn you!" Sobs fell from her, gut-wrenching cries as she lay next to Ezra and Wesley.

"Boudicca attacked. I was told to stay here with Wes. Guard his…body." Ezra's words fell from his mouth as easily as his tears fell down his cheek.

Ernest stood at the edge of the porch, drawing on the powers within him to hold off any hounds that attempted to attack. Tara, Cricket, and Thoren stood out front, fending off one ambush after the other, but Melinda couldn't see anyone else.

She glanced down once more. *I wish I could see his glamor again. See that smile. The wild cowlick curl at the back of his head. Anything to pretend he isn't dead right now,* she thought.

"Where's the queen?" Melinda straightened up, holding back tears. They burned, throat bobbing and ready to close any moment.

Ezra shrugged, pointing toward the front of the house. Before Melinda could begin her truck toward Boudicca, a soft call came from behind her. Turning, she saw two strangers. They reached out for her, hands welcoming.

"Who are you?"

Soft whispers escaped the girls' lips as the sounds of the battle behind her slowly disappeared. At last, she could only hear the ghostly figures before her.

"We are her daughters. Come to help you. Trust us." Once again, they reached toward her.

"Trust you? Your mother is the reason for all this death!" Melinda spat.

"We want to help her move on. Join us. We need a vessel in order to banish her." Eager hands still waited.

Melinda glanced around the estate. Unsure if she could trust the two girls, her attention snapped to their dwindling numbers. More and more hellhounds continued to funnel into the estate's lands, the Lycans decreasing every second that passed.

Hesitantly, she touched their translucent fingers. Carefully, she nodded. At once, she felt the two spirits of Boudicca's daughters retreat inside of her. Noiseless, everything around remained calm. Though battle and carnage raged on, she couldn't see it. Couldn't hear it.

As she walked through the battlefield, she found herself filled with grace.

Unstoppable, untouchable.

The power of the daughters was with her as hounds fell to their knees, lifeless before her. Never in her life had she felt anything like it. Power coursed through her like a living, burning entity, the girls guiding her. Toward the back of the house, Death followed her every step of the way.

43

WINIFRED

Winnie's screams ripped through the air. "Please Mum! Get some sense! Turn around and wait for me to get to you. To help you!"

Boudicca stood at the edge of the lake, floating amidst the flames. A row of hellhounds stood between her mother and the queen. That didn't stop her.

Winnie watched in horror as the earth swallowed the beasts whole. Vines pulled them under, suffocated by dirt and debris in mere moments. She felt the draw on her powers, the family's collective magic dwindling.

Boudicca let out a laughing cry, as if in awe of Milicent's power. "Now you know my pain," she spat.

Milicent's rage only fueled her path forward. A reaching hand shot toward the queen, vines grasping at her wrists and holding her down. Winnie took a stand next to her mother, calling on Gali and Aelius to aid in her attacks.

As her mother shot rock shards and spearing vines toward the queen, Winnie sent waves of water, ice, and fire. Crafting her own glacial daggers, they never pierced the woman's skin. When her masses of water didn't drown her and the flames didn't burn her to a crisp, Winnie let up.

"Nothing's working!"

Milicent's face turned toward her daughter. Enraged eyes dropped as if thinking.

Behind them, a presence entered. She could feel the power radiating their way before ever turning to see what or who it was. Melinda passed her, gliding effortlessly across the ground. Nearing the queen, a straggler hellhound barreled toward her. Before Winnie or Milicent could even think to protect the young woman, the beast dropped to the ground. Lifeless, it passed. She never even lifted a finger as the wolf took its last breaths.

Winnie could see it suddenly – the spirits with her. Jutting from her body, Melinda carried Boudicca's daughters inside her. Three souls inhabiting one, pure determination with only one goal in mind: Boudicca.

Winnie inched her way toward the queen, worried about getting too close to Melinda and her entourage of Death. The young woman peered behind her, a set of vacant eyes locking with Winnie's. Though they seemed lifeless, they burned brighter than any gas lamp or candle she'd ever seen.

At once, the trio turned back toward Boudicca.

"Mother. Stop this." Melinda's voice echoed through the field, eerie and indistinct. Bits of her own voice overlaid with the girls' made for a ghostly howl and chilled Winnie to the bone.

The queen snapped her attention to Melinda, as though she realized who was talking to her.

"My daughters?" Her face softened, eyes suddenly weary.

"This must stop."

"I'm doing all of this for you!" Boudicca cried out, struggling against Milicent's vines that held her.

"When you were alive, yes. But *this*. This is for you. We did not ask for you to continue your vendetta long past our lifetimes." The trio's voice grew in concern, harsher than expected.

"I must finish what I've started! I made a promise long ago. You don't understand. I cannot stop until Paulinus's lineage is eradicated!" Boudicca's words bellowed, attempting to send spears of flames at Melinda and the girls.

A gentle hand stopped the magic in its place, fire fizzling out in an instant.

"You were once a symbol of power and divinity. We admired you; looked up to your strength. Sought out your wisdom and reveled in your victories. But Melinda is an *innocent*. All of these people are *innocent*. Can you not find it in your heart to forgive?"

A long pause fell from the queen, glaring at Melinda. Winnie still stood, watching. Unsure what to do. How to help. Unsure if she should interfere, she instead helped her mother anchor the queen in place.

Several moments passed before she finally spoke again. "I…I don't know how to stop."

Melinda marched toward the family's stone altar, pulling Boudicca toward her. Vines traveled with the queen, slithering like snakes around her wrists.

As the young woman held up a delicate hand, a circle of flames surrounded the queen. Winnie could feel her tapping into the queen's powers, the ones they still shared. For the first time in the entire fight, Boudicca's skin finally burned.

Sizzling and bubbling, the queen's shrill scream resonated throughout Winnie's body, their blood curse linked and her own body heating in pain. Her skin didn't burn, but she could feel her spirit in torment.

"It's time," Melinda said, the daughters' voices echoing through the land.

"I…will…never rest!" Her words struggled to form, fighting back the pain of the flames that lapped at her.

"Rest. Find it in your heart to forgive."

Still Boudicca shook her head.

"Rest, or we will force you. You will not like the outcome." With every sharp word, flames burned brighter behind Melinda's vacant pupils.

"My own daughters dare turn on me. And you expect me to forgive?" As the words spat from her mouth, the flames around her grew taller.

"One last chance… Rest. Please. Come with us. Rejoin our father in the afterlife." Her daughters' words pleaded with the queen, though they were met with pure fiery determination to succeed.

"I can't rest. One way or another, they will *all* pay for what happened to you! To me! To our people!" Her head shook in vengeful stubbornness, body slowly consumed more and more.

"If we can find it in our hearts to forgive, so can you."

"I'm sorry, girls. But I can't stop. My rage will never cease. It is my greatest strength and my most significant undoing. You will have to kill me for I don't think I have it in me to choose peace."

Winnie thought she saw some semblance of humanity in the queen as she cried out to her daughters.

"If you cannot stop, then you are no longer the mother we cared for."

They nodded at last, Melinda's hand held out in front of her. A third eye appeared at the center of her forehead, a twin to the one forming on Boudicca's. The queen's shrill cries reverberated through the fields, her spirit ripped from Mary's body. The flames continued to costume her body, any semblance of the innocent mother she'd possessed gone. For good.

"I'll remember this! I always keep my promises!" The queen's words slithered from her mouth, thickening the air as she cursed them once more.

A burst of white light surrounded Boudicca, her body at last slumping and hair turning back to muted brown. Winnie watched as Mary's spirit stepped away from her body, sad eyes glancing back at her burning body. Another pocket of white light waited for her. Two small hands poked through the veil, childish giggles following as Mary stepped through the light and into the afterlife.

Melinda turned toward the fighting at the front of the house. Gliding across the bloodied fields, she inched closer to the hellhounds. Winnie chased after her, watching as beasts dropped like flies. One after another, they turned wildly. Noticing their queen burned like a witch at the stake, they turned to flee. A final burst of light left Melinda's body as she lowered back onto the ground.

Winnie could see the spirits of Boudicca's daughters slowly drift away, leaving only Melinda behind. As the hounds retreated, she glanced down at her tattooed arm whose lines continued to glow.

TARA

Tara looked out in the crowd, patting Cricket on the head with a smile cracking her lips as she took a deep breath realizing the fight was at last over. Staring back at her was the face of a devilish smile, blue eyes staring and scarred face gleaming at her.

He gave her a quick wink, the man who'd killed Augustine turning to run with the rest of the group. Her body shivered, thankful she hadn't encountered him once again during the battle. Thoren saw the man, voice bellowing above the crowd.

"Alaric!"

Tara stopped him in his tracks, worried he'd get himself killed in the moments leading up to their victory. Cricket threatened to run after him, but a sharp whistle stopped the mutt in his tracks.

"Let him go. We can get him another time," she said softly.

"He's responsible for Ezra's beating," he began with a grumble.

She cut him off swiftly. "I know. But now's not the time. You're injured."

Examining him, she saw the bite a hound had taken of his shoulder. She took a second to thank the Gods that at least she hadn't been bitten during the fight, knowing how disastrous it would've been for her.

She watched as Winnie ran from the side of the house toward Wesley. Tears streaming down her face, she stumbled onto the porch. Ezra sat leaned against the wall, cradling Wesley in his arms. All he could do was repeat the same phrase over and over again softly.

"He saved me."

Tara heard the words as she neared the commotion, too afraid to look at the boy she'd never really gotten to know. *I never took the time. And now I'll never be able to,* she thought. Cricket nudged her solemnly, sensing her distress.

"My brother…always saving everyone before himself." Winnie grabbed Ezra, pulling him in for a tight hug.

"Did we win?" Ezra asked, eyes sorrowful and unable to see past the group that surrounded the porch.

44

WINIFRED

Sitting at the edge of the porch, Winnie felt it. Without ever having to look at the masses of dead and dying. The lost souls wandering the estate howled in pain, recently deceased and unable to find the way onward just yet.

I could help them. Could talk them through the process of moving on. But I feel so…numb. I don't think I can move from this spot, she thought as she clutched her head.

The sun was slowly waking, the night before Samhain coming to an end. She watched as Thoren and Kane wandered the grounds, helping as many as possible with their healing songs. Many of Horace and Mohini's Lycans still clung to life, waiting for someone to save them.

As the siren brothers worked their magic, Milicent and Ernest walked through the rows with magical ointments trying to save those who'd incurred minimal damage. Her mother's stash was quickly depleting after hours of healing.

The guilt held Winnie in a chokehold. Her vision blurred, ears muffled, throat closing in on her as the cruel grasp of remorse held her by the jugular. It suffocated her, the thoughts that raced through her mind thrashing violently in her memories. Regrets swirled inside once again, wishing she'd never held Mary's seance in the first place.

Hellhounds littered the fields. Those still alive enough to speak pleaded for forgiveness. Many of Horace's people wandered, terminating those that still remained. It seemed no mercy was to be shown, a decision that didn't sit well with Winnie. At first.

A muffled cry sounded to the side of the house. It caught her attention, worried a Lycan was trapped somewhere and needing help. Finally leaving her spot, she turned the corner to see a woman, trapped beneath a large tree that had fallen over during Milicent's earthquake. Pinned, she had nowhere to go.

"Who are you?" she asked, examining the woman carefully. She didn't recognize her, but didn't want to assume the person in front of her was a hellhound.

"I…I'm nobody," she wheezed, pulling at the tree that held her.

"You're one of hers, aren't you?"

The woman didn't answer, only stared with a wild look in her eyes. Winnie took a moment to examine the hellhound. Her heart was torn – between helping her and ending her.

Crouching down, Winnie was face to face with the hound. A set of desperate eyes peered back at her, face contorted in pain. The woman attempted to cry, but it appeared no tears were left.

"Please help me," she choked out as the tree pinched her midsection.

"Why should I?" Winnie's icy rage glared at the woman, tilting her head to the side as any bit of remorse exited her body.

"She said she would kill us if we didn't do as she said! You have to believe me! We had no choice!" An anguished hand reached for Winnie.

She stumbled back, away from the woman's grasp. She surveyed the fields, seeing the dead Lycan in lines as Horace's people wept. Then her eyes returned to the porch where Wesley's lifeless body lay all night.

"Who were you? Before all this?" She took a careful seat in front of the woman.

"I told you, I was nobody. She told me she could offer me a life. A purpose. I believed her. I never thought it would turn out like this! Please! I'm in so much pain. Help me! I'll join your side, do anything you want! Just get me out from under this tree!"

"You think you can just join us after helping Boudicca kill our people?" she spat, feeling the navy lines of her tattooed arm heating.

As if sensing her anger, the hellhound tried to retreat. "Please! I don't want to die! You have to believe me!"

The tree trapping her was relentless in its grasp. Tears soaked her face as she looked around for anyone to help her.

"Your people didn't have any issue taking my brother from me. You almost killed many others that I love. I have no mercy left to give," Winnie muttered.

She reached toward the woman, shushing softly. The hellhound's weeps turned to a shriek as blazing hands touched her forehead. Skin sizzling, body thrashing. The sounds of her deafening cries pierced Winnie's ears as the beast slowly turned to ash before her.

"You're no better than I am."

The words echoed through her mind, though Winnie couldn't tell where they came from. That voice – she recognized it right away. Boudicca's. The lilt of her merciless rage burnt a hole inside, reveling in that glimmer of vengeance.

Behind her, a hand grasped her shoulder gently. Turning, she watched Kane's sad eyes examining the ashes before her.

"Winnie," he whispered.

At first, she couldn't move. Stuck in place, she suddenly couldn't tear her attention away from the ashes blowing in the autumn wind.

"Winnie, let's go." He pulled her to stand.

"Did I really just…"

Quietly, she hunched forward as they walked toward the house. As if trying to hide from reality, from the realization of what she'd done. *I watched her. She contemplated that decision. Chose to kill her even though she didn't have to. I remember what that's like,* he thought as he placed an arm around Winnie.

Their eyes made contact, though nothingness stared back at him. Distant, he wasn't sure if the Winnie he knew and loved was even still in there.

As they walked toward the house, memories of the attack on his island, his home, reminded him of the pain he still struggled to get past.

His mother's frail figured as she waisted away.

His father's agonized face watching her pass.

The way he'd thrown himself to their enemies in a fit of rage.

Gotten himself killed.

We were sixteen and eighteen. Too young to go to war. Too young to lose our parents. Too young to defend our home. And yet we did. And we survived. But at what cost?

He remembered the hole in his chest, the heat behind his eyes. The way he felt they could no longer cry when they dried up and ceased their endless flow. The pit in his stomach. The feeling of full-bodied nausea from shock.

Is that what she's feeling right now? Will this break her? She's too strong to let this be what changes her. It may take time, but she'll learn to forgive herself.

A small voice in the back of his mind countered his thoughts.

"Like you've forgiven yourself?"

He shook his head, trying to block it out. The pesky inner demon that often reared its ugly head whenever he doubted himself.

Reaching the edge of the house, she paused. She searched the fields once more. Countless still cried out in pain, waiting for healing though his siren songs no longer worked. Both brothers were tapped, unable to perform any more magic.

"Let them handle it. They brought a few healers," he whispered, tugging at her to go with him once more. They entered the house, turning to go upstairs.

Exhaustion overwhelmed him, realizing they'd been up all night. Thanks to Samhain. Thanks to the celebration that was supposed to be lighthearted and fun. And yet turned deadly. The sun peeked through the curtains as they entered her room. A shudder escaped Winnie before she swiftly walked to close the drapes.

She took a seat at the edge of her bed, still feeling lifeless. Deep bags hung under her eyes as she ran a hairbrush through her locks.

"I'll draw you a bath," he said softly, hoping it would draw her out of her trance.

They were both covered in blood and ash, reminders of the battle. Quietly, he filled the tub. Throwing in some salts and soaps, he wondered if he should speak to his own experience. At last, he decided not to. Better for her to focus on her own healing rather than worry about him.

Leading her into the bathroom, he showed her the tub. Incoherently, she undressed and stepped inside. Preparing to leave and give her time alone, she stopped him.

"Stay." Her words were soft, knees tucked into her chest as she covered herself by the water. With lost eyes, she stared straight ahead. Never acknowledging anything around her.

Grabbing the sponge that sat to the side, he gently wiped down her back. Nasty bruises and gouges lined her body, though thankfully no bites.

"I wish I could heal you," he said, head lowering with guilt. "In fact, if we're wishing for things, I'd like to go back in time and protect you from all of this."

"I deserve these injuries," she mumbled, almost unintelligible. The same words she muttered after the last fight.

"No you don't…"

"I'm the reason these people died. I should never have held the seance in the first place." Her eyes continued to stare, wide-eyed, off into the distance.

He couldn't tell what she was looking at or get a good read on what she was thinking. She only gazed away, unable to meet his eye contact.

"You are not responsible for the events that happened here tonight. Yes, you held the seance. So what? What happened to Boudicca was centuries ago. If it wasn't you, it would've been someone else. At least you had the resources to stop her," he countered.

Her eyes softened, looking down at the filthy water.

"Winnie, look at me." He gave her a moment before repeating himself. When she still didn't turn, he grabbed her face and pulled her gaze toward him. "This is *not* your fault."

He watched as she flinched, squeezing her eyes shut to hold back the tears that welled. Kane's heart broke, the sting of grief tangible in the air.

"I don't think there will ever come a time when I don't blame myself." She pulled her face away from his touch, placing her forehead on her knees. "I appreciate you trying, but I think I do want to be alone after all."

Dipping the sponge in the water once more, he stroked her back carefully.

"If that's what you wish, then I'll go. I'm just in the other room if you need me. Just remember that I…love you." He felt that same feeling he'd had the other night. A deep tear, as if ripped from his other half as he began to leave.

Her body tensed, still peering down at the water surrounding her. "How…could you *possibly* love someone like me?"

Her words hit like a dagger through his heart.

"How could I love you?" He scoffed, placing a careful hand on her back. "I don't just love you, I'm desperately *in love* with you. Infatuated even, by your bravery and strength. By the way you fight like hell for the people you love. You've never let anyone tell you what to do, something that's infuriated me at times. And yet, I've loved you since we were children. As we age and grow closer, that love has only turned into something I want to covet for the rest of my life."

A small smirk formed on her face, a tiny glimpse of the Winnie he knew peeking through.

"You made some tough choices. It doesn't change who you are. We did whatever we had to in order to *survive.* That doesn't diminish you as a person." He grabbed the side of her face once more, thumb gently stroking the side of her cheek.

"I didn't have to kill that last one," she muttered.

"If you didn't, someone else would have. That is the nature of war."

"I forget you've done this before," she mumbled, looking down at her tattooed arm.

A long pause sounded as he waited for her to continue. He could see the words eager to be spoken, too afraid to know the truth. The same question he'd once asked himself.

"Does it ever get easier?" Her eyes welled with tears and voice cracked.

"Do you want me to lie to you?"

A moment passed before she nodded.

"It does. One day you wake up and the pain and sorrow are gone. You no longer see the faces of the people you killed and you have forgiven yourself."

"Liar," she said with a half-hearted smile.

He offered one in return, a huff of air escaping him.

"It doesn't get easier, but eventually you learn to stop thinking about it. Push it down, and never drudge up those memories. It's the only way I've been able to survive."

Leaning in, Kane offered her a delicate kiss to the forehead. Getting up off the ground, he moved toward the door.

"I'll see you after we both get some rest," he added at last before heading off to his room to get himself cleaned up as well.

As he exited, he heard her. Softly, chanting.

"Push it down. Forget. Push it down. Forget." Over and over again.

45

WINIFRED

Waking in complete darkness, Winnie stirred. *How long have I been asleep? An hour? A day?* Her stomach growled as she reached for the gas lamp on her bedside table. Shivering, she flicked her wrist as her fireplace sparked. Filling the room with light, it was clear it was evening time. Pulling a robe around her, she wandered aimlessly toward the room Tara had used the last few days. The one that had once been Ezra's, vacant since the night of the healing circle.

Knocking carefully, she heard Cricket's small huffs wanting to bark on the other side. Tara shushed him, rushing to open the door before the shuck would wake the entire house. Her eyes softened as she saw Winnie outside her room.

"Hey," was all Tara could mutter, pulling her friend in for a tight hug.

The act alone sent Winnie into a weeping spiral. She didn't know what to say, only that they needed each other more than ever.

"It's okay," Tara shushed, pulling her to have a seat on her bed.

"He's gone," she managed to whisper once the tears subsided and there was nothing left for her to cry.

"I know, I'm so sorry lass. I should've stayed with him. Followed behind him when he ran to help Ezra."

"I…don't know who I am without my brother. I spent the last year ignoring his letters. Avoiding the manor. Months that we could've spent together, lost. Because I was upset with my mother."

A long pause followed, both sitting in their grief.

At last, Tara asked, "Why don't we get something to eat? We could both use some sustenance."

"I'm not hungry…"

Tara shook her head and insisted, pulling Winnie down the stairs with Cricket trailing behind closely. Wandering down the hall, passing a grandfather clock, she noticed the time.

Midnight.

"It's officially Samhain," Winnie whispered.

Tara offered her a sad smile, nodding as they continued to walk down the stairs.

Off in the distance, they heard soft murmurs coming from the sitting room. They entered, Milicent and Ernest sitting solemnly on the couch. Her mother laid out a picture of Wesley, candles lit to honor him. As she glanced up at Winnie, she smiled carefully before standing to embrace her daughter. She had deep, dark bags under her eyes. It didn't look like she'd slept at all since the fight.

Ernest joined them as Winnie wept. Even he shed tears, eyes fixed on the fire lifelessly. The sight of it threatened to crumble her like a sandcastle. The waves of grief threatened to ruin her entirely.

"There's food in the kitchen," Milicent said quietly, cupping Winnie's face and giving it a light squeeze as she wiped away tears.

Winnie spent another moment with her mother and father before heading off. She entered, noticing the gas lamps extinguished. Only small candles lit the way, an eerie silence spread throughout. Melinda sat at the windows, looking out aimlessly. Across from her sat a placemat and table setting, another picture of Wesley at the edge.

Placing a hand on Melinda's shoulder, Winnie never uttered a single word. Quietly grabbing a piece of bread from the counter, she leaned against the island. Mind wandering. Playing out the entire fight over again. Wondering what she could've done differently to save him. Save everyone.

Lost in a trance, it wasn't until a firm grip on her shoulder pulled her back out. Ezra. They never uttered a word as he hugged her tightly. She could feel the guilt radiating off of him as his sad eyes dropped to the floor, likely blaming himself just as much as Winnie took the regret to heart.

The following day, the Lycan left at last. Carrying their wounded toward their portal, they returned home. The dead lay wrapped in white, ready to go home as well. The smell of smoke clung to the air, the forest still slowly burning from Boudicca's attack. Thankfully, the flames never reached the estate. It seemed that part of Winnie's dream never came true.

Standing around the edge of the lake, the rest of the household waited. Milicent took special care to prepare the body. Winnie watched that morning as her mother chose the outfit. Dressed him. Cleaned his face up. Brushed the hair out of his face. *Not 'the body.' My brother,* she reminded herself.

Milicent insisted everyone stand back – away from Wesley. Laid out on a small float, they were ready to release his spirit. Send him on his way. Say goodbye. Placing a hand on his head, their mother said her final farewell. Winnie wanted to join but she'd insisted.

"I must do it alone."

Her words echoed through Winnie's mind. So strange. So foreign. *Why would we do anything alone from here on out? Doesn't this prove we need to stick together?* Her thoughts rustled aimlessly in her mind.

Kane held her tightly, a scowl on his face as he tried to remain strong. For her. If he broke, she knew she'd never be able to stop crying. *Wesley was just as much a little brother to them as he was to me,* she thought.

At last, the raft floated into the lake. Milicent turned to Thoren, offering him a small nod. When the body was far enough out, the siren bowed his head. Said a soft prayer. Begged for forgiveness as he lit the raft on fire.

Watching Wesley burn, Winnie's mind spun out of control. She felt like the air around her was too thick to breathe. The flames might as well have set her ablaze as well. Her world lightened, head heavy as dizziness overcame her.

It wasn't until she blinked that she realized – she was no longer staring at the burning raft floating away on the lake. Kane's grasp no longer held her. The sounds of her family's sobs no longer played through her mind. It was quiet. And still. And that's when she saw him.

46

WINIFRED

Squinting, she couldn't believe her eyes. On the other side of the lake, Winnie saw him. The body. Wesley. Not yet burning. Milicent's hand lay rested on his forehead, strange reflections seen from where she stood. Within seconds, she watched the raft go up in flames once more, noticing a version of her flinch in Kane's arms.

A strange tingling sensation resonated through her, like small lighting bolts sat under her skin. She rubbed her head, confusion washing over her as she watched herself turn and look at Kane. In an instant, she was gone. Disappeared. And as she blinked, her location changed once again.

When her eyes opened once more, she realized she was standing in the midst of Bethnal Green. At the center of her street outside her flat, she curiously looked around. The entire area was once again hustling with life, just as it was before the hellhounds attacked. She walked toward her flat, ready to open the door. Within seconds, it swung open in a fury as Liam darted.

Ezra followed soon after, attempting to run after the man before turning back toward the flat. Not long after, Boudicca's spirit left the dwelling as well. Winnie watched curiously as the queen wandered down the street, only to be surprised by two figures.

She saw them. One of them, a man with gleaming electric blue eyes. Alaric. The other, the mysterious woman she'd seen the day she astral projected into their camp. Still, she couldn't see the woman's face. They disappeared through a brick wall portal before she could run after them.

This is the night of the seance. What the hell is happening?

Ready to go inside and confront herself, she blinked. Once more, lightning zaps coursed through her body. Squinting, she waited for her vision to clear.

Curious eyes peered around as she realized the weather was no longer chilled, but peppery and hot. Standing in the tree line again, she glanced out over the lake. The trees surrounding her were smaller than before, most young saplings.

She heard the laugh first. Wesley's. Not his laugh as it was now, but the giggles he'd had as a child. A young Wesley sat in a canoe with an equally young Kane. Across the lake, young Winnie snickered, watching Thoren rocking the canoe and threatening to send them both overboard. Fishing. *Like when we were kids. How the hell did I get here?*

Young Wesley stilled, making eye contact with her across the lake. His hand reached up, offering her a soft wave. Acknowledging her existence.

Before she could raise her hand in response, she felt it another time. A bolt of electricity rang through her, snatched by time once more. But this jump felt different than the last.

The sharp sting of the portal felt tougher this time. Like she wasn't leaping through time but rather to somewhere new entirely. When she opened her eyes, nothing awaited her.

At first, she couldn't tell if she was seeing anything at all. The darkness, the void. It surrounded her, threatening to engulf her entirely. Just out of reach, she could see a small flicker of light.

"Winifred Fox." A loud, booming voice startled her. Suddenly, it felt like a million eyes were watching.

"Who's there?" she called out, still seeing nothing yet feeling everything.

"You have been summoned," the voice said, slowly morphing into several. It was as if multiple spoke at once in unison, an odd shiver running down her spine.

"Who are you? Show yourself!" she commanded. Though her body shook in fear, she tried her best not to show it in her voice.

Within moments, four figures appeared one by one before her. Their bodies were dim at first, as if not entirely in the same space as her.

The first entity to appear was a man, his skin various shades of orange and red. His hair was long, layered down his back in flaming curls. An emotionless face glared at her, eyes filled with charcoal. *Aelius, God of Fire.* Winnie shuddered, taking in the magnificence of the living flame.

Across from him emerged a woman. Her body was made of swirling water, dark navy skin glimmering like the ocean during a sunset. Thick strands of seaweed hung down her back, pearl white eyes looking her over affectionately. Small fish and other sea creatures swam within her tidal wave body. *Gali, Goddess of Water.*

Taking shape next, another man appeared. Below his torso was made entirely of swirling tornados. Pale gray skin and blank, empty eyes stared back at her. Debris and leaves seemed to fall around him as he floated, face stern. *Caelus, God of Air.*

Lastly, she joined. *Ina, Goddess of Earth.* With a body made of moss, vines, and insects, her hair was thick and full of life. Butterflies flitted about her, dragonflies and other little creatures swirling around. Sapphire eyes examined her carefully, a motherly affection engulfing Winnie like a warm hug.

At first, none of the Gods spoke. Their bodies moved like their elements, half corporeal and half in another realm. Realizing who she stood before, Winnie nervously kneeled before them.

She opened her mouth to speak, address them, yet nothing came out. *Am I seriously standing in front of the Gods I've been praying to my entire life?*

"Stand. There's no need to kneel," Aelius said. His voice matched his face – stoic and stern.

"You...summoned me?" She hesitantly asked, eyes glued to the beings before her. A lump sat in the back of her throat, unsure what to do with herself.

"We're here to discuss your brother," Ina said, voice soft and nurturing.

"Your heart called to us and we sensed your growing powers. We think we can be of service to each other," Gali interjected, drawing Winnie's attention toward her.

"I've been trying to talk to you for weeks and you've ignored me!"

"I've tried to answer your prayers, but somehow my words weren't making it through to you," Gali tried to say.

"You didn't have to summon us. We're always listening." Caelus smirked, the first sign of anything resembling emotions gracing his rock hard face.

"We're here to offer you a deal." Ina brought her hand up, an image of Wesley glittering in her hands.

The image of her brother almost sent her in a tailspin, ready to burst into tears once more.

"What kind of deal? Did you have something to do with his death?" An air of suspicion held in Winnie's tone, examining them cautiously.

"His death was fated. We had nothing to do with it," Aelius reassured. His apathetic face softened at once, as if sensing her pain.

"Should you agree, your brother will be saved from his fated death," Gali said softly.

Winnie scoffed. "You can't bring someone back from the dead. It defies the laws of nature. No one has that kind of power!"

"Well," Aelius began, though Gali interrupted him before he could explain.

"It's not as simple as just bringing him back. But we can ensure he will be protected," she replied.

"And what do you want from me in return?"

The elemental gods shared knowing glances between each other, as if having their own internal conversation amongst themselves.

"Should you accept our offer, we will guarantee your brother's safety. In return, you will complete a set of assignments for us to ensure the balance between the magic world and the common world are kept in check." Gali's words echoed through her.

"Yes! I'll do anything!" Winnie cried out, ready to throw herself at the Gods' feet.

"We were hoping you'd say that," Caelus said with a chuckle.

"What do you need from me?"

"First, you must decide. We will give you three options. Choose wisely. Once you've made your choice, there will be no altering your decision," Ina explained, waves of motherly affection flowing from her. Just being in her presence felt like the embodiment of love.

Before her, a glitter of images appeared once more. Three frames, each waiting for her to peer through them. Each a snapshot in time. An option. A different event.

"Touch each and you will see your choices." Ina ushered her toward the picture frames.

Reaching out, Winnie touched the first portrait. Pulled into the vision, she saw a potential outcome. Seeing the inside of her flat, she watched herself try and fill a pitcher of water with her magic. Just like the night of the seance, Mary's repetitive knocks sounded on her door, barging into the entrance of the room. Though before the grieving mother ever made it through the threshold to have a seat at the kitchen table, Winnie turned her away swiftly.

Overcome by grief, the mother ran down the street. Toward a familiar house. One Winnie lived at for quite some time before her former love betrayed her. Madam Stanhope's House of Spiritualists. Desperate, Mary pounded on the door. An overwhelmed Beatrix swung the door open in a frenzy, ushering the mother inside. Time seemed to speed up before Winnie as the seance went wrong just as it had for her.

Days and nights passed, unable to see what was happening. When all was said and done, flames consumed the house. Everything around it, too. The vision seemed to expand, showing all of London in flames.

"In this option, Mary sees Beatrix instead of you. Your rival does not know how to stop the queen and thus all of London perishes," Gali explained quietly.

"And what of Ezra and I?" Winnie asked, seeing Bethnal Green in flames, her flat included.

"Ezra perishes in the flames. You make it back to your family home just in time. But your brother is alive and well," Caelus added, voice solemn.

"That's a terrible option! Kill thousands to save my brother? I can't choose that!"

"Good thing you have two more," Aelius retorted.

Reaching for the second frame, Winnie watched a second time. Still in London, she tried to put the pieces together. Ezra ran down the streets of Bethnal Green after Liam, following him to an alleyway. Within seconds, the queen held him in her grasp. *This is the night Tara and Ez went to the pub,* she realized.

Holding his bruised and bloodied body in the air, only moments passed before his neck snapped and his body thudded on the ground. Off in the corner, Tara screamed. Cricket lept toward Boudicca, knocking her over with just enough time for his owner to escape. Without him…

"If Ezra dies in this moment, Wesley does not run after him in the battle. And he will survive the fight," Caelus explained.

"This option is just as terrible as the last! You're asking me to kill Ezra and Cricket!"

"In exchange for your brother, should you choose this option," Aelius reminded.

"What's the third choice?" A long sigh escaped her lips before turning to the final portrait.

For a third and final time, she peered into the memory. This time, she was not in London. In fact, she was at Fox Manor. Peering down onto the porch, Winnie watched Ezra place Wesley's body down. Her brother's features slowly changed, morphing into a creature she didn't recognize.

Soft green hues covered his skin, his features less distinguishable. Her mother glanced down at the creature in shock, ready to place a hand on his face to examine him. At once, the familiar face she'd grown up with returned, her mother jumping back in surprise.

"W–What is this?" Her words struggled to come out.

"In this version, your brother is…*exchanged.*" Aelius's words snapped Winnie from the vision.

"What do you mean *exchanged?*"she asked, her tone confused.

"Your brother will remain in the fairy realm, while a changeling takes his place," Ina explained, voice soft and comforting.

"You want to take my brother? This is almost as bad as the first two!" She scoffed, rubbing her head in confusion.

"In option three, your brother is alive and well, able to live his life. And your friends are spared as well. But you must choose. Sacrifice thousands, give up your friend and the beast, or swap him," Gali stated matter-of-factly.

"Can I have some time to think?"

All four shook their heads.

"This offer is now or never," Gali replied, face stern and unyielding.

"And if I don't choose?"

"Then you will return to your time and he will remain dead," Aelius muttered.

"Or, you can choose one of these and have your brother back," Ina explained softly, a patient smile across her lips.

"Where is this fairy realm? Will he be safe? How will I know he's alive? How will I get him back?" A slew of questions flowed from her mouth, unsure where to even start.

"We can show him to you, if that is the choice you make. You can have him back as soon as you complete a set of assignments for us," Gali explained.

"You mentioned that before. What are these assignments?"

All four nodded their heads once more.

"With your newfound gifts, you're able to travel to different times. A rare gift for one to possess," Caelus began.

Aelius continued where he left off. "Traveling to different times, you will complete a set of tasks that will ensure the balance between magic and the common world are kept in check."

"The hellhounds have grown too powerful and out of control. They must be stopped," Gali continued.

"When all are complete, you will get your brother back," Ina added.

"What kind of tasks?"

"You will be told what to do when the time comes. Each will serve you toward defeating Boudicca and her descendants, once and for all," Caelus responded, his tone impatient.

She paused for a moment. "Why are you doing this?"

"Your gift of dematerializing is one very few possess. It's been centuries since we last had someone of your talent on our side," Gali began. "I've known since you were very young that you were meant for greatness."

"What happened to the last one like me?"

"The last one was…unsuccessful. Let's just put it that way," Aelius scoffed.

"Why me? Why can I do this and others can't?"

"That part is unclear. We think it may be connected to your ability to travel to Oblivion. But you hold a very special set of powers that can alter the course of history. However, your life is dictated by destiny. Anything that must happen, will happen. No matter your meddling, the universe will ensure its will be done," all four Gods spoke in unison.

"What option do you choose?" Aelius asked impatiently.

I can't decide. The first two options are nonsense. They knew that offering them to me. I can either swap my brother or turn them down entirely.

"I've made up my mind," she said hesitantly.

Her mind raced as she stalled, still contemplating her options. *Can I truly swap him without weighing myself down with guilt? Can I choose nothing and allow him to remain dead when I could've saved him? I could exchange him and then I'll get him right back once the tasks are done. But what if…*

"Your inner monologue is growing tiresome. Stop stalling and make a decision," Caelus said, almost scolding her.

'I," she began, hesitating. "I choose option three." As soon as the words left her mouth, she regretted them. *Did I really just agree to exchange my brother for some creature?*

A small voice in the back of her mind stilled, reassuring her. *It's only temporary. The Wesley I knew will be back before I know it.*

"It is done," all four said in unison with a nod.

The palm of Winnie's hand burned suddenly as she let out a soft cry. The same arm that carried the mark of Boudicca now carried the mark of the elements. As though it were a brand, four quadrants lay on the inside of her hand, the symbols for fire, air, earth, and water burned into her skin.

"Wait!" she cried out as the elements started sending her back.

They paused, looking at her in confusion.

"Will any of my memories change?"

Caelus chuckled softly to himself before shaking his head. "No, Winifred. This is the choice you've always made."

They raised their arms and sent her back to the estate in an instant.

Looking out over the field, she saw her family still mourning the loss of Wesley. *I'll get him back once I complete my tasks,* she reminded herself. She looked down in her hands, seeing a thick leather bound book. She tried to open it, though the pages wouldn't budge. She looked up, noticing Kane running toward her.

"Where did you go? And what's that?" His eyes landed on the new item in her hand immediately.

"Um, a book?" A sense of sarcasm sat in her voice, surprising her as she turned it around in her hands. The cover held the same symbol as what marked the inside of her palm.

"What the hell's going on? You've never been able to teleport like that! I saw you across the lake and then you were gone." His eyes roamed her suspiciously, peppering her with questions.

"First I was…" she began to say.

In the back of her mind, she could hear the voices of the elements whisper, *"You cannot tell him about us."*

She groaned, rubbing her temples as a forming headache washed over her.

"What is it?" he pestered.

"Can I tell him about the deal?" she asked in her mind, knowing the elements were still listening.

"No," they responded.

She paused, looking at Kane as if trying to find the answers written on his face.

"Nothing," she reassured, pointing back to the funeral. "Let's go back to the others."

Kane, confused, walked ahead, glancing back at her for a moment before continuing his pace.

She stopped, examining the book once more. When Kane was out of sight, she placed the palm of her branded hand on the cover, the pages finally budging and allowing her to take a look inside. Within the book were pages and pages of a language that she couldn't read.

"How am I supposed to know what to do?" she questioned, wondering if they could still hear her.

"You will be shown only what you need to know in order to complete your tasks one at a time," the elements whispered in her mind.

The book was hundreds of pages long… *Did I just sign myself up for a lifetime of debt to the Gods?*

"How many tasks are there?" she thought back to them, though there was no response. Only silence and her own voice sat in her mind.

She flipped through the pages, seeing one entry begin to squiggle and move. The words, the language she didn't understand, changed and at once it was in English.

Her first assignment.

On the page stood one word and a date: Marvivia 1861

She walked back to the funeral, joining her friends and family. Carefully, Ezra inched toward her. Placing an arm around her shoulder, he offered her a soft smile. Watching him closely, she couldn't help but notice a dark, ghostly hand grasping his shoulder. *Death.*

Milicent joined her next. Hugging her tightly, her mother whispered in her ear, "This is not the end. There will be more to come. And we will not be able to stop them. I hope this was worth the life of my son."

THE STORY CONTINUES IN...

BOOK 2
of The LONDINIUM SAGA

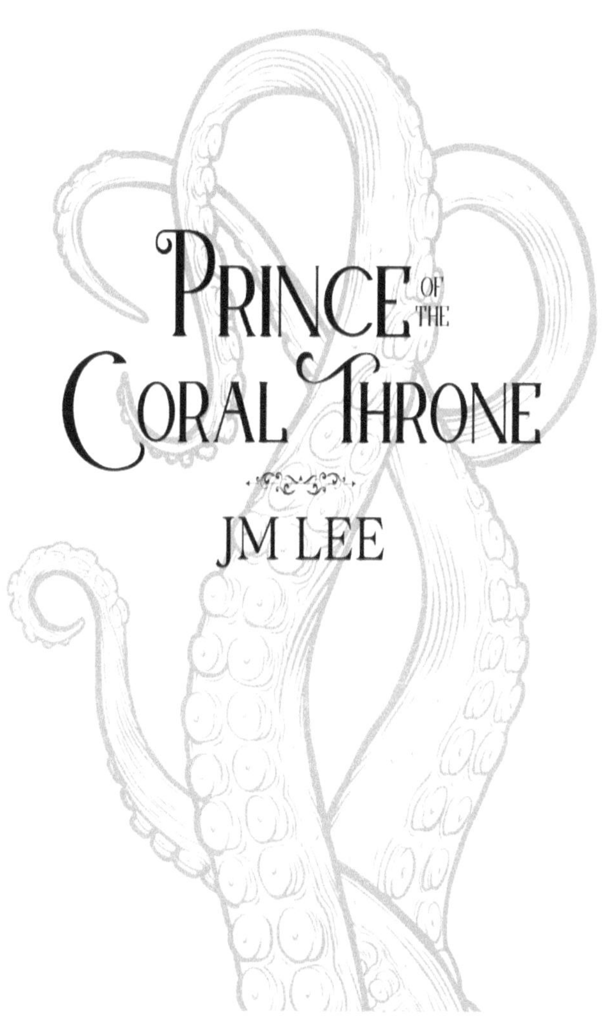

Author's Note

It should be noted that while I did everything in my power to ensure the history was as accurate as possible, this book is still fantasy. Queen Boudicca was a real person with real-life trauma that fueled her revenge on Rome. None of that is made up!

I encourage you to learn everything you can about this incredible leader and all she did for her people, her daughters, and herself. History is plagued by women's silenced voices. Learn about them, appreciate them, remember them. And above all, keep fighting.

And Boudicca, if you're a spirit seeing this in the afterlife – I don't think you're a villain. You're actually my hero. Much love!

Acknowledgements

There are countless people I'd like to thank as I close out this book. First and foremost, I have to thank my family and the friends who may not be blood but act like it. You've spent god knows how many hours listening to me obsess over this story. I've been dreaming about this book since I was 16 and now it's finally here.

I'd also like to thank the wonderful group of beta readers who tested out the book before others had the chance to look at it. Without your words of reassurance, advice, and guidance, this book wouldn't be what it is today. Thank you to: **Caeli, Emilee, my parents, Debbie, Sam, Jodi, Elizabeth, Rebecca, Shannan, Amanda, Kenny, Morgan, Lacey, Eric, and Kayla.** You guys mean the world to me!

Lastly, I'd like to thank two incredible artists who took my story and gave life to some of its characters. Thank you **Seth Cockerham** (@cockerhamdesign / www.cockerhamdesign.com) for the incredible art of the Elemental Gods. And many thanks to **Ayla Ginsberg** (@ayla.ginsberg.art / www.ayla-phoenix-art.com) for the hauntingly beautiful portrait of Bouddica. Readers, be sure to check out their instagram pages! You can see their artwork featured on my website (www.jmlee.info) and on my instagram:
@jmleebooks

About the Author

JM Lee is an indie fantasy author for both YA and new adult audiences. Her first book, When October Ends, was published when she was 13. In later years, she published the second and third book of the "Novus Proprius Chronicles" and a variety of short stories.

Currently, JM Lee lives in Virginia with her three dogs and a growing family. After finishing high school, she attended Western Governors University and majored in Education. She now teaches middle school English and hopes to inspire her students the way her middle school teachers inspired her. As a proud member of the LGBTQ+ community, she hopes to help others with her stories!

To learn more about her, visit www.jmlee.info or visit her instagram profile: @jmleebooks